ADVANCE PRAISE FOR *FORMULA*

"Gina Fava, author of ***Formula: Another HELL Ranger Thriller***, is at the top of the class for both the mystery and thriller genres; no easy task. Fava not only has a unique talent for storytelling, it's obvious that her meticulous research brings credibility, depth and real beauty to her novel that will undoubtedly satisfy both men and women. If you can't get enough of Daniel Silva, Dennis Lehane, and J.K. Rowling, add Gina Fava's HELL Ranger series to your bucket list."

— Stephen Besecker, author of *The Samaritan* and *Executive Power*

"Strap in. The HELL Rangers will take you on the ride of your life with *Formula*. With twists and turns from the first page to the last, Gina Fava races to the head of the pack."

— J.M. Leduc, Amazon bestselling author of the Sinclair O'Malley series

"Whirlwind pacing, breathless action, a sexy hero, a tough but stunning heroine, and an unlikely pairing of Formula 1 car racing with the sophisticated, secretive world of European wine making…This is FORMULA, Gina Fava's latest HELL Ranger adventure. Devlin Lucchesi doesn't know whether to bed his new client, Erika Aurora, or detain her. But he does want to find out what caused the death of his racing rival, Giancarlo Venchi. All he suspects is that it's about the water. Glorious Italian settings hosting luxurious lifestyles add to the glamour and glimmer. An electrifying mystery. "

— Sheila McCormick, author of *Cousin Andrew*

PRAISE FOR *THE SCULPTOR*

"Evil stalks the streets of Rome. A serial killer searches for his next victim amidst the ancient ruins and modern wonders. A smart, resilient, resourceful young woman crosses his path. How smart? How resilient and resourceful? Find out in ***The Sculptor***, a page-turning, spine-tingling heart-stopper that will keep you up all night. And when dawn comes and you turn the last page, you will agree that Gina Fava is one of the rising young stars of the thriller genre."

— William Martin, New York Times bestselling author of *Back Bay* and *The Lincoln Letter*

"After thrilling us with her action-packed debut novel, ***The Race***, Gina Fava takes a slightly lateral move to an intimate, suspenseful, at times creepy but always gripping, mystery tale in ***The Sculptor***. Just when I thought that I figured out the bad guy, Fava threw me a curve, and then another, until I reached the shocking, satisfying conclusion."

— J. H. Bográn, author of *Firefall* and *Treasure Hunt*

"Nonstop action, with vivid settings, sympathetic characters, and a serial killer to die for. Highly recommended."

— Douglas Preston, #1 New York Times bestselling author of *The Monster of Florence*.

"You will be riveted to the page as you discover along with Mara that everything she thought was true is a lie. Come along as she races to uncover the truth before she becomes the Sculptor's next victim. Gina Fava has a winner on her hands with *The Sculptor*."

— *Suspense Magazine*

"*The Sculptor* is a unique front-to-back thrill ride worthy of our primal senses. Fava's vast knowledge of the setting clearly shines through, and her desire to deliver a robust thriller for lovers of the genre has certainly come to fruition."

— Rob Watts, author of the *Crooked Road Through Cedar Grove* mystery series

"Another fast-paced thriller; kept me guessing right up until the hold-your-breath climax. An excellent read!"

—Steve Ulfelder, Edgar-nominated author of *Wolverine Bros. Freight & Storage*

PRAISE FOR *THE RACE: A HELL RANGER THRILLER*

"A high-octane thriller, rich with action, imagination, and intriguing suspense. "

—August McLaughlin, author of *In Her Shadow*, an Indies Excellence Awards finalist

"This is what you want to read when you think of a great thriller. The action sequences are really exciting and...You LOVE the characters. Tough one to put down for sure!"

—J. Korman, Amazon reviewer

"All the thriller essences of Dan Brown, and the cheeky humor of Harlan Coben."

—C. Florio, Amazon reviewer

"[I] found myself drawn into the story…and falling in love with the characters. It is exciting to me that this book is just the first in a series of HELL Ranger Thrillers."

—Amy Marbach, of *Bad Groove* car racing blog

"*The Race* got me hooked from the very first chapter. [I]t was riveting and always kept me on the edge of my seat, and it had me feeling like I was amidst the action. So hard to put down. The story was woven around family, terrorism and loyalty of friends. [B]est book I've read in a long time. I am anxiously awaiting more Hell Rangers books."

—Marsha Murphy, Amazon reviewer

"Thrilling action and intrigue at its best!"

—Steven M. Moore, author of *Survivors of Chaos* and *The Midas Bomb*

"[Fava] reeled me in right from the beginning and did not disappoint. Many times I found myself holding my breath to the next page…before I could let out a sigh of relief! All I can say is hurry with the next book- I can't wait to read it!"

—Marie Szalanski, Amazon reviewer

"This is one heck of a race. Plenty of plot twists, and nerve-racking thrills to keep you entertained all the way to The End."

—Joseph Handell, Amazon reviewer

FORMULA

ANOTHER H.E.L.L. RANGER THRILLER

ALSO BY GINA FAVA

NOVELS

The H.E.L.L. Ranger Series

The Race

Stand Alone Thriller

The Sculptor

NON-FICTION

Un Momento: A Taste of Italian-American Pastimes

FORMULA

ANOTHER H.E.L.L. RANGER THRILLER

GINA FAVA

Steepo Press

New York   Boston

FORMULA

By Gina Fava

PUBLISHED BY: Steepo Press

Cover Design: Bruce Skinner
Cover Photographer: Hyperion Photography

ISBN: 978-0989358798

For Tony and Joey,

with love

THE *FORMULA* PLAYLIST

Big Audio Dynamite, “Rush”

Kenny Loggins, “I’m Alright” (Theme from *Caddyshack*)

Van Halen, “Runnin’ With the Devil”

Men at Work, “Overkill”

Chris Isaak, “Wicked Game”

Fiona Apple, “Criminal”

Panic! at the Disco, “This is Gospel”

Foo Fighters, “My Hero”

The Cure, “Love Song”

Bleachers, “I Wanna Get Better”

Foo Fighters, “Walk”

Water will gush forth in the wilderness
And streams in the desert.
The burning sand will become a pool,
the thirsty ground bubbling springs.
In the haunts where jackals once lay,
grass and reeds and papyrus will grow.
—Isaiah 35:6-7

Water promises to be to the 21st century
what oil was to the 20th century:
the precious commodity that determines
the wealth of nations.
—*Fortune* Magazine, May 2000

Chapter 1

The car attempting to pass him on the right made him nervous. Devlin glanced over at the other driver, deadlocked with him for over an hour. He knew the guy wanted to steal everything he had. But he'd be damned if he was going to just give it up. Thing was, his tires were shot to hell, and he'd lose it all if he crashed. It was time to pull over.

Devlin "Lucky" Lucchesi wrenched his Formula One race car from the Monte Carlo track and sped between the guardrails of the pit lane. Giancarlo Venchi, the relentless clinger, pitted too. Venchi shot him the bird as he peeled into his garage, but he exhaled and let it roll off him. In spite of his moniker, he knew that luck had little to do with his decade-long Monaco Grand Prix winning streak. It was all about gumption. And he'd worked too hard for the cocky bastard to break his stride now.

Devlin maneuvered behind the painted stop marks and idled outside the Lucchesi pit garage. Nearly two dozen mechanics swarmed his vehicle like the undead on a victim. Every one of his crew was a brilliant pit technician, as well as an undercover special ops HELL Ranger. He trusted them with his life, in the pit and on missions.

It took them less than two seconds to jack the fifteen-hundred-pound car inches from the pavement and then unbolt and roll off the blistered Pirelli tires. Every crewman knew the importance of precision teamwork. In getting his vehicle back on track. And in getting his head back into the game. Not an easy task. Especially after Ella's death.

He spotted a bright orange "AURORA Vineyard" blimp flying low overhead, and it made him think of his son. "Guys," he told them through his mic, "remind me to pick up balloons and a cake for Marcello's birthday, would ya?"

The head of his crew, Benedetto Scotti, nodded. "Cake. Balloons. Got it." Seconds later, the jack men dropped his racing machine back to the ground onto fresh, warm super-soft tires. His crew dispersed. He gripped the wheel, ready to launch.

But something in his peripheral vision halted his momentum. He flicked his eyes to a side mirror. Giancarlo Venchi, Blue Rhino team's driver from hell, was back. And he was rampaging down the pit's common lane, aiming his machine right toward Devlin's men.

"Incoming!" Devlin shouted into his helmet mic. His crew dove for cover. Giancarlo's rear aerofoil clipped Scotti's metal brake sign and ripped it from his grip. Like a javelin, it catapulted through the air, nearly impaling one of his tire men before it slammed into another garage.

In the split second before disaster, Giancarlo veered his car sharp right. Barely averting Devlin's men by mere inches, the jackass motored out of the pit lane and back onto the street course.

"Scotti, talk to me, you guys alright?" Devlin asked. He checked the pit monitor. Scotti was rooted to his original mark on their pit apron, uninjured and wholly in control. The crew chief looked him in the eye, pointed toward the track, and said, "Get him!"

Devlin slammed his foot into the accelerator and roared up the steep, bumpy hill leading to the Massenet. Sure, he'd do anything to keep Giancarlo Venchi from stripping him of his title. But this was personal. No one messed with his crew and lived.

***

With only four and a half laps left, Devlin trailed Giancarlo by three seconds. The next team lagged a whopping eighteen seconds behind both of them.

Devlin thought of Marcello. After all that his son had been through the past year—no way he'd let him down. He pushed harder.

He flew up the long hill, lined with flapping banners that read "HydroVino," toward Hotel de Paris. The two cars shot past the casino. By then he'd closed the distance between them to mere tenths of a second. Together they plunged down the hill toward Hotel Mirabeau.

One more lap…

They rocketed past the harbor, in tandem, as if connected. He eyed the right-hand La Rascasse turn ahead. Cornering the curve, his legs felt like dead weights. The treads on his super-softs were bald and slick. The road beneath his low-rider felt a foot thick in marbles. His body shook with fatigue and dehydration.

The checkered flag hovered over the track in the distance. Devlin leaned forward, clenched the wheel, and pushed like mad to outrun him.

Neck and neck, they jetted across the finish line in a blur.

Devlin slowed his car to a halt near the foot of the Royal Box, where Monaco's crowned rulers awaited the award presentation. The crowd, cordoned off by metal stands and police officers, cheered with every replay of the close finish on the Jumbotron in anticipation of the winner declaration.

He unstrapped his harnesses and spotted a tall, buxom woman sporting credentials step past the barricade. He recognized her as the rep from Giancarlo's brand-new sponsorship. She handed Giancarlo a Blue Rhino champagne bottle. The smarmy racer grasped her arm, dipped her back, and kissed her for the cameras. She slapped her team's driver and marched off.

Devlin shook his head in disgust, yanked off the steering wheel, and climbed out of his steaming chassis.

Another equally statuesque blond, slightly more refined, stepped up to the blockade. Runa Aurora, one of three siblings behind the Aurora Vineyard name, typically presented their driver with a bottle of grappa on race day. But this was before Giancarlo had abruptly ended their sponsorship months earlier. Now Runa was stuck behind the gate without creds and cradling one of the cloth-covered bottles like an infant.

Runa, also Giancarlo's fiancée, was chastising him for kissing the other woman. But Giancarlo's grin only grew wider. He snatched the decanter from Runa's grasp, tore away the cloth satchel, flicked off the short cork, and swigged the 120-proof grappa like a pro. He held up the glass bottle, belched, and smashed it into pieces on the blacktop. "Now we're done, babe," Giancarlo boomed, "personally and professionally."

Runa stared at her fiancé, her jaw set and eyes blazing. Tears rolled over her flushed cheeks. Cameras flashed, and the press corps flocked to the jilted woman behind the gate, begging her side of the story.

Devlin whipped his helmet and balaclava into the monocoque and strode toward Giancarlo's car. The swarm around Runa blocked Giancarlo from public view, and Devlin confronted him. "Your behavior in the pit lane today was unacceptable."

Giancarlo smirked. "Assho—"

Devlin rammed his fist into Giancarlo's face. The driver's head snapped back. Giancarlo grimaced, focused, and put his fists up to fight.

The cloying smell of grappa on the driver's breath repulsed him. Devlin punched him again, a crisp, clean uppercut that delivered a message but failed to draw attention.

Stumbling, Giancarlo made a poor attempt at a roundhouse. Devlin grabbed the driver's arm and twisted it behind his back.

He socked him in the jaw once more, and Giancarlo crumpled. But he clutched the racer's chin with one hand and forced him to meet his gaze. "You almost killed my crew, you sonuvabitch."

Blue Rhino's driver mumbled in slurred, broken English. "It is…part of…the game. I never meant to—"

"You ever do something like that to my team again, I won't be quite as charming," Devlin said. The horde of reporters suddenly shifted to Giancarlo for his perspective of the broken relationship. In a suave PR move, he hauled Giancarlo to his feet in a choke hold as if they were old pals. The fans cheered, and Devlin sauntered away toward his crew.

On the way, the third-place finisher brushed his arm. Veronica Griffith, the only other American open-car driver besides him, flashed a grin. "Great race, Lucky, as always."

"You're hard to beat, Veronica. I thought you had me a couple times." He shrugged. "Not even sure yet if I whipped Giancarlo."

"Hope so. He's an embarrassment." She gestured to Giancarlo, now posing for pictures beside his vehicle. Walking toward the royal box, she said, "Rooting for you, Lucky." She winked at Devlin and sauntered away.

His face flushed with a heat as intense as his monocoque. He sprinted to his pit crew gathered on the finish line and threw himself headlong into their group hug amid the cheers and chants of the spectators.

Suddenly the crowd hushed. The Jumbotron must have posted the race winner. Devlin looked to the screen. What he saw shocked him.

Giancarlo Venchi was doubled over, writhing and gripping his abdomen with both arms as if gored by a bull. The driver reared back, clear physical agony contorting his features. He retched, and the crowd gasped when Giancarlo coughed up blood. Saliva foamed from his mouth. His fingers cramped into talons. His eyes rolled up into his head, and he collapsed onto the track. The spectators' earlier cries of adulation now turned to cries of terror.

Theories of seizure, choking, and asphyxiation flashed through Devlin's mind. He shouted to a stunned official to call for the track ambulance. The motorcade of security vehicles whisked away the principality's rulers. The Aurora blimp, ever-present during the race, was nowhere in sight.

Past animosities aside, Devlin pushed his way past reporters and crew to reach the driver, now on his back, writhing in violent convulsions. Four of Blue Rhino's men held down Giancarlo's arms and legs while the team doctor examined him. The physician pulled open the racer's mouth and searched for blockage with a pen light. He shook his head and began chest compressions.

Devlin nudged their pit boss. "I have medical training. Can I help too?" Their crew chief shrugged.

Another convulsion racked Giancarlo's body, until he lay limp on the track. The spectators had grown eerily quiet. Police motorcycles escorted an ambulance through the barricade toward the victim. One of the cops maintained order. Another one flipped open a notebook, and so began the official investigation.

Devlin overheard the team doctor say that the ailing racer had no known allergies and no preexisting medical conditions, the picture of health as of that morning's prerace physical. *So why the hell is Giancarlo Venchi on the ground fighting for his life?*

He took a step back to assess the scene and felt a crunch beneath the thin rubber soles of his racing boots. He glanced down to sidestep broken glass, likely from the smashed grappa bottle, and spied the discarded orange Aurora cork. The bottle's cotton shroud also fluttered against the base of the gate. A voice in his head convinced him to surreptitiously pocket both.

Giancarlo's pit boss held the ambulance door open while paramedics readied to load the gurney. The racer coughed and gurgled, then groaned with the effort.

Runa Aurora broke past the barrier, shouting her fiancé's name as she fought her way through the throng of Blue Rhino crew. The pit boss put his arm up to block her. Runa shoved him. "Get the hell out of my way," she said. The two exchanged words until the crew chief finally stepped aside.

Beside the gurney, Runa peered down at Giancarlo's face. His eyes were partly open, but there was no way to know whether he could see. She kissed his forehead. And, in a flash, she backhanded him. Hard. Then she spat into his already blood- and saliva-spattered face. A paramedic grabbed her arm. Before he removed her, she shrieked into Giancarlo's face, "Now we're done, you bastard." She broke free and pushed through the shocked crowd.

The paramedics loaded Giancarlo and slammed the doors. The ambulance sped toward the hospital.

Devlin looked toward his HELL Ranger crew. Scotti's gaze demanded answers. But Devlin's mind only raced with questions.

Chapter 2

The projectile shot through the open window of Erika Aurora's third-floor office and thudded against the opposite wall. She heard plaster crumble, must've been quite an impression. She looked up from her computer, shaking her head.

No shattered glass this time. Workers were already scheduled to replace another smashed pane and an adjacent one tomorrow with an industrial-strength composite. The cost of doing business.

Erika finished her tallies, stretched, and rolled back the leather chair from her mahogany desk. She strolled across her office and examined the object. A hefty chunk of terra cotta had sailed through the same window that a protester had shattered a few days ago. She marveled at the shrewd protesters. Their ability to hurl objects from behind the wrought-iron gates surrounding the estate was uncanny.

The Aurora Vineyard's CEO plunked the terra cotta atop her growing pile of spent ammo—cobblestone, slate, and other rubble—lovely natural specimens she now collected in an Etruscan urn in the corner. An idea for a new wine label formed in her mind. She snapped a picture on her smartphone. Her superior marketing acumen, that was the reason why Aurora Vineyard flourished.

She unstrapped her Sergio Rossis and kicked the crocodile heels under her chair. She backed up her computer and switched off the desk lamp for the night. She fleetingly wondered where her black Labrador, Tomba, had scampered off to. It'd been a couple days since she'd seen him.

She rolled her shoulders and poured a glass of water from the crystal decanter. Downed all eight ounces in seconds. Dinner. She really craved a minty leg of lamb and roasted potatoes, but the cantina staff had likely gone home. She also knew firsthand that the winery's dozen or so security guards were inept in the kitchen.

She dialed her brother and sister to see if they wanted to grab a bite, but neither picked up. Leif was spending most days skiing in the upper Dolomites or the Swiss Alps with his romantic entanglement, an expert skier who hung on her baby brother's every word. Erika could understand why. She'd been smitten since caring for Leif as a child, though she vehemently disagreed with him on nearly every issue. She was disappointed at not reaching him.

She was surprised at Runa's lack of response. Erika could usually track her down in the "alchemy" room, where her younger sister would bury her head in books, computers, and lab experiments, even before her fiancé's untimely death. As feisty and vibrant as Runa appeared to the world, Erika appreciated her smart, quiet reserve that she saved for her family.

Odd that she hadn't touched base with them all day. When their father, Augustus, had been diagnosed with pancreatic cancer a year ago, the three had grown closer than they'd ever been, and his death six months later had fiercely bonded them as a familial unit.

Until the news leak, which had solidly driven a wedge between all of them.

A security alarm signaled a breach of the estate's perimeter. Erika slipped on her Sperrys, accustomed to such an interruption these days. She felt confident that her security team would handle the situation, but it still piqued her curiosity. While she and her siblings had been away last week, some bastard had infiltrated an outer quadrant and killed Leif's cocker spaniel. Security claimed it'd been coyotes, but coyotes didn't inflict knife wounds.

She glanced at the panel of security monitors built into an armoire outside her private bathroom. One showed a single intruder with a hooded sweatshirt creeping along the garden path just outside the tasting cantina. Wait a minute…the intruder was now breaking into the cantina, two floors beneath where she stood. Where was her security team?

Three of the monitors showed guards rushing from various posts toward the cantina. But the agent usually posted there was nowhere in sight, and Erika doubted that the others would get there in time. She locked herself in her office and retrieved the Glock 42 from inside her desk drawer.

Footsteps ran down the hall just outside her office. She dialed the police and conveyed the situation.

The locked doorknob jiggled, then the intruder shook it harder.

Erika aimed the gun at the door, her hand trembling but not wavering from its target. One of her dearest friends had trained her in the use of handguns, and she firmly believed in the motto "Shoot first, ask questions later." If the door opened, she'd squeeze off a few rounds and *then* look under the hood.

"Erika, open up. It's Runa."

Runa. Erika indeed heard her sister panting on the other side of the door.

"Your door's locked. Open up," Runa said, out of breath. "You'll never guess who I ran into."

Erika slipped the handgun into the back of her skirt and opened the door. *And you'll never know how close you came to getting shot, baby sister.*

Chapter 3

Granted a reprieve from the dunk tank at his son's birthday party, Devlin had sought the quiet of the kitchen pantry to slice the massive Oreo cake. He clued in his pit boss, Scotti, on Giancarlo's cause of death: severe myocardial infarction. Alcohol poisoning, from the rapid consumption of copious amounts of highly concentrated ethyl alcohol, had attacked his heart. Too much grappa, too fast, end game.

"The Monaco ME just let you stroll in last week and check out the body?" Scotti plunked a scoop of strawberry gelato onto each plate.

"She and I have a rapport," Devlin said.

Scotti's eyebrow shot up.

"Not that kind of rapport. With me, anyway. She's granted me access to cases in the past. I've turned a blind eye to her dalliances with a lot of the HELL Rangers."

"Oh, thaaat medical examiner," Scotti said.

"Emily explained that Giancarlo had all the usual symptoms associated with severe alcohol poisoning. Blue-tinged skin, extreme hypothermia, severe dehydration. She showed me his toxicology report. Extremely low blood sugar level. Off-the-charts alcohol level." Devlin gestured to the scoop that Scotti had just licked clean. "You saving any of that for the kids?"

Frozen dairy dripped down Scotti's forearm and chin. It occurred to Devlin that the husky former Marine who'd introduced him to the racing world decades earlier now teetered on the brink of the big fifty. This formidable man had been a veritable father figure since rescuing Devlin from the murky waters of a terror-ridden childhood, literally plucking the drowning adolescent from New York Harbor and raising him as his own. Devlin could never imagine a life without this man in it.

Accustomed to hearty portions of good-natured ribbing from the crew, Scotti smacked Devlin upside the head. He stepped aside and left Devlin the chore. "Any indications of foul play or bodily trauma?" Scotti said.

"None. Other than a slapped face, thanks to his fiancée. And maybe...a slightly bruised jaw," Devlin mumbled.

"When did he—"

Devlin smirked.

"You socked him? I knew you couldn't let him get away with threatening the crew," Scotti said. "Good man. But you don't think that had anything to do with his death?"

Devlin shook his head. "Not a chance. Emily confirmed it." They grabbed dessert trays and edged to the back door. "Prior medical records showed no history of heart disease, alcohol abuse, or organ distress. Her physical exam confirmed the same. No sign of an aneurysm either. Tissue and blood samples demonstrated the usual traces of vitamins and minerals. No evidence of steroid use or bad medicinal interactions. Trace amounts of tobacco indicating a light smoker, probably an infrequent celebratory cigar. And there were slight elevations in carbon monoxide and methanol levels, of course."

Scotti nodded. "A by-product of the car-racing profession."

"We drivers are all a bit toxic at our core." Devlin winked.

In the yard, adolescent revelers darted in every direction across the lawn. The kids consumed the cake and ice cream in record time. Devlin cut the tethered ends of a net suspended between two cypresses, sending hundreds of water balloons raining down onto their heads. That's when the party really got started.

***

Devlin and Scotti joined Chiara, Vin, and Prost, seeking refuge from the ruckus beneath a pergola weighed down with bougainvillea vines. They settled into teak chairs circled around a metal washtub that overflowed with ice-cold Morettis. Scotti gave one of the beers to Devlin and addressed the small group. "Devlin's not buying into this 'accidental death' theory, folks. What are your thoughts?"

Devlin's sister, Chiara, swung her blond ponytailed head to face him. "Alcohol poisoning leading to a massive coronary? Seems far-fetched. The poor bastard was a picture of health. Death after only a few sips of grappa smells fishy to me." She scowled. "I know the official investigation is closed, but there has to be more to it."

Devlin nodded and swallowed his brew. Though he and his older, adopted sister had grown up in entirely different circles, Chiara's help in tracking down Ella's murderer had brought about a mutual admiration that he wished they'd shared earlier. He'd come to learn that her hunches often mirrored his. "I agree," Devlin said. "The guy was an ass, and he had his share of haters: ambivalent fans, disgruntled press, warring sponsors, indifferent crew chief, and a famous fiancée. Gotta be something to that."

Chiara shrugged. "He publicly cavorts with all sorts of women, and he dumps his bride-to-be on live TV. *I'd* have killed him if I were her."

Devlin nodded. "I placed a couple calls. One to Blue Rhino Team. They hung up on me. Another to the Aurora family. To extend my sympathies."

Prost said, "You mean to check out leads?"

"Exactly," Devlin said. "I briefly spoke with Erika Aurora, one of the three chief officers. Bright, professional. I didn't extract much, but I didn't push too hard this time. Runa was too bereaved to come to the phone. I'd like to touch base with the other sibling, too, and fish around."

Devlin didn't have much to go on besides a hunch of impropriety. Still, a fellow racer was dead. It didn't sit well with him that someone might be responsible for it.

"What's your theory?" Scotti's younger brother, Vin, spoke up. He tipped his head to the side. "You look like the cat that ate the canary, Devlin. What gives?"

Devlin smiled. The kid always had great instincts. As teenagers, Devlin and Vin had been close, but later the Marine Corps had stationed Vin in remote parts of the world for much of their lives. Last year a Syrian car bomb had left burns over half of Vin's body and sent him stateside. They'd reconnected when Devlin and Scotti had convinced the able-bodied hero to join their crew.

"Not a theory, Vin, more like a gut feeling." Devlin mused about those who seemed to despise Giancarlo. Then he explained how he'd secretly pocketed the grappa bottle's cork and wrapping. "My first impulse was to safeguard the evidence. If I hadn't picked them up, someone else might've. Maybe a perp, maybe just a souvenir hound. Either way, the evidence would've been gone."

"Why not give the evidence to the authorities?" Vin asked.

"We Rangers have worked with the Monaco police in the past," Scotti interjected. "Their ME is bright, but their CSI team is not as…thorough as we'd like."

Devlin nodded. "I ran a full analysis back at the Grotto. Headquarters showed Runa Aurora's and Giancarlo's fingerprints from when they exchanged the bottle. Otherwise nothing suspicious. No residue other than grappa, glass fragments, and road tar. I'm holding on to them, just in case."

"In case what?" Chiara sat up in her lawn chair. "Do I smell a HELL Ranger mission brewing?"

"God, I hope this one's kick-ass," Prost, another brother-in-arms, said excitedly. "With rescues, and mayhem, and another kidnapped pontiff. We need a sick one, Dev, c'mon."

Devlin stroked the stubble on his chin. "The one you guys did in Paris last week was sick."

"How the hell would you know? Your ass was stalled out in the Grotto. Examining a cork," Chiara said. "You were busy turning the engine, while we pushed the car. Same as the handful of lame missions right before that."

What is that incessant tapping? Devlin looked down to see his foot thumping a mile a minute on the flagstone. He stood and grabbed a few ice cubes to roll around in his mouth. The heat outside was sweltering. Back to the dunk tank, maybe?

Chiara stood. She put a hand on his shoulder and turned him to fully face the group, like an intervention. "We need some hot missions, Devlin. But that's not all. We want you to be a part of them again. Out in the field, getting dirty and righteous."

Marcello sped past them, laughing and shouting cartoon names at his compatriots, who chased him with water soakers back into the shady trees of the thick woods surrounding the villa.

Chiara looked Devlin in the eye. "Clearly, Marcello is in a good place again, satisfied. What he needs now is for his father to be whole again too, and…fulfilled." Chiara gestured to the group behind her. "We all think it's time you get back to doing what you're good at."

Devlin knew they were right. Ever since Ella's murder, and the death of the Rangers on that mission, he'd been avoiding complicated challenges that would endanger his crew. Like the man behind the curtain, he'd been orchestrating from afar and delegating only menial assignments. His crew deserved more.

Then again, he looked around at those he stood to lose. He shook his head and laughed. "You're all in cahoots. I thank you for your support. But your ganging up on me like this is unfair. Lupo would never—"

"I resent any statement that begins, 'Lupo would never.' It's unconscionable, my man." Devlin's best friend, Joe Buggiagalupo, entered the yard.

Relieved by the interruption, Devlin swung his gaze to Lupo and jet-sprayed a mouthful of beer all over the base of a fig tree.

The six-foot hulking marble-layer, known for his Popeye musculature, apparently had forgotten his pants. Instead, the beefy Italian wore a pair of bright yellow women's tights, a royal-blue satin sash, and a black-and-yellow striped tunic.

"What?" Lupo said. His tunic ruffle slumped. "Did I miss the water balloons?"

Chapter 4

The Tuscan hillside *paese* of Siena, Italy, fans out from the central shell-shaped Piazza del Campo town square. It extends outward, through the maze of cobblestone alleyways, stone houses, shops, and smaller *piazze* of the various *contrade*, or districts, until it meets the forest. The woods that guard its perimeter overlook the surrounding vineyards of the Chianti wine region.

Siena is divided into seventeen contrade, akin to the boroughs of Manhattan. Since the Middle Ages, ten of the contrade annually vie with one another for bragging rights achieved by a victory in a bareback horse race, called Palio, which is only seventy-five seconds long.

The race, held twice a year on July 2 and August 16, is preceded by as much pomp and circumstance as the postrace victory parties. Participants and spectators have been brought to their knees over a loss, or a win. They've paraded through the ancient cobblestone streets waving flags particular to each *contrada* in victory.

Joe "Lupo" Buggiagalupo's ancestors had believed that such pageantry and fanfare was a matter of civic pride. Thus, Lupo wore the tights and ruffles.

"I'm sorry I'm late, Marcello. Your godfather has been given the honor of planning Aquila contrada's prerace horse-blessing dinner, happening in just a few weeks. I was hung up haggling with a prosciutto vendor." Lupo pulled a bright yellow silk flag bearing regal eagles from around his neck. He draped and tied it securely around the boy's shoulders. Whispers of reverence and delight emanated from the pint-sized partygoers.

Lupo threw his fist in the air and shouted the name of their contrada, "Aquila!"

The young revelers chanted back, "Aquila! Aquila! Aquila!" and tore off for the inflatable waterslide.

Lupo cracked open a beer and leaned against the pergola. "What is it you were saying 'I would never…'?"

Devlin spoke up first. "You'd never throw me under the bus, like this bunch of—"

Chiara cut him off. "We're suggesting to Devlin that he get back in the game."

Devlin snorted. "You mean coercing, cajoling, berating…"

Lupo slapped a hand on his shoulder. "Listen to them. Get back in, full bore. You want to. You just don't know it yet."

"How the hell do you presume—" Devlin's cell phone rang. The screen indicated an area code in the lower Dolomite region of Italy. Where Aurora Vineyard was located. Devlin stepped to the garden, away from the chattering adults and giggling children, and took the call.

"Mr. Lucchesi, Erika Aurora here. Thank you again for extending your kind condolences to my family last week. You were the only race car driver to approach my brother Leif at the memorial service, and Leif made sure to share that with me and Runa."

"Call me Devlin. I hope your sister's well. It's never easy losing a loved one." A stab of pain in Devlin's heart proved he knew this too well.

"She's getting on as best she can. Personally, I'm glad the devil is out of her life. Too bad it wasn't sooner," Erika said.

Struck by her callous demeanor, Devlin prodded, "Is there something you wish to discuss, Ms. Aurora?" He tried to picture Erika's face from promotional ads and news pieces. Instead he kept envisioning her younger sister Runa from the postrace incident.

"Devlin, I'd like to hire you. On the recommendation of a mutual friend." The sound of her breath echoed in a glass, followed by a gulp. Sipping Aurora wine, perhaps? "Seems to think you might be the best man for the job," Erika said.

"What job are you looking to fill?" Devlin said, amused yet intrigued by her directness.

"I believe someone is targeting me and my company. And I'd like you to find out who it is, so that I may deal with them. Our friend feels strongly that you would easily and discreetly accomplish this task." A distinct breathy sip, and another gulp.

Devlin licked his suddenly parched lips. "When you say 'targeting,' do you—"

"I'm convinced that someone is trying to kill me, and sabotage and destroy my company," she said.

"Any proof?" Devlin had always been a voracious consumer of news. Ever since losing Ella, he'd spent countless sleepless nights devouring medical, business, and sports journals. He now recalled what he knew of Erika.

Erika Aurora had graduated top of her class at the renowned Bocconi business school in Milan. Like him, she was a member of Mensa. Erika was also a noted leader in the wine industry. A Master Sommelier of Italian wines, she was an astute entrepreneur whose company had maintained positive growth over the past decade, based primarily on innovative marketing campaigns. Erika was smart and successful. But was she paranoid because of her incredible success?

"I'm not paranoid," she said as if reading his mind. She breathed, sipped, and gulped again. He felt slightly aroused by it.

She continued, "There have been incidents at the winery that one would objectively construe as dangerous to my welfare. We have plenty of competitors, naysayers, activists, and whatnot. But things have happened lately that feel more…personal in nature." Devlin heard a glass shatter on her end. So endeth the arousal.

"I see. May I ask, who is this referral…this mutual friend?"

"Mr. Lucchesi, I mentioned discretion. I'm afraid I'm unable to discuss specifics now, but if you agreed to visit me here at the winery..."

Erika chatted on about the logistics of a meeting. Devlin knew that the opportunity to pursue the mysterious death of Giancarlo Venchi had presented itself in a nicely wrapped package. He could investigate the winery, the source of the infamous grappa bottle cork (still in his possession because, admittedly, he had an obsessive-compulsive personality). He would also interrogate the jilted fiancée and the younger brother. All of this would be done under the guise of helping a paranoid CEO, who happened to be a sexy wine sipper.

A sudden, high-pitched scream of a young girl pierced the jovial miasma in the backyard. More shouts followed. A half dozen boys and girls bolted from the periphery of the woods and into the grass, crying. Another five or six darted out of the forest behind them. All wore frosting-stained faces marked with terror. This was no party game.

"Marcello!" Devlin shouted. His son was nowhere to be found. Devlin ditched the phone. He grabbed the only weapons at his disposal, a water cannon and a bottle opener, and ran toward the source of the peril. Malevolent threats machine-gunned through his mind: terrorists, serial killer, ax-wielding lunatic, escaped prisoners...

On his heels, Lupo, Scotti and Prost ran with him, fanning out and calling for Marcello. Chiara corralled the children into the house, amid panicked cries of "*Cinghiale! Cinghiale!*"

Wild boar.

Devlin halted. He planted his feet and raised the pointed bottle opener in his fist, ready for attack. He imagined a bristly, humped behemoth of a swine with sharp tusks. “Brace yourselves,” he yelled to his crew. “They’re big, fast, and mean.”

The rustle of the trees indicated its location.

Devlin gestured to the crew their attack plan.

Suddenly, not one, but two…baby boar, the size of dachshunds, wiggled onto the lawn. They spotted Devlin, squealed, and ran back into the woods.

Devlin lowered his weapons and looked back at his crew. They were already rolling on the ground in laughter. Literally rolling.

Chiara opened the door, and the kids began trickling outside.

At that moment, a red-faced Marcello sprinted from the line of trees about a hundred feet north of where Devlin stood. Marcello turned and squirted his powerful super soaker about twenty-five feet into the trees. He bolted for Lupo, who stood in his line of sight.

Devlin heard it before he saw it. The low, guttural, fast-paced snort of a very large, very pissed-off mother boar. She rampaged from the woods in a blur, headed straight for Marcello.

Devlin raced toward his son. But as Devlin watched the black-haired beast dig its hooves deep into the earth like a racehorse, he knew he’d never make it in time.

Lupo lunged for Marcello. Before he could reach him, Lupo's feet landed on the slick waterslide. Lupo went ass over heels onto his back.

Closer now, Devlin shot his super soaker at the beast in an attempt to distract it, but the boar charged Marcello like a bull storms a matador.

Prost and Chiara hurried the children back into the house. Scotti rushed the boar from another angle, waving his arms in the air to divert it from Marcello.

Instead of running toward the house, where the children still pushed and stumbled to get inside the door, Marcello led the boar away from them, toward the opposite end of the yard. Amid his terror, a surge of pride welled inside Devlin. At the boy's sudden shift in direction, the boar stumbled. So did Scotti, who went down hard on his own flank.

The boar redirected and aimed its daggerlike tusks for the downed quarry near his path. It lowered its head, snorted, and charged Scotti.

Feet away now, Devlin chucked the beer opener into the rear quarter of the animal. It lodged in its sinew. The boar squealed in anguish, but still headed for Scotti.

Devlin rammed the animal cross-side and tackled it onto the Slip'n Slide. Man and beast slid together, upended, appendages flailing. Devlin heard a bone snap and prayed it wasn't his.

The grass at the end of the plastic yellow tarp halted their progress. The boar struggled to stand, and it pinned Devlin beneath its weight.

Devlin spotted the wild animal's broken leg and leaned toward it. The boar lost its balance. Devlin heaved the beast off him, onto its back. The boar continued to fight, and Devlin parried the massive tusks that threatened to impale him.

Lupo loomed over both of them. He hauled back and drove his marble pick deep into the neck of the vicious beast. The boar squealed and thrashed harder. Devlin could feel its powerful limbs gradually weakening beneath him, until finally the beast surrendered the fight.

Devlin stood. He gestured to Lupo, who used his body to screen the children from witnessing Devlin's next move. Devlin twisted the boar's massive neck and snapped it, thereby ending its rampage and its suffering.

Devlin shook his head. What was he thinking? For a moment, while on the phone with Erika Aurora, he'd been considering HELL Ranger fieldwork again. But it was too soon. His son obviously needed him.

Marcello ran back to Devlin, gave him and Lupo bear hugs. He scampered about the yard with his super soaker and a huge smile, excitedly recounting the adventure to his amazed friends. He stopped to hug Scotti, now back on his feet, and then dragged him by the hand toward the house, shouting, "*Andiamo, tutti!* Let's have more cake!"

But he never got that far.

"*Nonni!*" Marcello tossed his squirt gun and darted into the embrace of his newly arrived grandparents, who bore armfuls of birthday presents.

Devlin picked up the water gun and sprayed himself in the face.

Lupo glanced at his best friend shooting himself. "What's up?"

His family was right. His son would be fine. Marcello had rebounded well after Ella's death, as well as all the misadventures that had followed, from terrorists to wild boar.

The sabbatical he'd taken with Marcello, cruising around the cornfields and mountains of America, had provided them both healing. At home, his son was surrounded by an abundance of family and friends, who clearly knew how to take of care him. What Marcello needed now was for his father to be whole again. One look at Marcello's smiling face, forever haunted by green eyes identical to Ella's, and Devlin knew that there was no way in hell he'd ever let him down.

He scooped up the phone he'd discarded, dialed Erika, and explained his piggish interruption. "Ms. Aurora, I'll take the job." He flashed Lupo a killer smile and an eager thumbs-up.

Lupo slapped Devlin's shoulders with both hands. "Life just got even more interesting, didn't it?"

Chapter 5

Runa Aurora despised most people. Maybe not people themselves so much as *interacting* with them. She hated engaging the daily tourists who sputtered their rental cars and tour buses into her vineyard for tastings of Aurora's assorted wines and grappa. They'd smile at her as if they could truly distinguish the subtle nuances in flavor, color, clarity and aroma. Most couldn't. They'd imbibe too much (too ignorant to properly swish and spit). Then they'd buy a single bottle from her (often the cheapest) and chatter on about how they wished their friends could see them now. They probably guzzled down the bottle that evening with a cheeseburger at their cheesy hotel.

Worse were the ridiculous public events that she and her siblings endured to "ensure the vital growth of the company." From parading their vision at trade shows and conventions, to flashing their personas at movie premieres and sporting events, to brandishing their megawatt smiles in commercials and news shows, Runa wanted none of it. She knew her no-show at Giancarlo's memorial service last week had been a trending topic, yet she was relieved that her brother had stepped up to represent the family. The incessant dealings with sponsors, vendors, distributors, customers, and whoever else wanted a taste of the golden cup that was Aurora…it was too much.

How glorious life would be if she could spend every waking minute in the "alchemy" room, as Erika had always called it. The sorcery room…the room where the magic happened…the place where the witch kept her cauldron…Leif and Erika had always teased her about preferring to live her life behind its closed doors. Runa sat there now, experimenting with new concoctions and varietals of wines and liqueurs in the bowels of the winery.

This was Runa's domain. Like most nights, she toiled away in flip-flops and a tank top, her lustrous golden curls piled high atop her head. She preferred her black-rimmed Coke-bottle eyeglasses in lieu of her contacts. She absolutely couldn't work without Led Zeppelin blaring through her earbuds. Runa thrived when she was hunkering over beakers and microscopes, propagating vine cuttings, or stirring fermented brew. Whether Erika and Leif chose to believe it or not, her indefatigable R&D was the lifeblood of Aurora Vineyard. And over the past decade, while the three gradually took the reins from their father, they existed in a general state of accord.

Until someone leaked the news that threatened to destroy them all.

A blinking buzzer went off. She rose from her stool and entered an inner sanctum, reserved for delicate chemical procedures. She donned a long glove and removed a beaker from a nitroglycerin tub. A quarter of an hour later, she left the inner room and resumed her cuttings. She hoped to hybrid a delicate young pinot noir from the upper Piedmont region with one from Alto Adige.

She peered out of her laboratory's wall of windows overlooking the two-story factory. It housed the bottling works and the adjoining wine and spirits plant. The ceiling-high vats and interconnecting piping gleamed beneath the fluorescents. Only a half hour more until she needed to add a fresh flow-through satchel of their secret herb recipe to the grappa vat. She went back to splicing and grafting a little while longer.

On second thought, it wasn't the interaction with people she despised. It was people. She was a hater. And most people hated her. Her looks were the essence of perfection. Aphrodite would have been jealous. According to Erika, all three siblings bore the burden of their dead mother's superior aesthetics. Worse, Runa was an introvert. Speaking in public terrified her. She hid it well, and others, especially the media, perceived her as a cold bitch.

And forget about a love life. Of course, she had needs, and she'd sipped the wine of the finest fountainheads in the world. But she knew none of them had ever truly loved her. They usually wanted a taste of the "glamour" that was Runa Aurora or else a leg up in whatever industry they ran. The devil Giancarlo had even begged for a bloody Formula One sponsorship, and then offhandedly discarded it as he'd done with their relationship.

Giancarlo Venchi had truly been among the worst of all people. She'd thought she loved him. But an unknown source had provided her proof of his duplicity. And when she'd traveled to Monte Carlo to confront him, he'd broken her heart…in public, her true arena of pain. She despised him most of all.

Now the devil was dead. The bastard had it coming.

Her cell phone rang. "You again? Aren't you sweet?" Runa said. It took her lips a few seconds to form into a smile. She realized she'd been gritting her teeth at the thought of her dead fiancé.

"I appreciate your offer of condolences," Runa said. "But really, you can keep them. The world is a better place without Giancarlo Venchi in it."

As she spoke, Runa again glanced out the lab windows overlooking the plant. Erika stood atop one of the grappa vats. Runa hadn't noticed her sister come in.

Erika stretched her arm across the surface of the brew. Careful not to topple in, she dropped a new, bulging dry satchel of herbs into the grappa. She scurried quickly down the steel ladder, clearly anxious to avoid the potent vapors emanating from the fermenting yeast.

Erika headed in Runa's direction and walked past a shipment of boxed anniversary grappa. It was the same variety that Runa had delivered to the Monaco race. She swallowed hard at the memory of Giancarlo's final moments.

Erika hesitated at a wall stacked high with boxed bottled water. Her sister pulled a clipboard that hung from a nail and scanned it. Then she threw it down and shook her head in obvious disgust. The three siblings had agreed that their water line might someday represent the pinnacle of Aurora Vineyard's success. But a court-ordered injunction had halted all distribution of the product.

Runa knew it was because of the news leak.

Erika ascended the long, steep flight of metal steps to the lab. Runa wrapped up her call and hung up.

Erika rapped her knuckles against the open door. "I overheard some of your conversation. Is that our friend?"

Runa nodded. She carefully wrapped the tiny plant roots and cleaned and dried her instruments.

"Have you given any more thought to what we three discussed in my office?" Erika asked. "Our Sister is wise, and she has many resources to help you."

Erika made reference to the ancient Sisterhood of Amiata, a secret group dating back to the fourth century, of which she, Runa, and a select group of others belonged, through sick and sin. Bound by the ideal of guarding a sacred golden artifact, the sisterhood supplemented their objective with procuring lavish bounty by questionable means.

"I have the utmost faith in the Sisterhood. I'll do whatever she says," Runa said.

"I knew you'd see it my way." Erika extended her arm to Runa's. They clasped each other's Astrale watches and nodded. Erika turned and left without another word.

Runa turned to the sole surveillance camera in her laboratory and ensured that it was indeed disabled.

Chapter 6

Two weeks after the Fédération Internationale de l'Automobile (FIA) officially confirmed that Devlin "Lucky" Lucchesi had won the Monaco Grand Prix, the champion prevailed again. He solidly crushed the second-place Veronica Griffith by three full seconds at the Circuit Gilles-Villeneuve in Montreal, Canada.

Back in Italy days later, Devlin believed that Veronica's heart-pounding congratulatory embrace eclipsed both the victory and his overall circuit point lead.

"Anything going on with you two?" Scotti switched on the windshield wipers of the lorry that transported Devlin's noncritical racing parts (tools, jacks, extra tires). The crew chief was headed to the Monza Automobile Research Institute (MARI). There he would gather with the rest of the crew flying back from Canada, who bore the critical cargo (chassis, engines, computers). They planned to discuss wing improvements on a prototype with fellow engineers before the Baku European Grand Prix street circuit in a couple weeks. Devlin and Lupo had hitched a ride with him to Verona for Devlin's meeting with Erika Aurora.

"Going on with Veronica? Nah, nothing like that," Devlin said. He focused on the double yellow line of the *autostrada*. They passed a sign showing five kilometers until Verona. "I just like her smell."

"Her smell?" Scotti snorted at the remark.

Lupo sat in the middle of the cab. He sighed. "Nothing like the smell of a woman."

Devlin turned to Lupo and asked, "Hear from Ana Malia lately?"

Lupo shook his head. "It's been four months since that week in Barbados. She's been knocking back BBC assignments left and right. Haven't even sexted in two weeks. Miss her smell."

"What about that rich interior designer? Weren't you laying her marble?" Scotti asked.

"She's okay. She just wants me for my tool." Lupo exhibited his trusty marble pick. Handed down through generations of marble layers, it was the one he'd used to neutralize the wild boar. And to ward off a psychotic killer and a demented gorilla in the recent past.

"What about this vineyard owner, Devlin?" Scotti said. "I read the files you'd pulled on Erika Aurora. I've never seen a more beautiful CEO."

"No need for a hookup, boys," Devlin said. "How about that AS Roma game?"

"Missed it," they both answered.

Scotti drove into the expansive parking lot of Verona's exhibition center, known as Veronafiere, just outside the stone walls of the city proper. For the massive eighteen-wheel transporter, the historic city center of Verona was impassable. The morning rain had given way to noontime sun, and Devlin and Lupo planned to hoof it to their meeting.

Devlin shook hands with Scotti and donned his rucksack. A tattered book tumbled from the unzipped pocket of Devlin's bag.

Scotti shot down his long arm from the truck cabin and snatched the book midair, just before it dropped into a puddle.

Their eyes flew wide, and they stared speechless at one another.

A moment passed, and Devlin reached up and pulled his pit boss into a one-armed hug. "You always have my back."

"Always." Scotti shut the door, waved, and hauled off.

Devlin and Lupo crossed the convention center lot and headed for the traffic-clogged boulevard. Lupo broke the silence. "Is that the book from Ella's dad?"

Devlin solemnly nodded.

Ella's father, Maurizio, had lost his daughter and his wife, Ella's mother, in the terrorist bombing of Rome's train station over a year earlier. Soon after, Devlin and Marcello had moved into Maurizio's family home. Devlin was sure this had helped the healing process for all of them. Especially when Prost's mother, Filomena, had joined them to further facilitate Marcello's routine. The strong-willed, gorgeous Sicilian who'd been sitting Marcello regularly since he was an infant imbued laughter back into their lives. That's why Devlin cherished the book that Maurizio and Filomena had presented him the night of Marcello's birthday.

The seventeenth-century fairy tale collection by Italian poet Basile, *Pentamerone*, had been Ella's favorite storybook. Maurizio had recently unearthed the book from Ella's childhood bookshelf. He'd gifted it to Devlin, for the message she'd penned inside the front cover. A line from Shakespeare's *The Tempest*, it read: *I would not wish any companion in the world but you.* Devlin had initially ascribed it to the whimsical flourish of a young girl. Until he'd noted the date beneath it—his and Ella's wedding date. Had she meant the book as a gift for Devlin that day? Had she meant it as an affirmation, one that she'd likely have shared with their firstborn, Marcello, or to their second child had their lives not been cut short? The book with its inscription was an enigma, and Devlin would always treasure it.

He and Lupo rounded the corner of the immense exhibition center. Devlin was stunned by the dramatic lighting and signage splattered about the façade, all announcing the upcoming Worldwide Water Summit.

He'd experienced the Vinitaly Wine Expo here last April. The plethora of press, vendors, and celebrities that had overrun the streets of Verona would likely return for this summit. In fact, he surmised that for a global water value conference, replete with activists, financiers, legal eagles, desalination plant operators, utility contractors, and government trade and environment ministers, the fanfare might even be kicked up a tick.

Devlin frowned. "I thought the summit was happening in Rome this year?"

Lupo shrugged. "Dunno. But look at the swarm of reporters camped out here already. I wouldn't want to see this place jammed tight with people in a few weeks."

Devlin nodded. "Good luck getting an espresso, right? Speaking of which, I could go—"

"Shh!" Lupo froze. "Do you hear that?"

Lupo's eyes darted back and forth. He scanned the hordes of reporters spouting their noontime news coverage.

"All I hear is people talking," Devlin said.

"Exactly. Shh!" Lupo put his finger to his lips to silence him.

Devlin listened. What would magnetize Lupo's attention so fully? And then he heard it.

An authoritative yet feminine voice purred with tigerlike intensity and knowledgeable candor. It was the unmistakable lilt of a BBC reporter.

"...one of the world's largest annual wine conventions. And in just a few short weeks, Veronafiere will host the Worldwide Water Summit. Leaders deny reports that the summit was abruptly moved from the Eternal City to Verona due to continued gorilla sightings, of the unrecovered primates that allegedly escaped the Rome Zoo over a year ago. Nevertheless, organizers here contend they'll be ready...

"Tune in this weekend for my exclusive interview with Erika Aurora, CEO of the legally embattled Aurora Vineyard…

"Reporting live from Verona, Italy…for BBC News…this is Ana Malia."

Chapter 7

Romeo Montague declared, "There is no world without Verona walls, but purgatory, torture, hell itself." The bronze bust of Shakespeare that protrudes from the city's fortification attests to this. Even Julius Caesar fancied the burg as his favorite place to kick back. Ana Malia agreed.

Ana had always identified with Verona. Both were classic yet cosmopolitan, savvy yet artistic, productive and sophisticated. Both she and the city exuded the beauty, wisdom, and high-spirited attitude that made people fall in love with them. At least her part-time lover, Lupo, would agree with that appraisal.

Four months ago, she and Lupo had rattled their cabana for one long, glorious week in Barbados. Since then, not a single phone conversation. Only occasional sexting and sporadic voice mails.

It seemed so fitting that today, wrapping her report outside Veronafiere, Ana had locked eyes with Lupo at long last. "My God, you're beautiful," he'd mouthed from across the boulevard with his unmistakable boyish charm. Just one look, and she'd wanted him all over again.

Minutes later, she was slathering his face with kisses. Lupo enfolded her in his arms like a warm blanket, and Ana knew she loved him. So why couldn't she ever get up the nerve to say it?

She stepped back from Lupo and faced Devlin. "Lucky…you look like you're doing well, my friend."

A strong hug convinced her that, even after losing so much, Devlin was at least on his way back to good again. "I knew *you'd* be here, Lucky. But this guy…" She gestured to Lupo. "How'd you rustle *him* up?"

Devlin tipped his head. "You knew I'd be in Verona? How's that? I'm actually here to meet—"

"I know. You're here to see Erika Aurora. She's been detained, and she sent me instead." She flashed him her Bulgari Astrale wristwatch, symbolic of the Sisterhood to which she, Erika, and Runa belonged. "The Auroras asked me to help. As you remember, Sisters always have each other's backs."

Devlin nodded his understanding.

Ana grasped Lupo's burly forearm and beamed. The watch strapped to his wrist was nearly identical to her own. "You still wear it?" she asked.

"Since the day you gave it to me," Lupo said. "I've never taken it off."

Ana smiled at the memory. As far as she knew, Lupo had been the only man ever gifted one.

***

Ana laced fingers with Lupo. "C'mon, I'll explain everything on the way to the vineyard." She led both men to the BBC television van, and they climbed aboard. They exchanged pleasantries with Letizia, Ana's camera operator, with whom Devlin and Lupo had become familiar in Rome.

They pulled onto the SS12 highway leading out of the city. Devlin stole a last glance at Verona's exhibition center. It was nearly the size of Rome's new rail station, the one rebuilt after the terror attack that had killed Ella. Though Ana and Devlin had maintained a solid professional relationship prior to the violence, they'd forged an everlasting bond of friendship through the events that unfolded.

"You'll find the Auroras are an interesting family, Devlin," Ana said. "I hope you'll all be useful to each other." Devlin shot her an inquisitive look. Ana ignored it and pulled a couple water bottles from a shoulder bag. "Contraband," she said. "The commerce department doesn't allow sale of this product."

She handed Devlin and Lupo each a bottle that bore the Aurora Vineyard insignia and orange label. The high-grade plastic containers were shaped like ancient pottery urns and stopped up with corks. Devlin held his up to the window and examined the fine specks of glitter inside the liquid that shimmered like a kaleidoscope. "Specks," he said. "Metallic ones. Almost like the gold flecks in Goldschläger schnapps."

"Platinum," Ana said. "Aurora Vineyard has infused their bottled water with minute flecks of platinum. Straight from the Fountain of Youth."

Chapter 8

The gondola lift descended the picturesque Italian Dolomite mountain range at a whisper, giving Leif Aurora a few minutes of solitude from the rigors of vineyard business.

The mountains always soothed him. Leif had spent most of this past winter skiing the lower Alps of Switzerland while working toward his MBA at the University of Lausanne. But he preferred to ski the Dolomite ridge just north of Verona, what he called "Leif's Peaks," where his vineyard home was nestled. Growing up over the past quarter century, he'd always loved hiking, cycling, and hang gliding during the warmer months. This summer he planned to blaze new trails with the hot young thing he'd met at school. Provided his pain-in-the-ass sisters allowed him a minute's free time from running the business.

Cursed by the movie-star good looks of his deceased mother's lineage, Leif was also burdened with intellect and charisma. People were naturally drawn to him, which facilitated his prowess for brokering deals. Hell, his sisters had had him negotiating contracts as soon as he'd hit puberty.

He knew that was the reason that his company prospered. Erika could crunch numbers and brainstorm marketing ideas all she wanted. Runa could concoct potions day and night, but the real chemistry was with people. He had the knack. And Erika and Runa relentlessly fostered his ingenuity for the good of the company. Even now, in the face of the news leak that threatened the vineyard's existence. Or maybe because of it.

Yet, for as long as he could remember, Leif had always longed for something more. Grateful for the affluent lifestyle his company provided him, he still sought to give back. His master's in business had been a given. The flip side of his dual major, environmental studies, had gotten him thinking. The latest research had suggested that worldwide water conservation had reached crisis mode. He'd fought Erika tooth and nail to accept this fact, and to adapt. His improvements to Aurora Vineyard's water conservation techniques over the past year had taken a ridiculous amount of persuasion. But he knew he'd have to push Erika and Runa harder to accept his further demands.

In the past few years, their wine and grappa revenues had far surpassed industry standards. Perhaps his theory of dropping Erika's brass-ring product line, bottled water, would not be such an undue burden to their company as she insisted it would be. Perhaps the planet's limited freshwater supply was a resource that should be free to the world, not controlled or paid for.

His lover strongly upheld this conviction, so why shouldn't his family? Just because Erika had helped raise him didn't mean she had the right to hang like an albatross about his neck. And forget Runa. Her aloof, cynical ways had never provided him any support. Leif planned to change the direction of the company and achieve something more than just the bottom line that drove his sisters. Erika believed that they should have the right to bottle and sell the waters of the Fountain of Youth. But why not ensure the water's accessibility to those who needed it?

Glimpsing the distant shimmering pool that was Lago di Garda, Leif smiled. At long last, he knew how to achieve this goal. And nothing would get in his way.

***

Awaiting the arrival of the aerial tram in the stuffy, sun-laden lower station, Ana Malia removed her cream suit jacket, revealing her own ample mountain range. She tossed back her nutmeg hair and glossed her pouty lips while Devlin and Lupo enjoyed the view. Then they turned and looked at the Dolomites.

"Wait until you get a load of the Bloodsucker," Ana said.

"I'm intrigued," Devlin said. "What's that?"

"When Augustus Aurora died and Erika assumed control of the vineyard, in her eyes anyway, the press gave her the moniker 'Bloodsucker.' She squeezes out every last drop of juice from her vineyard's grapes, right down to their skins," Ana said. "Plus, she's bled the life out of the small producers that once dotted the region."

"Augustus died over six months ago, yet his will was read sometime in the last couple of months. Why?" Devlin said.

"Aurora was represented by in-house legal counsel for decades. Some shyster. When Augustus died, Erika outsourced. Now they keep on retainer Frigo, Orologio & Blatz, out of Milan. When the shyster refused to turn over the will, the new firm caught up with him in New Zealand. The will was finally read, leaving the company to the kids. No big surprise. Until..."

Ana popped the cork on her bottle of Aurora water. She gulped a few hearty swigs. Water dripped down her bare throat and cascaded over the cleavage beneath her white silk top.

Lupo sighed.

"You gonna make it?" Devlin asked him. Lupo shook his head slowly.

"No surprises in the will...until the aquifer came to light," Devlin said.

"Exactly," Ana said.

"That's what caused the uproar," Devlin said. "Among the press, the industry, the government, the competition. Aurora had been sitting on an unmarked aquifer for decades, one that the Italian government had never recorded, or even knew existed. Until..."

"Until someone leaked it." Ana nodded. "When everyone got wind of it, the Italian courts moved in and ruled for an injunction. Aurora would have to cease and desist all tapping of the aquifer in its production and consumption."

"That meant no bottling of the aquifer's natural springwater," Devlin said. "And no irrigation of their acres upon acres of grapevines."

"How the hell does a winery run with no water?" Lupo held up his bottle. "And if that's the case, then what the hell am I drinking?"

Ana said, "*That*, as I told you, is contraband. Aurora labels it 'FONS' after the god of freshwater springs. It's sourced from the aquifer running beneath their land and packaged as 'Pure Water from the Fountain of Youth.' Not a bad marketing ploy, if you ask me. Erika shipped me a case, bottled before the embargo, as a gift." Ana finished the bottle and tucked it into her Prada handbag.

"They also continue to bottle their renowned fine wine and grappa with a bit of innovation," she said. "Aurora has set the environmental standard for vineyard irrigation via container technique, trapping overland mountain runoff, snow, and rain. The ban has propelled them to the forefront of water conservation."

"You can't tell me runoff water supports their entire irrigation system," Lupo said.

"They supplement, considerably, by importing water for production," she said.

Devlin exhaled. "Sounds costly. And frustrating. Especially when you're sitting on a free, plentiful water source."

Ana nodded.

"Why impose an injunction?" Lupo said.

"The courts are being pulled in a hundred directions and need time to sort out a decision," Ana said. "That's why I'm here. Erika, Runa, and Leif have agreed to grant me an exclusive interview. My goal is to provide the rest of the world Aurora Vineyard's perspective. I hope to turn up the heat a bit. Pressure the courts into making a decision, one way or another. Either privatize the aquifer, or decree it a public water source, instead of keeping everyone in limbo."

The gondola lift came into view, about five hundred feet away. It hummed along on steel cables nearly fifteen hundred feet above the valley below.

Ana stood and donned her suit jacket. Lupo assisted, brushing her hair back from her chest with both hands. Ana smirked.

Devlin stood and tossed his rucksack over his shoulder. "These other interested parties…the ones disputing whether the aquifer is considered public or private—water rights activists, governments, competitors—who's to give them a voice in the public forum?"

"I've interviewed them all. Aurora is reluctant to bare details to the media, except to me. But the rest of them will talk to just about anyone. That's also where the Worldwide Water Summit comes into play. World leaders, activists, public and private companies, legal representatives, and anyone else who's interested can come to the annual event," Ana said. "It's a venue to discuss ideas on revolutionizing water rights and conservation."

The aerial lift slowed to a crawl. At one hundred feet out, it entered the station and stopped. A dashing young man in his early twenties smiled, waved, and opened the door to exit the lift.

"One more thing, before Thor gets here," Lupo said. "Who leaked the existence of the aquifer, causing all this turmoil?"

Ana opened her mouth to speak, but the blond god had already crossed the tarmac in long, sultry strides. Bearing platinum-speckled gifts of FONS, he welcomed them.

***

The tall blond Viking-Italian who looked like Thor pissed off Lupo from the moment he'd introduced himself. He'd clasped Ana Malia's hand to ease her aboard his ship, and Lupo's stomach churned. Standing not even ten feet across from them, Lupo nearly retched with every stitch of Ana's laughter that the Versace-clad goon elicited as they sailed in the air toward his realm.

Lupo discreetly checked his look in one of the long rectangular rearview mirrors. He spat into his hand and slicked down his side cowlick. Devlin rolled his eyes and patted Lupo on the back. Not even his best friend could keep Lupo's bile from rising.

The buzz of a single-engine Pilatus Porter distracted him. Lupo glanced out the right wall of open windows and calmed his breathing while he watched. The plane puttered at a higher elevation than the lift, over the bright green landscape speckled with shade from spattered dark clouds. His gaze settled on the gondola station at the top of the mountain a couple football fields farther down the line. He hoped to wrestle Ana far away from pretty boy as soon as they arrived.

Leif said, "Mr. Buggiagalupo—"

"Everyone calls him Lupo," Ana said.

Lupo nodded.

"Ana tells me that you're heading up Aquila contrada's prerace festa. Quite an honor. Only the best and brightest are awarded such a privilege," Leif said.

Maybe the Viking kid wasn't all bad. "Now that you mention it," Lupo said, "I was hoping to discuss the possibility of Aurora's presence at all of the Palio festivities this year. Perhaps you'd like to sponsor the event? Showcase your wines and grappa?"

Leif nodded. "I'm pleased you asked me, Lupo. Between the Palio ceremonies, the race, and the celebratory dinners, Aurora would love to make its mark in Siena this year. You'll love our wines. You'll see when you taste them, paired with our exquisite six-course pranzo. We'd love to bring our special anniversary grappa to Sienese tables, as well. All for a bit of signage here and there. I think we can make this work."

Lupo and Ana beamed. Lupo had anticipated a good deal of cajoling, but that business deal was easy. The Viking was his new best friend. "Aurora sponsorship, and wine and grappa service. That's…wonderful. Thank you."

"The same anniversary grappa that your company presented Giancarlo Venchi shortly before his death in Monte Carlo?" Devlin asked.

The smiles dropped from Lupo's and Ana's faces. The air had officially been let out of the Viking sails. Lupo glanced out the window to escape the awkward tension flooding the compartment. Across the distance a wingsuit flyer disembarked the sport craft he'd spotted earlier. Then another. Even amid the assembling rain clouds, Lupo wished he were out there right now, flying free.

"It's the very same grappa that Mr. Venchi voraciously imbibed, I'm afraid." Leif Aurora grasped Devlin's shoulder and held his gaze. "Words can't express how sincerely aggrieved my family and I are over your colleague's untimely death. I'd hoped that I'd sufficiently conveyed that to you at his memorial."

"You did," Devlin said. "But you can understand my wariness over serving your grappa to the people of my town, as its consumption contributed to his death."

Leif bowed his head in deference to the slight and smiled. "Giancarlo Venchi's alcohol poisoning likely stemmed from issues unrelated to a few swigs of our decades-old recipe. You might consider a discussion with his new sponsor, Blue Rhino, instead. I understand they'd been supplying him with more than just bottled water, providing those pharmaceutical rumors are true."

"Provided Aurora did not originate those rumors, perhaps after he abruptly halted his sponsorship relationship with your company," Devlin said.

Leif's eyes went wide. "Mr. Lucchesi, I resent the accusation. I can assure you that Runa's ex-fiancé was nothing more than a fu—"

Something that sounded like a dumped load of pine logs slammed atop the tram and thundered through the cabin. The aerial lift shook and jostled like a yo-yo against the steel cables from which it dangled.

The rearview mirror on the wall behind Ana detached with the impact and shattered at her feet. She yelled out and gripped the inside rails to keep balance. Lupo lunged across the interior to prevent her from toppling out of the open windows that surrounded them.

Only the rear- and forward-facing windows remained stationary. When Leif lost his balance, his head smacked into the glass. Blood trickled down his face.

"What the hell was that?" Devlin didn't wait for an answer. He pulled his long sleeve over his hand and picked up one of the shards of broken mirror. He angled it outside the open window to view the rooftop.

Ana pulled a handkerchief from her leather satchel and pressed it to Leif's bloody forehead. He accepted the offering and then pulled a cell phone from his pocket. "Need to reach the gondola engineer." Leif dialed. "Luca, standby with security. We have another incident," he muttered and hung up.

"Two men, in wingsuits," Devlin said. "No weapons visual…yet." He pulled his 9mm Tanfoglio from his backpack.

Lupo heard the men's voices from the roof, shouting words in German that he didn't understand. They must've been the two guys who'd jumped from the leisure craft. "Maybe it was an accident?" Lupo said.

Devlin unlocked the handgun's safety. "Two guys don't jump from the sky and crash-land on the same tram at the same time, by accident."

"Behind you!" Lupo shouted, too late.

One of the jumpers catapulted in through the window like an aerial gymnast. He kicked Devlin from behind, slamming him against the wall.

Lupo tackled the jumper and pinned his arms behind his back. He spotted the other intruder peeking in, dangling down from the rooftop. The lanky beanpole of a man spat German phrases at the people in the cabin.

Devlin turned and gripped the dangling man's gloved hands. Then he hauled him onto the glass-strewn floor. The helmeted jumper grasped a glass shard and swung it toward Devlin's face. Devlin whacked the arm aside, then knocked out his attacker with a right uppercut.

Devlin whipped around and faced the jumper still pinned to the wall. "What the hell do you want?" he said to the man in German.

The German looked about the cabin and nodded toward Leif and Ana. He spewed a tirade, of which Lupo only grasped two words—Blue Rhino.

Leif and Devlin both countered in German, and the man calmed down. Leif took hold of the man and nodded to Lupo, who reluctantly released him with Devlin's approval. Devlin patted down both men, but his weapons search came away empty.

The tram station atop the mountain loomed. Leif again called the gondola engineer, to abort the security detail and to halt the tram's progress. He seemed surprised that his sister Erika now controlled the tram. Lupo overheard that she'd stepped up to oversee security. Soon the lift halted, and Devlin and Leif discussed a few more things with the now-conscious foo fighters.

Lupo looked out. The gondola hovered a few hundred feet over a brook that trailed through a clearing and into a spattering of pines. A fine mist had settled. Lupo looked at Ana, who winked at him. Not a bad place for romance. He sauntered over and kissed her on the mouth. "Why do we always find ourselves in these situations?" he said.

Ana shrugged, kissed him some more, and rubbed against him. "You seem to like it, though," she whispered. She glanced across the gondola, and her sultry eyes went wide.

Devlin opened one of the gondola doors. The man whom Devlin had slugged, now fully revived, squatted in the opening. A moment later, he waved to Leif and Devlin and jumped. His wingsuit spread wide, and he glided out over the tall pines through the misty rain. Apparently, they'd patched up their differences.

The aerial gymnast whom Lupo had pinned now shook hands with Leif and Devlin. He glanced at over at Lupo and threw him an obscene gesture. He simultaneously reached into the pocket of his hoodie, pulled out an aerosol can, and sprayed the front of Ana Malia's dress suit with red spray paint. Leif,

Devlin, and Lupo all shouted and lunged for him, but the jumper ran out the open door. He pedaled through the air for a moment and spread his wings. A flood of curses followed.

Lupo shook his head and sighed. After clashing with the Race, an extremist group who'd terrorized Devlin's family last year, nothing shocked him. But he sought an explanation.

Leif, whose head was still bleeding, explained that the two men were a couple of confused activists in need of a cause. They'd come to confront the Auroras, who they'd heard were hosting the press today.

"What were they protesting? Silk suits?" Ana shook her head. She removed her stained jacket and pressed it to Leif's forehead, as his handkerchief had surpassed its limit.

Devlin laughed. "First, they argued against water privatization, with which Leif empathized. Then, they claimed there'd been animal rights violations, asserting that the beautiful Auroras must be secretly testing beauty products on animals."

Leif joined him in laughter. "Yes, and the one must have confused you, Ana, for my sister Erika, which is why he sprayed you. Forgive me, Ms. Malia, I promise to replace your jacket."

"But the best part..." Devlin said. "The two idiots were recently fired from Blue Rhino Water Company and actually asked Leif for a job in the plant. What a crock."

Leif dialed Erika to restart the tram but could not get a cell signal. He glanced toward the gondola station, but the booth appeared empty.

"Here, try mine," Ana said. She reached into her leather satchel.

"Is that a Toujours bag?" Leif asked her.

She smiled wide. "It is!" She handed him her phone. "I'm impressed. Most men don't notice what name I'm wearing."

"My friend's mother runs the company. I see the bag matches your Toujours shoes," Leif said and winked.

Lupo huffed. Fashion talk. Leif Aurora knew just how to win over Ana Malia.

Apparently just as frustrated with their idle chitchat as he, Devlin pulled out his own cell phone. He dialed Erika, now in his contact list from their recent conversations. The call went right to voice mail. "I can't connect with your sister. How about we contact your security team to restart the tram?"

Leif stood and thrust his hand toward Devlin. "Before I do, I'd like to clear the air. I know Erika brought you to our vineyard to discuss the possibility of sponsoring your Formula One car. And I want to make things right between us before you meet her."

Lupo didn't flinch. He was privy to the knowledge that Devlin's wealth preempted any need for sponsorship. Plus, since his wife's passing, Devlin's sole inscription located on his tail fin, "ELLA," was the only label he allowed on the race car, for sentimental reasons. Clearly, Erika hadn't told Leif that she'd hired Devlin to investigate Aurora's recent security scares.

Leif continued. "In light of our teamwork on this eventful tram ride, I'd like to reestablish a friendlier relationship—"

Devlin did not shake Leif's hand. "Mr. Aurora, I appreciate the olive branch. However, a fellow driver died. Your product was involved, directly or indirectly; I don't know which. With all due respect, I plan to find out."

Leif shook his head. "Devlin, I can assure you, when it comes to my company, there is nothing untoward—"

Glass tinkled. Then a cracking sound, like someone had stepped through a thin layer of ice.

"Shots fired. Get down!" Devlin shouted.

***

Devlin made a mental note *not* to take the scenic aerial route to Aurora Vineyard next time, but rather to drive the winding roadway of terra firma up the mountain. Provided he lived long enough for a next time.

Not a second after he'd shouted his warning, Devlin dropped to the floor. Leif Aurora lay prone on his stomach beside him, poised as if ready to launch into push-up reps. Lupo dove for Ana, who crouched low, sheltering beneath the three-foot gondola chassis that surrounded them. Lupo covered her body with his in the corner and looked to Devlin for instructions.

"Sniper. In the trees. Starboard side of our ship." Devlin pointed to the bullet hole in the rear window of the tram. Veins of cracked glass spidered away from the hole. Devlin fumed. His best friend had been standing inches from the spot seconds earlier. He again grasped a shard of glass in his sleeve-covered fist and used it to gain a visual on the shooter or shooters.

Bullets whizzed through the open windows of the cabin. Two more metallic dings. Devlin was relieved that the bullets had not pierced the tram's hull, or the people taking cover behind it. The shots emanated from the same general direction, in slow bursts. In all likelihood, a single shooter, with a silenced pistol.

"Leif, call security. Call anyone. We're sitting ducks out here. We need to get this thing moving." Rain spattered against the roof now. Devlin found it difficult to view whether or not anyone stood inside the gondola station ahead.

"My phone isn't getting any signal due to the cloud cover," Leif said. The remaining three checked their phones and groaned a consensus of bad reception.

Bullets continued to fly through the tram in sporadic bursts.

"How many are there? And what the hell do they want?" Ana said.

"I'm fairly certain there's only one of them." Devlin turned to Leif. "Is a visit to your vineyard always this dangerous?"

Speechless, Leif merely shrugged.

"What can I do, Dev?" Lupo asked.

"Not sure yet, bro. Still thinkin'." Devlin pulled his Tanfoglio from his pack again. Any attempt to shoot a sniper hidden in the trees from that distance with a hand pistol was an exercise in futility. Still, forcibly demonstrating that they too were armed might chase away an amateur. Using the mirror fragment to gauge an approximation, he spied a couple bursts of gun flash through the rain, amid a canopy of pines. Aiming there, he peeked over the edge of the tram's chassis, pulled a few bursts from his own gun, and prayed.

No retaliatory fire. Using the mirror, he checked his progress but saw nothing of the shooter in the rain-soaked hideaway.

Devlin shot a few more times. He kept track of his rounds to ensure he had a few extra in the magazine, just in case.

Again, no return fire from the sniper. Had he scared him or her away? Had they simply relocated, only to fire again? Or was the shooter simply waiting them out?

Using the mirror again, he glimpsed movement. A single person of unknown gender, masked and dressed in a black hooded sweatshirt and pants, dropped down from one of the shorter trees in the grove. Without a backward glance, the figure dashed away from the cliff overlooking the valley and darted along a path leading into the woods.

"If we're ever getting out of here, we need to make our move now," Devlin said.

"What the hell does that mean?" Leif said.

"It means I'm not waiting around for someone else to try and kill us," Devlin said. "Lupo, help me out."

The two men edged closer together, keeping their heads below the level of the open windowpane. Devlin opened his pack and removed gloves. He gestured upward, and then he shrugged at Lupo. Lupo nodded in unspoken understanding, like always.

The two men stood. Devlin maneuvered atop the edge of the metal pane. Lupo gripped his torso and boosted Devlin up through the open window of the gondola's port side. Lupo secured Devlin until he could find a handhold atop the slick rooftop. Devlin spotted one and grabbed hold. He yelled to Lupo, who hoisted him higher until Devlin pulled himself up and out, onto the roof.

Rain pelted him. He looked down. Stupid move. Over a hundred yards above the ground, he knew that all it took was one slip and he was done. He walked to the center of the tram, where it clamped to a couple steel cables. He clasped one of the cables between his gloved hands, followed it until his feet just touched the roof, and exhaled.

He pulled himself up, all six feet and two hundred pounds of muscle, and started to move. One hand after another, he gripped the slick steel cord and inched forward. He made steady progress. The heavy downpour slowed him, but his adrenaline pushed him. He knew the only way to get his friends out of harm's way was to traverse the hundred feet or so remaining between him and the gondola station. Once there, he'd drive them all in, preferably before the shooter returned.

Almost there now. His water bottle slid from an outside pocket on his backpack and plummeted. It smashed open, spattering its contents against the rocky cliff side below. Yeah, next visit to the Dolomites, he'd opt for the boring car ride.

Just a couple dozen more feet, and he was home free. He allowed himself to enjoy the refreshing mountain workout. And then a compressor sounded, and a motor. And the whir of the tram. Headed right for him.

Once a soothing mode of joyride, now a lethal machine, the massive gondola threatened to collide with him. If he didn't haul ass to the station, the lift would knock him from the cable. Otherwise it would crush him before he had a chance to clear it. Hand over hand, faster now. Like a demon trapeze artist, or a mountain climber, or whoever the hell hung from cables in midair, he needed to move or die.

The cable ended in a garage cut into the mountain beneath the windowed control station, his sarcophagus before long. Hand over hand, and he was running out of cable.

He looked to the window of the station. Through the rain, Devlin saw a figure standing at the controls. But why couldn't they see him? Or did they? Hand over hand, and he was running out of time.

He could smell his gloves charring against the friction of the steel rope. His arm muscles burned and ached with the effort. The weight of his soaked clothes threatened to wrench him from the line.

About fifteen feet from the garage, he heard the gondola whir directly behind him. He felt the tremble of the moving car through the cable. Devlin's whole body shook, and the tram smacked him full-on, ramming into the back of him.

But Devlin was ready. Gripping the cable, he pushed off from the car with both feet. He thrust his legs upward and back-flipped, until landing his full bodyweight with a shudder atop the gondola's rooftop.

He glanced ahead. Only ten feet remained between him and the end of the line now. He could hear his friends' shouts through the tram's roof below him. They were either cheering him on, or else trying to gain the engineer's attention. Either way, there was no time to finagle his body back inside the tram before it charged into the bay.

Five feet from the entrance now, the cement roof of the encroaching garage threatened his extinction. He put his head down, clamped his body flush against the length of the roof, and prayed.

The tram rushed into the garage and screeched to a halt. Darkness engulfed him.

The shouts of his friends below could not stir his burning muscles. Devlin lay there, completely spent.

Lupo jumped onto the tarmac from the open door of the gondola. He scrambled atop the metal windowpane and peered onto the roof. "Holy shit! Are you okay, man?"

Devlin nodded, too exhausted for words.

"Well, let's go, then." Lupo jumped down to the platform floor. "Time to eat. Chop-chop."

Chapter 9

Devlin's first course of business was to run the gondola engineer out of town. Then Erika, who'd invited him. And then Leif, for all of his olive branches. Devlin didn't trust anyone at Aurora Vineyard. He had already suspected their possible involvement in Giancarlo's death. But the past hour inside, and outside, of the gondola had driven Devlin over the tipping point.

Devlin, Lupo, Ana, and Leif ambled out of the aerial lift's garage and up a long flight of stairs to a central courtyard. Devlin panned the area from left to right. Behind the cliffside tram garage was an empty gravel parking lot. Beside the lot, a long, narrow ribbon of cypress-lined road stretched west from anywhere and east to nowhere. An array of stone buildings, ranging from castle to cantina, spread before him. These were joined by flowered terraces and enclosed by a tall wrought-iron fence. Over five thousand acres of pristine vineyards sprawled beyond the fence and blanketed the landscape like a patchwork.

Erika Aurora was the first to greet the disheveled bunch in the courtyard. The Bloodsucker threw her arms around her brother. "Leif, I was so worried. Oh Lord, the blood on your face! What happened to all of you?"

Leif stumbled away from her reach. He looked toward the sniper's pine tree perch, then over to the gondola station. The rain had slowed to a drizzle again, and the control center sat visibly deserted. "Where's the security detail? Where's the engineer?" Leif asked.

Erika ignored his questions and embraced Ana next. "Oh, darling, what do you need? What can I do?" Erika stepped back. "My goodness, let's run inside and get you all dry clothes and something to eat."

Devlin stepped forward. "Ms. Aurora, I'm Devlin Lucchesi. Would you mind telling us what the hell is going on here?"

Erika thrust out a hand, and Devlin took it. He was exhausted. He was enraged that his friends' lives had been imperiled. But, damn, if the person before him was not the most ravishing woman he'd ever laid eyes on, then he just wasn't human. He'd planned to castigate her from the start. But when he grasped her hand, and she enveloped him with those warm hazel eyes, he was instantly disarmed.

Lupo must have known it. When Devlin instinctively took a step back from Erika, his wingman spoke up before Erika could answer.

"First, activists hijacked us," Lupo said. "Second, your control tower stranded us. Then a sniper tried to shoot holes through us. And when Devlin tried to get help, whoever manned the tower almost rammed him. We're feeling a little…unwelcome. Can you tell us why?"

Erika dropped Devlin's hand. She held his gaze a moment longer, warming him everywhere.

She appraised Lupo's hulking form. "Please forgive me. Lupo, is it? Devlin mentioned you'd accompany him. A pleasure to meet you under these bizarre circumstances." Erika gestured for them to follow her toward a large building, a rustic stone castle that appeared centuries old.

Erika continued, "I'd replaced Luca, our engineer, and sent him on break while I personally awaited Rasmus, our head of safety personnel. Then Leif canceled the need for backup, assuring me that all was well, and asked me to stop the tram, which I did. I was then summoned for an emergency conference call, and I phoned the engineer to handle your return. It appears that Luca and I were both delayed, and stranded you, for which I sincerely apologize.

"But you're telling me someone shot at you? I'm as shocked as all of you." Erika turned to Leif. "Oh, honey, the blood. You're wounded…we need to get you to the hospital."

"I'm fine. Bumped my head is all," Leif said.

"You did lose a lot of blood, Leif," Ana Malia said. "You really should see a doctor."

Leif wrapped an arm about Ana's shoulders and squeezed. "Thank you, really, for your trusty suit jacket compress. But I'm fine."

Lupo rolled his eyes, clearly frustrated with Leif's incessant flirtation with Ana.

Devlin shook his head. "The sniper ran, and the gondola returned safely. But we do have an active shooter situation."

"Yes, let's get all of you cleaned up and refueled back at the villa," Erika said. "I'll call my security chief for reinforcements on the property. We'll get to the bottom of this."

A blond man of about twenty, dressed in a cowboy hat and red faux-leather boots, abruptly exited the stone building. His long legs spanned the distance to them in seconds. When he reached Leif, he frowned at the sight of his bloodied face. In a subtle French accent, the man said, "What the hell happened to you?"

Leif took a step forward, and the man enfolded him into his arms. They stood together in silence for a few moments.

"Everything's okay now," the man said, rubbing his back. Leif nodded, and together they turned and walked hand in hand toward the stone façade.

Erika gestured to Ana. The two marched up the hill to the main building, while Erika shouted orders into her phone.

Lupo hung back, his mouth agape. He finally turned to Devlin. "I did not see that coming."

"What's that?" Devlin asked.

Lupo said, "We hike up here for a weekend gig to check out some wine company's involvement in your friend's death. We stumble into bizarro world. First off, we're attacked. Not once, but twice. But did we get any answers? No.

"Next, my eyes and ears tell me that the Viking Thor's putting the moves on my lady friend. But really, Thor just likes her leather shoes. He prefers the company of some dude who didn't stay long enough to divulge his name, or give us any indication of what the hell is going on around here."

Lupo took a breath. "Then one of the company's bigwigs saunters off with her 'Sister' in tow. But again, no answers."

Lupo shook his head. "Gee, maybe we should ask the other chief officer, Runa, for the lowdown? Negative. No sign of her either. Devlin, I feel like I'm crazy. Tell me what to do."

Devlin gestured toward the ridge of pines, his sidearm ready. "Let's get our own answers."

***

With the others momentarily occupied, Devlin and Lupo hustled to the sniper's perch directly across from where the tram had stopped midair. They ransacked the pine grove for clues.

Devlin snapped a few pictures of the earth beneath the high hide. The shooter had left broken branches and twigs, some of which Devlin pocketed for hair and fiber samples. Though he and Lupo hadn't turned up a single bullet casing, the perp had left behind the mother lode of footprints, now caked firmly in the rain-sodden soil. The prints came from an athletic shoe, in an unusually small size, for either a man or a woman. Lupo carefully tracked the steps leading away from the branched pine. Devlin followed, but the trail went cold at a shallow pond.

"Some solid evidence," Devlin said. "Let's get back before they miss us."

Lupo agreed. "How about calling the police?"

Devlin nodded. "Best to keep as few mechanics under the hood as possible. How about dinner?" Devlin turned back once more and gazed out at the location where the tram had stopped. Who had shot at them? And why did they want them dead?

***

The party of six sat at one of the ten long wooden tables in a rustic room which Erika called *la cantina*, an intimate dining tavern adjacent to *il castello*, the main castle. Comprised of stone and crisscrossed brick and wooden beams, the cantina was where Aurora Vineyard typically entertained day travelers, guests, business interests, and VIPs for a multicourse midday pranzo paired with a showcase of their reds, whites, aperitivi, and digestivi.

The antipasto course, fresh pink salmon marinated in lemon, pesto, and fennel, sated them long enough for the conversation to turn back to the shooting.

"Erika, you've heard our side of the story. What's yours?" Devlin asked her from across the table.

"I don't have an explanation, Devlin. We've been walking a tightrope since the injunction went public." Erika paused and blatantly glared at Philippe from across the table, clearly indicating her belief that Philippe, an ardent believer in the mantra of "free water for all," was responsible for leaking the existence of the aquifer to the authorities. Philippe returned the hardcore stare and sipped his tap water.

Erika continued, "Due to the public controversy over rights to the aquifer, we've amassed some enemies. But I'm shocked someone's resorted to shooting at us now." She looked at Ana. "I must apologize for endangering your life, Ana. I can only assume that the shooter thought it was actually me inside the tram. If something had happened to you…"

Ana sipped her dry prosecco. "I'm just fine. Besides, I was able to raid your closet in the aftermath." She winked at Erika.

Aurora's prized Sauvignon Blanc was poured. Philippe lifted his water glass and offered a toast in English, laced heavily in his French accent. "I'd like to thank you, Devlin and Lupo, for saving Leif's life. From what I gather, things became quite dangerous up there. I'm grateful for your efforts. To Devlin and Lupo."

Erika raised her glass. "I second that."

Devlin nodded graciously. Over a *primo piatto* of lobster risotto and the best fava beans that Devlin had ever tasted, Lupo regaled them with the tale of how the two of them had met while fending off a group of thugs decades earlier. During the story, Devlin eyed the tall, lanky Frenchman who had hair the color of sandpaper. He wondered exactly what Philippe had been up to at the time of the shooting. When Lupo finished his story, he asked him.

Philippe rolled his eyes. "Americans are quite suspicious of the French, *n'est-ce pas*?"

"Only the rude ones." Devlin smiled.

Philippe pursed his lips. "It so happens that I was telephoning with my mother, who was concerned about the shooting."

Devlin said, "She'd become aware of the shooting as it was happening?"

Philippe rolled his eyes again.

Erika clarified. "Philippe's mother, Marisse, and I are friends. She and I have been business acquaintances for a few years. She runs Toujours leather company in southern France, and I adore leather jackets…" Devlin's eyes darted to the short brown one she wore that accentuated her long brown hair and slight, round shoulders. He forced his gaze back to her sparkling hazel eyes. Not a hardship.

"When Leif and Philippe began dating exclusively almost two years ago at university, she and I chatted more often," Erika said. "Today, she and I spoke, the same conference call that detained me from running the tram. When I heard the shots, I quickly told her and hung up. As a mother, she must have panicked and called Philippe to ensure his safety."

"Not that she always cared," Philippe muttered under his breath. An awkward silence, along with a limoncello sorbet, cleansed their palates.

Noting the family discord, Devlin attempted to provoke a reaction. "Toujours is a Fortune 500 company. You must be very proud of your mother."

"Of course, I am," Philippe said. "She worked her way up from clerk, became educated at the same college I later attended, École Polytechnique Fédérale de Lausanne, and now she is a…head honcho, I think you Americans call it."

"Wonderful. Do you follow in her footsteps for work?" Ana asked.

"I ski."

"What did you say?" Gnawing on a lamb cutlet, Lupo paused with a befuddled look. He washed it down with a gulp of 2002 Syrah and awaited an answer.

"I ski," Philippe said again.

"You graduated with a degree from EPFL. Your mom could get you a corner office at the famed Toujours leather emporium. And…you ski?" Lupo said.

Devlin fought back a smile at his friend's directness.

Leif spoke up. "He's a brilliant chemist, but he chooses to spend his spare time skiing, like I do. It's our favorite hobby."

"Besides shoving the environment down everyone's throat, you mean?" Erika said. "Philippe has encouraged Leif to…embrace an eco-friendlier perspective these past couple years."

"A few months ago, I was awarded the Green Medal for Pioneering Wine Making, Environmental Respect, and Territory Enrichment, which I'll publicly receive at the global water summit," Leif said.

"It's a beneficial perspective. But tough on the bottom line, *mon frère*," Erika said. "Maybe consider spending more time skiing and less time lobbying for—"

A loud, thundering engine sounded directly overhead the cantina. Leif ran to the door and opened it wide for the others to look out.

Blinding sunlight spilled in, partially obscured by an aircraft. The small biplane flew low to the ground, and its small engine echoed loudly against the stone buildings of the compound. A colorful banner trailed behind the plane, and its graphic message shocked Devlin. It was a plastic water bottle, pouring out blood-red liquid into the thirsty upturned mouths of children.

Ana shook her head and looked to Erika.

Countering the looks of dismay on her guests' faces, Erika said, "Raspberry cheesecake and vin santo? Any takers?"

Lupo shrugged. "I'm in."

***

After an hour of overindulgence, the dinner guests dispersed. The sun began to set in the mountains, and all that remained of their menu was a grappa digestivo. Lupo and Ana had wandered to an outside terrace for a cigar with Leif and Philippe. A dozen or so security personnel patrolled the area.

Devlin remained at the table with Erika and awaited service of Aurora's notorious anniversary grappa. The one that had served as Giancarlo Venchi's last supper.

A server set a tray with seven glasses and a bottle of Aurora grappa on the table in front of Erika. He retired back into the kitchen behind closed doors, leaving just the two of them in the cavernous yet cozy terrace room.

Blazing hearths at both ends cast seductive shadows on Erika's smooth apple cheeks. She lifted the bottle, cloaked in its traditional cotton-cloth garb, and uncorked the stopper.

Devlin picked up the familiar cork, identical to the one he still carried in his pocket since the Monte Carlo Race, and sniffed it. He recoiled, struck by its intense, pungent aroma.

"Be careful, Devlin. Methyl alcohol can kill you." Erika winked.

Devlin knew she jokingly referred to the "head" of the grappa batch, the first hit of the fermented liquid that contained a lethal dose of methyl alcohol. Uneducated moonshiners had often fallen victim to the poisonous initial shot during Prohibition, but professional vintners knew well enough to cast it away before bottling. He stole a glance at the "120 proof" on the label. The whiff he'd just taken of the pomace brandy might've burned out all his nostril hair. And that was just from the cork.

Erika poured them both a snifter of the brew. She raised hers. "*Salut!*" she toasted and drew a hearty sip.

Devlin imagined the liquid warming her sensuous throat, but one sip from his own glass shot him back to reality. *How the hell did Giancarlo guzzle those few gulps without exhaling dragon fire?*

The beautiful business mogul smirked and poured him a glass of Aurora's bottled water as a chaser.

Devlin emptied the water glass. "Forgive me. I'm not much of a grappa drinker, no matter the brand."

Erika smiled.

"But the water is delicious," Devlin said. "I enjoyed the story you told over dinner of the aquifer's discovery. I'm sorry about your recent difficulties in accessing its benefits."

The amused expression dropped from her eyes. "I only wish we'd tapped our 'Fountain of Youth' decades earlier, prior to the agc of unmitigated political correctness. Society might've demanded the sale of their precious beverage, and perhaps the court of public opinion would have thwarted the Italian court system's injunction," Erika said. "Instead, the battle over public versus private water usage taints our reputation, interferes with our day-to-day affairs, and threatens our company's lifeblood."

"Do you suffer flybys often?" Devlin asked.

"These days, probably a couple times a week. They don't bother me anymore, but it leaves a bad taste in the mouths of our guests." Erika sipped her grappa. "Did you love the banner? That one comes by most often. Word on the street: our staunchest competitor, HydroVino, is the culprit."

"I had no idea the wine industry was so cutthroat," Devlin said.

"You'd be amazed." Erika rolled her eyes. She dipped an almond biscotto into her glass of grappa and nibbled it pensively. "Please don't think me a monster for not embracing my brother's environmental enthusiasm. His innovation deserves accolades, as our water conservation standards now set the bar for the wine industry.

"However, our company alone, because of the injunction, is unfairly burdened by such measures, and our cost of doing business far exceeds that of our competitors. Not to mention the exorbitant penalty of back taxes the courts are seeking to impose, based on some arbitrary date decades ago, when we weren't even on the measurement grid.

"What's worse," she continued, "we're impeded from selling a product that would ensure our company's prosperity for generations. Our customers are withheld a life-affirming, beneficial product that would improve their lives, and—"

"With all due respect, Erika, it's bottled water."

"Aurora provides the invigorating waters of the Fountain of Youth for all who seek to consume it."

"It's bottled water."

"Whoever chooses to believe in its youth-affirming properties deserves the right to imbibe those waters, Devlin. If a consumer chooses to fork over twenty-five euros for an hourglass-shaped bottle containing platinum-speckled springwater, then damn it, Devlin, why shouldn't I be the one to give them what they want?" Erika said.

He nodded. "If not you, then someone else will."

She thrust both hands in the air. "Exactly." Erika exhaled, releasing the tension she'd bottled inside of her since welcoming them earlier.

Devlin took another sip of grappa, aerated the grape liquid in his mouth, and swallowed. He realized that this product also contained platinum-colored specks. He looked up to find her watching him.

"My father thought of infusing our grappa with platinum years ago. He applauded my idea of waiting until the release of our special anniversary edition. I thought it only right to sprinkle it into our upmarket springwater line, too." She stared into the swirling contents of her snifter.

"I appreciate your capitalist point of view, Erika," Devlin said. "As well as the conservationist point of view shared by Leif and Philippe. What's your sister Runa's take on it?"

"Runa's never been one to take sides. She's typically a solitary person who doesn't get involved. Which is why her romantic relationship with Giancarlo was initially surprising. Later it made sense. She's a hot-blooded woman who happens to be an introvert—marrying a man who was around only for the occasional booty call but away the rest of the time suited her well."

"Where's your sister now?" Devlin said.

Erika sighed. "Probably in her laboratory. I apologize for her absence at our table. As I mentioned, she keeps to herself." She stood, downed the remainder of her liqueur, and came around the table to offer him her hand. "May I show you around, Mr. Lucchesi?"

Devlin gulped. Since his wife's passing a year ago (or was it almost two, now?) he'd had fleeting moments of attraction to other women. But Erika Aurora was the first for whom he'd ever felt distinctly…desirous, for something more than just flirtation.

She leaned forward. Her smell, a mix of cognac, lavender, and musk, aroused him. "Afraid I'll bite, Mr. Lucchesi? C'mon, how about a tour of my grounds?"

Chapter 10

Twilight invaded the Dolomite Mountains like the marauders of ancient centuries, hard and fast. Lights from distant hill towns twinkled in the distance.

On the pretext of investigating the company's enemies, Devlin planned to interview every Aurora family member over the next couple days before heading back to Siena, to ready Marcello for ten days of sleepover robotics camp. His true aim was to glean intel on Giancarlo's mysterious death. If cause arose for further inquiry, he'd summon a posse of his fellow HELL Rangers. They had a few weeks' reprieve before the next Formula One circuit in Azerbaijan, so he'd start with Erika, the woman who'd reached out for his help.

Erika shoved her arm through his and guided him back toward the tallest building in the complex. Amped up security personnel discreetly stalked the grounds. "Aurora Vineyard lies at the base of the Little Dolomites on a seven-thousand-acre estate. My father married my mother and adopted the three of us when we were little. She died, and we nearly went bankrupt. I decided that the best way to mend a broken heart and save my family was to pour whatever I had left into making this the best damn vineyard on Italian soil, if not the world. When an earthquake uncovered the aquifer, I felt like it was a sign from God, that He too wanted our tiny vineyard to flourish. Because of our ample water supply, we survived in times of drought and flourished in times of prosperity.

"My father was no genius, Mr. Lucchesi, but I am. After my schooling, I'd thrust this company onto the world stage by the tendrils of our grapevines. And damn it, I will not let someone else tear it from my clutches. Do you understand? I will do anything it takes to keep enemies away from my company," Erika said.

Devlin was aroused again, but also intrigued. This woman would clearly go to any lengths to protect the reputation of her company. Including murder?

Erika rambled on about terroir, and noble vines, and clonal research. All the while Devlin added up in his head what he had to go on. Erika was a beautiful, brilliant businesswoman who would clearly stop at nothing to guarantee the success of her company.

Leif was a gregarious, affable company leader whose environmental agenda guided his every business move, no matter the cost.

Well, nearly every move. Philippe, Leif's life partner, seemed to sway Leif's business judgment toward more alternative pursuits, like political lobbying and skiing. Unless that was a cover for someone intent on snatching the purse strings away from one chief officer, Erika, by sidling up close to another, Leif?

And then there was Runa…or, rather, where was Runa? The introverted scientist had refused to leave her lab to meet a BBC reporter and two investigators that had infiltrated her property seeking answers to her ex-fiancé's mysterious death. Even after they'd been shot at…and, come to think of it, where had she been during the shooting?

These questions continued to vex Devlin even as he and Erika sidestepped animal tracks, the shape of which clearly indicated wild boar in the area. The two of them entered the castle's main entrance. After passing through the atrium, they breezed into the bright and cheery *enoteca,* a small boutique for tastings and the sale of company wares.

Next they ambled into an enormous barrel room, where massive oak barriques aged and stored the finest wines until bottling. Posters bearing the Aurora labels for every varietal hung from the pristine rafters like tapestries.

After the barrel room, they exited into the main courtyard and headed toward an adjacent stone building. "Your estate reflects a perfect marriage of tradition and technology," Devlin said.

"Thank you. I'm very proud of my company and our fine reputation with wine aficionados. The flyovers, the graffiti, the picketers…they're a nuisance, just a part of doing business, I get it. But some things that have happened lately…are hitting a little too close to home."

"Such as?"

"Someone managed to make it past our guard and spray-paint the glass shower door in my personal bathroom with 'Die, Erika.'"

"Sounds like an inside job to me. Someone not only breaches security, but they have personal knowledge as to the location of your private bathroom in this gigantic compound?" Devlin said.

"Rasmus and his security staff are the same team we've had for the past ten years…best and brightest, and completely checked out," she said.

The two stepped into another enormous two-story building—the bottling plant. Apparently closed for the evening, this manufacturing room housed a dozen forklifts, thousands of cases of empty bottles, and ceiling-high machinery used for bottling, corking, and labeling.

"I have an enormous pile of rocks and bricks, courtesy of vandals who remind me nearly every day of just how big a threat we are to our competition, and it makes me smile," Erika said. "But one night, a rock crashed through my bedroom window. It was actually a metal tin, with my name written on the lid in Sharpie. Glad I never opened it, because the police found a live scorpion inside."

They crossed a steel ramp into an even larger room. Here the cloying, robust aroma of fermentation seemed to seep into his every pore. Erika proudly swept her arm from left to right. "After harvesting, this is where the magic happens. Only the best grapes are fermented here, in premium oak-and-steel staves. Wines are vinified in this room, grappa next door."

Devlin craned his neck to gaze up at the pipes running overhead and down into the oak-and-steel vat that towered beside him. A maze of pipes crisscrossed those and dropped into two dozen similar vats. The enormous casks spanned the room in rows like docked vessels in a harbor. Devlin nodded. "Very impressive." He asked a few questions about harvesting, filtration, and the reduction of sulfites to appease her, but then tactfully turned the conversation back to the threats. "You mentioned police involvement?"

"Yes, ours is an ongoing case, with few developments. I threatened a lawsuit, didn't go far. Attempted comingling with my security team, but no-go. Tried bribery, too. But the police in this region are too busy with border patrol and avalanches to pay any mind to minor complaints by an upscale winery. Plus, ever since the courts got involved in determining our rights to the aquifer, the cops refuse to pee in another man's pool." Erika stopped and turned to face him. "That's why I called you, Devlin. Ana recommended your particular set of skills very highly."

A door opened and slammed shut. Hurried footsteps echoed down the hall, and a man shouted orders into a walkie-talkie. The man turned the corner and came face-to-face with Erika. "We've found your dog."

"Is Tomba okay? What's happened?"

The sixty-something uniformed guard, built like a tank, shook his head. "Not sure. Rasmus found him lying next to his water bowl outside the enoteca. Alive, but convulsing."

"Where's Tomba now?" Erika said.

"Rasmus's cousin drove him to the vet, who verified that it's severe dehydration. The vet wants to keep him overnight for observation."

"Thank you. Please, go home to your family now; you did well."

The guard strode away, and Erika turned to Devlin with a look of concerned confusion. "That dog has been my rock since my father died. If anything happened to him…I just don't get it. My cocker spaniel is the picture of health."

"Convulsions are serious. A sure sign of dehydration, or heatstroke," Devlin said.

"For two years, Tomba has lived in those woods. He comes home for food and companionship every few days. Probably subsists on pond water in the meantime. I don't know why he's suddenly dehydrated. And heatstroke? In the mountains? Middle of June, and the temperature hasn't broken seventy-five degrees yet."

"Let's check out his water bowl."

Minutes later, after examining the stainless steel bowl with gloves he'd pulled from his rucksack, Devlin shook his head. "I'd like to run a few tests in my own lab." He pointed to a few spots on the rim. "Possible traces of platinum."

"Grappa or bottled water?" Erika glanced at him. "Who'd fill Tomba's bowl with anything but tap water?"

Devlin shook his head. "Not the grappa. We would have smelled it on the bowl. I'm thinking your bottled springwater," Devlin said. "Any reports of allergic reaction to the platinum specks in the water or the grappa?"

Erika shook her head. "We added the platinum to market the water as an upscale luxury item, nothing more. No added health benefit. And no detrimental side effects to ingesting it either. It's a minimal amount of metal. Smaller than the amount of gold dust added to Goldschläger. We ran clinical trials, federal testing, all the usual precautions on both beverages, and nothing turned up. We've never had a complaint filed either."

Devlin nodded. "Both gold and platinum are found in trace amounts in the human body every day. I would imagine it would turn up in dogs, too."

Erika agreed.

"Unless maybe," said Devlin, "a minority of individuals, or dogs, are simply unable to tolerate minuscule amounts of platinum? And perhaps convulsions follow?" Maybe Giancarlo was one of those individuals, whose intolerance to the minute dose of platinum had caused him to suffer the same traumatic convulsions as the dog.

"Runa's a chemist," Erika said. "If platinum is capable of producing a dangerous reaction, she'd know."

Chapter 11

"Giancarlo deserved death," a sultry female voice echoed from high atop a metal ladder, scaling a Slovenian oak barrel filled with twenty-four hundred gallons of fermenting grappa.

Devlin and Erika stood in the doorway, and Erika gaped at the comment.

Standing atop four-inch high heels beside the vessel's steel base, Ana Malia looked up from her notes and stared at Runa. "I'll be sure to leave that bit out of my news report."

Devlin and Erika had shifted their tour directly to the grappa plant, just outside the laboratory, in the hope of connecting with Runa Aurora. He sympathized with Erika's visible embarrassment over her sister's shocking first impression. Nonetheless, Erika charged forward with introductions.

Dressed in leggings, an embroidered plaid western shirt, and Converse sneakers, Runa reluctantly descended the ladder. She offered Devlin a handshake. Her dripping hand imparted more effervescent spirit than her demeanor.

Ana stepped forward. "Devlin, pay no mind to my old friend's sister. Runa's crabbier than usual because I let slip that

Philippe's mother is paying us a visit tomorrow, to check up on her son's welfare after the shooting."

"Is that so?" Erika asked. Devlin sensed a deeper onset of tension in the room. Erika said, "I'm excited to learn about Toujours' upcoming fall line of leather jackets. But does Philippe's mommy really need to come running for every little thing? I mean, things are a bit hectic around here lately."

Runa grunted. "I hate the bitch. Come to think of it, I hate Philippe, too."

Ana changed the subject in her classically optimistic manner. "Well, you'll both love this news. My editor called. There's buzz going around that the courts are going to make a final ruling on the injunction in the next few weeks. My guess is they plan to use the Worldwide Water Summit for their grand reveal."

"What's the word? Will they lift the injunction? Or is it permanent?" Erika said.

"No word either way just yet," Ana said. "But you'll hear it here first, I promise you." She winked.

Runa said, "You both know that cocksucker, tree-hugger Philippe was the one to leak the news of the aquifer, which then led to the court's inference into our R&D." Runa glanced up at a second-floor wall of windows that overlooked the room. "If they shut us down, or try to close my lab, I'll kill them all." She turned to Devlin. "No one messes with my micro-viticulture of monovarietals and cuvees. Not the courts, not Leif, and most definitely not Philippe."

Devlin nodded, rendered speechless. Not by her smooth porcelain skin, her perfect complexion, her slim, shapely curves, or her luxurious blond hair. It was the venom that dribbled from the corners of her mouth when she spoke.

"Anyone care to see my latest hybrid?" Runa asked, not stopping to take note of whether anyone followed. She ascended the steep metal stairway leading to the room of windows.

Devlin trailed her, figuring this was why he was here, though he vowed to steer clear of sharp lab instruments. Behind him, he heard Erika mutter to Ana, "She can be quite tiresome when she's in a mood."

The reporter asked candidly, "Is she ever not in a mood?"

The group settled just inside the lab's doorway. Runa babbled on a few minutes about her research, with wit as dry as the herb bag she now concocted for one of the vats. Devlin swept his gaze over every corner of the room. He attempted to gain insight into the publicly jilted fiancée, Runa Aurora, who was the one person who truly bore a motive for Giancarlo's death. Aside from her surly countenance, he noted an OCD-like preoccupation with orderliness, but nothing struck him out of the ordinary.

Until he spotted the vials and beakers stacked against the back wall of a workstation, and the rubber mat hosting a dozen or so syringes lined neatly in rows below it. A thought struck him, though surely the concept had always lingered beneath his consciousness.

Runa, a skilled chemist, had ample opportunity to concoct some sort of lethal formula. She might've injected it into a bottle of Aurora anniversary grappa and presented it to the man who'd embarrassed her in front of millions with his sordid breakup, and then drummed it up to accidental alcohol poisoning. Solid theory. Especially since the toxicologist had found no traces of any other lethal substance besides the excess of alcohol in Giancarlo's blood. Runa Aurora had means, motive, and opportunity to murder Devlin's racing colleague. Now he just needed the evidence to prove it.

Minutes later, Runa abruptly stopped talking. She breezed past them and marched toward one of the vats with the herb bag in her hand. They all followed the socially inept scientist to the plant's ground floor, but they waited while she climbed the ladder to the top of another sky-high barrel. It was then that Erika asked her sister the question that burned in Devlin's mind. "Runa, in your expertise, would you consider it possible for a minority of the population to develop an intolerance, or a severe allergic reaction, to the minuscule amounts of platinum in our grappa, or in our FONS springwater?"

"And might convulsions necessarily follow, as if the victim had effectively been poisoned?" Devlin asked.

Runa wobbled on the ladder. She tipped forward precariously over the fermenting brew but caught herself before pitching into the vat.

She looked down at them. "Yes, definitely. Occupational asthma—if one worked in a platinum mine his whole life and breathed it in every damn day." Red-faced, she stormed down the ladder and confronted them. "I've told you, Erika, time and again, there are no detrimental side effects to ingesting the miniscule amount of platinum in our water and grappa. Now get out! I mean it. My time is precious, and I have tests to run. It's clear to me that you're all here to ascertain my guilt over my fiancé's death. But you can all fuck off. Giancarlo deserved what he got. And Erika, you and Leif might consider supporting me on this.

"As for you, Mr. Lucchesi, keep your nose out of my business." A timer sounded, and Runa pointed toward the lab. "That buzzing signals that another one of my patented designs is ready, a design that I have created for my company. If you'll all just get the hell out, then I can get back to keeping this company afloat."

***

Erika escorted Devlin and Ana across the grounds and into a cul-de-sac of six small but extravagant private villas, into which Leif, Philippe, and Lupo had settled earlier. Ana hugged them both and said goodnight, promising to meet Erika in the morning for their television interview, once Ana's camerawoman arrived.

Erika showed Devlin the way to his quarters, and he turned to leave. But she grabbed his arm and stopped him. "Runa thinks that I don't know she's turned off the surveillance monitors in the grappa room, and in her laboratory. I don't let on that I know, because I suspect her of ill will, and I'm hoping to catch her in the act some other way."

Devlin nodded, knowing she had much more to say.

Erika said, "Did Runa murder Giancarlo? Maybe. Is my sister attempting to hijack Aurora for some other gain, or to appease someone else? Maybe. Is Runa planning to supplant Leif and me, and retain full control of Aurora? Another maybe. I don't know Runa's plan, but I do know that I will stop her any way that I can, sister or not.

"One more thing: No cops," Erika said. "I brought you here, Devlin, in the hope that you'll take me up on my offer to help me. From what? I believe, from my usurper, whoever that may be. I believe today went a long way in convincing you that someone is attempting to wrestle my company away from me. And I will not allow it. No cops, because government intrusion always leads to disaster. Instead, I want you."

Erika Aurora turned from him then and sauntered away. Devlin wasn't swayed to take on the problems of corporate warfare. Let the grape leaves fall where they may, without him.

But there was something else that grounded him here. Though Devlin's motto on the racetrack was to leave every car racer behind, Giancarlo Venchi was the exception.

A HELL Ranger never left a fallen man behind.

Chapter 12

The crime scene, Runa thought as she jogged past the sniper's pine grove. Earlier that day, from her exterior lab window high in the castle tower, she'd spotted Devlin and his muscular friend fervently examining the spot. Later, Ana had told her about the shooting. Runa glanced through the pines and across the valley in the direction of the aerial tram station. But she could only make out the building's outline in the midnight haze. Such a fuss over nothing.

Runa preferred jogging through the *paese* further down the mountain only late at night, to avoid people. Tonight's run felt therapeutic, especially since her spontaneous midday trot through the woods had proved fruitless.

Minutes later, she arrived back at the castle and headed straight for her sanctuary. Inside the grappa room, she plucked a bottle of FONS from the plethora of unshipped contraband and guzzled it down. She wiped her mouth with the back of her hand, and it came away flecked with platinum. Erika and Devlin's interrogation about allergic reactions to platinum pissed her off.

She kicked a stack of cases and flung the empty bottle into the corner. Fuming, she climbed the stairs to her lab two at a time.

Once inside, her heartbeat slowed, and she resumed normal breathing. Calm, unadulterated isolation; clean, orderly lab instruments; and the aroma of violent, earthy fermentation always soothed her irritability.

She kicked off her running shoes outside the laboratory and shut the door. Donning a pair of work gloves, Runa reached inside the cold vault for a handful of delicate fresh spices. She dropped them onto a cutting board and went to work chopping them into precisely measured increments. She rolled her neck and sore shoulders as she worked. Stress cramps in her neck exacerbated her cantankerous nature, more so than usual.

Erika and Leif hate me. Of this she felt certain. Acrimony had flourished between them ever since news of the aquifer had hit the press, sending the company into a tailspin. She'd never seen that coming. She'd always felt pretty close to her brother and sister as a child, but now she felt a genuine divide between them, a growing incurable animosity.

Jealousy? Aurora would be nothing without her, and they knew it. When she'd mentioned to them that their fiercest competitor, HydroVino, was attempting to poach her, she'd expected an overt reaction. Instead, no reaction at all. Did they think they'd be better off without her? Did they think she wouldn't go through with it? She didn't know. But she hated them both for their ambivalent response.

Runa gathered the fruit and spices in the cotton cheesecloth and tied it with a jute ribbon. She cleaned and dried her tools.

Speaking of tools, ever since Leif committed to that asshole ski bum Philippe, the whole dynamic of the family's chemistry has gone downhill. Runa slipped the scalpel that she was holding back into its sheath.

And Philippe's far-left agenda has wreaked havoc on Leif, who's so damn impressionable. Philippe's tearing our company's harmonic symbiosis to shreds. Instead of replacing the scalpel in its usual drawer with the others, she pocketed it. Someday soon, she'd make Philippe pay.

Just like Giancarlo.

Runa tucked her tiny feet into her sneakers and tied them. She traversed the warehouse room and checked the grappa plant's overall temperature. It was slightly elevated. She made a mental note to check the cooling unit before turning in for the night.

She picked up the empty FONS bottle that she'd chucked and threw it in the recycling bin. The receptacle overflowed with all the other empty Aurora water bottles she'd drunk. *Who cares, no one else will ever drink it.* The writing was on the wall. The injunction would remain permanent, and Aurora would fold. That was why she was entertaining the HydroVino offer. When Aurora went belly-up in the coming weeks or months, HydroVino and other industry leaders would kill each other for a chance to woo her. After all, her research was what had put Aurora Vineyard on the map in the first place. That was the beauty behind everyone finding out about the hidden aquifer's existence. She was glad it had worked out the way it had. Advantage: Runa.

She climbed the steel ladder to the top of one of the grappa vats that she hadn't nursed for some time. Must have been weeks since she'd fed the brew some fresh spices. A little bit of vanilla bean. Some cinnamon sticks. A bit of clove, and some allspice. Into the blend, she'd thrown in some star anise and orange zest to see what would happen. Might suck, might not.

Not many things had gone her way in the past, and she felt that she was ripe for a leg up.

Especially regarding Giancarlo. He'd ravaged her ego, torn it to shreds. The other women…the showboating…bad form. She'd fallen for his rough, bad boy nature in the sack. But she thought he'd save his hard-edged, sexy brutishness just for her. Not to be. And when he'd dumped her via Jumbotron in Monte Carlo…he deserved death.

Runa sought with her hand for the hook inside the slippery steel lip of the vat. She planned to sink the herbs into the frothing, foaming turbulent bath for a couple nights. The fumes of this leavening batch were particularly strong, and she felt woozy. She shook her head. She gripped the ladder and turned away to fill her lungs with the fresh air that circulated about the room from the ventilation system. It didn't make her feel any better, and she knew it must be getting late. She'd been up since dawn, and she was exhausted from an eventful day. Best to tie it off quick and go to bed.

She turned back, skimmed the rim of the barrel with her fingers again, and this time found the hook. As she tied the jute string into knots, she envisioned Giancarlo floating there in the muck. Bloated and purple from asphyxiation, the bastard wouldn't have lasted five minutes before choking and suffocating to death from carbon dioxide overdose. She'd have left Giancarlo there, deteriorating for weeks, floating atop the solid pomace of seething, volatile grape skins, pits, and leaves until the turbulent solution fermented his corpse into grappa. The sight of him would frighten every one of those other sluts he'd bedded. What a horrific way to die.

She thought of Philippe, smiled, and made a mental note.

She turned away from the brew again to suck more fresh air into her lungs. As she did, a shove from behind jolted her. Runa lost her balance and grasped the handles of the steel ladder. She cried out, but an herb bag was thrust into her mouth to silence her.

Who the hell violated my sanctuary?

Runa breathed in deeply, fighting to fill her lungs with air. But the cloying musk overwhelmed her, slowed her movements. *I'm going to die! I can't move! No strength.* Runa struggled to raise her arms and fight off her aggressor, but with each breath, her strength ebbed. *I'm suffocating. I can't breathe. I can't...*

A piercing pinch in her shoulder told her that the attacker must have thrust a needle into her arm on top of it all. *Why?*

Her vision blurred. *Leave me...alooone. Can't feel...my lips.* She was drunk. Her thoughts blurred in her mind. Her knees gave way, and Runa stumbled on the ladder's platform.

Strong arms grabbed her. *Save…me. I can't…do it*, Runa thought.

The person lifted her in their arms. Man or woman? She couldn't see. Not able to focus. Not blurry, but hazy. The world was swimming. She felt nauseous. She felt burning in her throat. Her stomach churned. The fumes. So heavy. She threw up in her mouth, but the bag blocked its outlet. She coughed. She was choking on her own vomit. Her head swam. The world rocked and swayed like a tiny boat on big waves.

The arms dumped her. Let her go, into the swirl of bubbling, churning foam. Chunks of pomace scratched and bubbled against her skin, matted her hair.

With all the strength left in her body, she willed her arm toward her face and knocked the herb bag from her mouth. She opened her mouth like a drowning swimmer, gasped for air, but the air she breathed was poison. Every breath brought her closer to death.

Lying spread-eagle atop the surface of the brew, she wondered if things would get better in the morning. She'd sleep, and maybe she'd see Giancarlo.

They both deserved it.

Chapter 13

Devlin snapped awake around four in the morning, ready to run.

Car racing, HELL Ranger missions, and fatherhood demanded regular bodily conditioning to keep up with all three. So he ran. Anytime, anywhere.

This morning Devlin combined fieldwork with running, and he headed for the sniper's pine grove that he and Lupo had examined earlier. Minus Lupo, whose villa Devlin had found unoccupied. He envied his best friend, who was likely wrapped in the arms of his lover beneath the warm covers of her bed.

With every footfall on the uneven terroir, Devlin puffed plumes of breath into the cold, dark morning air. Though the winery's security lighting cast a glow on the main property, Devlin switched on the jogger's headlight that Marcello had given him for Christmas. He scanned the premises but didn't detect any other personnel. He wondered if any of the grape pickers worked beneath the moonlight in the surrounding vineyard, but none caught his eye. He checked in with one of the security guards who radioed the others of his presence.

Rounding the corner of the cantina building, he spotted a BBC van on the cobbled drive. He ran past it and instinctively touched the hood of the vehicle, cold to the touch. Ana Malia's cameraperson had likely arrived late last night for the morning interview with Erika Aurora.

Discerning the path through the woods with his headlamp, Devlin continued toward the shooter's hideaway. His cell phone rang at a quarter past four, and he tapped his finger against the Bluetooth speaker in his ear.

"Good morning, sunshine." Scotti's melodic tone coincided with the patter of Devlin's soft soles against the mossy woodland carpet.

"I know you always call me when you're up early baking, but you're in Verona on business. Sleep in a little." Devlin swiped at a low-hanging branch and sidestepped a rock before arriving at the sniper's location in the pine grove.

"Sleep is for the dead," Scotti said. "I'm catching up on paperwork. And I'll have you know, I brought three of my puffed almond pastries with me for the guys at the Monza Institute. Now, what's the word?" Scotti and Devlin had shared early-morning briefings for as long as Devlin could remember.

As Devlin updated Scotti on the previous day's events, he scoured the dew-laden earth for further signs of the shooter. Devlin turned and faced the valley. He traced the approximate location where the gondola had ceased its progress and where the shots had been fired. He turned off his lamp and closed his eyes.

When he finished conveying the details of the story to Scotti, Devlin asked him for a minute of silence.

Devlin opened his eyes and triangulated the position of the shooter in the tree, and then he focused on the farthest radius beneath the tree where bullet casings may have flown. He switched on the headlamp, gingerly stepped a few paces northeast, and scanned the ground. Less than a minute later, Devlin spotted them. Two bullet casings, a few inches apart and tucked beneath the broad umbrella of a delectable porcini mushroom. He pulled two baggies from his sweatshirt pocket. In one, he scooped up the casings, careful not to touch them. In the other went the mushroom. He told Scotti about his findings, and Scotti promised him mushroom risotto when they both got back home.

Devlin wrapped up his conversation and jogged back through the woods toward the villa. He stopped abruptly.

He was not alone. He sensed someone there in the woods with him. Lurking nearby, watching him. He pulled his Tanfoglio from his waistband, backed against the nearest oak, and listened. His eyes searched in all directions through the misty gloom of early morning, but he failed to spot anyone. He controlled his breathing and restricted his movement, mostly hidden in the brush surrounding the oak. Moments passed, and he wondered whether he'd imagined it. But he'd learned long ago to rely on his instincts, and he remained still, waiting for the person to indicate its location. Was it a family member, Lupo, or a security agent? Or was it the sniper, returned to finish what he or she had started?

Just then, he heard it. A low, guttural snort, followed by a high-pitched squeal, emanating from about fifty feet south. Through the brush, he spotted a mother razorback and her piglet scurrying away from the complex.

Sus Scrofa. The scientific name for wild boar. Devlin released the breath from his lungs that he hadn't realized he'd been holding. In recent years, the population of swine had risen dramatically throughout Europe. Like coyotes and bears in America, they were pests seeking food, and similarly wild and dangerous. He made a note to mention his sighting to the Aurora family. Pests were bad for business. Then again, so were company agitators and snipers. Apparently, Aurora Vineyard had its fair share of them all.

Upon his return to the main grounds, he shoved through a "mostly unlocked" side door of the bottling plant, right onto the main floor of the shipment room. He surveyed a hundred-foot wall lined with cases of the distinctive FONS water bottles, marked for shipment to the World Wide Water summit. Devlin peered through the shrink wrap that encased the bundles. The labels denoted a representative of the summit as recipient, and the destination for the shipment read: Verona, Italy.

Why were thousands of cases of Aurora's water, clearly earmarked for the summit, sitting in the shipping warehouse when a legal injunction barring its sale and distribution had been imposed? And imposed long before the summit's venue had made the change from Rome to Verona? Clearly, Aurora planned to circumvent this injunction, legally or otherwise, in a publicly grandiose way. He felt sure that this move would likely have been Erika's decision. Once again, her boldness intrigued him.

Devlin passed from the water plant to the grappa room and spied another enormous shipment of wrapped bundles. Again he found more bottles of FONS that proclaimed to offer a taste of La Fontana della Giovinezza, the Fountain of Youth. On an adjacent back wall, stowed behind one of the enormous grappa vats, stood another mountain of unshipped boxes. A ladder from floor to ceiling leaned haphazardly against the cases. The heavier, taller platinum-hued cardboard boxes indicated that their contents, also destined for the water summit, held the special anniversary-edition grappa. *A real treat for summit participants*, Devlin thought. *The drink of choice that Giancarlo Venchi imbibed just before convulsing and dropping dead at the finish line of the Monte Carlo racetrack.* Devlin patted the pockets of his track suit and kicked himself. He'd left behind any sort of tool that might disengage a sample bottle from its thick wrapping.

Devlin glanced up the stairs of the warehouse toward Runa Aurora's laboratory. He'd spotted dozens of sharp instruments there yesterday. After she'd immersed him and Ana with her bitchy demeanor by the grappa vat, he felt justified in misplacing one of her prized possessions.

As he crossed the floor of the grappa plant, a call came in from Lupo. Devlin hit his Bluetooth, and he scaled the stairs and entered the lab.

"Did you know that Ana's hair never fails to smell like peaches?" Lupo said.

Devlin smirked. "Peaches?" He scanned Runa's shiny, flat metal trays laden with various vinicultural instruments. The vintner's scalpels and trinket hammers could just as easily represent the tools of a surgeon, or a torturer.

"I haven't had breakfast," Devlin said. "And now I'm craving peaches." He opened a few drawers and looked for something sturdier, like a pair of scissors. All he found was a few boxes of sterile syringes. Should've sought cutters in the shipping manager's office. "So, lover boy, how is Ana?"

Lupo sighed. "She's amazing." His groggy attitude suggested he was still in bed. "But alas, duty calls. Letizia, her camerawoman from the BBC, drove up the mountain late last night. They're doing the Erika Aurora interview right now in Erika's office."

"It's five in the morning. Why so early?" Devlin flicked a set of switches that lit up a closet, as well as another small room, an inner sanctum of the laboratory. He peeked through the window of the sealed door to the inner lab. Vials and centrifuges and a bunch of other expensive technical devices filled the room, along with what looked like a dorm-room-sized refrigerator. He presumed a lot of potion work went on in that part of Hogwarts. He took a few steps back toward the closet in the outer room.

"Had to be early," Lupo said. "Ana's headed back to Verona later this morning. She's got some afternoon interviews with summit reps. Ana's a dynamic woman. So is that Erika chick."

"The whole Aurora clan is pretty astute...Erika, Leif, and Runa. They're really messed up. But despite their dysfunction and that annoying Philippe guy, the siblings have built up a damn good company." Devlin unlatched the closet to find that it was actually a tall, narrow refrigeration compartment.

Lupo yawned. "Maybe staying at each other's throats drives them to outdo each other. Makes a stronger company."

The refrigerator housed hanging vials of every color, shape and size. "Sometimes ruthlessness pays off," Devlin said.

The vials were methodically labeled with chemical symbols of various components, corked, and classified in specific arrangement. Devlin continued, "Maybe our invitation to figure out who's encroaching on the Aurora company from the outside is just a ruse. Maybe Erika, Leif, Runa, and even Philippe are vying with each other for solitary control of the company. That, and maybe they're trying to keep us from deducing they're all equally viable suspects in Giancarlo's death."

Lupo yawned again, louder this time. "Mmm...that Runa is a prime suspect for so many reasons...hated her boyfriend...mean bitch...hates everybody..."

Devlin distinctly heard the low hum of Lupo's snoring on the other end of the line. Devlin grinned and clicked off the call. He reached to shut both doors of the cold store, and a row of glass vials containing a distinctly rust-brown liquid caught his eye.

He swung open both doors again. A single ampule had been removed from that particular row. Each remaining bottle on either side of the vacancy was similarly colored, but strangely unlabeled. He wondered what particular chemical had resided there. Its absence seemed an oddity, based on Runa's meticulous nature. It could have been anywhere in the chem lab. Yet he was struck by a gut feeling that this missing vial was somehow an anomaly.

He pocketed another in the same row for later examination. He closed the fridge and flicked off the side lights. He peered back down at the table of metal instruments, snagged a sturdy enough blade, and descended the steps.

Devlin headed back toward the grappa shipment behind the vat. He was determined to extricate meaningful evidence about this special liqueur that Runa had served up to his dead colleague. It struck him that Lupo had mumbled something about Runa Aurora's wicked character. It reinforced Devlin's hunch that Runa may have altered Giancarlo's grappa with the contents of the missing vial from her lab, as payback for their public breakup.

Devlin slipped on the wet floor. He almost went down, but he caught himself before crashing his ass onto the cement. He looked down and noticed a puddle near the base of the enormous grappa vat. And just beneath the lip of the copper pot was a large, flow-through bag. Using the scalpel, he scooped up the dripping wet bag and held it before him. Herbs, fruit peels, cinnamon sticks. His stomach growled. Damn, what he wouldn't do to throw this shit on top of some steel-cut oats right now.

Something slipped from the bag and clattered to the floor near his feet. He blinked and took a step back. It was a syringe, similar in size and shape to the others he'd seen packaged in boxes in the lab drawer. With his sleeve, he picked it up and held it beneath the glare of his headlamp. Empty. But for a minuscule amount of rust-brown liquid. The same color as the fluid from the missing vial in the lab.

Devlin tore a fresh piece of cardboard from an unassembled shipping box. He nestled the syringe safely inside and added it to that morning's growing collection of evidence in his rucksack. Forgetting the grappa shipment for the moment, Devlin doubled back.

He gazed out at the room, inspecting the eight massive vats inside the plant. A ladder extended from floor to ceiling beside each copper barrel, save the one he was standing beside now. The missing ladder was likely the one that leaned against those unshipped cases he spied now behind the vat.

He strode to it, righted it, and ensured the stability of its base against the boxes. He climbed to the top of it. Nothing appeared out of place with the stack.

He turned to inspect the vat from which the ladder had been moved, took one look into the grappa fermenting in its cauldron, and abruptly retched. He forced his gaze back to the roiling contents in the twenty-five-hundred-gallon pool before him. A bloated, discolored corpse floated atop the brew. The color and length of the splayed blond hair, the approximate size of the cadaver, and the telltale vintage plaid cowboy shirt clearly indicated that the victim was Runa Aurora.

***

Devlin approached Aurora's stone office building and slowed to a jog. He steered his way up a couple flights of stairs toward the room he'd seen brightly lit against the gathering dawn. He heard voices from the hall and crept silently toward an open door. He peered in from the doorjamb, unobserved by Erika Aurora or Ana Malia. The two sat facing one another in winged Queen Anne chairs beside a large mahogany desk. He also recognized Ana's colleague, Letizia. She stood behind a camera and filmed the two sharply dressed women entrenched in conversation.

Despite the shock of just discovering the interviewee's dead sister, Devlin was intrigued by the tail end of Ana's remark, "…think that's why UNESCO has dubbed you 'the Bloodsucker?'"

If the moniker annoyed her, Erika never showed it. She thrust her chin out and licked her lips. "My family is fighting for its birthright. My father discovered the existence of the springwater aquifer on our land. We, and future generations, shouldn't be forced to relinquish it. The 'Bloodsucker' nickname is apt, in that I reap the marrow from my land, and I share the resource with those who hunger for it. Is it so wrong that I should be compensated for my efforts in alleviating the world's thirst? I think not."

Ana added a professional closing. The women shook hands, and Letizia said, “That’s a wrap.” The red light above the camera went out.

Devlin cleared his throat to announce his presence. Erika turned and offered him a confident smile. But when she saw his face, her radiant expression faded.

“Who died?” she said.

***

Devlin shared the news of Runa’s death with Erika, who maintained a sullen yet dignified demeanor. Erika informed her brother Leif, who did not. Ana retrieved Philippe, whose consolation proved ineffective in assuaging Leif’s grief. And the two men retired to their villa with a bottle of Xanax.

Local and Veronese authorities cordoned off the warehouse and began their investigation. Devlin explained how he’d encountered the body by propping the ladder beside the vat for a look at the company’s brew. Devlin omitted his discovery of the syringe, and the sniper’s bullet casings, preferring his own examination of the evidence later.

By the time the sun began to set on the vineyard, Runa’s cause of death had played out as Devlin expected. Though they promised a formal toxicology report, the ME and the CSI team surmised accidental overdose by carbon dioxide poisoning. The victim had fallen from a ladder into the vat, become asphyxiated by the toxic fermentation fumes, and drowned in her own vomit.

As the CSU packed up and left, their mumblings of the vic's possible suicide attempt over the breakup and death of her fiancé sent Erika into an uncontrolled rage. But Ana steered her back into the cantina to uncork some medicinal pinot noir.

Ana's suggestion that Erika call her friend, Marisse, to comfort her for a few days brought on another short-lived explosion of anger. Erika explained that although Marisse sold great leather, she was really just a clinger who came by to check up on her mamma's boy, Philippe.

That evening, Letizia offered Ana, Lupo, and Devlin a ride out of the Aurora nuthouse and back to Verona. Devlin couldn't snatch up the proposal fast enough. He needed a breather from this mess. Time to collect himself.

When he and Erika were left alone in her office just before leaving, Devlin knew. Whatever backwoods circus show was going on under this big tent called Aurora Vineyard, it would truly require the full application of Devlin's HELL Ranger acumen.

She came around the desk to face him, leaned her backside against her desk, and crossed her long legs. *Just when I thought it was safe to drink the grappa...Erika Aurora's going to drown me in it*, he thought.

"Clearly, I need you, Devlin. Much has happened at my vineyard—the threats, the shots fired, the flyovers. But nothing is as grave as the death of my sister. Today you witnessed firsthand the ineptitude of the police, with that cursory review they called a probe." She threw up her hands. "How can you turn your back on us?"

Devlin agreed. "They didn't even ask for surveillance footage. And they just about ignored your security chief's input."

Erika sat down beside Devlin on the couch next to her desk. "Contrary to what the police have deduced, my sister's death was not accidental. I believe that someone murdered her. Just like I'm convinced that someone poisoned your colleague, Giancarlo, with our product." She leaned forward, as if letting him in on a secret.

"Devlin, someone is out to destroy my company. They might be plotting to kill us off one by one. Or their angle might be to jeopardize our reputation, or to somehow usurp the power that my company wields in the industry. I don't know who it is or why they want to destroy Aurora, but I know that I need your help to find out. Now, more than ever."

Devlin stood and walked across the room. He reached for a bottle of water, but thought better of it. He'd sworn that he wouldn't leave Giancarlo's death with unanswered questions. A sniper was still at large. An owner of the company, formerly his prime suspect, was dead. Hard evidence existed—bullet casings, syringes, and a tainted dog bowl—that might pinpoint real answers to a case that clearly demanded them.

He turned to face Erika. She stood with her arms crossed and her eyes narrowed in determination. Was it an outside job or an inside one? Was the real perp standing in front of him, manipulating him into believing otherwise? Only one way to find out. He opened his mouth to accept her offer. But Scotti rang, and he picked up the call.

Devlin told Scotti, “Tell Lupo to get the band back together and meet me in Rome. In forty-eight hours, at the Grotto, we’ll get the HELL Rangers started on our next big, kickass mission.”

Chapter 14

"Lucky!" Devlin's son wrapped his arms around him and pulled him close, nuzzling his head into the crook of his father's shoulder. Devlin lifted him and swung Marcello side to side. He melted into the bear hug, stunned at how tall his son had grown in just the few days they'd been apart.

Less than thirty seconds later, Devlin's young lightning rod zapped back and forth across the bedroom, packing for robotics camp. Initiated by Marcello's grandparents about a week earlier, the chore had been relegated to Devlin upon his return to Siena that morning, out of sheer frustration and exhaustion.

Marcello motored on, "Zander and Rocco are leaving for the station early tomorrow, Lucky. So we have to get there way early, too. Maybe we can take the Vespa; it's so much faster. No, we'll have to take the car; it's bigger. Because I can't go to camp without my comic books. And I need to have all my comics, not just a few, because Zander and Rocco are bringing theirs too. Maybe I shouldn't bring my Hulks…they'll get wrecked. What do you think, Lucky? Hulks or no Hulks?"

The fact that Marcello insisted on calling him by his racing nickname, Lucky, never failed to crack him up. Marcello had practiced the trend during their vacation touring America's racetracks. Devlin had learned to appreciate the apt moniker even more one late night watching Godzilla movies with his son. Dangling on the precipice of sleep, Marcello had whispered in his angelic voice, "So very lucky you survived that creepy Ishmael dude. Your racing name…fits you…love you…" While Marcello dozed on his shoulder, Devlin had wept over the loss of his wife, and for the bittersweet joy that he and his son had continued to live on.

Now, Devlin teetered on the edge of Marcello's bed. The Iron Man comforter was crumpled in a ball at his feet, and the sheets were pulled back to leave room for a suitcase. Six pairs of swim trunks, two pairs of flip-flops, a hooded sweatshirt, and an overflowing box of comic books filled the case. Devlin's head spun. He'd prayed every day since Ella died that his son would achieve this state of little-boy normalcy. Devlin scooped up a pile of comics and smiled. "Definitely bring the Hulks."

***

The next morning, way early as requested, Devlin packed them into the big car and safely hugged the apex of every Tuscan hill on the drive to the Chiusi train station. Chiara and Prost followed behind in Lupo's tiny Fiat. The grandparents followed in an Aston Martin. At the station, Devlin parted with his big boy for a whole ten days. Marcello planned to learn "every single awesome thing about making robots, ever," until his return in time for the Palio festivities in early July.

After hugging and kissing their grandson, Filomena and Domenico took off for the Amalfi Coast for some much-needed R&R. Chiara and Prost waited for Lupo's incoming train from Verona. When Lupo arrived dressed in his bright yellow tights, and royal-blue-and-red Palio plumage, the three packed into the Fiat and headed to Siena.

A pang of regret struck Devlin when he realized that Chiara, Prost, and Lupo would miss his scheduled meeting at headquarters in Rome. He dug out his phone to question Lupo, but then he chalked up his melancholy to missing Marcello and pocketed it. Just because his son was growing up too fast, it was no use taking it out on someone else. Time to man up and handle disappointment.

Devlin drove the long and winding road to Rome, formulating a to-do list for the noon powwow in the Grotto. He'd spent some time over the past year at the headquarters conducting research for small cases. But this was really the first time the HELL Rangers would all meet there since strategizing the rescue of his son and disarming the bombs planted throughout the Eternal City. Acid boiled in his esophagus, and he turned up a little Zeppelin to ease his apprehension.

An hour later, Devlin entered the dining room of the lair, hidden deep in the bowels beneath Borghese Gardens. The aroma of roasted chicken made him salivate. Forget nerves; now he was pumped. He felt like he'd come home.

An aproned Scotti exited the kitchen and hugged him. Devlin handed him the wrapped porcini. Scotti grinned with satisfaction and shifted his heft back into the kitchen. "We have an hour before dinner. Go putter."

Devlin shrugged and descended the few floors down to the level that supported the tech room and forensics, devoid of any other brothers-in-arms. He unpacked the platinum-tainted dog bowl belonging to Erika's dehydrated pet, along with the baggie of bullet casings from the pine grove. He unwrapped the syringe he'd found at the grappa plant and corked it with a sterile plastic test tube stopper. He set to work dusting for prints and searching for specimen samples. He was about to test the composition of the rust-brown liquid when a text from Scotti informed him dinner was ready.

Back upstairs, Devlin frowned as Scotti poured some red wine from a decanter into two measly glasses. He glanced quizzically around the kitchen at the unusual absence of chaos.

"Change of plans," Scotti said. "It's just you and me for dinner. Lupo did attempt to assemble everyone under one roof like you'd requested, but the guys had already scattered."

Devlin's acid reflux had subsided considerably while he was puttering. Now it was back.

"I'm catching a train back to Monza tomorrow morning," Scotti said. "Got a call from the suits at Formula One this morning. Good news, they like your braking specs. Bad news, having a tough time convincing them to implement the changes before the Baju Grand Prix. I'm gonna zip the prototype up to MARI and convince them."

Scotti continued, "Either way, Hamilton, Montoya, and Helio never left Monza, so we'll wrap up and meet you in Verona in a few days. Lupo's bringing Prost and Chiara. And a bunch of the others are on their way back from the mission you'd assigned them in Syria. Looks like you're on your own until then."

That same melancholy stupor that struck Devlin at the train station threatened to railroad him. But the hearty aroma from the porcini risotto and roasted chicken that Scotti had busted his ass making shook him from his reverie. Devlin plucked the proverbial pacifier from his mouth and raised his glass. "*Salut*, my friend."

Scotti smiled and toasted him in return.

"Can I join you ladies, or is this a private affair?" a voice said from the open door of the kitchen. Scotti's younger brother, Vin, sauntered to the table and poured himself a glass, but not before Devlin crushed him in a one-armed hug.

The strategy meeting would have to wait, but some quality time with the man who'd always felt more like a father than a pit boss, and his kid brother, could never hurt. Since retrieving Devlin from the flotsam and jetsam of the New York Harbor decades earlier, Buffalo-born Benedetto Ilio Scotti had molded Devlin into the car-racing covert agent that he was today. With the same patience, guidance, and humor he'd used to save Devlin from his tumultuous childhood, Scotti had coaxed him from the anger and pain of Ella's death, back to the land of the living.

Scotti and Devlin cleared the kitchen, and Scotti filled him in on their dealings with the Formula One board of regulators. By the time Devlin realized that Vin had left them for dead, Vin reappeared with a file in his hand. "Saw you were playing with chemicals earlier, so I finished it up for you. Figured it was important."

Devlin wiped his hands and opened the folder. Vin had completed the chemical identification Devlin had begun earlier on the rust-brown liquid. Devlin sifted through the details, fascinated by the speed and accuracy of Vin's results. Until he remembered that, after serving in the Marines, Vin had graduated at the top of his class with a biochemistry degree from UC Berkeley.

More fascinating were the results of the report. At the bottom of the page, Vin had circled four letters in red ink: MeOH.

Shorthand for the chemical symbol for methyl alcohol.

***

Nearly a decade ago, Scotti and a few HELL Rangers had discovered their favorite bar, Nickel City Moonshine, late one night on the hunt for women and beer in Rome's Trastevere neighborhood. Enamored with the name, Scotti and the boys had ducked inside for a quick grappa. They'd been amazed by the extensive autographed memorabilia of Scotti's hometown teams, the Buffalo Sabres and the Bills.

The barkeep, Chuck Darcy, had turned in his Buffalo season tickets years earlier to marry an evil temptress from Rome. When the bitch left him, he'd stumbled into a broken-down tavern, slapped down his life savings, and rededicated the sports bar to his hometown teams. On most nights, Chuck regaled patrons with stories of the Bills' four-straight Super Bowl runs and the Sabres' elusive quest for Lord Stanley's Cup.

Tonight, Chuck digitally fed the live Sabres game (an afternoon competition across the pond) through the handful of flat-screens plastered around the backer bar. Though cheers from American tourists and study-abroad students occasionally drew their attention to the game, Scotti, Devlin, and Vin spent most of the night poring over the lab findings. Hunkered down at a wooden table in a "quiet" side room, they discussed the methanol found in the syringe at the grappa plant.

"Methanol is wood grain alcohol, highly toxic and unfit for human consumption. Commonly used in antifreeze, solvents, and jet fuel," Devlin said. He cradled his empty pilsner glass and shook his head in disbelief. "I actually found it in a syringe, carelessly discarded on the floor. With partial residue, as if it had been full but then been expunged. Pretty sure that's not standard winery protocol."

"Sounds like something left behind, by someone with bad intentions," Vin said.

Scotti sipped a grappa with an amber beer chaser on the side. "The ME confirmed Runa Aurora died of lethal asphyxiation. On a combination of fermentation toxicity and the rancid contents of her stomach. Let's say someone expelled the syringe into the woman's bloodstream, poisoning her, and that they dumped her body into the grappa to make it look like an accident. Are we really dealing with an idiot perp who remembers to dump the body, but who carelessly handles evidence and forgets that a tox screen will turn up poison anyway?"

"Either the perp's an idiot, or the syringe is unrelated to Runa's death and it was left behind by someone else with a different purpose," Devlin said.

A pert waitress with a black bob scooted by, and she rubbed her ass against Vin's arm before turning and reaching for his empty glass. "Can I get you something else?" she said. "Really, anything at all, you name it."

Devlin asked for another pilsner, and she assented without taking her eyes from Vin's face. For as long as Devlin had known him, Vin had had the knack. In spite of his war-damaged face, or perhaps because of it, women were drawn to him. Another beer was ordered, digits were passed between the two horny kids, and the discussion continued between the three men.

"Why the rusty-brown color?" Devlin said. "The stuff I found looked like the broth in Scotti's minestrone."

Scotti threw him a glance.

"I ran three tests. All showed the basic ingredients for grappa, like grape seeds, skins, and water, as well as the scant amount of platinum that Aurora uses. Aside from that, all signs point to methanol," Vin said. "Oh yeah, and cow shit."

"Cow shit?" Devlin frowned.

Vin laughed. "I swear I'm not pulling your leg. I found cow DNA. Grapes absorb nutrients from the soil in which they're grown. The pomace in the grappa probably retained a bit of cow manure during production."

Devlin flicked his eyes back to the report, to the circled red letters of the methanol symbol at the bottom of the page—MeOH. Then he scrolled his eyes to the fine print near the middle of the report and nodded. "Methanol, grappa, platinum, and cow manure? That's it?" He felt like they were missing something important.

Vin reiterated, "A modicum of platinum and cow excrement, grappa residue, and a trace amount of methanol. Methanol is typically clear in liquid form, and so are most grappas. Even so, amber-brown coloration can be attributed to a number of things: faint pigments from the grapes; possible oxidation present in the water; or even absorption of the hue from the barrels in which they're stored. Or even cow shit."

Vin sipped his Labatt Blue and continued, "What I find most unusual is the efficacy of the formula itself. Whoever concocted this little potion found a way of maximizing the potency of the methanol, by nearly a thousandfold."

A cheer rippled through the bar. Devlin glanced up and saw that the Sabres had scored, sending the game into overtime.

"Explain?" Devlin asked.

"Methanol is a natural endogenous compound found in humans in trace amounts. Usually it's metabolized, and we exhale it. Take a bite of an apple, you can end up with a gram of methanol, but the body processes it, and you don't die," Vin said. "But if you increase the amount to ten milliliters of pure methanol, the common foreshot in moonshine production, then a human goes into convulsions. Without treatment, it's possible that blindness, brain damage, and death could result."

Vin pointed to the lab report. "In your syringe, someone devised a formula that imparts only a barely detectable amount of methanol, which ordinarily wouldn't affect an average adult human. But then he or she boosted the methanol's potency, enough to cause a violent reaction and death within minutes."

"Similar to Giancarlo's extreme reaction after drinking the grappa in Monaco. That too was chalked up as an accidental death, as the minute amount of methanol quickly metabolized," Devlin said.

"Exactly," Vin said. "And the same may be true in Runa's case."

The flirty barmaid returned with drinks and briefly interrupted their brainstorming session. She winked at Vin. "I'm off in five minutes if you want to take me home," she said. Vin flashed her a smile, and she sauntered off.

Scotti stifled an amused grin. He held up his grappa to the candle flame on the table. "Moonshine is dangerous stuff. In the old days of Prohibition, the guys distilling whiskey in their garages didn't know that they had to remove the "foreshots" or "heads," the first few ounces of the batch that drips from the condenser, containing the methanol from the mash." Scotti sipped his drink with the determined face of a daredevil. "There's an Italian law on the books that says winemakers have to sell their pomace to grappa producers, because it's a tricky process removing the foreshot during distillation."

Devlin's eyebrow shot up. "Aurora Vineyard produces both—wine and grappa. What do you think they do with all their methanol stores from the woody stems and seeds leftover from grappa production? Maybe sell it to commercial industrial users, like cleaning solvent companies…"

Scotti piped up, "Or space programs and…"

"And Formula One," Vin said. "Methanol's good fuel, but highly combustible. I know they used to use it in open-car racing, like Formula One and IndyCar. But now I think it's been banned for safety, because it's so flammable."

"Methanol by-product in a grappa plant," Scotti said. "Sure sounds like a clever way to get rid of CEOs, company usurpers, or an ex-boyfriend…"

Devlin's eyes flicked back and forth between the brothers. "Maybe a chemist…or perhaps a knowledgeable vintner…" Devlin set down his beer. "Someone, inside or outside the gates of Aurora Vineyard, decided to encapsulate this poison formula into vials and syringes?" Devlin tugged at the locks of tar-colored hair that scraped his collar, looking at Vin and Scotti, but not really seeing them. "Perp dopes up his victim with just enough methanol to send them into convulsions and/or cardiac arrest…"

"By injecting it into a bottle of anniversary grappa at a car race…" Scotti said.

"Or a needle into the bloodstream before a swan dive into a grappa vat?" Vin said.

"Yes. Just enough lethal alcohol to kill…but an amount small enough that it would quickly metabolize and appear as an accidental overdose." Devlin slammed his hand on the table. "Gentlemen, I think we've got ourselves a potential murder weapon."

"He shoots…he scores!" Chuck shouted from behind the bar in the next room. Cheers and high-fives circulated through the establishment. The Buffalo Sabres had won, and Devlin bought a round of grappa for the entire bar.

Chapter 15

What I wouldn't do to take a bite out of that sweet ass, Erika thought. She eyed a tall younger man dressed in a well-fitted Armani suit kneeling before the casket of her dead sister Runa. *What kind of a sicko thinks such things at her sister's memorial service?*

Erika glanced around the interior expanse of the centuries-old church, centered in the tiny town at the base of their mountain. She sighed, wishing she were anywhere but here. Mourners, qualified by the Aurora security team, had gathered since dawn for the noon service. Now that the ceremony was over, attendees lingered in the church and in its adjoining parish hall, chatting and nibbling refreshments as if at a trade show.

Erika reminded herself again to drop the aloof sneer and replace it with a demure countenance of anguish over her sister's loss. But she couldn't summon a look of pain, because she didn't feel any. She felt numb. Maybe that's why they called her "Bloodsucker." She sucked the life out of those around her like a vampire and still wasn't satisfied. She glanced at the tall drink of water who now rose from the casket's kneeler, and imagined sinking her teeth right into those glutes, as tight as a pair of bongos. She gasped, and covered it with a cough, when she realized she'd been ogling her new private dick, Devlin Lucchesi.

He's here, she swooned inwardly. She did all she could to calm her heavy breathing. He steered deftly through the traffic of lamenters, straight for her. The fleeting thought, *I'm his finish line*, skittered through her mind a second before he arrived. He embraced her in a demonstration of condolence. He hadn't noticed that she'd copped a feel of that great ass when she'd run her hands down his back to disengage, or he hadn't shown it anyway.

"You're early. I didn't expect you until tomorrow," she said.

"I expected that you might need a bit of comfort today, but you seem to be holding up well," Devlin said.

"Thank you, that's kind of you. Don't worry; it won't be a wasted effort. This gathering is a great opportunity for reconnaissance, as many of our competitors and compatriots are here," Erika said. "I feel certain that someone under the roof of this church today is the one that's out to destroy Aurora."

She hooked her arm through his and treaded toward a stand of red sympathy roses off to the side that provided an ample yet discreet view of the crowd. There they stopped to review their targets. She leaned in toward him, and he clutched her close for support, as if sharing a moment of grief. The girth of his bicep beneath her fingers nearly made her weep. She was clearly no longer numb.

She began her evaluation farthest away from where they stood. Erika said, "At three o'clock, you'll see a man who looks like an adult Charlie Brown—short, pudgy, no hair, big nose, and a desperate, dejected grimace permanently etched into his face. Jasper Feckle, owns Blue Rhino, the water company that sponsored your deceased colleague and Runa's ex-fiancé, Giancarlo. They stand to gain if we go under, because they're always vying for the same contracts and sponsorships. I'm the Lucy to that ugly Charlie Brown—wherever I go, he follows, and he never has an original idea in his head."

"I can understand why Blue Rhino would want to eliminate Aurora as a competitor. But what's his motivation for murdering the racer that he sponsors?" Devlin said.

"Devlin, with all due respect, I hired you to ascertain who's after me and my company. Please conduct your personal investigation on your own time," Erika said.

"With all due respect, Ms. Aurora, don't ever tell me how to do my job. Or the last you'll see of me is the dust from my tires."

Erika felt her nipples grow hard beneath her silk chemise. No one had ever dared speak to her that way. "Fair enough."

He softened his curt statement with a smile and forged on. "Tell me about that woman over there." Devlin gestured to a tall blond woman, one the tabloids had rumored was romantically connected to Giancarlo during his engagement to Runa. "I'm not sure I understand why you'd allow 'the other woman' into your sister's funeral service."

"Leif and I call her 'Legs'. She's Charlie Brown's daughter. Leif thought it best to include our competitor's future owner—keep our enemies close, ya know?"

Devlin nodded. "She's Blue Rhino's future owner, and she's the slut that stole away your sister's fiancé's sponsorship…maybe she—"

"Scratch her off your list," Erika said. "Legs just flew in from working the Victoria's Secret Angels runway in Las Vegas. No way she's responsible for Runa's death."

Erika reached for the scribbled note attached to the extravagant flower arrangement. "Love, Ana Malia," it read. Leave it to Ana to shower her with love in the face of adversity. Ana had insisted on ditching her Verona work assignments to support her friend through Runa's funeral arrangements. But Erika had sent her away, in favor of a bottle of red and her accounting ledger to muddle through the loss.

"How about the guy hanging on Hot Legs' arm? I know him. He's the pit boss for Giancarlo's squad. Acted like an asshole in Monaco when I tried to help resuscitate his convulsing driver," Devlin said. "Maybe the two of them—"

Erika shook her head again. "He was with Legs in Vegas. Saw pictures of them on the red carpet. What do you say we head over to the sandwich trays, and I can introduce you to another competitor, Jacques Vitreuve?" She and Devlin strolled to the mountain of finger sandwiches piled high on a spinning table near the center of the parish hall. "Vitreuve runs

HydroVino on the Italian Riviera, in San Remo, just a sneeze away from Monaco."

"French guy, Italian winery?" Devlin said, snagging a roast beef and caviar nibble. Devlin winced, opened the sandwich, scraped off the caviar, and popped the rest of the panino into his delicious mouth. She pictured him in a caveman loincloth and salivated.

"Jacques's former French vineyard apparently dried up," she said. "He moved to San Remo and bought another plot of land, which thrived. He recently incorporated bottled water into his portfolio, and now I want *him* dead, the wily French frog."

Devlin halted halfway to popping a cucumber sandwich into his mouth at her declaration.

"I want his company to die, not him," Erika said. "And I'm sure the feeling is mutual. He's as likely as anyone to want me out of the way. Plus, though he's a decade older than me, he's always had a thing for my younger sister. A year ago she finally acquiesced to date him, but when Giancarlo came along, Runa dumped him."

Devlin swallowed the sandwich and narrowed his eyes, taking better stock of Jacques Vitreuve. Devlin seemed intrigued with the Frenchman's prospects as a suspect in Giancarlo's and Runa's deaths, not to mention as a usurper for her company, she was sure. Erika had always speculated Vitreuve might prove the worst kind of threat. Now, at her sister's funeral, she felt justified by the notion.

Devlin tipped back his glass for a swig of water. The goblet was jarred by a flying elbow coming in fast toward Erika for a sympathy hug, and the contents spilled down his white shirt beneath the sensuous Armani fabric.

"Erika, my darling. My deepest sympathies for your family's loss." A slender woman in her late forties, dressed in an elegantly cut suit, broke her embrace with Erika and turned to Devlin. "Forgive me my manners, sir." She dabbed at his shirt with a handkerchief. "In my grief and haste, it appears I've become clumsy."

Devlin smiled good-naturedly. He grasped her dabbing hand with tenderness and kissed it. "Ma'am, think nothing of it. It's my fault for getting in the way. And it's nothing a cleaning won't remedy." He offered his hand. "Devlin Lucchesi."

Before the woman could answer, Erika interjected. "Marisse LeFleau? My God, woman, you look wonderful. It's been entirely too long since we've seen each other. Devlin, this is Philippe's mother. She and I chat now and again about her most beautiful leather creations, and—"

"And I keep tabs on my son," the woman finished with a roll of her eyes. In perfect English with just a lilt of French accent, she said, "I am what they call 'a helicopter mother.' *C'est la vie.* I am what I am. I love my son. He is my world." She shrugged. Devlin and Erika laughed. "But you're right, Erika," Marisse said. "It is too bad we see each other but once or twice a year if we are lucky. *Quel dommage!*"

Philippe sidled up beside his mother then and kissed her cheeks in greeting. As they did, Erika pondered the plastic work Marisse must have had to appear so youthful. She peeked beneath Marisse's short blond bob and behind her ear for skin tucks, but she couldn't catch a glimpse.

Devlin offered his hand and condolences to Philippe, who nodded and shook it. Philippe whispered into his mother's ear and marched off like a spoiled child.

Marisse sighed. "Will you two please forgive me? It appears that Philippe requires a ride back to the university, *tout de suite.* I'm heartbroken to hear that your poor brother, Leif, has been unable to leave his room since his sister's loss. Please let me know if there's anything I can do for him or you, Erika."

Erika shook the woman's tiny hand. "I understand completely. And thank you, Marisse. I'll be in touch soon."

Marisse kissed her cheek and settled her aubergine leather pocketbook on her shoulder. The woman bid good-bye to Devlin and walked the length of the room with all the sophistication of Grace Kelly.

Erika turned back to Devlin and slumped her shoulders. "I'm sorry about your wet shirt. I can get you one of Leif's."

Devlin waved her off. "No one's ever died from a splash of water. Now tell me more about…" Devlin suddenly cocked his head at the frescoed ceiling. Flying angels stared down as if taunting him. "I hear a helicopter. Hovering overhead the church."

Erika grabbed his hand and led him to the entrance. With the other, she texted Rasmus Laukkanen, her chief of security.

Outside, a helicopter indeed lingered overhead. The whir of its rotors elicited the chapel's participants like the Pied Piper of Hamelin. While everyone gawked at the chopper, security stood armed and ready to fire if the need arose.

Erika glimpsed Devlin move his hand to the back of his waistband, likely to secure his own handgun. How had she earlier missed the bulge of his piece while caressing his backside with her eyes?

The helicopter surged forward, ready to move away. But then it halted, as if to taunt them. Suddenly, a barrage of water balloons exploded from the interior of the chopper, like corn from a popper. The balloons rocketed down from about a hundred feet up and crashed to the ground at the revelers' feet, splashing red liquid in every direction. Most people scattered. Devlin and Erika took cover behind a wide marble pillar. Many were drenched. A banner unfurled out of the door that read, "Bloodsucker, DIE!" and then the chopper tore off.

Security radioed the local authorities, but Erika knew the chopper would be long gone by the time they arrived. "Damn activists," Erika muttered under her breath.

Devlin dabbed his finger in a red puddle, sniffed it, and dabbed it to his lips. He nodded to Erika's security chief, who stood nearby. "Water, with red dye. Not a security issue, just a public nuisance." Rasmus nodded and stormed off with two other guards. Devlin and Rasmus had more or less joined forces on the day of Runa's murder, respectfully residing on the same wavelength.

For the next half hour, an impromptu reception line formed outside the church. It was comprised of those who had come to eat and drink her food, and who now were taking off at the first sign of inconvenience.

"Erika, *ma chère*, we must let bygones be bygones, *n'est-ce pas*?" Jacques Vitreuve kissed both her cheeks. She restrained herself from vomiting at the cloying stench of his aftershave.

"It is tragic what has happened to your sister, such a lovely bird of paradise, taken too quickly," Vitreuve said. "Say that you will visit. Come to San Remo, bring your family…Leif, Philippe, your friend Mr. Lucchesi, come and relax. Let us put aside our differences in the face of this tragedy and start anew, *ma chère*."

Erika knew she was grimacing but she couldn't command her facial muscles to relax into a smile, not with Jacques Vitreuve, Aurora's staunchest competitor. Devlin must have noticed her discomfort, and he said, "What a lovely invitation, Erika. One you should consider, in my humble opinion." She felt Devlin discreetly squeeze her arm, and she knew that he meant a meeting on Vitreuve's vineyard was a wise strategic move. She nodded her acquiescence and was grateful when Vitreuve accepted this slight confirmation and left.

Erika shook hands, hugged, and accepted well wishes right down to the very last one. Then she kicked off her heels and plopped down on the church steps. Devlin, who'd stood by her side through it all, pulled a bottled water from his inside jacket pocket and bent to offer it to her. The label read HydroVino. Devlin had handed her Jacques Vitreuve's product, one that her competitor must have finagled into her own sister's memorial right beneath her nose. Erika turned to castigate Devlin for his thoughtlessness and was instantly disarmed by his boyish grin.

"Gotcha," he said and winked.

She smiled. She should have known Devlin had been toying with her, trying to calm her down. It had been a longer day than she would've thought, made longer by the damn activists that refused to let her be, even at her sister's funeral. And by the heavy feeling that this situation was not going away anytime soon.

"Anyone else worth mentioning as a potential suspect in that long line of interesting people?" Devlin said. He stood on the pavement, with his hands in his pockets, swinging his elbows back and forth. She supposed that's what he must've looked like as an impatient child. Adorable.

She shook her head. "I've arranged for you to stay right on the vineyard's property, with a room and a computer for you at the villa. I'll also get you a key to my office. You can comb through every competitor's file, every threat, every negative newspaper article ever written against me." She clutched her heels by the straps and stood, stifling a yawn. "But right now, I'm taking a bath."

Chapter 16

A cold shower is so clichéd, Devlin thought, *but damn if it didn't work.*

Saved by a church officiant who'd required Erika's attention after the service, Devlin drove like a demon up the winding path to Aurora, cleared security, and headed straight for the room in which he'd bunked days earlier.

After twenty minutes beneath an icy power head, Devlin felt a tad more respectable. The things he'd envisioned doing with Erika Aurora and her tiny, tanned feet had consumed him the entire ride up the mountain. Now he chastised himself for his feelings of impropriety toward a client during an active investigation.

He quickly unpacked his duffel into the claw-footed chest of drawers. He flipped open his computer on the matching desk by the window overlooking the courtyard. The evidence files he'd collected from the lab tests at the Grotto fell to the floor, as did the small book that Scotti had given him almost a week earlier. Ella's childhood storybook, the one she'd inscribed on their wedding day. He picked it up, and Erika Aurora's face flashed through his mind.

"Damn it." Devlin slammed the book on the desk. He was a monumental ass. His wife had just stepped into her grave, and here he was flirting with disaster. What an ass.

A call from Scotti saved him from further self-flagellation. His pit boss updated him on the positive discussions at the racing institute in Monza. Devlin told Scotti about the goings-on at the memorial service.

"Anything else you want to tell me?" Scotti said.

"No. Why? What do you mean? No," Devlin said. "Why are you pressuring me?"

"Uh-huh," Scotti said.

"What's that supposed to mean?" Devlin's voice reverberated through his cell phone. It sounded more high-pitched than he would've liked. "What?" he said an octave lower.

"You're lonely," Scotti said. "And that's okay."

"What are you, my psychiatrist?" High-pitched voice was back. "What are you talking about?"

A limo pulled into the flagstone drive below the window. The driver opened the door for Erika Aurora. She exited the vehicle with a briefcase and one of the smaller arrangements of funeral flowers. She walked to the villa's entrance, barefoot. He might need another shower.

Scotti's voice interrupted. "Marcello's away at camp. The HELL Rangers are scattered for the moment. And you're...a little lonely."

"No, sir. I'm working," Devlin said. "I've been alone on missions be—"

"Not alone. Lonely. It's been a long time since Ella's passed. And no one would blame you for desiring another woman's companionship, you know."

"With all due respect, sir, I don't think I'm ready for this conversation." Devlin ran his finger along the binding of Ella's book. "I need to get back now."

Scotti said, "I'm always here if you need me."

"I know." Devlin hung up, grabbed his laptop, and headed for Erika Aurora's office.

***

Angry voices emanated from the open door of Erika Aurora's office. Devlin knocked, and the voices stopped. He poked his head around the doorjamb. "I could come back later."

Leif sat facing Erika at her desk, his left leg slung over the arm of his leather chair. In a robe and slippers, Leif ran a hand through his unkempt hair. Erika smiled and waved Devlin in, while Leif regarded him with swollen, red-rimmed eyes. Leif's attempt at a smile was nothing more than a thin crack on the face of a porcelain doll. All in all, it was a vast improvement from Leif's hysterical bereavement a few days earlier.

"I have meetings tomorrow that can't be avoided," Leif said to Erika. "Along with my deposition at the injunction appeal in Verona. After that, I'm meeting Philippe at school. He's on break before the next term, and we could both use some rest."

"Restful skiing, probably?" Erika said, rolling her eyes.

"Yes, you know the slopes soothe us both. Philippe has been working on his clean water dissertation, and ever since Runa's…" Leif trailed off, clearly struggling to keep it together.

Devlin diverted him. "Tell me about Philippe's dissertation."

Leif sat up in his chair and crossed his legs. "Philippe's a hero, with amazing ideas on clean water. His thesis explores changing dirty runoff into clean, potable water. Dirty runoff from the muddy rivers of Africa, to the polluted Ganges, to the hurricane-ravaged waters in Haiti, to the swampy bayous of New Orleans…" Leif stood and glared at Erika. "To the by-product wasted in the production of wine."

"Excellent theory, expensive application," Erika said. "Convince Philippe to expand the cost-benefit analysis portion of his thesis. If he can come up with a way *not* to bankrupt the companies and governments that employ the process, then he'll be a real hero."

Leif balked and stormed toward the door.

"I'll expect to see you in San Remo to meet with Vitreuve on Friday," Erika said.

Leif paused at the door, shot up his middle finger, and left.

Erika pointed to a desk in the corner of the room. "Your workstation, Devlin." She swept her hand across the tall wood-paneled filing cabinets. "Your evidence lockers. Have at them." She pointed to her collection of assorted rocks, bricks, and shards of glass. "Free gifts, deposited in my private sanctuary over the past month by vandals. Test them all you like. Just return them to the pile, because they drive me to work harder." She dropped three keys into his palm. "One is for my office, another my files, and the last is for the lab. What's mine is yours."

Devlin nodded and pocketed the keys. He walked to his workstation and deposited his laptop, which knocked over a pile of manila folders. "And these?" he said.

"Possible leads. A few activists that have been particularly vocal over the past year, especially after news of our private aquifer leaked. I think one or two of them are responsible for those vile 'Bloodsucker' campaigns. Others might just be a nuisance. We'll see," she said.

Erika walked to his desk and handed him an envelope. "A messenger from the medical examiner's office brought this."

Devlin unfolded the single sheet of paper inside. Runa's toxicology report. He skimmed it. "Confirmed accidental alcohol overdose. Faint traces of methanol and platinum commonly found in the average human," he read aloud.

That coincided with the possibility that the methanol syringe had been expunged into her bloodstream before Runa's death. Nothing confirmed it, as she was indeed found floating in a vat of alcohol. Still, there was nothing to contradict the theory either. Whoever wanted Giancarlo and Runa dead probably enjoyed damaging their reputations too.

Erika handed him a thick red file folder, banded together with a large elastic to keep it from busting open at the seams.

"This is a file on HydroVino. In the last hour, I made a few calls and set up a meeting with Jacques in San Remo for Friday. We'll call it 'positive company relations.'"

Devlin nodded. "I have four or five of my team coming to Aurora Vineyard in the next few days. I'd like them to work with your security personnel and evaluate threats firsthand."

"A few of them arrived before you did this morning…Lauda, Hunt, Ascari, Sneakers. Clever racing nicknames, but why the name Sneakers?" Erika said.

"Believe it or not, it's a tribute to his warrior attitude. Remind me to tell you the story sometime," Devlin chuckled. His special ops team that he'd stationed in Syria must have finished off their mission early and hightailed it up the mountain. Funny that Scotti hadn't mentioned it.

"While we were at the church, your men spent the morning coordinating with my team," Erika said. "They inspected the vineyard for potential breach sites and whatnot. One of them is already in the lab running tests on the red water from the dropped balloons. Nice kid named Vin."

***

Devlin found Vin bent over a sink in the vineyard's lab, Runa Aurora's former stomping ground. He was scraping metal shavings from a glass slide into running water and chomping on a piece of bubblegum.

Vin shook hands with Devlin, skipped the pleasantries, and immediately clued his boss in. "As we know, the trace amount of methanol that I tested at the Grotto was not pure. It was definitively tainted by oxidation. Platinum's considered a noble metal, highly resistant to corrosion, so that's out," Vin said. "When I arrived today, I ran four tests on the water that's piped throughout the vineyard." He ran the sink and filled a glass of water. "All of the water here, whether for bottling, production, cleaning, irrigation, or human consumption, is tapped from the private aquifer that runs beneath the vineyard. The mountain runoff, rain, and even some of the production waste ends up in the water table, filling this natural aquifer, which then nourishes the entire property. And there's natural oxidation in this water, which is likely filtered out when it's bottled."

"So the amber-brown color is either from rusty water, or cow-shit-flavored grappa?" Devlin asked.

Vin smirked, "Exactly." He held up a bottle. "Aurora's anniversary grappa, the same one Giancarlo swigged before his death. It matches the liquid in the syringe, minus the concentrated methanol. I tested samples from a dozen bottles. Some contain cow DNA, others don't. It's likely that various batches are comprised of different pomace, some flavored with cow, some not. But that's not what's at issue here."

Vin blew a massive pink bubble, which popped. "It's the extreme toxicity in the minute trace of methanol foreshot that poses the real conundrum. How did someone amp it up so high?"

Devlin shook his head. "I don't know. Is it possible someone added to the formula some other trace elements that are present in the aquifer's water, and they metabolized before we could test it? Or maybe a temperature change, or some other such process, affects it. Maybe the pairing with the platinum has something to do with it."

Vin nodded. "All are sound possibilities." Vin ceased his work and stared at Devlin, clearly struck by a viable theory. "Maybe a synthetic additive or a synthetic process?"

"So…mad scientist theory?" Devlin said.

Vin smiled and shook his head. "Bottom line, someone's found a way to trigger a reaction that makes a minute amount of methanol extraordinarily toxic, and virtually undetectable."

Devlin nodded. "Sounds like a formula for disaster. And I know where to find vials that match the syringe." Devlin rummaged in his pocket for the lab key. "Erika mentioned that you were running tests on the red water from the dropped balloons?"

Vin blew another bubble and popped it. "Confirmed your theory that it's nothing but water and basic food coloring. Available everywhere."

Devlin nodded. "Aside from our industrial-strength moonshine, our evidence is pretty slim. Erika's dog fell sick from a water bowl laced with platinum specks. Any trace of methanol would now be gone, but it's a good possibility that our perp tried to do away with her dog, too."

Vin spat his gum into the bin. "Who'd take out a friggin' dog?"

Devlin shrugged. "Couldn't lift any prints from the dog bowl. Nor the bullet casings that all came from a nine-millimeter handgun." He unearthed the keys from his pocket that Erika had given him. He walked to the flat-panel refrigerator on the back wall. "Never heard of a pro sniper shooting long range with a handgun."

"Sounds amateur, and a little desperate." Vin cleaned and dried his workspace and neatly put away a few instruments into drawers. He dropped a metal chisel off a hook on the opposite wall, and the metal clang drew Devlin's attention. That's when Devlin noticed the tiny green light.

It was a green indicator on a live surveillance camera, one that hadn't been functional the last time he'd surveyed the lab. This signaled that someone had deliberately turned it back on. He glanced through the windows overlooking the plant, and he spotted tiny green beacons dotting each of the four surveillance cameras in the warehouse.

Devlin's thoughts returned to the task at hand. He tried to insert one of the keys that Erika had given him into the lab's refrigerator panel, but it didn't fit that keyhole. As he finagled another, he considered the enhanced security, for the lab door and the fridge that had at one time stood entirely accessible by anyone. He wondered who had implemented this newfound security, and whether it was legitimate, or if it was to dodge culpability in the face of Runa's death.

Finally, Devlin unlocked the fridge and opened it. All was as it should be. All but the handful of vials that contained the dirty-brown liquid, the same found in the syringe. They were gone.

Since Runa's death just a few days earlier, someone had entered the premises and absconded with the vials that, in all likelihood, matched the contents of the syringe, bearing the lethal methanol formula.

Chapter 17

The lights of San Remo glittered like diamonds in the sunset when Devlin's train had pulled into the station. The city on the Italian Riviera was renowned for its gorgeous beaches, casino-driven nightlife, and sumptuous atmosphere. Yet its opulence paled in comparison to Erika Aurora, sitting before Devlin now in the moonlit night. Together they sipped HydroVino bottled water from a glass, on the clay patio in the olive grove of her sworn enemy, Jacques Vitreuve.

Though she'd demonstrated a distinctly edgy attitude toward her rival vintner throughout their welcome dinner, Erika Aurora never failed to exude a radiance that transcended her professional demeanor. Maybe Scotti was right. Maybe when the Aurora investigation was over, Devlin would focus his personal attention on this woman in the royal-blue dress. It hugged her body as tightly as he'd like to wrap his own body around it. Maybe someday, provided the woman wasn't behind bars, or dead, by the time it was all over.

Jacques Vitreuve was a five-and-a-half-foot-tall, salt-and-peppered native Bordelaise. He'd relocated to San Remo back in the late 1980s, "because I wanted to buy a vineyard, and I found this one for a song," he'd said. Vitreuve had proved himself a hospitable *padrone*, with a charm and wit that had kept them all laughing through their four-course meal.

The tour that Jacques had provided upon arrival for Erika and Devlin, as well as Leif and Philippe, who'd flown in from Switzerland, had been short. The vineyard was small, and its operations were more condensed than Aurora's. Nestled inland, but with a gorgeous view of the Mediterranean, the vineyard had started as an olive oil producer in the 1920s. Now it was comprised of a single-label winery, a cozy grappa cantina, an olive oil cellar, and a roadside enoteca with an office. Jacques and a small staff resided alongside it in the family farmhouse. But it was Vitreuve's brand-new state-of-the-art water-bottling plant, a few miles down the road, which was the bee in Erika's bonnet.

When Vitreuve excused himself to fetch a bottle of grappa from his small cantina, the rickety door slammed behind him. Leif leaned forward across the table. "I thought the little bastard would never leave us alone. The guy's mental."

"Totally paranoid," Philippe agreed.

"He just doesn't want us skulking about, looking for trade secrets," Erika said. "As if he has any."

"Oh, he's got secrets," Leif said. "We flew into the airport, but instead of meeting his chauffeur, we rented a car. We hauled ass to his water-bottling plant, to check it out before we got here."

Erika's eyes widened. "Distribution hasn't even started yet on their line of bottled water. How'd you get in?"

Leif leaned back in his chair. "Funny how far you can go when you're two flamboyant boys in ski gear who only speak Swiss." Leif smiled and threw his arm around Philippe.

Erika smiled and leaned forward. "And? What's the skinny?"

Leif discreetly opened one side of his suit jacket to reveal a bottle of water that eerily resembled Aurora's characteristic urn-shaped FONS water bottle.

Devlin wondered if he'd have to push Erika's brown eyes back into her skull.

"Silver-speckled water! That sonuvabitch!" Erika said. "That's why he declined to take us there. It looks just like our platinum FONS." She stood and paced back and forth across the clay, huffing and puffing. "Good faith gesture, my ass. Dinner as sign of condolence, my lily-white ass."

A vision of Erika's lily-white ass flashed through Devlin's mind.

"Shhh, there's more. Sit down, before he sees you stalking around," Leif said.

Erika sat.

"Tell 'em about the grappa," Philippe said.

Erika gestured toward the cantina from which Jacques would soon emerge. "We saw the grappa room. Bit production. So what?"

Leif donned a devilish grin. "There's another one. Bigger. Almost as big as ours."

What? Erika mouthed through gritted teeth.

Philippe nodded. “Large foundation. Four copper vats of grappa, and two stainless steel bins of methanol waste.”

Devlin’s interest was piqued at the mention of the methanol waste. Of course, every distillery produced methanol waste, the natural, toxic “heads” and “tails” of the distillation process. From Devlin’s research over the past couple days, he’d learned that some companies simply flushed it. Others stored it for sale to industrial companies.

Both Aurora and HydroVino stored it. But the fact that these two competitors stood in obvious time-sensitive contention, based on Aurora’s indefinite injunction, got Devlin’s heart pounding. To what lengths would these two companies go to procure market leadership in the grappa and water markets?

“Clearly, Vitreuve is taking advantage of our injunction against the sale and distribution of our bottled water, and he plans to launch his first,” Leif said.

“But the fact that’s he’s planning to make a run on our grappa business—it’ll be too much of a burden on our bottom line. That little frog has to be stopped,” Erika said.

Leif and Philippe exchanged a look of mischief. But they stifled their giggles when Jacques exited the cantina with a bottle of spirits. “*Mon Dieu*, I forgot glasses,” he said and turned back inside.

Leif nodded toward Devlin. “You’ll want to hear this. There’s more grappa. *Our grappa*. A stash of six cases of it, hidden in what's supposed to look like an abandoned shed in the back of the water-bottling complex."

Leif pulled open the other side of his suit jacket and handed Devlin a bottle of the Aurora company's grappa. "It's *our* anniversary special-edition grappa. The same one that your friend Giancarlo drank before he died. Why is Vitreuve hiding six cases of it in an abandoned shed on his winery?"

***

The screen door slammed again behind Vitreuve, who now carried a tray of glasses in one hand and a bottle of HydroVino grappa in the other. Devlin secreted the Aurora bottle beneath his fleece jacket, while the rest of the bunch abruptly switched to a conversation of the annual bicycle race traversing the roads between Milan and San Remo.

Devlin considered Leif's point. Why was Aurora's staunchest competitor stashing a few cases of their special grappa? Corporate espionage, maybe. Vitreuve had had no moral compunction about producing and distributing a copycat water label in the face of Aurora's injunction.

On the other hand, Devlin wondered if Leif and Philippe had actually stumbled on a smoking gun. It was the same type of grappa given to Giancarlo before his death, and the same found in the lethal syringe found in close range of Runa's dead body. With full access to a lab and large stores of methanol, had Jacques Vitreuve tampered with this bottle that now rested uncomfortably against his lower abdomen? He'd have Vin test it upon their return to Aurora to see if the bottle's contents matched that of the poisoned syringe.

The tense conversation floundered, and Devlin figured now might be a good time to shake things up even more. From his back pocket, Devlin pulled a capped syringe. It was a blank that Vin had filled with nonlethal Aurora grappa, and Devlin tossed it onto the middle of the table.

Leif stared at the syringe, as if eyeing a snake that was about to strike. Were those beads of sweat on his forehead?

"What the fuck, Devlin? Keep your shit to yourself," Philippe said. "You want a taste of the angel, do it on your time. I'm recovering, you sonuvabitch." Philippe stormed from the table and headed into the farmhouse.

Leif shook his head and threw Devlin a disparaging glare. "Thank you for your generosity in our time of mourning, Jacques. Philippe and I will take our leave." He stood and also headed inside.

Erika and Jacques maintained complete control in the face of Devlin's maneuver. Zero reaction. Two damn good poker players.

"Devlin, I do not understand..." Jacques finally said.

"Have you ever heard of Jell-O syringes? You fill them with grappa and gelatin. I hear it's a hit on the party scene in San Remo," Devlin said. "I apologize if my presentation was ill-conceived."

Jacques laughed, then he rumbled louder. "That is an excellent contribution. Thank you, Devlin." Jacques's laughter died off, and he excused himself to grab a pot of coffee. He probably believed that Devlin had had his fair share of alcohol for the night.

"What was that?" Erika said when he'd gone.

Devlin explained to her his discovery on the day of Runa's death, and his subsequent findings. Yet, under the guise of investigation, Erika Aurora did not break. Or had there been a fleeting look of panic and a slight red tint to her cheeks when he'd first cast the syringe on the table?

Leif and Philippe certainly hadn't been the picture of composure. He had no idea that he'd inadvertently struck a chord with a recovering heroin addict. After days of combing through hundreds of files and running logistics with his crew, Devlin simply thought he'd try something outside the box in San Remo.

Devlin's phone signaled a call from Lauda, one of the other HELL Rangers investigating at Aurora. Devlin had left him in charge of the monotonous death threats and vandalism tactics that had become par for the course at Aurora. He also handled any violent picketers or gate crashers that demanded to share their gripe with the "water-guzzling profit-seekers" or "the Bloodsucker." Per Devlin's request, Lauda also continued following the activists' paper trails.

"I think I might have found something interesting," Lauda said. "One of the most prevalent water rights activists, the one that's always arrested for harassment and trespass, is tied to a shell corporation based in Lausanne, Switzerland. Isn't that the same town where Leif's partner lives? I got an address. You want me to check it out?"

One of Aurora's biggest protesters, the one with enough dough to hire choppers on a regular basis, had been traced to the same town in Switzerland where Philippe lived. Hardly a coincidence.

"I'll send Hamilton," Devlin said. "Scotti told me that he, Ricardo, and Helio are finishing up in Monza. They're all due to arrive at the vineyard in two days. Tell him to swing by Lausanne." The two men signed off.

Devlin's mind raced.

Two related deaths, staged as accidental, but with clear indications towards murder. Possible means by which to carry out both of them reside in a high-caliber methane formula.

Likeliest suspects include: Erika and Leif, both vying for total control over Aurora; Philippe, who perhaps wants to share in a bigger piece of the Aurora pie with Leif, and influence its future with a disparate corporate vision by getting Erika out of the way; Jacques Vitreuve, an underhanded competitor out for a bigger market share in the industry; and a significant water rights activist with deep pockets, who's persistently attempting to destroy the Aurora corporation, thereby releasing its aquifer into the public domain.

All solid suspects, with mounting evidence. So, why did he feel like he was hitting a wall?

Seconds later, an explosion thundered through Vitreuve's San Remo vineyard.

Chapter 18

The force of the blast could be felt by those strolling the beach four miles south of the San Remo vineyard, news reports relayed. When Devlin revived just enough to ensure that all four limbs were intact, he could understand why.

Devlin found Erika facedown in a crescent-shaped mound of poppies. Her arms were splayed wide, and their overnight duffels were piled on her head like pillows.

"Erika." Devlin rolled her over and patted her face, until she moaned and struggled to sit up. "Erika."

"I'm okay. What happened?" she said. "Leif?"

"They already left, sweetheart, a few minutes ago, remember?" Devlin said.

Erika shook her head to set it right. "Pissed. Stormed out. Taxi. Mm-hmm, I remember," she mumbled.

Devlin smelled smoke and peered further down the road. He pointed to a fire that smoldered just above the residential rooftops. "A gas main explosion? Or an incendiary device?"

"Or highly flammable methanol?" Erika said. Devlin turned to see Erika's unsettled glare. Were her brother and his partner responsible for the explosion? Especially in light of their admitted trespass into the grappa plant up the road with the methanol storage?

Jacques came running out of the house. A HydroVino security van sped around the corner to meet him. He grabbed the door handle and then looked over at the pair. "Are you two alright?" he shouted.

Erika appeared shaken but unhurt. Devlin patted his torso, relieved that he'd sneaked the bottle of grappa into his bag earlier. Lucky for him, the stone wall at the end of the drive had cushioned his impact. He suffered a goose egg and scraped elbows of only minor proportions. He signaled for Jacques to attend to the business of determining what the hell had rocked his vineyard, and the owner sped away.

Seconds later, another explosion, smaller than the first, rocked both of them to their knees.

"Devlin!" Erika shouted. "What the hell?"

Shots fired.

He threw her down, sheltered her body with his. "We need to take cover in the house," Devlin shouted. She nodded.

Amid the sporadic gunfire, Devlin yanked Erika to her feet and snatched up their bags (No way was he parting with possible evidence.) He grabbed her hand and tore off toward the farmhouse.

Inside, Devlin closed the curtains around the kitchen and turned off the lights. When he reached the window facing the rear garden courtyard, he said, "Over here."

Erika hunkered low behind Devlin, as if bracing for more overhead shots. Devlin pointed to a beaten-down decades-old Peugeot parked at the edge of an interior vineyard of Concord grapevines. The keys dangled from the ignition. "We run for it, yes?" he said.

Without waiting for a response, Devlin took her hand and ran. He threw the bags into the backseat, while Erika slammed herself into the passenger side. He turned the key, and the tiny car roared to life. Together they sped down a dirt path and out into the small vineyard. They sped past rows of vines until, about a mile from the farmhouse, they turned out into the deserted main road.

"Explosions," Erika shrieked. Her eyes stood wide open. Her face was beet red. Her hands trembled at her sides. "Shots fired, here and in my vineyard. Poison syringes. An injunction against the company that my daddy entrusted to his children." Erika rambled louder and louder. "Death threats and vandals. And, oh God, my poor sister, dead." She turned and glared at him. "Devlin, when does it all stop?"

As Devlin drove, he stole a glance at Erika. Real fear showed in her eyes. Her hair stuck out in every direction. Her dress was torn. She'd never looked more beautiful, or more vulnerable. He touched his hand to her cheek. This was truly the face of an angel. Or a really good con artist.

He pulled off the road, into the underbrush. He pulled a sweater from inside his duffel and wrapped it around her shoulders. Devlin pulled her close, and she clung to him.

After a minute, her breathing slowed. Her hands stopped shaking. The sweater slipped from her shoulder. She pulled back from him slightly, and she rolled her eyes. "I'm so sorry that I freaked out. It's been quite a week."

He smiled and tangled his fingers in her hair. She turned her mouth up toward his, and he felt her breath on his lips. She wet hers. And that tiny pink tongue eclipsed every last bit of his resolve. He pulled her close and kissed her. When he felt her kiss him back, he should have pushed her away, but he didn't.

After a few minutes, she pulled back gently. She lowered her gaze. He noticed the curve of her neck, and knew he wanted to taste more of her. He lowered his mouth to her bare shoulder, and then he noticed the neck of the grappa bottle sticking out of his leather duffel in the backseat.

What the hell was he doing? Taking advantage of a vulnerable client, in the middle of an investigation. Holy shit, he was an asshole.

He squeezed her shoulders gently, and he turned back to face the road. He gripped the wheel, and he pulled back onto the country road, headed for the train station. "Forgive me. That will never happen again. You're a client, and I know better."

Erika shook her head. "We're both a little edgy. And I'm sorry, too. It was unprofessional. And it won't happen again."

"Agreed," Devlin said. "Let's just put it out of our minds. Get back to business." She nodded.

Later, back at the Aurora Vineyard, Devlin lay in the bed of his private bungalow, alone. He spent all night trying to put Erika Aurora out of his mind.

Chapter 19

"Lucky!" Marcello, Scotti, and the crew cheered from the Lucchesi garage in the pit lane of the Monte Carlo Grand Prix circuit. Their fervor sustained Devlin in the last lap of the race.

Devlin was neck and neck with the tenacious Veronica Griffith heading into the tunnel. He stole a glance to his right. The driver, Giancarlo Venchi, edged closer and sneered at him. Giancarlo jerked hard right and smashed headlong into the wall, exploding into a fireball.

Devlin steered toward the pit lane to aid his dying colleague. But Ella appeared like a specter at the finish line and beckoned him with outstretched arms. He lurched the wheel back to the road and gunned his engine faster, charging straight for her.

But a voice in his helmet microphone coaxed him like a siren to see things her way. She cajoled him to forget about Ella, Marcello, Scotti and the crew. Enticed him with an invitation to change teams...

Devlin awoke drenched in sweat. He glanced at the clock, which read 4:00 a.m., and then pulled on his running shoes. Once outside, he dialed Scotti and told him about the dream.

Scotti laughed. "You're nuts. Just sleep with the lady. Then you can get some real, uninterrupted sleep and get on with your life."

"Which lady?"

"Does it matter?" Scotti said.

Devlin smirked and shook his head. Ordinarily, he would have dispensed similar advice. But Veronica Griffith was a colleague. And Erika Aurora was his client. Schtupping a client violated his personal code of ethics. Plus, what would Ella think? *Nothing, you ass, your wife is dead*, Devlin thought.

Acting like a proper father to his son was Devlin's main priority. Romancing beautiful women, especially one that might just be a murder suspect, was not part of the plan. Devlin sprinted faster.

"Funny you mentioned Veronica was in your dream, because she arrived in Monza yesterday," Scotti said.

Devlin envisioned Veronica in her racing jumpsuit. He wondered what she looked like out of the jumpsuit. "Why was she at MARI?"

"Veronica Griffith and Ryan Hunter-Reay both showed up with reps from the American IndyCar contingency," Scotti said. "They're in talks with Formula One to schedule some exhibition races on each other's circuits. Word on the street is the two organizations may merge in a couple years. This year they're planning special races to get fans pumped up over it."

"Similar to when the NFL plays in Europe before launching expansion teams," Devlin said.

"Exactly," Scotti said. "IndyCar's showcasing a huge new race in the States. Veronica, the Queen of IndyCar, wants you, the Formula One king, to race with her."

Veronica and he on a fun run? Ample opportunity for merging.

"If you still need me on the Aurora case, I'm coming up there tomorrow by lunchtime," Scotti said.

"I always need you." Devlin gave Scotti a rundown on recent events. "Your little brother's been a huge help. I'm really impressed with Vin's findings. Late last night I dropped off the Aurora grappa stash that I found on the San Remo property of HydroVino. He'll probably get it done this morning."

"Knowing Vincenzo, he stayed up all night working on it. He reminds me a lot of you, Devlin," Scotti said. "I don't know how you got the bottle out of HydroVino in one piece after the explosion. But let me know if it matches up to the grappa in the methanol syringe. In the meantime, hit the sack."

Devlin ended the call, chuckling at Scotti's last suggestion. He jogged to the lab and found Vin there working. The kid had already finished tests on the grappa bottle pilfered from the abandoned shed at HydroVino. "I have a lot to report. First off, your bottle…it's a match," Vin confirmed. "The poisonous formula in the syringe is equivalent to the grappa you gave me last night."

Devlin ran his hand over the scruff on his chin. He should've shaved; he was on a job. "So the Aurora anniversary grappa bottle that I snagged from a hidden stash on HydroVino property holds the same liquid found in the syringe with the super potent methanol?"

Vin nodded.

"Is HydroVino our perp? Or did someone plant it there to look like it?"

"Dunno," Vin said.

"And this is the same Aurora anniversary grappa that poisoned Giancarlo?" Devlin said.

Vin nodded again. "Absolutely the same. The super potent grappa in the syringe…I found minute traces of it on the cork that you found on the Monte Carlo track. The one that popped from Giancarlo's bottle."

Devlin scratched his stubbled chin. "Is it the same grappa with platinum residue left behind on the dog bowl?"

"Not sure," Vin said. "There were platinum particles on the bowl. The vet's report showed traces of methanol and platinum in the blood. Shows the dog might've just lapped up too much liqueur on the premises, as grappa intake would yield negative effects on any canine." Vin shrugged. "Crazy that anyone would put grappa in a dog's bowl. But there's just not enough evidence to prove someone tried to off the mutt with the poison formula."

Devlin nodded. “Mm-hmm, but the traces of poison found in the syringe, and the cork from Giancarlo’s grappa, and the HydroVino stash all definitively match. We’ve got a real pattern here of criminal intent.”

Devlin gestured to the boxes stacked beside the grappa vats downstairs from the lab. “Erika told me that the negative feedback over Giancarlo’s death forced her to halt all shipments of this limited-edition grappa to the public. And she removed distributed inventory from store shelves, at least until the media dies down. But after what you just told me, Aurora may need to issue a total recall, and ban this particular product’s distribution altogether. Have we tested those other batches wrapped up in the plant?”

“I randomly selected a few, but none tested positive. Want me to check them all?” Vin said.

“That’s a lotta booze,” Devlin said. “We’ll call in more guys to help.”

“Before you do, you should know something else.” Vin pulled a container from a locked cabinet. “This is the original syringe that you found beside the vat. Since I first tested it, I’ve run the same applications every single day, every six hours.”

Devlin nodded.

“Our ‘super methanol’ has increased in potency, exponentially, since my first run.”

Devlin’s eyebrows shot up. “That’s some dangerous shit.”

“Brace yourself. There’s more.” Vin tipped his head. “It’s commonly known that methanol in liquid form metabolizes over time when exposed to air or the elements.”

Devlin nodded.

Vin held up the syringe with a gloved hand. "I've extracted minute increments of super methanol from our base, and then I exposed it to air and water, every six hours, for the past few days." He locked eyes with Devlin. "Not only has it grown more potent, but neither air nor water dissipates the methanol in our samples of the foreshot."

Devlin's stomach dropped. He exhaled in a rush, as if tackled. The import of Vin's last statement rocked him to his core.

He continued to stare at Vin, opened his mouth to speak, shut it. Vin nodded.

Devlin finally spoke the words neither of them wanted to admit. "This lethal formula represents a biochemical weapon of catastrophic proportions.

"If it ever entered the water supply, millions would die."

***

Vin hopped a train back to Rome headquarters. Devlin prayed that the Grotto's lab would provide the tools Vin needed to develop an antidote against the formula.

By midday, Devlin shut down his workstation in Erika's otherwise vacant office. He put down the files he'd been combing through for the hundredth time. His resolution: determining who was responsible for producing the poison formula was a real ballbuster.

At that, he wondered where Erika had been all morning. She'd mentioned water summit preparatory meetings. But after enduring their night of explosions and shootings in San Remo, he figured she might be sleeping it off.

Devlin headed to the cantina for a bite. Inside, he encountered Leif and Philippe at a corner table. He grabbed an espresso and sat down with them.

"Philippe, I'm truly sorry about last night," Devlin said. "Tossing a syringe on the table was a callous stunt to get a reaction from Monsieur Vitreuve based on my investigation." *Not to mention a reaction from you two and Erika*, he thought. "I had no idea that you're recovering from substance abuse. Please accept my apology."

"You're just like all the rest who do not understand my suffering, Devlin. Apology not accepted." Philippe nodded to Leif and strode from the cantina.

Leif put his hand on Devlin's shoulder. "I appreciate your gesture. In time, Philippe will forgive you. He's just…sensitive."

Devlin nodded. "I'm sorry if what I did made you uncomfortable, too. I had no idea."

Leif waved him off. "No need. How could you know? Not many do. Really, I think only Erika and I, and Philippe's mom, know about his drug problem. Erika's never been a fan of Philippe, mainly due to his opposing beliefs in water conservation. Though they're similar to mine, he's considerably more vocal about them." Leif sipped his coffee. "But she's always been kind and supportive of his recovery, and he respects her for that."

Devlin nodded. "Are you responsible for his rehabilitation?"

Leif smiled. "Actually, no. Philippe did that all on his own. When we met at school, he was already a year into the program. And I'm happy to say, he's never looked back."

"I'm sure you had a lot to do with his continuing efforts," Devlin said.

"Yes, I'm his biggest fan. Other than his mom, of course. But they didn't always have such a great relationship. Their rocky early years actually pushed him into using."

Helicopter mom drove the mamma's boy to drug abuse. Shocker. "What happened? Why was it rough?" Devlin asked.

"Philippe never knew his father. He died when Philippe was first born, leaving Marisse with a company to run and a newborn to raise. She had a tough time of it, and so did he. She sent Philippe away to boarding school, and he found drugs," Leif said. "But then Philippe spent a summer working in a desalination plant in China, and he returned a staunch water conservationist. He put drugs and alcohol behind him, in the face of all the suffering he'd witnessed overseas that was far worse than his own. Now he's on an accelerated doctoral program at EPFL in water resource management. I'm very proud of him for accomplishing so much at a young age."

"Young?"

"He doesn't even turn twenty until January." Leif blushed. "Looks like I'm robbing the cradle."

Devlin smiled. "Does Philippe ever join up with those water activist groups, like the ones that hijack ski gondolas or spray-paint leather coats?" Devlin chuckled, so did Leif. "No, really, does he?" Devlin said.

Leif smiled. "Philippe is a good man. He has strong convictions, and he's sometimes unconventional in his expression. But he's a good man."

"Unconventional, as in blowing up Vitreuve's water-bottling plant?" Devlin had put it out there. He'd received news from Hamilton that morning that Vitreuve's water plant was shut down, effectively halting production and distribution. Ham also mentioned the abandoned building that had held the Aurora stash—destroyed. Including any evidence that might've tied Vitreuve to the case.

"Neither Philippe nor I had a hand in setting those explosives last night, if that's what you mean," Leif said.

"But you two admitted sneaking around the plant when you'd first arrived. That's how you stumbled upon the stash of Aurora grappa," Devlin said.

"That's why we snuck around, Devlin. I believe that Vitreuve has it in for Aurora, and I was right, based on my findings. We snooped, but we didn't sabotage." Leif swigged the last of his espresso and rose from his chair. He'd just signaled an end to their discussion on Philippe's activism and Aurora's competition.

Leif's phone rang. "Glad you called, Lupo. I've been wanting to iron out the remaining details for Palio. The wine and water for the pre- and postrace dinners. Yes, I've got details, if you've got numbers. Great." Leif turned to Devlin. "Will you excuse me?"

Devlin nodded. He stayed in the cantina, pondering the banners that bore the labels of Aurora's finest beverages, including their infamous anniversary grappa.

Whoever had set off the explosives last night in San Remo, was it the same person who'd shot at him and Erika? Was it a team effort? And how did all of this tie in with the poison formula that had been found at Aurora, HydroVino, and Monte Carlo?

Chapter 20

Ascari's older brother had been torn apart by a wild animal in the Coliseum while deactivating a bomb. The younger brother's resemblance, in looks and in gumption, rattled Devlin. The kid even chomped on cigars like his older sibling. It was a no-brainer when the younger Brooklynite had assumed the same moniker upon joining the HELL Ranger crew last year.

Ascari, Sneakers, and Vittles had joined Devlin a few days earlier at the vineyard, maintaining its security in tandem with the Aurora personnel. They'd successfully kept protesters at bay behind the property gates, especially near the tastings and sales rooms. They'd worked with local airport authorities to prevent further flybys, though Ascari had resorted to an irrigational water cannon a couple times, too. And they'd arrested a spattering of trespassers who'd breached the outer vineyard boundaries.

Two more of Devlin's crew, Lauda and Hunt, who never got along, were remanded to opposite ends of the complex to help guard the manufacturing plants. Over the past few days, the HELL Rangers vetted Aurora Vineyard's entire staff, from security personnel, to the chefs, to the staff nurse, to the bottlers, to the couple dozen field-workers.

Ascari, Vittles, Sneakers, and Devlin now stood peering into the deep valley beside the Aurora mountain, which Devlin had traversed in the aerial tram a week earlier. Devlin updated them on all of it.

Ascari propped his foot on the metal safety barrier and spat tobacco off the cliff. "You never did find the sniper, then? Bet it was one of the shitheads we dragged down to the station this week."

"I don't know. Seemed more of a personal vendetta situation than an angry activist to me," Devlin said.

"They sure have a lot of enemies here," Sneakers said.

Devlin nodded and smiled at the tall Kenyan, glad that he'd teamed up with them. Once the fastest soldier on two feet that Devlin had ever known, Sneakers had temporarily been dubbed "Sneaker" when his foot had been blown off in a bombing. Relegated to desk work during his many months of rehabilitation, he was now back and better than ever thanks to a prosthetic à la Usain Bolt. Recently, after a night of foot races and beer pong, he'd been renamed Sneakers.

"Great security team and staff, though, who all have nice things to say about the owners. Must get paid well," Sneakers said.

Devlin smirked.

"Called Ham like you asked," Ascari said. "He's headed to Switzerland to check out the address of the activist corporation we traced there."

Devlin nodded.

"Lupo called. He's batshit crazy right now, organizing the Palio activities. Thinks he's in over his head. Prost and Chiara are helping him out. Says he'll come help us if you need him," Sneakers said.

"Hell no, there's no way I'd take him from his big gig. Means a lot to him," Devlin said.

Sneakers smiled. "Think we'll make it back in time for the horse race?"

"About a week away? We'll do our best, never any guarantees," Devlin said. "Marcello's back from camp a few days before that. Would be nice to get him there. See his godfather in action."

Marcello's camp discouraged parental contact, to keep the kids more focused, but Devlin longed for Marcello's bear hug and boisterous laughter. Devlin wondered if this twisted mission would be over in time for the festivities, or whether he'd be forced to call in more men and delay his return.

Devlin gazed out at the snowcapped higher elevations of the Dolomites. He spotted the highest peak, Marmolado, only a few football fields away. It loomed in stark contrast with the mild, vegetative mountain that stretched beneath his feet. He squinted. Were those a couple of snowboarders zigzagging their way down the steep and rocky piste? Crazy. But then, who was he to talk? He maneuvered a wheeled machine around tight corners at top speed for fun.

Devlin tossed a rock over the side of the Aurora mountain and listened to it ping-pong downward against the shale. He considered his and Vin's conversation about the potentially tainted anniversary grappa, and the need to test and possibly destroy the remaining batches. A moment later, Erika sauntered up between him and Sneakers, and he mentioned the conversation to her.

At Devlin's news of the ramifications threatened by Aurora's tainted grappa, Erika stared at him, absorbing it all. "How can we be sure that all of the batches have been tainted? Testing each and every bottle, or otherwise destroying the entire lot of the sequestered batches in the warehouse, would require significant time and money."

She folded her arms, and a slight breeze blew her hair back from her face. "But the health risk posed by one poison bottle—whether to a solitary person, or as part of a widespread outbreak should the contents leach into a water source—that would be a disaster."

Ascari mentioned the AC Milan game to Sneakers and Vittles, and the three HELL Rangers slinked a few steps out of earshot. Devlin didn't blame them. He wanted no part of this conversation either.

The platinum grappa was evidence. Erika had been right to pull it off the shelves and sequester the remainder inside a locked warehouse. But contemplating the logistics of testing thousands of bottles gave Devlin a headache. Likely best to destroy the lot of them after the investigation. No simple matter, and Devlin did not envy her responsibility. But if Erika Aurora had indeed been the one to taint one or more of these bottles, then her next steps might be telling.

Unfortunately, the matter was dropped when Erika's cocker spaniel, Tomba, came bounding over to them with four muddy paws and a snout full of bristles.

"Oh, my poor baby! Look at you!" Erika Aurora bent down and scooped up the whining, shaking cocker spaniel into her arms and held him close against her silk dress. "Oh, my sweet boy, let me get those bad briers out of your nose." She pulled the floral silk Hermes scarf from around her shoulders and swaddled the anxious canine in her arms.

"Gentlemen, please excuse me while I help Tomba," she said. The HELL Rangers had been watching the pair of snowboarders jet down the ridge. "Please help yourselves to lunch. Chef's incorporating broccoli rabi into every course," she shouted back over her shoulder.

"I love broccoli rabi," Vittles said. Ascari removed the cigar from his lips, flicked it over the cliff, and smiled. He, Vittles, and Sneakers took off at a run for the cantina. Sneakers got there first.

"I'll help you with Tomba," Devlin said as he followed behind Erika. She scurried to a laundry room on the main floor of the villa. Once inside, they settled the dog into an oversized utility tub. As he shampooed the wily pooch, Erika donned eyeglasses and went to work removing briers and nettles from his nose with tweezers.

"You recovered well after our scare at HydroVino last night," Devlin said.

She gave him a smile that he felt everywhere. "I'm okay," she said. "Been in meetings with water summit organizers in Verona all morning. Met with the lawyers handling the injunction, and the ones handling matters at the summit. And I saw Ana. She never fails to brighten my day." Erika's face radiated a warmth that Devlin had trouble attributing to a murder suspect.

"Chatted with Leif earlier about the Palio event and some other things. Surprised he didn't join you for the meetings?" Devlin asked.

"Haven't seen Leif all day. Shocked he blew off presummit meetings, considering his leanings on water conservation. Probably just gearing up for the main event. On top of that, I did manage to run into Vitreuve, that smarmy bastard." A look of murderous intent swept across her features. She quickly doused it with another compassionate look at her dog.

Dr. Jekyll, and Ms. Hyde.

"Vitreuve had the nerve to accuse me of blowing up his plant!" Erika looked up at Devlin over the top of her tortoise-shell frames. "Okay, so then what? Does he think I shot at myself while I was running for my life from his property? He's such an ass."

Erika grabbed the faucet nozzle and rinsed suds from behind Tomba's ears before seeking more prickers with her tweezers. "Vitreuve and I and a few other reps rotated between buildings at Verona's convention center this morning. One building is dedicated to desalination discussions. Another's for water treatment technologies for oil and gas companies. Another's for business innovation, and transition to circular economy. Plus, water conservation strategies."

She sighed and began rinsing the dog's torso. "The prelim meetings are boring. But the main event is usually pretty entertaining. We drink wine. They hand out awards. Al Gore goes on about his carbon footprint. The president of Mexico does the salsa; he's a helluva dancer. But this year, with the injunction hanging over my company like a dark cloud, I'm…a little…nervous."

The dog suddenly shook his body, dousing them both.

Devlin glanced at Erika, who peeked at him over her glasses. She grinned at him through the mud and soap suds, and he laughed out loud. She burst out laughing too, and then she aimed the faucet sprayer at his face and let loose like a fireman.

His mouth dropped open in surprise. She dropped the sprayer and put her mouth on his and caressed his tongue with hers.

A few seconds later, the dog saw his opportunity and jumped out of the tub, ending their kiss. Devlin slammed the door with his foot before Tomba could escape the room. Erika scooped the cocker spaniel into a towel.

"Thanks for the help. I had fun." Erika flicked her eyebrows at him and left the room. Toweling the dog, she strode down the hall of the villa and into her room. The door slammed shut behind her.

Devlin walked to his bedroom and took another cold shower.

***

A half hour later, Devlin went back outside to the courtyard. He jogged past the dog, skirted a parked tour bus, and sauntered into the cantina. He joined Ascari, Vittles, and Sneakers, who were sitting in the back and working on their dessert: broccoli rabi and orange gelato paired with Moscato.

Devlin looked to the front of the cantina, where a raucous group of ten men and women of various ages laughed and sipped wine at a long wooden table. A group leader sat at the end, writing in a journal propped atop a backpack. "Tourists?"

"Erika took in a tasting tour. Her head of security had it scheduled, and bags were checked before they came in," Vittles said.

Devlin nodded. "Part of running a winery is having people taste your wine, I guess."

Ascari handed him a prosciutto panino and stood. "You missed a great lunch, but Erika brought you over a snack. Thought you might be hungry." Understatement of the year. Devlin tore into the sandwich.

"We gotta fly," Ascari continued. "Got a call from security just before you walked in. Couple of boarders just breached the outer perimeter." Probably the two who'd shredded down Marmolado earlier. Just passing through, or a threat? "Sit, eat. We got this." Devlin knew they would.

When Ascari, Vittles, and Sneakers exited the cantina, Devlin glanced over at Erika from his seat. She stood at the long bar in front of the tasting table, holding up one bottle after another. She expertly described tasting notes for each red and white to the attentive bunch. She suggested that each person consume a piece of cheese, bread, or carved meat. Then she urged them to sip the wine slowly, swish it around their palates, and then spit the liquid into a spittoon.

None did. They swallowed. Which is why the group had grown exceedingly louder, as more wine and time wore on. Erika soon led them outside, and Devlin was happy to see them all go. He was relieved that a tour bus awaited them, and none of them would be driving. He could still hear cackling laughter even after the heavy wooden door slammed shut.

Which is why he didn't immediately notice a woman shouting outside in the courtyard, who now seemed to be crying out in pain. He bolted to the door and opened it. A rotund woman with a Leaning Tower of Pisa tee shirt lay on the ground, struggling to right herself. Heart attack, or too much to drink?

He rushed outside to assist her. But he noticed that most of the upper-middle-aged tourists were cowering on the gravel drive beside the bus.

He looked to Erika, who stood beside the bus. Erika's head bent close to a tall, beefy woman with short red hair who looked like the leader of the group, the one previously jotting notes at the tasting table.

The tall redhead suddenly twisted Erika's arm behind her back in one quick move. Erika instinctively gasped in surprise, but immediately stomped her high heel into the woman's foot and struggled to break free.

Red growled, and she whipped a metal object from the rucksack on her back. Not a gun, but shinier. Not a chisel, but shorter. Not a knife, but curvier.

A corkscrew, with a sharp metal end.

Devlin reached for his piece, and a litany of foul language ran through his head. No gun. He'd left it in his room after his shower.

He dove forward to tackle the beast of a woman but stopped short. Because in one swift motion, Red had yanked harder on Erika's arm, pinned it even tighter behind her back, and stuck the corkscrew to Erika's neck, just enough to jab her. Erika cried out.

Red bellowed a baritone warning: "Stay back, or this bitch gets it!"

Devlin halted and put up both hands, not wishing to endanger Erika further.

Red backed away from the bus, dragging Erika with her. The corkscrew's end must have penetrated Erika's skin, because a thin trickle of blood ran down her neck. Devlin knew that one jarring swipe of the pointed bottle opener into the jugular vein was all it would take. Erika's life would cut short to mere minutes before she bled out.

Devlin evaluated his options. His HELL Rangers were on the other side of the vineyard dealing with the rogue snowboarders, out of reach. The bus passengers and the elderly driver were crying or rocking back and forth beneath the bus, useless. No gun on his person. Red held all the cards. Time to talk. He needed to stall the attacker until he could maneuver close enough to safely pull Erika from her clutches. Then he'd take down the bitch redhead with his bare hands.

"Tell me what you want," Devlin said to Red, splaying his arms wide to prove he carried no weapon. He crouched down slowly and eased the woman in the Pisa shirt to sitting. Her face was badly abraded, and grimy tears streamed down her face, but she was otherwise unharmed. He said, "Let's just talk."

Like a stampeding boar, Erika's cocker spaniel leaped through the air from behind the bus, teeth bared and growling like a leaf blower. The dog charged Erika's attacker. Tomba sunk his incisors into Red's face, and the corkscrew dropped to the ground. Devlin kicked it behind a tire.

Erika twisted and writhed to break free. She lurched in the direction of the bus. Her melon slammed into the steel bus with a clunk, and she cried out. Devlin lunged forward and broke the captor's hold on Erika's wrist. Out cold, Erika slumped into his arms. He lowered her to the ground.

On his knees, Devlin seized Red by the ankle. With one arm, he yanked hard and knocked her forward. The redhead face-planted into the gravel parking lot. Erika's dog gnawed at the nest of red hair just above her rucksack.

Still on his knees, Devlin slid his other hand from behind Erika's head. It came away bloody. He clutched a discarded jacket and tucked it behind her head.

The redhead pushed up from the ground and jerked sideways, toppling the dog into her beefy hands. She hurled Tomba toward the bus like a football.

Devlin thrust out both arms and snatched the small dog from midair, before it could smash into the vehicle. As he did, Red made a run for it, straight for the cliff.

Erika mumbled. Tried to sit up. But Devlin sprinted away.

He headed for Red, only a few feet ahead of him, but the bitch was fast. Apparently also a runner.

He lunged forward, but the straps of her backpack slid through his fingers, too slick with Erika's blood.

The edge of the mountain loomed ahead of them. Devlin had forty yards to catch the attacker, or barrel the bitch over the cliff. "Who the hell are you?" he shouted as he ran. "What the hell do you want?"

"The waters shall forever run impure. Made foul with the blood on your hands!" Red said.

Who says shit like that? And what the hell does it mean? Devlin thought.

Twenty yards until the precipice. He was closing in on the demon sprinter with the ridiculously muscular calves, but he knew he'd better do it quick.

He spied Sneakers, in his peripheral vision, cutting through the dusty vineyard. Like Roadrunner, the Kenyan's arms and legs pumped, making time like no one else could. He toted a hunting blade in his right fist.

Sneakers reached for her with his left hand. He swiped and grabbed her pack, and he stopped her in her tracks.

He heard Erika call his name, catching up just behind him.

Devlin pushed harder. He couldn't wait to get some answers. "Waters run impure…Blood on your hands." What was that about? Protest? Murder?

Canine rescue again bounded out of nowhere, and Tomba tore straight for the redhead. The woman took advantage of the diversion and broke free of Sneakers' hold. As she did, the knife that jutted from Sneakers' other fist snagged the outer pocket of her rucksack and clattered to the ground.

Again, she ran. So did Devlin. So did Sneakers. Right for the cliff.

Sneakers sprinted past Devlin and grabbed for the woman. But Tomba caught up with her first. The dog was inches away from chomping her ankle, when Sneakers tripped over the dog and went flying. He pinwheeled through the air, but Sneakers regained his balance and landed on his feet.

By the time Sneakers landed, and Devlin avoided running into him, Red had bent down and scooped up the cocker spaniel.

"No!" Erika shouted. "Put down my dog!"

Red smiled. And ran. Clutched in the crook of Red's left arm, Tomba snarled and barked at her. With her right hand, Red reached out for the metal barrier of the cliff. She vaulted the fence and landed on the rocky precipice on the other side.

"Oh my God, no," Erika said, fear cracking her voice.

"Don't do it!" Devlin shouted. "Don't jump. We can talk. Tell me who—"

Red jumped from the cliff, a smile planted firmly on her face. One hand muzzled the dog from biting. Red's other fist tugged at the strap of the backpack. But after few more yanks on the strap, the redhead's smile disappeared. Replaced by a look of confusion, and then terror. The tear on the pack inflicted by Sneakers' knife had damaged more than mere aesthetics. It had apparently rendered useless her parachute.

Tomba's barking echoed across the mountains, as Red plummeted down into the valley below. The woman shouted a few words on her way down, and then no more.

The dog's barks ceased. Erika shrieked Tomba's name once and then crumpled to her knees. Silence ensued. Which left the redheaded woman's final words echoing in Devlin's ears: "The Bloodsucker made me do it."

***

Beside the cliff, Erika leaned heavily against Devlin. As she clung to him for support, he spotted Rasmus, the head of security. Rasmus and six other fully armed security personnel, including Sneakers and Ascari, surrounded the tour bus.

Devlin escorted Erika toward the group. By the time she met them at the bus, she'd regained her composure. "Gentlemen, holster your weapons. We have guests."

"Ma'am, one of them attacked you," Rasmus said.

Erika discreetly tugged the cowl of her cashmere sweater over the bloodstains on her neck. "The situation is under control," she told Rasmus. "Please take our clients into the cantina. They require the utmost accommodation." Erika rested her hand on the shoulder of the woman in the Pisa shirt and smiled at the group. "Grappas all around."

Rasmus issued orders to two of his men to contact the local authorities about the attacker who'd plummeted into the valley. Then he ushered the dozen or so travelers, buzzing about the ordeal, into the cantina.

Devlin touched Erika's shoulder. "We need to get you medical attention."

"I have an in-house nurse that I've already texted," Erika said. "She'll give everyone here a once-over, and we'll be back on our feet before we know it." She gave Devlin a quick hug and walked through the cantina door with the others.

A professional reserve had clearly steeled Erika's nerves. Her forced smile ensured that it showed outwardly. But he knew deep down that, after being physically attacked and having lost her beloved dog, Erika Aurora had to feel pretty distraught.

Alone, Devlin hung back to examine the crime scene. He scoured beneath the tour bus on his hands and knees. Perhaps Red had left behind her notebook with some viable leads. Maybe the corkscrew was rampant with the attacker's fingerprints, which might lead him to her true identity. He needed to ascertain what the hell had just happened.

Clearly, the redhead had planned to escape after the attack, not plunge to her death. Had Red been another zealous activist who'd simply gone too far? Or had she been the devoted lackey of a bigger outfit? *The Bloodsucker made me do it.* Perhaps the activist that his crew was checking out in Lausanne had hired her? Or maybe Jacques Vitreuve of HydroVino, or some other competitor, was pulling the strings.

Devlin extracted the discarded wine opener from behind the tire with his sleeve. After a painstaking check under, on, and around the bus, he made his way to the jump zone to check for more evidence.

Did the attacker wish to place the blame on Erika for an incident that might inspire fear or scandal, or had it been a foiled plan for something worse? Something like a coup, designed by a CEO like Leif Aurora. Was Leif advancing his opposing agenda as the sole vision of his company in bold fashion against his only living contender, his older sister?

The Bloodsucker made me do it.

After nearly an hour, Devlin trudged back to the cantina. One question stood out among the rest. Had Erika Aurora, aka the Bloodsucker, plotted this entire skirmish to dissuade him from considering her a suspect in the case?

***

The tour group exited the cantina, boarded the bus, and drove off, amid hugs and waves and promises to return. Another notch marked in the belt of Erika Aurora as a renowned show woman and masterful businessperson.

Devlin gave Rasmus the corkscrew to run forensics, and the Aurora security team retreated back to their on-site headquarters. Ascari, Sneakers, and Vittles left to apprise Lauda and Hunt of the day's events, with plans to follow up on the tour bus company.

This left Devlin standing alone in the middle of the empty courtyard, with the Bloodsucker.

In the setting sun, Erika slowly walked to him from the cantina. She'd since changed out of her bloodstained suit. Now she wore blue jeans and a tight black Aurora Vineyard tee shirt. Her ponytail revealed a fresh square bandage on her neck. She was sexier than he'd ever seen her. Yet the tears that glistened in her bloodshot eyes signaled despair. When she reached him, she bent her head to his shoulder and let out a quiet sob.

Shocked by her vulnerability, he embraced her.

"I'm not sure how much more of this I can take." Erika sniffled. She wrapped her arms around his neck and clung to him as if he were a life preserver. "I can't handle any more explosions, gunshots, BASE jumpers…and, for God's sake, I can't handle any more death." She cried freely now. Her shoulders gently shook up and down, her head still pressed against his chest.

"My sister, Runa, is dead." Erika locked eyes with him. "I've been attacked. My company is being terrorized. And now my dog, the only one in my life who loved me unconditionally…is gone."

She lowered her gaze, wiped her tears, and swallowed hard. "I can't be strong right now." Erika peered up at his face again. Her eyes, once filled with anguish, now appeared…hungry, reckless, primal. "I need someone to be strong for me."

She dropped her embrace from around his neck, down to his arms. Her fingertips squeezed his biceps, dug into them for a moment, continued to descend.

She gave him a kiss; he devoured it. She dropped her hands down to his backside, gripped it hard. They kissed again. Without another word, they walked to the villa and slipped inside her bedroom door.

***

As the sun finally settled into its lowest point, Devlin and Erika lay nuzzling.

"I'd fantasized a bunch of times, but I never thought you'd live up to my expectations, Lucky," Erika said.

"What do you think now?" Devlin asked.

"Not sure."

"Not sure?"

"Have to try again." She kissed him.

"Again?" He kissed her lips, salty from his skin.

"Again."

Chapter 21

And again.

The sun came up, and Scotti rang Devlin for their morning briefing. For the first time in a long time, Devlin declined the incoming call.

He and Erika pulled each other close.

And tried it again.

***

Over an hour later, Devlin awoke, alone in Erika Aurora's king-sized four-poster bed. He replayed some of last night's finer points in his mind. There were a lot of them.

He pushed the sheet back and swung his legs to the floor. He glanced at his thighs, his feet, his arms, his chest, and oh God, what clsc? He counted twenty-four hickeys, not including those likely on his backside. Was that why people really called Erika Aurora "the Bloodsucker?"

He needed his jeans. He needed coffee. And he needed to run.

A knock at the door and a "*Caffè, signore*" pushed Devlin to scramble his jeans on faster. He pulled on his shirt to cover his marked torso. He opened the door to a uniformed server who rolled in a tray of espresso and biscotti and left.

Devlin downed the espresso, and the caffeine jolted him fully awake. What the hell was he doing?

He'd slept with Erika Aurora, a suspect in his investigation. Suspected of corporate espionage, murder, and potentially genocide. A woman perhaps cunning enough to hire him in order to deflect her culpability onto others.

He'd shagged Erika Aurora, a possible victim of those heinous crimes. One whose family member had died, and who had hired him to prove that her company was being sabotaged and that she was being personally threatened.

What kind of a professional does the deed with a potentially deranged suspect, or worse, a vulnerable victim, in a murder investigation?

Devlin shook his head in disgust. He threw on his running shoes and fled the room to embark on a monumental walk of shame.

He headed right for the woods to clear his head. He startled a flock of birds, who took flight into the sky, and he thought of Ella. He'd defiled her memory. She was barely in her grave for more than a year, and he'd just had sex with a client. He could feel his face burning with disgrace.

How the hell would he ever confront Erika Aurora again? If Erika was a victim in this mess, would she feel demeaned that he'd breached her trust? On the other hand, what if she was the perp? Would she feel driven or enabled to commit more crimes, knowing that she'd easily manipulated him into sleeping with her?

He looked down at the missed call from Scotti on his phone. He exhaled deeply and ran faster. He needed to hash this out with the one man who would talk sense. Scotti would help him figure out a plan.

But before Devlin dialed, he spotted Ana Malia crossing the drive from her rental car in the direction of Erika Aurora's office, crunching through the gravel in four-inch heels. She spied him. Sheepishly, he waved. She waited for him to emerge from the woods.

When he did, she looked him up and down, and she beamed. "You got laid! It's about damn time."

His face burned again in humiliation.

Ana waved off his exasperated glare. "Let's go find Erika and Leif. I've got a big hit of info."

Chapter 22

"Good news!" Ana propped her briefcase atop Erika's desk.

Erika and Leif both leaned against the edge of the desk with their arms crossed and eyes wide open in anticipation.

Devlin stood by the door, curious about what would've pulled Ana Malia away from live coverage of a summit meeting just three days ahead of its commencement. He also couldn't help but eye Erika Aurora's tanned legs. But the size of her small feet, wedged into pointed stilettos, grounded him. He glanced at Leif's Bruno Magli leather loafers and noted the extraordinarily small shoe size of the Aurora family. The sniper who'd shot at the gondola upon his arrival boasted a below-average footprint, too. Add that to Erika's late response in shutting down the gondola. The theory that Erika might have been the one to shoot at them still proved a credible one.

Ana pulled a file from her briefcase and slapped it down on the table. "You know that gorgeous blond counsel from that bigwig firm you hired to handle your injunction fight? He's on his way over here with really good news." She reached for the tiny cup of espresso on the desk with the lipstick smudge, swigged it back, and gulped. "But I got here before he did," she said with an impish smile.

Leif threw up his hands. "What's the news?"

"The injunction against Aurora has been lifted," Ana said.

Erika beamed. "Does that mean full rights and ownership of my dad's aquifer?"

"Whoa, girl. One step at a time…that's still an ongoing battle. Whether your aquifer is private property, with all attendant rights and ownership, is still up in the air. The court hasn't passed judgment on whether it's private or public," Ana said. "But your lawyer has successfully argued that 'Aurora Vineyard suffers insurmountable damages from its ban on production and distribution' while they hash it all out, so the courts have lifted the injunction."

Leif stood. "Which means that—"

Ana cut him off. "Aurora is free and clear to produce and ship any and all product lines. Anywhere, anytime."

Erika and Leif turned and locked eyes, and spoke in unison. "Just in time for the water summit."

***

The next few hours played out like the opening night of a theater production. All hands were on deck in the conference room. Department heads, production and shipping managers, and security personnel all coordinated their efforts to move forward with their original idea of sponsoring the beverage needs of the Worldwide Water Summit.

Upon the imposition of the injunction, summit organizers had scrambled to secure another beverage supplier. They did, yet no exclusivity was granted. When the injunction lifted, Aurora promised to provide their water, wine, and grappa product lines to the thousands of attendees, entirely free of charge. Free meant exclusivity, and organizers dropped the competitor. Though theirs was a risky and expensive marketing proposition, Erika and Leif hoped it would ensure that the Aurora name was on the minds of all the worldwide leaders in water value.

When the enormous *porchetta* salads and sandwiches were delivered midday, Erika realized she was famished. Her kickass crew continued to work through lunch, but she took a few minutes on the balcony to clear her head.

She knew that Aurora's renewed sponsorship of the summit was a major coup. Her father would have been so proud. From the veranda, she gazed reverently at the aquifer marker in the center of the courtyard, the discovery of which had led to the creation of their growing empire. She couldn't believe it was nearly twenty years ago to the day.

Good labor was always important. At twelve, Erika's real father had died penniless. Back then, she and her pregnant mother had traveled across northern Europe into Italy with baby Leif in tow, never stopping long enough to put down roots. When a shabby orange "AURORA" signpost beckoned them into a vineyard outside Verona, her mother had asked Augustus Aurora for work. He'd asked her to marry him. This had been good for all of them, and Erika had finally felt stable.

Not all labor was good. Erika's mother had died giving birth to Runa. Nearly a year later, a migrant worker with the long raven hair, crooked teeth, and bouncy chest had stumbled onto their fledgling estate in the dark of night. She would toil in their vineyard by day and visit Augustus in his alchemy room in the evening. This was bad for all of them, and a then fourteen-year-old Erika felt adrift again.

On the day of the aquifer discovery, the sun had shined high over the Dolomite Mountains. Erika, with thirteen-month-old Runa strapped to her back, quit tending the vines for their midday *pranzo* meal. Together with a handful of Spanish, French, and Polish time-tested laborers, they tramped back from the vineyard's western acres and into the yard of the humble villa. A half dozen other less-experienced migrants had already returned. She halted midstep, shocked by their behavior.

They splashed dust and dirt from their clothes and sloshed water over their faces, arms, and boots. Not with the runoff rain water set aside for washing, or for feeding the chickens and pigs. But with the barrels of fresh drinking water placed in the shade behind the house. This clean water was meant solely for human consumption, as it was very hard to come by during the drought.

"Crisis" was the word she'd heard her adoptive father use many times a day, especially during summer and fall. Augustus and his neighbors, vendors, and workers all sweated bullets over things called "efficient irrigation," and "major shortage," and "diminished yields." She knew that these words signaled doom for her family. Wasting precious drinking water just might drive her soft-spoken father over the edge.

Working in the winery's bottling room with the raven-haired farmhand for most of the morning, Augustus must have witnessed the workers' shenanigans from the dusty cellar window. He burst through the villa door and out onto the flagstone terrace with a beet-red face, waving around grape-red hands and shouting words she was never allowed to use. Augustus chased the workers from his property, all the while snapping his suspenders over a wine-splotched undershirt and kicking crumbled soil with poorly cobbled shoes.

Though his anger was directed toward the dripping-wet laborers, his outcry also startled and provoked his innocent, established work hands. They too sputtered away on their broken-down motor scooters and three-wheeled pickup trucks. All except the ratty-haired woman with the big chest. She stood alone in the dirt road with her back to them.

When the buzzing of the last motor scooter had faded into the distance, Augustus's shoulders slumped, and he ran his purple-stained fingers through his hair. Erika stood with her mouth agape at her father's unusual outburst. Runa, still strapped to her back, patted her hair for comfort. Her father turned and hugged them both, apologizing to his daughters through tears.

The lone migrant worker turned and grimaced at them with her jagged teeth. Her eyes blazed through her veil of bedraggled black tresses. She put her hands on her curvy hips and demanded, "Now what? Must I work this field all by myself? What will you do now, you filthy bastard!"

Silence settled in, and Erika watched her father's face turn pale with surprise.

"Froggie!" Giggles overtook the silence, from her brother, Leif. He ran from the vineyard and out into the quiet dirt road, hands outstretched and shouting, "Froggie! Froggie!" Leif slammed into the woman's legs, toppled, and wrapped his arms about her for balance, while still clutching a slimy amphibian. He threw back his smiling face and shouted, "Froggie!"

"Off me, you little piece of shit!" The woman thrust the child from her legs, hauled back, and slapped him so hard that Leif fell to the cracked ground.

"Father!" Erika shouted. But Augustus Aurora simply stared at the laborer. He blinked wildly, seemingly unable to process the abuse of his child.

Erika scooped her brother from the ground and into her arms, cradling him. She glared at the bullish woman and summoned every curse word she'd ever learned. But she never had the chance to hurl her venom, because the earth began to shake.

The ground around them rumbled with a sound like thunder. Erika stumbled and fell, still carrying her brother and sister. "Father!" she shouted again.

The land continued to convulse. Augustus fell to one knee, arms flailing for balance. The raven-haired farmhand fell onto

Augustus. Baby Runa wailed. Leif's whimpered cries of "Froggie! Froggie!" rang of fear.

A crack formed in the road, and a jagged line ran from it, all the way up the drive toward the vineyard. The ground gave a final, roaring shudder, and then it ended. The deafening rumble faded to nothing. The earth had ceased moving beneath her splayed-out hands and bruised knees.

Augustus gasped. A red handprint had swelled across the right side of Leif's tear-stained face.

Erika's eyes narrowed at the troll who'd marked him. Spittle flew from her hips as she spoke her words through gritted teeth. "Make her leave, Papa."

Augustus hefted the vile woman to her feet. He whispered words to the migrant worker that Erika didn't hear and then pushed her to the road. He turned his back on her, and walked his children home. The defeated woman strode off, flagged down a passing car, and sped away. Clearly good labor was best cultivated among family.

Together the Aurora family ambled toward the vineyard, following the jagged crack etched into the earth. Augustus steered them to the barrel of freshwater. He cupped handfuls and washed away their dirt and fear. They walked to a row of grapevines at the edge of the vineyard, into which the crevice had run. Together they shoveled handfuls of purple grapes into their mouths.

Church bells tolled in the nearby town. High noon.

Another rumble, lesser than the first, shook the earth again. The crack beneath their feet widened. A faint gurgling sound emanated from the dusty soil. It strengthened in intensity, until the earth again stood still and the bubbling, babbling sound dissipated.

Erika looked down. Her once dusty feet were drenched through her sandals. They were washed clean by a large puddle that ran the length of the crevasse.

Her father dropped to examine the ground. "It can't be!" he said. Flat on his stomach, he reached his long arm down into the fractured, muddy soil, then pulled his arm from the depths and licked fresh springwater from his fingers. "Water!" he said. Eyes bright, he thrust a pail into the ground. A moment later, he hefted it from the fissure and slurped the clear liquid inside.

He'd jumped to his feet, clasped his children's hands and danced with them, splashing in the puddles underneath the scorching midday sun. In the courtyard, amid rows of tethered vines, Erika had finally felt rooted to something vital, and in her heart, she'd claimed Aurora Vineyard as her own.

Now, overlooking the same courtyard in which they'd danced, Erika spotted the aquifer's marker, emblazoned with the date of the earthquake. She knew her father would have been proud of all they'd achieved since that day.

"Erika, time for another one of Ana Malia's interviews," Leif told her. He stepped beside her and looked down into the courtyard, then smiled back at her. She squeezed his hand, and together they walked to the table where Ana Malia sat waiting for them.

With cameras rolling, Erika told Ana, "The true formula for success is timing and ingenuity. It's something my family taught me." She then shifted her penetrating gaze to the camera and proclaimed, "Aurora is back, with a vengeance."

Chapter 23

Devlin had finished his comprehensive review of Erika's files yesterday morning. With Erika and Leif scurrying about her office knee-deep in summit details today, Devlin moved his workstation to Runa's empty office for privacy. And to scour the place.

Devlin spent a few hours inspecting Runa's desktop, but it turned up nothing. Devlin stretched and peered out the window, considering another espresso. When he spotted Ana outside in the courtyard shaking hands with Ascari, he decided to join them.

"Dev, I was just coming to see you." Ascari glanced skittishly at the reporter.

Devlin nodded. "I see you two just met, but Ana's okay. She respects the HELL Rangers' work, so you can speak freely. In fact, she was a huge help with the Ishmael situation."

Ascari darted his eyes to Devlin. At the mention of the man who'd killed his older brother, Devlin saw a mix of pain and anger in the young man's face. Devlin nodded his reassurance.

Ascari glanced at Ana and his gaze softened. "Any friend of my brother is a friend of mine."

The twenty-something Brooklynite pulled the unlit cigar he'd been chewing from his mouth. "We're regularly reviewing surveillance all over the vineyard, like you asked, Devlin. Nothing new on that front," Ascari said. "We checked into the tour bus company of the cliff jumper. Reputable firm with no prior issues. Scheduling error allowed the perp to breach their security and pose as tour director. Police haven't recovered her body yet. But Rasmus ran a check on the corkscrew fingerprints. Identified her as a Swiss national with no prior record. Interpol uncovered no terrorist ties. She's previously associated with the Dig Deep and the Flow On water conservation groups. They claim no responsibility for the incident, say she acted on her own."

"They're pretty straight-up organizations," Ana said. "Probably kicked her out."

Devlin thought for a minute. "So the woman was a radical activist with violent tendencies. Good work. What else you got?"

"Rasmus wanted to let you know that on the night of Runa Aurora's death, the HVAC system was manually shut down. No prints, though."

"No air-conditioning. No ventilation." Devlin nodded. "Likely increased the rate that the carbon dioxide built up in the air. Especially at the top of the fermenting vat, where Runa's body was found. Pretty knowledgeable perp, probably wanted to speed up the asphyxiation process. Who turned it back on?"

“The system is on temperature default and a timer. It either kicked back on automatically when the plant’s temperature rose too high, or it clicked on in the morning.” Ascari shrugged. “That’s all I got.”

“Authorities confirmed that the bomb that went off at HydroVino was foul play,” Ana said. “The buzz going around pre-summit prep is that Aurora’s responsible. Vitreuve, in his stupid high-pitched voice, would not shut up about how Leif and Philippe left your dinner party early, so of course they must have done it.” Ana rolled her eyes and exhaled a long trail of smoke. In spite of her incredulity, Devlin still wasn’t ready to discount this theory. Ana continued, “Oh, and Vitreuve’s convinced that Erika’s in on blowing up the plant too, because she stole his Peugeot and ran for the rail station before police could arrive.”

“We ran because we were being shot at,” Devlin said.

“*Oui*, but there’s no surveillance at his farmhouse, so Vitreuve claims it was all a ruse,” Ana said. “He’s spreading word that Erika Aurora staged the shooting to steer away blame for the explosion.” Ana shook her head while she lit another cigarette. “I’d call that quite the accusation since there are no bullet casings, no footprints, and no leads. Pure slander, wouldn’t you say?”

Ascari shrugged.

Devlin shrugged too, but his mind reeled. Slanderous, or truth? There were no leads, which indicated another professional-style hit. Or perhaps there was veracity in the theory that Erika had staged the shooting, again to shift culpability for another crime. Plus, setting the explosive at her biggest competitor's water plant days before release of its latest product would suit her.

Was the Kansas City Shuffle indeed Erika Aurora's MO? Did she feign status as the victim while perpetrating a crime elsewhere?

***

Devlin bid good-bye to Ana. She took off for Verona to handle the BBC's coverage of the summit in the upcoming days.

Devlin spent the next couple hours exploring the rest of Runa's office beyond her desktop, but he found nothing that would shed light on the case. The documents in her file cabinets and desk were sparse. The personal belongings on her shelves were minimal.

Clearly Runa's world had revolved around her laboratory, of which he and Vin had taken complete inventory earlier. They'd spent days there evaluating encrypted computer files and any notebooks or handwritten scraps on which formulas might have been jotted. They'd unearthed hundreds of creative ideas for revolutionary wine hybrids and grappa herb concoctions. Nothing there suggested criminal activity involving the lethal formula in the syringe.

For the second time that day, Devlin wheeled back the leather chair behind Runa's office desk and stretched. He cracked his knuckles once, and then another round, frustrated by the lack of evidence.

Leif strode past Runa's open doorway with files cradled under one arm as if carrying a football. He headed in the direction of Erika's office, chatting loudly in Italian on his cell phone. Moments later, Leif retraced his path toward his own office, his arm devoid of paperwork but still conversing on his phone. He tripped, and Leif stooped to tie his black leather shoe. Devlin couldn't help overhear Leif finalizing the logistics with Lupo on the weekend's Palio horse race. Lupo would be thrilled about the lifted injunction, with Aurora's new FONS water added to the event's beverage list.

The pending summit and the overlapping Palio race now spelled a deluge of activity for Aurora Vineyard. Devlin shook his head. *When it rains, it pours…*

"*Sì, certo. Arriverò a Siena presto. Adesso, vado alla fabbrica del'aqua,*" Leif said, moving down the hall. Devlin gathered that Leif was headed to the Aurora water-bottling plant to handle things from there.

While Leif Aurora was temporarily distracted with business in another part of the vineyard, Devlin seized the opportunity to nose about the CEO's unlocked office. But one step into the hall, and Devlin smacked headfirst into Erika Aurora.

"Oh!" Erika giggled and rubbed her forehead. "Thank you for a wonderful evening, Devlin. You were lovely." She straightened her posture and stuck out her hand. "I crumbled last night, too weak to handle the pressure. That's not like me, and it won't happen again. I won't allow last night to affect our working relationship."

He smiled and shook her hand. He wanted to say something meaningful, but before he could she said, "Gotta fly." She squeezed his hand and released it, then strode down the hall and out the stairway exit.

That confrontation was much easier than he'd anticipated. Erika's summation of the night before represented his thoughts exactly. Like him, she'd succumbed to a moment of personal vulnerability. But they'd regained their business composure, and that was that. Back on track.

So why were guilt, shame, and a touch of foreboding still churning his stomach? He shook it off. *Stick to the plan.*

Devlin dipped into Leif's office for some recon and shut the door behind him. He scanned the usual places—desk, file drawers, a logged-in computer. He knew he could spend hours there investigating. One of these days he would do so, probably when Leif took off for the summit meeting. But with only about a half hour on his hands, he'd take what he could get.

Devlin pulled on a thin pair of gloves from his jeans pocket. He poked under the desk for secret drawers. None. Checked behind curtains and artwork for compartments. None. Next, he slid back each panel of the wine bar cabinet. Just like in the movies, he found a safe. He sighed. Why did people always put their safes in clichéd locations? Did pride make them think they were invincible? Standard safe, easy to crack. Devlin set to work on the lock.

Minutes later, he shimmied the door wide and rifled around the safe's two-by-two-foot interior. He found a journal, a handful of file folders, a long Cartier watch box, a packet of securities, and some handwritten letters. The folder contained deeds, patents, and wills belonging to the Aurora family members, including their father, Augustus. One was a deed in Leif's name for a cliffside property in St. Moritz, Switzerland, likely a ski chalet. A packet of bonds, all made out to Augustus, totaled nearly two million dollars.

Devlin brushed aside a rubber-banded packet of correspondence between Leif and Philippe that reeked of Drakkar cologne. Instead he aimed for the back of the deceptively deep safe for another packet of letters. These were worn with age, and he was curious to learn the sender and recipient. But he mistakenly cuffed the rectangular Cartier box, which emitted a sound like marbles rolling back and forth inside. He picked it up, rattled it, and opened the box. He could not believe what he found inside.

The door to the office opened. Leif Aurora stood on the plush carpet threshold, his phone to his ear, his back to the room. "The World Health Organization recommends a minimum of twenty liters of water, per person, per day for basic survival…hold on…"

Devlin heard Erika walk by Leif in the hall and mumble something. He took those few seconds to shut the safe and close the panel on the wine bar.

"Thanks, I needed these numbers," Leif said. Erika's voice trailed off down the hall in conversation with another, and Leif resumed his call. "Yes, and recommends fifty to a hundred liters per day for hygiene and sanitation." Leif's leather shoe shifted past the threshold. "So why can't we—"

Devlin pocketed his gloves and slid into the leather chair facing Leif's desk, just as the youngest Aurora pushed wide the office door.

Leif frowned at him.

Devlin put up a hand in greeting.

"Let me call you back," Leif said into the phone and hung up. He put on a smile and crossed his arms. "Devlin, what can I do for you?" Leif's eyes flicked subconsciously toward the wine bar, and he walked behind his desk.

"I just wanted to take a minute and thank you for working with Lupo on this Palio event. It means a lot to him," Devlin said.

Leif took a deep breath and smiled wider. "It means a lot to Aurora to sponsor Palio. Both our company and the event embrace the concepts of competition and tradition." He sauntered to the wine bar. "May I offer you a drink?" He reached down and slid one of the lower panels aside, revealing a bottle of Jack Daniel's. He lingered a moment, perhaps considering whether or not to check the integrity of the safe. Then he snatched up the bottle. "In America, this is good stuff, am I right?" Leif said.

Devlin nodded. "That's true." He and Scotti had been known to enjoy a little Jack Daniel's after racing the Circuit of the Americas in Texas. He'd tried reaching his pit boss a few times over the course of the morning and had left voice mails.

The fact that he'd ignored Scotti's early-morning call while rolling around in the sack with Erika Aurora brought back in full force that guilty churning in his stomach. He patted his abdomen. "Thanks, Leif, I'm going to pass on the drink. Something I ate last night."

Leif ambled back behind his desk. "You only came in here to thank me for sponsoring Palio? Surely, there must be something more."

Devlin was about to delve further into Aurora's plans for the water summit when a call from Scotti shot right to his voice mail. Screw the idle chat. He stood, shook hands with Leif, and left quickly. He had to talk with Scotti about what he'd just found in Leif Aurora's safe. Something that just might crack this investigation wide open.

Now back behind the closed door of Runa's office, Devlin pulled aside his untucked shirt. He dislodged his gloves from his jeans pocket and unfurled them to reveal the booty he'd uncovered from the box inside Leif Aurora's safe.

Four capped syringes. Filled with brownish-amber liquid. Each resembled the syringe he'd found beside the vat where Runa Aurora was killed. The syringe that had tested positive for the lethal chemical formula.

Chapter 24

The four potentially lethal syringes found in Leif Aurora's office safe did not bode well for baby brother.

But before Devlin could make any presumptions, he needed to ascertain the authenticity of the contents. He needed Scotti's brother, Vin, to compare the samples. Might as well kill two birds and call Scotti, to give him and Vin the sitrep.

Before he dialed, he decided to check the recent voice mail from Scotti. His pit boss was probably close to arriving at the vineyard and was giving him an ETA. He realized that he'd been truly worried about Scotti since dropping his call that morning, and not having heard from him the entire day.

As he rewrapped the evidence, he listened to the voice mail. It started with a clear indication of someone fumbling with the phone, and then a hang-up. He smirked. Thank God he hadn't stopped what he was doing with Erika Aurora for a phone call that ended in a disconnect.

He then played the only other voice mail, the one he'd received while sitting in Leif's office. It also had been dialed from Scotti's number, but when he played it, a woman's voice spoke to him.

"Devlin, this is Veronica Griffith. Call me at this number. I have some news." The voice mail ended with a muffled voice in the background, like on a PA system, paging a doctor. Veronica was calling from a hospital.

***

Devlin's fingers flew across his iPhone as he tapped out Scotti's number. Again he heard Veronica Griffith's voice.

"Devlin, oh thank God. I've been trying to reach you," she said when she answered.

"Veronica, what's wrong? Are you alright? Where's Scotti?" Devlin said.

"We're okay. But Scotti's in the hospital. Around five this morning, he was driving me from Monza to the train station in Verona. Just outside the city, he complained of chest pains. I drove him to the hospital. The doctors think he may have suffered a mild heart attack."

Devlin crumpled into the chair in front of Runa's desk. His elbows rested on his knees for support. He kneaded his temple with shaking fingers. The world had begun to spin at the mention of a heart attack, and it still hadn't stopped. Devlin breathed, in and out. In and out. Tried to stop his heart from pounding so hard. Gradually the spinning and the pounding slowed.

Veronica continued, "When the chest pains started, Scotti gave me your number, and I tried to reach you. But some guy cut me off on the autostrada, and my phone flew out the car's open window. Then I couldn't access Scotti's cell until the nurses returned his belongings just a little while ago." Veronica's voice trembled, but she cleared her throat. "He's feeling much better. They're running all kinds of tests now, but when he gets back, you can talk to him, okay? Devlin, are *you* alright?"

Devlin had refused Scotti's morning call because he was being selfish. Rather than speak to his closest friend, he'd chosen to mess around in the sack. With a woman he should not be messing around with. Had he spoken with Scotti, he might've sensed that his pit boss wasn't well, and then Devlin might've been able to do something. Instead, Scotti had suffered a heart attack on his way to meet with him. My God, it could have ended in disaster.

"I don't know what he would've done if you hadn't been there for him, Veronica. I don't know what I would've done if..." Devlin couldn't bear to finish.

"Don't talk like that, Lucky. He's going to be just fine. The doctors are amazed at how well he's recovered, and they want to send him home tonight. He's in really good hands. I'm going to stay with him for the tests. And then—"

"Stay with him, please. I'll leave now. I can be there in less than an hour."

"Devlin, of course I'll stay. And, honestly, there's no need for you to come." Veronica lowered her voice to a whisper. "I pretended to be his daughter, so the doctors are telling me everything. They plan to keep him for a few more tests, and then I can take him up to where you are tonight. I'd like to stay with him just until tomorrow, if that's no trouble. Scotti and I go way back and…I care about what happens to him, you know?"

"I know you do, believe me," he said. "You've always been good to him on the circuit. You've always shown him the respect he deserves. But I can't ask you to cart him up here. I'll get to the hospital—"

"Dev, I'm not 'carting him' anywhere. This happened on my watch. He's a good man, and I feel responsible for him. I think you can understand that," Veronica said.

Devlin's head cleared. After all that had happened to his family at the hands of a terrorist on his watch, he understood exactly what she meant to "feel responsible." Devlin told her, "I'll leave him in your hands until you get here tonight. On one condition."

"What's that, Lucky?"

"I'd like to talk to his doctor. Then to Scotti when he gets back from his tests."

"Of course," she said. "Call you back soon."

Devlin dialed Vin and told him about his older brother's status. Vin explained that he'd already made arrangements to hop a train for Verona. The two men spent the next twenty minutes sharing anecdotes about Scotti. Their pit boss would kill them both if he found out they'd been commiserating over him, so Devlin told Vin about the four new syringes. Vin promised to compare them to the original the next morning at the vineyard lab.

When they hung up, Devlin heard Leif and Erika arguing outside the office door. It was Erika's words that Devlin discerned first. "...And our aquifer is naturally fed by the mountain water supply that millions already tap into..."

Leif shouted at Erika, "By 2050, an estimated eight billion people will be consuming the world's depleting water supply, then what?"

Devlin secreted the wrapped syringes back into his pocket. He walked to the door, but he did not intrude into the hall. After the day he'd had so far, he was staying out of World War III. He waited until the siblings finished.

Erika retorted, "Then we'll filter our refuse. We'll dot our coasts with desalination plants. We'll...ugh, why does your goddamn phone keep ringing? Just answer it..."

"Philippe, hey, hon. I miss you too...you're where? Let me grab my car. I'll meet you there. Erika, we'll talk more later." Leif's voice retreated, and the thumping of feet down the hall signaled his departure.

Devlin opened the door to find Erika alone in the hall.

"Sorry about the noise, Dev," Erika said. "This summit is going to spell death for me."

Chapter 25

"He left me!" Erika Aurora wildly clicked and tapped a text with her thumbs so fast that Devlin feared she'd suffer a stroke from the effort.

Devlin said, "Maybe Leif left early for the summit, to get a head start on the logistics at the convention center and—"

"Nope. He's not answering his phone or returning my texts. My asshole brother took off for Bolzano to go night-skiing with Philippe, right in the middle of a shipping and production crisis!"

"Are you sure? He might—"

"Anywhere else, and he would've called his driver. But Leif keeps his Range Rover on standby in the garage. It's packed with his skis, boots…everything down to his hand warmers and his hand-carved grappa flask, for Chrissakes. When he can't take the heat, he runs for the mountains. So typical…" Erika flung her hands in the air and headed down the hall. She muttered the rest of her rant, employing vocabulary she could only have picked up from truck drivers or sailors. The bustling conference room door slammed shut behind her just as Devlin's cell phone rang.

"Devlin, I have a scruffy, tattooed young man sitting here with me. He says he wants to talk to you, but that was before a beautiful young nurse came in to take his blood pressure. Shocker, it's skyrocketing." Devlin could hear Veronica smiling on her end of the receiver. "Scotti's wrapping up his exit paperwork. I glanced at the directions you sent me, and it shouldn't take us more than an hour to get to the vineyard."

"I appreciate this so much. Tell me what I—"

"Lucky, if you thank me one more time, there'll be hell to pay, I swear," Veronica said. "Hey, you know that old saying, 'What do the Scots wear beneath their kilts?' Well, I now know what surly pit bosses wear beneath their hospital johnnies…"

Devlin laughed. "What do they wear?"

"I do not peek and tell," she laughed. "But the wee Scots have nothing on this Italian stallion!" She laughed, and he joined in. He'd only ever shared brief professional encounters with Veronica, but she'd always been able to make him laugh. She was sweet and salty. Like Ella.

A pang of guilt slammed him out of nowhere. He'd already slept with Erika. Now he was flirting with his racing colleague. He could envision Ella rolling her eyes at him, telling him to get his head out of his ass.

"Hold on. I've got Scotti here," Veronica said. "See you soon, Lucky."

Devlin rubbed the stubble on his chin and exhaled. Sometimes the pain of losing Ella overwhelmed him. But lately, it was more the torment of her lingering in his head. If only he could find peace in her memory…and let her go. What was he afraid of? Falling apart?

Scotti's voice, tired but strong, spoke to him. "Give me a sitrep," he said.

"Is that all you think about is work? I'm pretty sure you should be resting," Devlin said.

"Your failure to update me is increasing my heart rate," Scotti said.

"First off, I've made the decision to skip the Baku circuit," Devlin said.

"You can't cancel our appearance at the race. It's our first year in Azerbaijan, and—"

"And nothing. You just had a heart attack," Devlin said.

"It was a scare. My pressure was elevated, with minor palpitations. Doc told me to limit my cannoli intake to five a day. That's all. We're going to Baku."

"You're going without a driver, then," Devlin said. "You need rest. Veronica's going to bring you to the vineyard tonight, where I can keep an eye on you. Then Vin and I are taking you home to Siena to kick back for a little while."

"I do not 'kick back.'"

"You will," Devlin said. "I'm also suspending this Aurora case while I help you recuperate. End of story."

Scotti growled. "It's bad enough Montoya and Helio hauled ass to Verona. All over a few friggin' palpitations, for Pete's sake. I told them to stay put in Monza and show your prototype to the IndyCar contingent, but do they listen? Course not. Your race car's sitting in a trailer taking up most of the goddamn hospital parking lot just so they can hold my hand while I check outta here."

"They're worried about you," Devlin said. "Quit your bellyaching."

Scotti grunted his disdain. "The Aurora case. It stalled out?" he said.

Devlin filled him in, right up to the point where he'd discovered the syringes inside the vault, leaving both of them confounded over the most likely suspects—Erika? Leif? Or both siblings acting in cahoots?

"No more talk of this case. You need rest," Devlin said. "I can't believe you had a heart attack. I—" Devlin choked up, momentarily unable to speak, grateful that it had not been Scotti's time yet. Devlin swallowed hard. "Just get your ass up here, old man, I miss you."

"Me too, son, me too," Scotti said.

***

Devlin had about an hour until Scotti checked out of the hospital, then another hour until they all arrived at the vineyard. He figured he might as well make the most of the time he had with the Aurora case before his self-imposed sabbatical.

He stepped out of Runa's office. He overheard Erika loudly barking orders to her people inside the conference room down the hall. Unhindered, he stole back into Leif's office. He shut the door, pulled on his gloves, and spun the combination lock on the vault once more.

Back to the journal. He flipped open the hardcover leather-bound book and fluttered through its yellowed pages. The journal belonged to the vineyard's *padrone*, Augustus Aurora. The timeline began when Augustus had first met Helena, the biological mother to Erika, Runa, and Leif. Skimming through the first entries, Devlin gleaned the fact that Augustus was a man in love. The vintner's life truly hadn't begun until the day the little family had wandered onto his fledgling plot of land.

He flipped through more entries, pages dealing with the man's grief over his wife's death at such an early age, a subject with which he had become only too familiar. After some time, Devlin arrived at the notation that described the discovery of the aquifer—the exact place of the sun in the sky, the calendar date, the weather, and the latitude and longitude of where the spring had sprung. Devlin envisioned the spot in the center of the courtyard. It was now designated by a weathered metallic plate that resembled a New York City manhole cover.

The day of discovery—nearly twenty years ago to the day, he noted—was one of rebirth in the eyes of the Aurora business. What had once been a sole grape farmer eking out a pittance of production had evolved into a profitable market leader, all due to the newly tapped water source that naturally flowed beneath the terra firma.

The next few chapters of the journal outlined the company's rapid rise, where Augustus highlighted the significant contributions of his children in its development. The final few entries petered out slowly, signaling his deteriorating health, until the man had succumbed to the ravages of cancer.

He shuffled through the pages one last time. What grabbed his attention was a collection of a half dozen pages near the beginning of the journal, bearing drawings, scribbles, and handwritten numbers. Most were chemical formulas that he recognized as part of the winemaking process. Others were drawings for wine labels. On one page Augustus had scrawled a list of names and contact info of distributors, publicists, suppliers, security personnel, and employees. Devlin could tell that Augustus was old school, a man who relied on paper and pen rather than computers to store such vital company intel.

He spotted a page with a scrawled date that hearkened back just before the discovery of the aquifer. On it was a chemical symbol written in bold letters of green ink that read: MeOH. His heart pounded faster. The symbol stood for methanol, the main ingredient in the poisonous syringe. The noted abbreviation was not an unusual one for a wine and spirits producer. Except that the symbol was written on a page that folded onto itself. When he unfolded the page, the inside bore more letters, constructed into a formula. He snapped a photo and texted it to Vin, asking him to decipher it.

Certain now of the journal's worth as evidence, Devlin decided to add it to his Aurora collection and examine it fully later. But he couldn't help rifle through one more time. One page, doodled in just before the aquifer discovery, showed a caricature of a woman. Drawn in black ink, she sported witchlike hair, sharp fanged teeth, and a pronounced bosom and backside. He actually laughed out loud at its absurdity.

He rubbed his eyes and pocketed the journal. Next he reached for the back of the safe, toward a packet of letters. Not the ones that smelled like men's cologne. But a rubber-banded packet of more official-looking correspondence on pristine business paper.

At that moment Erika Aurora pushed open the door to Leif's office. Her mouth dropped open, and her eyes went wide, clearly surprised to find him there.

He stood and surreptitiously shut the door to the safe with his foot. "I just…stumbled upon a safe," he explained. He felt his face flush warm. "Thought I might investigate…was trying to crack the combo. Think I just got it."

"Well, I did hire you to investigate who's taking over my company," Erika said. "And there are company documents in that safe." A mix of anger and amusement visibly stamped her face. She tilted her head, and the corners of her lips curled upward. "You're not my company's usurper, are you?"

"Don't be silly," he said. "I'm just thorough. Like I said, I merely cracked the safe. I planned to seek your authorization to ascertain its contents."

Erika smiled. "I'm sure you did." She walked to the cabinet vault. "I must say, I'm impressed. Besides my father, who's long gone, I'm the only one in the world with the combination. Just me." She peered up at him through her silky long eyelashes. "And now you."

"I'm sorry. It's a parlor trick. I crack safes," he said. "Would you like to open it now? Maybe sort through the contents together?" Devlin boldly pushed forward. If she was the only one with the combination, then logically she was the only one who could've stashed the syringes inside the safe. Feeling the bulge of the wrapped syringes in his pocket, he was curious what would happen when she learned that they were no longer inside the repository. He pulled back the chair to allow them both access. "Please, be my guest. Open it."

"Sorry, I was coming in here to retrieve files for the shipping company. I just don't have the time right now, what with the summit in three days."

He held his ground. He taunted her with his gaze to open the damn safe.

"Besides, I rarely open the vault," she said. "In fact, the last time I did was months ago. A bauble of sorts from Lausanne." A sly grin spread across her gorgeous mouth. "You know how to work the tumblers, Devlin, but would you like to know what the combination signifies?"

He raised his brows, curious.

"My father was a stickler for remembering dates. The combination is the day, month, and year that my mother, Helena, stumbled upon Augustus's vineyard. With Leif and me alongside her, and her belly pregnant with Runa. Of course, I'm the only one alive who knows the exact digits. And now you."

Erika retrieved a file from atop Leif's desk and strode to the door. She held it open for him, clearly dismissing him from the room. "We'll peruse its contents together some other time."

Likely until she could rearrange or remove its contents to her liking, he figured.

He followed her out of Leif's office. She turned and locked the office door. Devlin informed her of Scotti's condition and pending arrival.

To his surprise, she embraced him. "I'll contact housekeeping and ensure Scotti has everything he needs," Erika said and headed back to the conference room.

Devlin's phone pinged in the fluorescent-lit corridor. He glanced at the screen. A missed call from Hamilton, and a couple texts from Vin. His HELL Rangers were resourceful.

Devlin left the office building and strode directly to his bungalow. Before examining his spoils, Devlin scanned Vin's texts. Change of plans. Vin was on his way to the vineyard as agreed, but via Land Rover, not train. And Vin was bringing reinforcements.

The HELL Rangers formerly on a mission in Syria had returned to their underground headquarters in Rome. There, the young military biochemist had filled them in on the investigation into Giancarlo Venchi's death and the corresponding hijinks at Aurora Vineyard. The four HELL Rangers had insisted on joining Vin, to help Devlin, and to visit Scotti. Their arrival was imminent.

Next, Devlin returned Hamilton's call. Ham reported, "The water rights activist who attacked Erika and those tourists before jumping the cliff was part of a company called Watery Grave. Their headquarters are based in London. They have known subsidiaries in Berlin, Paris, and Burlington, Vermont."

"Okay, that much I have already from the police. Learn anything new from the address uncovered in the Aurora files?" Devlin said.

"I traced that address to a property in Lausanne, Switzerland," Ham said. "If it's truly another subsidiary of Watery Grave, it's a ridiculously small one. The trail ends at a tiny chalet in the college ski village there."

"Lausanne?" Might the ski chalet be the so-called bauble that Erika had mentioned procuring?

Devlin unzipped the locked compartment of his backpack that held his Aurora evidence and Ella's keepsake book. He compared Ham's property address to the one on the deed inside the Aurora vault. Perfect match. "Why would Aurora Vineyard own a subsidiary of a known water rights activist that consistently, overtly attacks them?" Devlin said.

"Dunno. But there's more," Ham said. "Even if it is a subsidiary, it's unclear whether it's fully operational. Someone leases the property and appears to live in the chalet, as a full-time student. Maybe it's a one-man show? I did some digging at town hall and came up with a name."

"A full-time student who lives in a ski chalet in Switzerland?" Devlin said. "I'd bet my race car that it's Philippe LeFleau."

"Bingo."

"Nice work, Ham. Tomorrow I need you to follow up on another hunch. But be sure to get some shut-eye. There'll be some travel." Devlin issued Hamilton further orders. They chatted a few more minutes on Scotti's condition, then on football in the Barclay League, before hanging up.

Philippe LeFleau. Why did the outspoken activist lease a property owned by Aurora Vineyard? Was he a one-man subsidiary of this larger activist organization? Was he a lone wolf acting of his own accord?

Maybe his partner, Leif, had set him up there for school. But did Leif know that the property was associated with one of the world's largest water rights activists, one that regularly harassed his own company?

Devlin cracked open a bottle of FONS. It was "A Taste of the Fountain of Youth," according to the Aurora marketing label. He gulped down most of the platinum-speckled liquid and belched. He didn't feel any younger.

Was Philippe playing both sides of the fence? Might Philippe be the one who was planning a coup of the Aurora company? Or perhaps Philippe, Leif, and Erika were working together somehow, for some nefarious, ulterior motive involving the super potent methanol formula?

He opened Augustus's journal to the page with the methanol symbol. Then he unfolded the page to reveal the theorem hidden inside. Devlin compared this chemical formula to the one typed into the final part of Vin's text message. A match.

Vin's text also read: "Formula script in your photo matches the syringe by Runa's vat. Both high-octane methanol... Both lethal poisons." So the equation in Augustus's journal represented the super potent, lethal liquid contained inside the syringe found beside Runa's death chamber.

The dated journal entry showed that Augustus had developed the lethal formula in his winery's lab. But to what end? The formula's chemical composition, as well as its tangible expression in the form of syringes, was not only found near Runa's corpse, but also in Leif's office, inside a safe whose combination was admittedly only known to Erika.

Devlin reconsidered his earlier promise to Scotti about suspending the Aurora case. Against the backdrop of the mounting evidence, Devlin knew it was time. Time to call a meeting with the surviving members of the Aurora clan.

Chapter 26

Full-on crisis mode, Erika Aurora thought, *that's what this day has been.* She squished her painted toes into the plush carpet by her office window and sipped a smoothie. She'd stashed her Christian Louboutin pumps beneath her desk twenty minutes ago. They would stay there for the night, damn it, because of the day she'd had. Concealed in darkness, she surreptitiously lifted the sash and peered across the courtyard to the doorstep of Devlin's villa. She paused to chew the almond bits whipped into her raspberry yogurt and eavesdropped on the conversation that Devlin was having with Rasmus.

Devlin told her security chief that four more HELL Rangers were expected on her property tonight. *More Rangers…it's a friggin' military reunion!*

Not that Erika wasn't grateful for their added security measures. Devlin and his men worked well with Rasmus and his team. If she didn't have the summit looming, she might've even slept peacefully that night. But crisis mode meant sleep deprivation for as long as it took to get the job done right. If only her pristine vineyard didn't feel so much like a military installation. *Cripe, by the time Scotti arrives from the hospital tonight, Devlin and Rasmus might as well just fire up the BBQ and throw a party.* She sighed, pissed at feeling like an ornery den mother.

Devlin was getting under her skin. And not in the way she craved.

After Runa had served Giancarlo the company's grappa as his last supper, Erika had expertly hired Devlin Lucchesi to deflect the backlash to Aurora involving the racer's death. Then she'd retained Devlin's services to successfully keep up appearances after Runa's passing. The man was a truly skilled professional. She'd grant him that. It also helped that he knew exactly how she liked her grapes pressed.

But now Lucky Lucchesi was overstepping his boundaries, snooping around in places that were off-limits, like her father's safe. How dare Devlin invade her privacy? Cracking the code on the Aurora vault, to which she'd been the only one privy for the past two decades, was scandalous. She'd gotten careless with him. Horny and careless. But now it was time for Devlin, and his army of tramps, to haul ass off her property.

Her phone vibrated. She glanced at the lit screen. Leif. She clenched her fists.

She saw Devlin glance up at her through the darkened window. He must have noticed the light from her phone when it rang. She nodded to him. He raised his index finger, suggesting that she stay put and wait for him there. Damn it.

Erika answered the call with guns blazing. “Leif, you dropped everything into my lap. How could you bolt for the hills to ski with Philippe at a time like this?”

“I’m sorry. When I stress out, I ski. And you drink smoothies, right? Bet you’re drinking one now.”

“Now is not the time to play nice, little brother,” Erika said. “I’m headed to Verona in the morning. Activists, corporate heads, newspeople…they’re already hustling there in droves. You know as well as I do that water rights issues are more contentious now than they’ve ever been. And Aurora’s charging in with our brand-new bottled water line, dredged from our controversial aquifer. There’s still so much work to be done. Promise me you’ll at least make it back in time for the summit’s opening speeches?” Erika said.

Silence.

“Leif, promise me.”

“I’ll be there in a few days. By the first full day of presen—”

“Leif!”

“Don’t worry, I have to be there to accept my award anyway. And Philippe and I are just a stone’s throw away. In Bolzano. I’m not even an hour from Verona, should something pressing arise,” Leif said.

“We’re under the gun over whether our family’s aquifer will be deemed public or private…I’d say that’s pressing. We’ll be hounded every minute for interviews and meetings. Please, reconsider?” she said.

She heard Philippe in the background voice something unintelligible, and then the two men giggled. Leif dropped the phone and laughed some more, and she heard him wrestle with the receiver. The call dropped, and she cursed him aloud.

She dreamed every night about ways of killing off the arrogant, troublesome mama's boy Philippe LeFleau. Leif's boy toy kept interfering in situations that did not concern him. But sometimes she also wished Leif would just walk away. Gather up his water conservation principles and just leave her to run the company on her own. Then she could handle crisis mode just as she saw fit.

Erika knew in her heart that it was just a matter of time now. One day Leif and Philippe would take off skiing and never look back. Perhaps that day was closer than anyone would think.

A knock on the door signaled Devlin's arrival from the courtyard. She opened it. A determined, forthright man stood there. He exuded purpose and confidence in his ripped jeans, tee shirt, parka, and bulging backpack.

Erika rested her hand on his chest and exhaled sharply. "I'm overworked. I need to blow off steam. Wanna screw?"

Chapter 27

"You'll never know how tempted I am by your offer," Devlin said. "I'm flattered. But our time has passed. And I need to review information about your case, and I'm certain you won't like it," he said.

Erika Aurora removed her hand from his chest and took a step back.

He stepped forward into the room, into her space. He slipped the backpack from his shoulder and propped it on the desktop.

Erika walked behind her desk and slid on her pumps, increasing her stature by nearly half a foot. She gripped the edge of the desk, her knuckles turning white.

Devlin flipped the dials on the backpack's locked zipper. The phone in his pocket vibrated with a call. "Will you excuse me, Erika? Lupo typically texts rather than calls. It's probably important."

"Please," she said. Erika turned to flip through her file cabinet.

"Dev, I've got my godson here." Lupo spoke into the phone in a singsong, jovial voice. "Says he wants to say hello to his daddy."

"But Marcello's not due back for a few more...*Ciao*, Marcello! How's my boy? Everything okay? You're home a little early," Devlin said.

Marcello's groggy, tentative little voice said, "*Ciao, babbo*," and nothing more. Devlin gripped the desk. His son had taken to calling him Lucky for almost a year now, full of adolescent spunk and bravado. Now Marcello was reverting back to calling him "daddy" in Italian. Something was wrong.

"Marcello, are you hurt? Tell me what's the matter," he said. Fear and foreboding roiled in the pit of his stomach.

"I'm tired, *babbo*. When are you coming home?" Marcello yawned, and the tail end sounded like a whimper. "I miss you. And...I miss...Momma."

Devlin's stomach dropped. His son had come home early from robotics camp. Not because he was sick or hurt. But because he was suffering the loss of his mother. And he missed the only parent that he had left. *My God*, he thought, *what was I thinking, abandoning my child at sleepaway camp after all he's been through?*

"Marcello, I'm coming home. Scotti and Vin and me. And a whole bunch of the crew. We're all coming home tomorrow," he said into the phone.

At the mention of his leaving, Erika looked up from her filing. Abject concern was etched on her face. Concern for the company or for his child?

"Why can't you come home *now*?" Marcello yawned again. Devlin envisioned his boy's face. It was clearly transitioning into the awkward years of puberty, but it still maintained the babyish nuances he cherished. Before he could answer, Marcello said, "Zio Lupo wants to talk again. Come home now so we can go to Zio Lupo's horse race together, okay? Promise?"

"I promise, *amore*." Devlin pressed his fingers to his eyelids to ease the tingling behind them. "I'll come home, and we'll go to Palio together. You and me, okay? I love you."

"*Sì, babbo, buona notte*," Marcello said.

He said goodnight to his son, and Lupo spoke next. "Hey, man, little dude's just really tired from a rollicking good time at camp. There's nothing to worry about. He just needed to hear your voice. Now he's gonna sleep it off. He'll be right in the morning," Lupo said. "Prost's mom and Ella's dad are both here. Making him toast with Nutella and some caffè latte. He'll be fine."

Devlin hung up and slung the backpack onto his shoulder. "Erika, we'll discuss your case later. My family needs me." Tomorrow he would haul his crew back to Siena for a much-needed reunion.

Erika opened her mouth to speak. But another incoming call on his phone, this time from Vin, interrupted them. Likely a status update. Devlin pushed up the window sash higher and looked out into the courtyard, expecting Veronica and Scotti to pull in any minute. It was still too early for Vin or the others to arrive. Devlin answered.

"Devlin…Scotti's had another heart attack. Big one. He's…" Vin's voice choked. There was silence on the other end.

***

Memories slammed Devlin so hard that he collapsed into the leather seat behind him. Scotti's face, beaming at Ella as she walked down the wedding aisle toward Devlin. That same expression when Scotti had grasped Marcello in his strong, capable hands and first cradled their infant son close to his heart. The smell of tar, gasoline, and champagne on Scotti's race suit, whenever he'd crush Devlin in an embrace after a win or a loss.

Graham, Devlin's trusted medic, took over the call from Vin. "The hospital called Vin, as next of kin. We'd just arrived in Verona, and we sped over to the hospital when they called."

Devlin muttered, "But Scotti sounded so strong. There were tests. He was filling out paperwork to leave…"

Graham continued, "Veronica was wheeling Scotti out of the hospital when he suffered a full myocardial infarction. They rushed him into the ER, and…"

He struggled to form words. "And what?"

"Devlin…Scotti might not make it."

***

The ride from the vineyard to the Verona hospital felt like the longest of Devlin's life. Rasmus drove Devlin and Erika. Another Aurora guard sped the four HELL Rangers over the long, winding path down the mountain. But when they reached the highway leading into Verona, traffic crawled with incoming visitors to the water rights convention in the city. Devlin maintained contact with Vin and Graham nearly the entire ride, helpless but informed.

Graham told Devlin that Scotti had first suffered a mild coronary artery spasm on the way in from Monza with Veronica. This likely led to a temporary blockage, one that was undetectable in his blood tests and EKGs. The damage would've caused the major heart attack that Scotti suffered while leaving the hospital.

Doctors had then rushed Scotti into emergency bypass graft surgery to treat the blockage. It would be hours before anyone knew whether Scotti would pull through. All Devlin could think about was Scotti lying on a table with his chest cracked open, a dozen hands fighting to keep the man alive. Devlin refused to think about failure.

***

Rasmus dropped Devlin and Vin at the entrance to the hospital. The rest of the HELL Rangers met them inside the waiting room. Devlin threw his backpack onto a hard plastic chair and paced. He tuned out the world and waited.

An hour later, a woman cut into his line of sight, directly in front of him. He gazed up at her from his chair for a few moments before his brain registered her face. Veronica Griffith.

Devlin's fellow race car driver stood before him in a short brown leather jacket, blue jeans, Converse sneakers, and a U2 concert tee shirt with coffee stains down the front. Her long hair was held back in a clip. Her eyes were red and puffy, and her lips were chapped and swollen. She reached out her arms toward him, zombielike, as if begging for solace and refuge from the last living human on earth.

Devlin knew he had no solace to share. Yet he stood slowly and reached for her, then took a step forward into an embrace. The comfort they both craved was found in that moment. They wrapped their arms around each other completely.

He felt the tension in her shoulders ease. She rested her head on his chest, and he cradled her there. This woman would forever be a hero to him, for her patience and unfettered care toward the man who was by all accounts his father.

"Thank you," Devlin said. "A thousand times, thank you."

Veronica pulled back to glimpse his face. A smile cracked her solemn lips, and she nodded. The two of them separated, and she plunked into a seat by a window.

Devlin turned to Vin. "Erika Aurora. Is she here?"

"Rasmus drove her down the road, to the convention center hotel," Vin said. "She's preparing for tomorrow night's summit speeches. She said to keep her posted on Scotti's condition."

Devlin nodded. So far, there was no confirmed link between the high-potency-methanol syringes and the deaths of either Giancarlo or Runa. Though the formula itself posed a serious hazard, Vin would continue to work on an antidote back at the

Grotto. Devlin would inform local authorities of the formula's danger, and he'd ensure Rasmus contained or destroyed all of Aurora's special grappa stock.

He was chucking this investigation. His family needed him. Marcello, Scotti, Lupo. He never should have taken on the probe at all. He had been wrong to think it was safe to go back in the water. He was in above his head, and it was time to go home and take care of his own.

***

Two hours later, Veronica gestured to a set of double doors, out of which a doctor strode into the waiting area. Devlin and Vin stood.

The surgeon pulled off her cap. Her face was cold, focused, unnerving. "Your brother's surgery was a success," she said to Vin. "No problems. He's headed to ICU, where we'll monitor him. No visitors until morning." She shuffled quickly down the hall toward Scotti, who lay still upon a gurney, his heart fragile but mended.

Vin collapsed back into his chair. The rest of Devlin's team headed for the cafeteria. Devlin remained standing, staring at the double doors. A hand on his shoulder made him turn. Veronica Griffith smiled at him through her tears.

Chapter 28

After receiving further assurances from Scotti's surgeon, Devlin eventually settled into the ICU waiting area.

A few hours later, he awoke. Veronica slipped him a package of peanut butter crackers and a cup of coffee. He skipped the crackers and downed the rancid brew. Revived somewhat, he ran his hand through his hair and stretched his legs. What he wouldn't do for a shower.

He turned to Veronica and thanked her for the java. For a woman who'd hung in there as long as day-old bread, she still looked remarkably fresh.

"My crew. Do you know where—"

"Vin snuck into his brother's room and fell asleep in a chair," Veronica said. "The rest of the guys never left the cafeteria."

Devlin stood and peered out the window. Fog ensconced the terra cotta rooftops and cobblestone streets of the old city. Bands of first light played across the clouds, daring to penetrate the haze, but Verona remained asleep.

"Ryan Hunter-Reay called to check on Scotti's status. Thought you might like to know," she said. "The two really hit it off in Monza. All the guys did. In fact, your crew in Monza arrived while you slept. They also crashed the dining hall."

He realized that he was still clutching the crackers. Famished, he tugged at the wrapper with fumbling hands.

Veronica took his hand and pressed a gift into his open palm. A stainless steel box cutter with the words "Jack Daniel's" inscribed on the side stared up at him. The blade sliced through the wrapper like a scalpel through flesh. "Where the hell did you find this?" he asked, outwardly impressed.

She smiled, lowered the tip of the blade back inside its safety sheath, and slid the cutter into her back pocket. "My dad. Owned a liquor store outside Boston. Carried that blade everywhere. He'd forget he had it. Until he needed it." She looked off toward the window. "When I first left home and hit the circuit, he gave me this one, his favorite."

Devlin nodded. "Let me guess…he told you to watch your ass. So you keep it in your back pocket."

"Exactly."

For a few minutes, they nibbled some cracker squares. Then he asked, "How is it that you ended up driving Scotti to Verona from Monza in the first place?"

"My cousin's staying in Montepulciano for a week with friends. They invited me to join them," Veronica said.

Devlin sat up. "I had no idea. You've been tremendous, but if you need to go—"

She raised her hand again. "My cousin wishes Scotti a full and speedy recovery. The folks in Montepulciano understand completely. I'll head down there when I'm good and ready." She winked.

He liked this woman.

He peered outside the window again. Sunshine flittered across the rooftops, and a warm glow overpowered the dissipating fog.

Veronica left to freshen up, and Devlin paced the room. He toyed with the idea of sneaking a visit into the ICU, but he stalled when his phone vibrated. Panic struck when he saw that his son was calling him at five in the morning.

"Marcello, *dimme*, what's wrong, *figlio*?" Devlin shut the door for privacy. "Are you hurt?"

A giggle on the other end. "Lucky, I'm fine. Chill, dude," Marcello said.

Mischief was back. Devlin smiled. "What are you up to?"

"I'm taking all of Filomena's underpants and Nonno's socks out of the laundry basket, and I'm putting them in the freezer." Devlin heard the freezer door shut, followed by more of his son's stifled giggles.

Devlin couldn't help laughing. "Marcello, that's an awesome prank. But what are you doing up so early?"

"Lupo, Filomena and Nonno tucked me in last night. They told me about Scotti's heart, and how he got it fixed, and that he's okay." He heard Marcello pause to take a drink, followed by a small belch. "I know Scotti always calls you early in the morning. But he probably can't talk right now. I wanted to make you feel better, so I called you instead."

Devlin put his hand to his mouth and squeezed his eyes shut to keep himself together. Paternal love threatened to crush him.

Marcello continued, "After I dialed you, I found the basket of underwear. And things got outta hand." He laughed. "I can't wait to tell Tonio and Gio. I'm going over to their house later…maybe we can put their parents' stuff in the freezer too!"

He collected himself. "I thought you were feeling…a little down…about camp. You sound much better."

"Lucky, I'm sorry I acted like a baby. You know when I get tired, I get kinda crabby. Plus…camp really sucked. It was soooo boring. Everything they tried to teach me, I already learned it all from you in the Grotto."

He beamed.

"I'm gonna ask Tonio and Gio if they want to start our own camp. So we can teach kids really cool stuff. Like the kinda stuff your crew does. So, um, I love you, but…you don't have to rush home anymore. I might be kinda busy, ya know. Just come home when you're ready."

At that moment, Marcello's resilience, wit, and enthusiasm bolstered his spirit more than ever. "I understand, *amore*. I'll just finish up a few things here and head back soon," Devlin said.

"'Kay, Nonno's coming …gotta go…love you, bye!"

After another giggle, the call ended, and Devlin felt ready for his own bit of mischief. To hell with visitation hours. Time to ambush the ICU.

He grabbed his backpack and meandered down the hall. He paused at the drinking fountain outside Scotti's unit to scout the area. Snoring emanated from the room. A single nurse at the station grabbed a file, and she shuffled down the hall in the opposite direction before disappearing into a room.

He slinked into Scotti's room. The bed was hidden behind a curtain. Devlin spotted Vin sitting in a wooden chair in the corner, snoring like a buzz saw. Scotti must have been used to it growing up, because when Devlin pulled back the curtain, he was sleeping peacefully.

Devlin picked up Scotti's chart and checked his vitals. Steady progress over the last few hours, he was relieved to see. Then he gazed at the man lying in the hospital bed. Down, but not out, this warrior, his hero.

A snort and a gurgle behind him made him turn. Vin stretched, glimpsed Devlin, and smiled. "He's doing okay," Vin said. He yawned and stood. "When they check on him, I pretend I'm asleep in case they toss me. But they murmur positive things under their breath about his improvement."

Devlin patted him on the back. "You're a great brother."

Vin nodded. "He's lucky to have you, too. I need a coffee run. You want some?"

Devlin declined, and Vin left. He took the seat that Vin had left vacant, and he pulled it next to the bed. He grasped Scotti's hand. He always knew it to be strong and capable. Now it felt heartbreakingly weak and fragile. Oxygen tubes trailed into Scotti's nostrils. Tubes ran into his arms. But his spirit appeared stable and robust, as warmth colored his cheeks and REM sleep animated his lids.

Scotti's doctor entered. She appeared startled by his presence. But Devlin wasn't ready to leave. "Please, just give me a few more minutes," he said.

The doctor smiled. "The nurses are getting ready to move him out of ICU. Good surgery, no complications. He's had a good night, no issues. He'll have to stay in the hospital about a week, but so far, he's doing well. The man is strong as an ox. But be sure to keep the ox on a low-fat, low-carb, low-salt diet, will you? You just might get to keep him around awhile."

Emotion overwhelmed him once more.

"Take your time," the doctor told him. "I'll come back in a little while."

He nodded and smiled his thanks, and she left the room. After the situation involving Ella's death and Marcello's run-in with danger, he wondered if he could've endured losing Scotti.

"You've looked better, son," Scotti mumbled in a hoarse voice. It sounded like a haze of pain meds was making him reasonably comfortable, and even more direct than usual. A smile crept over Scotti's face, and Devlin grasped the man's hand even harder.

"You've had a heart attack. But the doctor said you'll be okay."

"Of course I will. I'm not done here yet," Scotti said. He pulled his other hand across his body, winced, and placed it atop Devlin's. "Sorry I'm such a pain in the ass."

Devlin smiled. “I’m used to it.” He gestured to the machines. “They’re moving you out of this room soon, into one that doesn’t beep and blink so much. Then you get to hang around for about a week or so. Doctor says you’re strong as an ox.”

“Strong like you. Only you don’t know it,” Scotti said.

“I know I’m strong enough to muscle you home, old man. And force-feed you a reasonable diet from now on.”

“Don’t you dare bring up the notion of whole-wheat pasta again…I will take you down,” Scotti said.

“Calm yourself. Don’t start your heart pumping more than it has to,” Devlin said. “I’m taking you back home and making sure—”

“You will do no such thing,” Scotti said. “You’ve got a job to do. And it’s not finished.”

“Oh, I’m done. With this job, with racing. You people need me, and I’ve been—”

“You’ve been living, finally,” Scotti said. “That’s what we’ve needed you to do. Now get to it.” A little too much color rushed to Scotti’s face, and Devlin feared riling him. He checked the vitals again, but all appeared normal.

Scotti nodded toward Devlin’s backpack on the floor beside the chair. “You carry that thing around with you everywhere you go?”

“Took it with me from the vineyard. I’m taking you home to Siena after you’re well enough to travel. The bag has all the evidence I’ve collected. I plan to give it to—”

"Don't even say the words 'local police' for Pete's sake. You know better. Now show me what you have," Scotti said.

Devlin laid it all out, from the bullet casings to the syringes. He went through each specimen, providing Scotti with background on all of it. "Bottom line: while Aurora's hashing out their water rights and family issues, someone's busy trying to usurp the company. They don't need me to figure it all out. In fact, I think dysfunction is the driving force of that company."

"But your racing colleague, Giancarlo, is dead. Runa Aurora is dead. Some perp shot at you and Erika. Someone blew up Vitreuve's water plant. These Aurora people may end up killing each other. Or an outsider may kill them all. You have to do something about it, Lucky. This isn't like you to walk away."

Devlin shook his head. "My family is my responsibility. And my family needs—"

"Your family needs you to be true to yourself." Scotti waited a few seconds for the concept to sink in. "Ella was killed. But there was nothing you could've done to prevent it. She's dead. And you can't live your life as if the things you do or don't do are going to bring her back. Stop being afraid to live your life, just because she's gone."

Devlin stood abruptly, knocking his chair to the floor. He walked into the hall, ran his hands through his hair. He squeezed the muscles in his neck to ensure blood was flowing to his brain. Because, clearly, Scotti felt that he wasn't thinking right.

After a few minutes, his hunched shoulders relaxed. Then he sauntered back into the room.

"Give me the book," Scotti said.

Devlin shot him a puzzled look.

"The book, in your pack. I just saw it when you rifled through the evidence. The book that Ella gave you on your wedding day," Scotti said. "Read the inscription again."

He pulled the copy of *Pentamerone*, Basile's fairy tale collection, from his pack. He opened it and reread the handwritten inscription inside the front flap. "*I would not wish any companion in the world but you*," it read.

"Ella loved Shakespeare, you know that," Scotti said.

He smiled. "She memorized every word of every play."

"By that logic, Ella would've been acutely aware of other significant quotes from *The Tempest*. How about, 'He that dies pays all debts'?"

He waited for an explanation.

"Ella's gone. She's debt-free," Scotti said. "Wouldn't your wife wish you to be free of all debts, too? Unencumbered by this guilt you've developed about moving on with your life, and living it to its fullest."

Devlin shrugged. "She'd be pissed if she knew I was acting like this." Dumping a mission before its successful completion. Avoiding relationships for fear of offending the dead. Worrying about things that were outside of his control.

Ella never would've married a man who carried on like that. She'd be destroyed if she knew that she was the reason for it. *If you love me, let me go*, she would've told him instead. He looked at the inscription. Maybe she already had.

"Here's one more quote from the play to chew on: 'We are such stuff as dreams are made on; and our little life is rounded with a sleep.'"

Devlin must have looked at Scotti like he'd grown three heads. Scotti chuckled and said, "Ella use to read Shakespeare aloud to Marcello when she was pregnant with him. I caught on."

Devlin nodded.

"All things come to an end," Scotti said. "Don't be afraid of falling apart. You already did that. Now you need to put yourself back together. Ella never had the chance to fully live out her life. Shouldn't you honor hers by living yours to its fullest?"

He closed his eyes. After a while, he opened them. He smiled at the strong, willful man before him. Scotti had saved him once, following tragic circumstances in Devlin's early life. Today, even as Scotti edged back from the precipice of death, he'd saved him again.

He grasped the man's shoulder. "Scotti, I…"

Scotti clasped his arm. "I know. Me too."

Vin arrived with the doctor, two nurses, and a gurney. "Your pit crew has arrived," Vin told Scotti. "Let's get you moving."

Devlin packed Ella's book, and the evidence, back into his bag. "Let's get you settled into your new room, old man. Then, the HELL Rangers and I are running across town to the summit." Scotti stared up at him, a smile edging up the corners of his mouth.

"I'm finally confronting Erika Aurora with the evidence against her," Devlin said. "And I plan to get answers."

Chapter 29

Dante Alighieri has nothing on Lupo, Ana Malia thought, gazing at the statue of the lovelorn poet standing in the Veronese Piazza dei Signori.

In the semidarkness before sunrise on the cool, crisp morning in June, the journalist had paused her morning run to stop and smell the cappuccino, and she compared the two men.

Dante spoke to her mind through his powerful verse. Lupo touched her heart like no other man ever had. Lupo also touched her in places that Dante never could. She missed Lupo, working so hard to assemble the perfect Palio activities hundreds of miles away in Siena. She couldn't wait to finish her assignment and wrap her arms and legs around him. Just a few more days. Until then, Dante's quill would have to suffice.

Ana jogged past the gloriously intact Roman amphitheater in the heart of the old city center. She passed through the sixteenth-century Porta Nuova stone gateway that separated the old world from the modern industrial outskirts. Past the wall, she turned south down the Via delle Nazioni thoroughfare toward the Veronafiere event center, just off the autostrada highway.

The BBC had stationed her at a motel about a block away from the south end of the convention center. Populated with members of the press, low-level academics, research speakers, and technologists, this cold-water-only establishment stood in sharp contrast to the plush oasis that adjoined the convention center on the north end.

Ana preferred the oasis. She'd paid a hefty premium to change her reservation because she believed that to get a story, you had to follow the money. This hotel housed the summit's royalty—top-level corporate execs, bankers, investors, lawyers, trade ministers, and delegates from over seventy countries. The establishment catered to the upper crust, people like Erika and Leif Aurora, of Aurora Vineyard. And Philippe's mother, Marisse LeFleau, head of Toujours leather company. Sting, Leonardo DiCaprio, and former United States Vice President Al Gore also topped the list for the duration.

Ana jogged to her room and showered with the hotel's luxurious peppermint body gel. She brushed her teeth, blotted her lipstick, and tucked her trinket gun and permit into the top of her skirt. Though security would be tight at this global event, nowhere is ever secure enough. She firmly believed that the only way to stop a bad guy with a gun was a good guy with a gun. Personal experience had proved that.

***

Ana Malia and her camerawoman, Letizia, crossed the street to the rear of the convention center. The only door open here at the crack of dawn was the media entrance. She always arrived for the pregame show, hopeful to snag that rare early-morning interview. At a global water summit, awash with world leaders eager to get their hands muddy, the early bird was bound to turn up a lot of worms. She flashed their credentials and then acquiesced to a satisfying pat-down that provided more action than she'd seen in over a week.

Ana had only drunk three cups of coffee so far, so she and Letizia stopped at a food cart parked between two immense lecture halls off the main atrium. One hall focused on new frontiers in desalination, and the other on technology in the wastewater revolution. She spied one of the main speakers, Dr. Abdulmaran Al-Ibrahim. The sheik ran Salina Water Conversion, a massive conglomerate, and he was just arriving with his entourage.

Ana groped around in her bag for her tape recorder, and kept groping. Where the hell was her recorder, and damn it, where was her phone? How much had she and Letizia drunk last night? She never should've downed that second bottle.

She wished Erika Aurora had joined them last evening. She and Erika had been known to party hard in the past. But the Aurora CEO hit the sack early after dropping Devlin at the hospital. She'd allayed Ana's fears over Scotti's condition and then turned in. Clearly, Ana should have followed suit.

Ana left Letizia behind to arrange an interview with Amal Clooney. Then she ran back to the hotel as fast as her Gucci heels would carry her. In her room, Ana gathered her iPhone, tape recorder, and a handful of mints. She swigged from a FONS water bottle nestled in the ice bucket, locked her door, and dashed to the stairs. When she passed the spa door, she promised herself a treatment later that night.

Suddenly, a woman's scream from behind the sauna room door startled her. Another scream, louder than the first, was sharply cut off to a muffled cry.

Ana dropped her bag. She palmed her Beretta Nano and grabbed the door handle. Locked. Or rather, impeded. Someone had shoved something heavy against it.

Ana kicked off her heels, braced herself, and shoved hard with her left side. The weight behind the door barely budged. Her left shoulder groaned with pain, but she slammed against the door harder. Something bulky, like an armoire or shelf, scraped along the sauna's tile floor. She pushed again and forced a larger opening that released a wave of steam from inside the room. But not large enough for Ana to slip through.

The woman cried out again.

"Hold on, let me get help," Ana shouted.

"Ana, please, someone's trying to—" The woman's voice inside abruptly halted its plea, as if she'd been struck. It was Erika Aurora.

Adrenaline shot through Ana like fire. She summoned every bit of strength, took a running start, and slammed the full weight of her body against the sauna room door.

The blockade budged, just enough. Now with the 9mm thrust in front of her, Ana finagled herself into the room, low to the carpeted floor. As she did, she heard a door slam shut further inside the impenetrable fog of steam.

On her knees, Ana quickly gauged her surroundings. With visibility clearer down low, she figured the area to be a ten-by-ten waiting room. She spied an inner door, wide open and billowing hot vapor—the steam room. Beside the open door, she spotted Erika Aurora sprawled on the floor.

Erika lay on her back in a robe, unconscious, her head lolled to one side. A few feet away from her, another woman lay on the floor beside a clearly marked exit. She was also dressed in a bathrobe, with a towel wrapped around her hair. She was facedown and groaning.

Ana crawled to Erika and knelt beside her, checked her pulse. Alive.

Ana pivoted on one knee, the gun pointed toward the inner sanctum of the sauna. Ana could not assume that the door she'd heard slam was the attacker leaving through the exit. Instead, the perp might've stupidly cornered him or herself inside the steam room. She crept quietly to the spa's threshold, prepared to shoot if necessary.

But the other female victim who was lying on the floor began to speak. Trying to catch her breath, the woman spoke slowly, in English laced with a French accent. "The bastard ran out the exit. He's gone."

The victim sat up, braced herself with one hand against the wall. She rubbed the back of her neck with other, kneading a spot beneath her toweled head, and groaned again. "Came out of the sauna. Walked in on them in the waiting room. He'd blocked the main door with the chest of drawers. He stood behind her, with his hands around her neck. Erika was struggling. He knocked her out when I came in. Tried to turn on me, but—"

The woman finally turned to face her. Ana's eyes widened with surprise. Marisse LeFleau.

"I kicked him in the privates very well." The Frenchwoman smiled. She gathered herself and stood erect, straightened her robe. "Then you, my dear, must have scared him away, thank goodness. He threw me against the wall, and he ran." The woman's lip quivered, and tears sprang to her eyes.

Ana stood and embraced her. "Thank you, Marisse, for saving Erika."

***

Ana ensured that the hallway beyond the emergency exit was clear. She stooped low beside Marisse, who was stroking Erika's hair. Ana called her friend's name. Erika's head rolled to the side, and her eyes fluttered open. She winced and reached for her forearm.

Marisse grasped the arm and rubbed it for her. "There, there, *ma chère*, you must bc so sore from the awful man's rough handling." Marisse rubbed the other arm, too, and then cradled Erika into a hug and patted her back.

Ana had no idea that the French were so affectionate.

Marisse rocked Erika a few more moments in a motherly fashion, settled her head on a towel, and then excused herself to the restroom to change.

Ana continued to call out Erika's name, while the fallen woman slowly regained consciousness. When she finally appeared lucid, Erika's body trembled, and she struggled to focus on Ana's face. Ana seethed with rage at how hard the attacker must have hit her defenseless friend to provoke such a terrified reaction.

All at once, Erika's eyes rolled back into her head. Frothing saliva dribbled from the corner of her mouth. Her trembling body suddenly convulsed with violent spasms. Erika was having a seizure.

***

Ana had all but dropped Erika to the floor as she'd raced to dial emergency on the spa phone. Ana had shouted for Marisse's help, and she'd come running.

In mere minutes, an ambulance was transporting them to the Verona hospital down the street. Ana dialed Devlin on the ride over and asked him to meet her at admissions. "What happened?" he asked when they arrived.

Sitting amid the rows of waiting room chairs, Marisse relayed the story of the attack on her and Erika in the spa room. Through it all, Devlin patted Marisse's shoulder, conveying his sympathy.

Ana finished the story, pacing back and forth along the worn linoleum, and told him about the seizure in the spa room, as well as the subsequent one in the ambulance.

He gawked at her.

"Devlin, what's the matter?" Ana had witnessed only a few of the significant peaks and valleys of Devlin's life. But that short span of time had brought with it a real understanding of the man's character. Right now, something was up.

Devlin shook his head and stood up from his plastic chair. "Lucky you were there for her, Marisse, to protect Erika from her attacker." He turned to Ana. "Thank God you came when you did."

Ana saw something flicker in his eyes. Clarity.

He offered Marisse his hand. "I believe that you require some medical attention, as well. That bump on your head could indicate a concussion." Marisse instinctively touched her forehead and winced. Devlin led her toward the nurses' station, where a nurse immediately sat Marisse in a wheelchair and began checking her vitals.

Devlin strode back to Ana. "Are you going to be alright?"

"Lucky, I'm fine," Ana said. "But my friend is in there fighting for her life right now. You look like you know something about that. What the hell's going on?"

"I need to find Vin," Devlin said. "Erika's going to continue having seizures until one proves fatal. If she's been poisoned with the same formula as Giancarlo and Runa, then Vin's the only one who can save her."

***

Minutes later, Devlin and Vin came running down the hospital corridor. Ana led them to Erika's emergency unit. Devlin busted into the room, where dozens of doctors were attempting to save Erika's life.

They'd been in there for over half an hour and had yet to provide Ana any news. Whatever Devlin was doing in there now, she hoped he'd at least come back with some intel.

Ana paced, and Vin tapped away on his keyboard. She stared at the floor, running through highlights of the relationship she shared with Erika over the past few years. They hadn't known each other long. Circumstances involving the artful manipulation of money and men had joined them in an enduring bond of Sisterhood. She toyed with the Astrale watch firmly clasped to her elegant wrist that symbolized their connection. She prayed that her Sister in crime would make it through her ordeal, through sick and sin.

A thought occurred to her. She turned to Vin. "Forgive me, I'm so selfish. How is Scotti? Devlin told me he made it safely through the surgery. Is he doing alright?"

Vin smiled shyly. "Don't fret. You have a lot on your plate right now. He's doing well. Thank you."

Ana smiled. She gestured toward the ER. "Any idea what Devlin's doing in there?"

"Your friend may have been poisoned with methanol and suffered an overdose, leading to the seizures. It's likely the same poison that was used to murder Giancarlo Venchi and Runa Aurora. Based on our findings, I concocted an antidote in the Grotto. Planned to store it in the Aurora lab. When Scotti's heart attack diverted me to the hospital, I brought it with me," Vin said.

"Wow. Lucky for Erika," she said. "Thank you."

Minutes later, Devlin exited the ER's double doors. For a brief moment before they swung shut, Ana spotted Erika resting peacefully atop a gurney. The doctors and the nurses in the room were wiping sweat from their brows and scattering.

Devlin beamed at Ana. "She's going to make it. They're taking her to a room where you can see her in a little while.

Ana exhaled the air that she'd pent up in her lungs while waiting for a miracle. Vin and Devlin had given her one. She hugged them and kissed their cheeks. "Thank you. I'm...speechless."

Devlin hugged her tightly. "That is a first."

***

A short while later, Devlin and Vin checked in on Erika, from whose bedside Ana had refused to budge.

Ana couldn't believe how good Erika looked. The color was back in her face, and she appeared strong. The doctor's prognosis was for a full recovery, though she warned of possible dehydration. With a short-term regimen of fluids and bed rest, Erika's long-term health wouldn't be hindered by the methanol overdose.

From Erika's bedside, Ana called Letizia and filled her in. She promised to return to the summit by noon. In the meantime, she instructed Letizia to watch her back.

When she hung up, Vin was describing the antidote cocktail to Devlin and Erika. "Fomepizole, sodium carbonate, folic acid…"

"And a touch of platinum?" Erika said. "Why's that?"

"I felt it was only right to mirror the original," Vin said. "And, still there are no side effects or complications?"

"So far so good," Erika said. She gingerly reached for Vin's hand. "I owe you my life." She looked at Ana and Devlin. "All of you. If you two hadn't been there…and Marisse. She really came through for me." Erika leaned back against her pillow and sighed heavily. "Asshole ambushed me in my goddamn skivvies. I didn't know what hit me. Never even saw the asshole's face. When I find out…"

"Easy, girl. Rest now," Ana said. "You sure you don't want me to call Leif? Let him know what's happened to his big sister?"

"No way. He left me to go skiing. He's due back by tomorrow morning for the convention. When he returns, I'll lay on him the biggest guilt trip ever." Erika sat up straight in her bed. "Speaking of the summit, I need to get out of here. I have work to do. Shipments to coordinate…"

"Plenty of time for that later." Devlin rested his hand on Erika's shoulder and gently eased her back to the pillow. "You need rest. You have a phone. Coordinate with your staff from here, where the doctors can keep an eye on you."

Erika yawned. "You're right. I need a nap. When I wake, I'm downing a whole pan of lasagna and then going over to the summit to work. Come hell or high water."

Devlin smiled. "Deal. And like you asked, I've convinced the hospital that you overindulged on booze, rather than suffered a poison attack. They'll release you much quicker, with a lot less paperwork. But the HELL Rangers and I are working to find the bastard that did this. You sure you don't want the police involved?"

Erika shook her head. "No cops. Don't trust them, you know that. It'll unduly influence the court's ruling on the aquifer. Besides, that's why I hired you. Unless…with Scotti, if you can no longer…"

Devlin smiled. "Scotti and I talked. He'd kill me if I quit now. Funny thing is…before the attack, I was planning on laying out my evidence against you. You were my prime suspect, Erika."

Erika gaped at him. "All this time. Even after we…" She blushed and shook her head. "I understand. You were doing your job. And I appreciate your candor. But now, who do you think really is behind all this?"

"I have a few suspects in mind. And with you in the clear, the case against them becomes much stronger." Devlin told her about the syringes he'd found in Leif's office safe, the one to which only Erika allegedly knew the combo.

"Who else could have known the exact date when my family arrived at my father's estate?" Erika shook her head. "Someone else must have cracked the code like you did, Dev. I've been so careful…" Erika trailed off into thought.

"And the syringes?" Erika said. "Someone must have placed the poison in there to frame me, or maybe frame Leif. But who, and why?"

Devlin stood and walked to the window.

After a few moments passed, Erika said, "You think it's my brother, don't you? You found the syringes in his safe, and…well, he's nowhere to be found. Leif says he's off skiing, but is he? Or did my own brother attack me?" Erika swallowed. "Or Philippe? He could have just as easily attacked me, pretending he was away on some mountain. Dear God, I hope Philippe hasn't hurt Leif…or what if…"

Ana looked at Erika's sullen expression and finished her statement for her. "What if Leif and Philippe are in on this together?"

The door to Erika's hospital room opened. Ascari stepped into the room, chomping on an unlit cigar. "You feeling better, little lady?"

"Physically, I'm getting stronger every minute," Erika said.

"That's good. Because your head of security called me," Ascari said. "Told me that your shipment manager thinks something's very wrong. He said that Philippe signed Leif's name for a huge shipment of water headed to the summit. Water that Aurora planned to give away at tonight's opening gala dinner."

"Philippe? Signed for Leif?" Erika said.

Devlin and Ana's eyes met.

Erika swallowed hard. "What if they've tainted Aurora's bottled water with the same formula that they used on me, my sister, and Giancarlo? My own brother and his controlling, loony-activist lover…they're really planning to destroy Aurora."

Erika looked up at Devlin, startled by the even bigger picture at hand. As if reading her mind, he said, "Leif and Philippe plan to poison the world's leaders gathered at the water summit."

Chapter 30

Leif trembled in the bitter wind as he gazed out over the Val de Sole, nearly three thousand meters atop the Presena Glacier. The Tonale pass, less than two hours north of Verona, was among his favorite places for summer skiing, because he and Philippe could still hit a handful of off-piste runs in June. Summer or not, it was still damn cold.

Yesterday evening's escape from his company's overbearing chaos had left him thoroughly drained. He'd met Philippe at their chalet, had had rough, angry sex for awhile, and then crashed dead asleep. So it wasn't until late this morning that he and Philippe had hit the slopes. Another gust chilled him, and he remembered the flask of grappa in his backpack. He felt around for it near the bottom of the pack, anxious to ward off the cold with a few long gulps of sweet grappa nectar.

Philippe had finished adjusting his Tyrolia binding. He now stood upright, one hand on his hip. "Are you going to be able to ski the eight kilometers to the lodge? Or do I have to wrap you in a thermal blanket and drag you down?" Philippe lowered his goggles.

Leif smiled behind his balaclava. He adored Philippe, right down to the sarcasm that dripped from his lips like warm absinthe. "I'm freezing," Leif said. "My nipples are like rocks, and the rest of my extremities have shrunken to a quarter of their normal size."

"Mine too, but you don't see me shaking like a leaf."

Leif rolled his eyes. "A few sips of grappa will set me right." He finally located the monogrammed stainless steel flask and yanked it from its stronghold beneath a mass of tangled extra gloves. "I know better than to ask if you want some. We'll get you some hot cocoa back at the lodge."

"*Très bien,*" Philippe said. "Missed you this morning. Rolled over around three and found the bed empty."

Leif nodded. "Couldn't sleep. Too much on my mind. Drove for a while."

Philippe smiled. "Me too. Driving clears the conscience." Philippe spat into the snow. "Glad you're joining me for a morning ski run. Hoped you hadn't bailed on me. Lovely to see your handsome face on the tram this morning."

Leif winked at him.

Philippe nudged Leif and pointed to the inlet off the Noce River. "On your way down, snap a picture of that bountiful water source. May be the last we see of it after Erika's finished hoarding all the resources in the Dolomites."

Philippe was a drama queen. Ever since the reporter Ana Malia had blabbed about the Italian court lifting the aquifer injunction, his partner had been incorrigible. Last night, Leif had pulled into the resort lot with such high hopes for relaxation. But from the moment they'd met up at the chalet, Philippe had insisted on ranting about Aurora's involvement in the summit. Thus the rough angry sheet-twister, followed by the escapist sleep therapy, topped off by his early-morning roguery.

Leif removed his gloves and unscrewed the cap. "I know you're upset. But the decision about private use or free public consumption of the aquifer…it's up to the courts. There's nothing we can do. So let's enjoy our quick jaunt before the convention." Leif uncapped the flask. He lifted it for a swig, but Philippe's reaction stayed his hand.

Philippe lifted his goggles and glared at him. "The summit is where we need to make our point. Force our agenda down the throats of those who don't understand. That work that you escaped from…the coordination of 'boutique water' shipments…all to impress water resource leaders—it's devil's work. Rather than enabling transport, you and I need to sabotage those shipments of FONS. We should give those summit representatives something they'll really remember."

Leif stared at Philippe, startled by his sudden vitriol.

Philippe continued, "The act of bottling water and selling it is vulgar. Especially when there are humans unable to obtain fresh, clean water. Seventy percent of the Earth's surface is covered with water. Only two-and-a-half percent of it is fresh water. And less than one percent is easily accessible…"

"I'm aware," Leif said.

"This minuscule percentage includes *your* aquifer. Shouldn't everyone have a free, natural right to drinking water? The fact that Aurora sits on this water source and hoards it, wastes it, and charges for it…that's obscene. And that doesn't even touch your wine production, where four hundred bottles of water are needed to produce just one bottle of wine. How do you live with that, Leif?"

Leif carefully placed his hand on Philippe's chest. He hoped this amiable gesture would calm his activist lover, and prepare Philippe for his reasonable rebuttal. Leif countered, "It would be obscene if we polluted it, which we're not. Also obscene if we refused to tap into it at all. Rather, we're protecting it, bottling it, and sharing it with whoever chooses to drink our brand."

Another aerial tram arrived. It released three skiers, including a mountain ranger, only a few feet away from them at the top of the slope.

Philippe replaced his goggles over his eyes. He shimmied the straps of his ski poles into his grasp.

Leif lowered his voice and continued, "You know I've engineered a revolutionary way to make our wine and spirits without wasting a single drop of the water. Based on the Coca-Cola model of water conservation, out of the billions of gallons of water we employ each year, Aurora returns the equivalent of ninety-six percent of it back to nature. And we're on track to reach ninety-nine percent by next year. Whatever we don't consume in our clean, filtered process simply flows back into the land and is reused."

"You should be giving it away!" Philippe shouted. The ranger glanced over at them. Leif waved an apology for the disturbance. Philippe said, "You're impeding a societal movement toward free access to freshwater. You should be ashamed of your corporate theft."

Leif didn't feel the cold anymore. His blood had risen to a boil. "I am not a thief. Aurora is offering up its reserve for a cost, just like the providers of electricity, natural gas, oil, propane, you name it..."

Philippe smirked. "Oh, please. My mother says the same thing about her precious leather being a salable natural resource, too. Water is a vital asset that the world can't possibly live without. It should be free."

Leif shook his head in disagreement. "Water is a resource that should be preserved and regulated for the benefit of the world. But there's a cost associated with protecting and distributing it. Why shouldn't Aurora reclaim our cost, and also profit from our marketing and research?"

Philippe inhaled sharply, but Leif cut him off.

"Hear me out," Leif said. "Twenty years ago, almost to the day, the earth shook and water sprang from a crevice beneath my family's feet. I remember it because it scared me to death. Sometimes it still does. Our family was granted a gift. And I feel a tremendous responsibility to conserve this indispensable gift and to provide it to anyone who wants to procure it for a cost. Just like an artist might do with the gift of his voice. I accept the responsibility, and I will own it until the day I die."

Leif raised the flask to his mouth, but stopped to look his lover in the eyes. "Whether you like it or not."

Philippe gasped.

Leif wondered, *Have I gone too far?* He loved his company, and he'd always butted heads with Erika over her need to maintain Aurora's bottom line. He consistently pushed for strict conservation methods in their company's production. He urged Erika, and formerly Runa, to consider new and exciting water protection and replenishment projects all over the world. Her reckless lack of consideration in water usage exasperated him at every turn. Leif dreamed of the day when he might run the company in a more socially responsible manner, without her intolerable intervention.

But where he'd once felt buttressed by Philippe's support the past couple of years, Leif felt stifled. Philippe had become an increasingly staunch activist, especially in light of the summit. Philippe no longer believed in progress. Instead he embraced anarchy, both in his speech and in his methods. Leif recalled the explosion at Vitreuve's water-bottling plant, and another shiver coursed through him. Perhaps he and Philippe had reached an impasse. Something had to give.

Leif tossed his head back and ingested a gulp of the fiery grappa down his gullet. "I love my company, and I'm prepared to do whatever it takes to protect it."

Philippe leaned in close. "You sound just like your wretched sister. It's barbaric what you're saying… raping the land of its resource, hoarding a life source from the rightful masses, whoring your wares to the highest bidder. Water deserves another destiny, and I plan to be the one who leads the fight against you. No matter what."

Chapter 31

Devlin returned from Erika's private hospital room to find that nearly a dozen pit crew members had stationed themselves wall to wall around Scotti's room, in full-on strategy mode. The HELL Rangers' headquarters had come to Verona. Computers, maps, and diagrams were strewn about the room. But Devlin's pride in their proactive thinking was supplanted by his grave concern for Scotti's health.

He glared at the heart attack patient. "What the hell, Scotti? You just had surgery." He spotted Vin lower his head, and he pointed his finger at him. "You did this."

Vin stood. "I take full responsibility. My brother ordered me to gather the troops for this mission, and I did it. Or else he'd kill me."

Scotti spoke up. "I could not be more proud of him. Vincenzo stepped up, got the job done." He gestured to the crew. "They're all staying, because it makes me feel better. End of story. Move on." He crossed his arms, signaling resolution of the matter.

Clenching his fists, Devlin opened his mouth to sling a retort. But he glanced over at Veronica Griffith, who leaned against the wall trying hard to fight off laughter.

Devlin shook his head and sighed. He ambled over to an empty chair, turned it around, and sat down hard. "Okay, man, I'll play your game." He winked at Scotti and continued. "Based on recent developments, Erika Aurora is no longer a viable suspect. She's a target. Based on our evidence, the theory that someone's picking off Aurora's chief officers is extremely plausible. Whether someone's either overtaking or sabotaging the company…it's still unclear.

"Erika previously denied protection. In light of her attack, she's reconsidered." Devlin focused his gaze on Ascari. "Until Rasmus shows up, you stick to her like glue."

"Where's Erika now?" Ascari said.

"She developed a fever," Devlin said. "The doctors are running tests for the next hour. When she gets back to her room, either you or I will always have eyes on her."

Ascari nodded affirmation.

"Also, this case may have more far-reaching consequences—the water summit," Devlin said. "It's possible whoever poisoned Erika and Runa, and for whatever reason Giancarlo Venchi, may have sabotaged a shipment of Aurora FONS. That's their line of bottled water. It was sent to the water convention last night."

"Did the organizers confiscate all Aurora water shipments?" Scotti asked.

"Aurora is an official sponsor, so their wine and spirit product lines pass through standard security protocol," Devlin said. "For the past couple weeks, all shipments have been safely checked and warehoused in the convention center pending the summit's commencement."

Scotti nodded.

"In the last couple days, though, Aurora was given the green light to distribute their FONS water," Devlin said. "After Erika greased a few palms, the organizers allowed exceptions to the protocol, and they allowed last-minute deliveries."

"Shit," Vin said.

"Luckily, Rasmus spied Leif's forged signature on last night's drops," Devlin said. "Rasmus contacted convention organizers, and they canceled them. Rasmus confirmed those shipments never made it off their delivery trucks. Aurora's warehouse intercepted it, and they plan to quarantine those pallets for testing. His team is now scrutinizing all outgoing product from their shipping warehouse."

"I think we ought to partner up with the convention's security team, as well as the Aurora detail," Scotti said.

"Agreed," Devlin said.

"Where's Hamilton, by the way?" Scotti asked.

"Traveling. Switzerland, San Remo, France…" Devlin said. "He's gathering intel. I acted on a hunch a while back. Hoping it might pan out. I'll let you know."

Scotti nodded.

Devlin continued, “Now, here’s what we know about the perp…”

“Or perps,” Ascari interjected.

“Exactly.” Devlin nodded. “Our culprit may have acted alone, or partnered up. There’s a lot we don’t know. But here’s what we do know…

“Number one on our agenda is to track down the whereabouts of Leif Aurora and Philippe LeFleau.”

Chapter 32

At what point had our chemistry turned to poison? Leif wondered as he stared into Philippe's cold expression at the top of the mountain.

Leif recalled the time Philippe's mom had dropped off her son outside the couple's newly acquired cottage just off ECLA's main campus after winter break.

Leif had stood in the doorway, peering through the falling snow. His heart had nearly burst at the sight of him. Philippe had stepped from his mother's limousine in his bright red faux-leather cowboy boots, ankle-deep in fresh granular and his arms outstretched. Their romantic chemistry had never made Leif feel more alive than at that moment.

Now atop the Dolomite mountain, again standing face-to-face in the falling snow, Leif realized that their once-magical formula had turned toxic.

A tremor coursed through Leif's body. Had it grown colder since he'd first peered into his lover's gaze? Tanned, rugged, and framed by locks of gold, Philippe's face had once promised love and acceptance. That same visage now glared back at him with malice and contempt.

Leif tipped back another gulp of grappa to warm himself. He shuddered when he replayed Philippe's noxious phrases in his mind: *wretched like his sister…barbaric…raping the land…whoring his wares…*

And the worst thing? Philippe had vowed to fight against him, no matter what.

Bile rose in Leif's mouth, literally. It burned his esophagus worse than the grappa he'd just imbibed. His realization that they'd transitioned from romantic witchcraft into vile devilry must've triggered a psychosomatic reaction. Leif truly felt sick.

His body tensed, spasmed, and then tightened again. He crouched, his innards recoiling. His facial muscles contorted. His whole body shook. It was so much worse than just the effects of the freezing cold. Even worse than his shock-induced trembling when his father had died.

Philippe glided backward a few strides away from him on his skis. He huffed, clearly appalled at Leif's reaction. Leif's physicality must have signaled that he was grimacing at his lover, and crouching low in preparation to ski away from their confrontation.

But Philippe was reading him wrong. Leif fought to open his mouth, or shake his head, or reach out, but his body refused to obey his mind's commands. Philippe turned to leave, but Leif was unable to stop him. He was having a seizure.

Leif felt his throat closing, though the bile continued to burn through it to his mouth. His saliva had kicked into overdrive, and Leif feared drowning behind the mask of his balaclava. His fists, now viselike arthritic claws, gripped his ski pole in one hand and his grappa flask in the other. He was unable to drop either one of them and flag Philippe for help. Leif shimmied back and forth on his skis, his body quaking with tremors that threatened to tear him apart. All he could do was stare at Philippe through his goggles, and beckon him with his eyes to please, for the love of God, help him!

Philippe broke his cold stare and turned away from Leif. The Frenchman glided soundlessly to the edge of the tree-lined mountain and thrust his poles into the terrain. With his back to Leif, Philippe said, "We're done."

Would those be the last words he would ever hear Philippe say to him? A violent shudder raced through him, and Leif collapsed to the ground. His muscles contorted and spasmed. He drowned in his own poison. His body had failed him. His lover had failed him. All he could do was lie there and watch Philippe, who was turned away, facing the slope and stretching his back in preparation for the run.

A voice cried out above the bitter wind. Was it another skier from the gondola? Had one of them spotted him? Would they get help? Would the ranger be able to save him before his body gave out?

It didn't matter now. The love of his life had turned his back on him, in every possible way.

As he lay prone, Leif's eyes rolled back in his head. He smelled the loss of control over his bodily functions. Another tremor, worse than any before. Powdery snow fluttered onto his face. He felt it melt on his cheeks. The water trickled over his lips. Funny how this same water from the Dolomites that had transformed his life, now seemingly destroyed his life. Would the taste of it be the last sensation he'd ever register?

Leif's eyes rolled back into place, in line with a view of Philippe. Though his vision had grown hazy and blurry now, Leif prayed that the sight of Philippe would sustain him in his final moments.

Philippe thrust off from the edge, heading toward the moguls that were his favorite part of the glacier. But as Philippe took off, he turned one last time to glance at Leif.

Leif's heart leapt. Philippe had stolen a last look. Something deep inside of Philippe must've forced him to look back. *It's chemistry*, Leif thought. *He may be angry, and we may have grown apart. But there will always be chemistry between us.*

Hands were on him now. The other skiers had gathered about him and were seeking to help him. The ranger thrust a wooden stick into his mouth and uttered commands into a walkie-talkie. Leif couldn't discern the words. He simply locked his gaze on Philippe.

Through the darkening haze of his receding vision, Leif could tell that Philippe finally realized something was amiss. Philippe attempted to halt his forward motion, corrected, then bobbled awkwardly. Bad form, or genuine concern? Leif prayed it was the latter. But no, Philippe was indeed falling. Badly.

Philippe's thrust forward from the edge had clearly packed some speed, because his lumbering correction sent him on a demolition course for the trees. Leif watched in horror as his left leg snagged, and Philippe accelerated wildly toward an enormous pine tree.

Smack!

Leif's whole body shuddered again, as if mimicking the force of Philippe's impact with the pine. He screamed a tortured cry inside his mind as his lover's body collapsed to the ground and lay still.

Leif cursed his shaking body, and he willed Philippe's to move. Another skier raced over to Philippe. She gasped and put her hand to her mouth in despair. Slowly, she looked back at Leif with pity in her eyes.

Leif's eyes rolled back into his head, and he took comfort in that. He no longer wished to see Philippe's broken, lifeless body. Instead he chose to remember the vivacious college activist with the little red cowboy boots and the rugged smile who loved to ski.

In his final breaths, he clung to Philippe's one last look back, all in the name of chemistry.

Chapter 33

Devlin was thrilled to see Erika Aurora back in her street clothes. Rejuvenated by Vin's antidote, a power nap, a clean bill of health for both her and Marisse, and a container of takeout lasagna, Erika Aurora appeared ready for battle.

Marisse had bid them both farewell, with promises to chastise Philippe for dragging Leif away to ski, and to meet up with Erika to share some grappa at the summit dinner.

A short time later, the hospital officially released Erika, too. Devlin outlined the plan that the HELL Rangers had discussed for the past two hours. As he and Erika strolled the corridors back to Scotti's room, suggestions were made, logistics were ironed out, and the plan was ratified.

Things were different between Devlin and Erika. Friendlier, lighter. Not quite so intense. Her siren-like attraction had diminished for him. Now that they were genuinely working together to achieve the same goal, things were more stable, and professional. They both seemed to prefer it this way.

Erika was finally introduced to Scotti, whom she hugged, and Veronica, whom she greeted with a curt nod. Erika sidled up next to Vin and professed endless gratitude for providing her the antidote. While the two told the crew about his lifesaving efforts, Veronica gestured to Devlin to follow her out of the room.

In the privacy of a hallway alcove, Veronica gave him a quick hug, wished him luck with the case, and told him that she'd see him on the circuit.

Devlin had expected that she'd leave once Scotti improved. But he'd never anticipated how crushed he'd feel when she did. Unlike the purely physical attraction that he'd felt toward Erika, his affinity toward Veronica Griffith was based on something more. It went beyond her competitive racing prowess, philanthropy, and physical beauty. What she'd revealed in one of his darkest hours—her selflessness—had meant everything.

"Before I go, I have something for you," Veronica said.

He appreciated the confident way she flung back her long brown hair and slipped her hand into the back pocket of her tight-fitting jeans. He waited for that familiar pang of guilt, but it didn't come. In fact, he could get used to looking at this woman, a lot. He'd never stop loving Ella, who had left their lives too soon. But now he knew that moving toward meaningful relationships felt a hell of a lot better than moving away from them. It's what Ella would've wanted.

Veronica slipped a cold metal object into the palm of his hand. Her Jack Daniel's box cutter.

He looked up into her dark green eyes and shook his head. "Your dad gave this to you. No way I can accept it. Thanks, but—"

She straightened her shoulders, raised an eyebrow, and put up her hand to silence him. "My dad always said it would bring me luck. And it did." She winked. "Now it's yours."

He grasped both her hands in his and accepted the token. He thanked her for everything, and Veronica kissed his cheek. She stepped into the elevator, and before the doors closed, she told him, "Take care of the old man. I plan to kick both your asses next race."

***

Devlin returned to Scotti's room. Erika now stood beside Ascari, her unofficial bodyguard whenever Devlin was detained or until Rasmus arrived. The crew was visibly eager to execute their mission for safeguarding Aurora and catching the mastermind behind the poison formula. As always, he maintained cautious optimism. Personal experience had proved—well-made schemes usually went to shit. Best to prepare for it.

That's why when the call came in from Lupo, he knew something must've gone wrong.

"Ana told me everything," Lupo said. "I'll ask you again…do you want me, Chiara, and Prost to come up to Verona? Help out with Scotti and the summit?"

"Thanks, but no. Much of the gang is already here. Montoya and Helio raced back here from Monza…"

"What'd they do…drive your race car?" Lupo laughed, then got serious. "No, really, did they?"

Devlin shrugged. "They were toting the race trailer from Monza back to Rome. When they got word of Scotti's heart attack, they hauled ass to the hospital." He glanced out Scotti's window to the enormous eighteen-wheeler carrying his Formula One car. It took up an entire row of parking spaces in the lot. His men had character, and expedience. Not a bad crew.

Devlin continued, "Our men that settled that Syrian hostage crisis, they're here now, at the summit. We also have the boys we'd posted at the vineyard, along with the Aurora detail. Don't worry, we got this," he said. "Besides, you've got thousands of spectators about to pour into Piazza del Campo for a horse race and pregame. You can't up and leave the day of the big rehearsal dinner…Siena's mayor would have you shot."

"The insanity has already begun," Lupo said. Devlin put the phone on speaker as Lupo continued, "The streets are packed with people from every contrada, waving their banners and drinking."

Lupo went on, "Chiara and Prost took Marcello to *la tratta*, and Aquila scored a kick-ass horse in the prelim, a real hot racer. Then his grandparents took him over to the Aquila stables and watched the horse get blessed. The jockey shook his hand and now he won't wash it. Marcello's having a ball. He's dressed up in the Aquila garb, even slept in it. May not take it off 'til this whole thing's over."

Devlin laughed out loud. The Aurora family thrived on dysfunction. His family thrived on resilience. He felt ready than ever to take on this mission.

He ended Lupo's call just as Ascari hung up with Rasmus, who'd been coordinating plans to obtain more weapons. But the rattled look on Ascari's face terrified him. Because like his brother before him, Ascari never got rattled.

"We have a situation," Ascari said. "There were shipments of FONS water held in quarantine at the vineyard, in the grappa plant."

"I'm aware of them," Devlin said. "Erika insisted on locking them up after Runa was killed. A few thousand cases of bottled water. And a similar shipment of grappa, too."

Erika nodded.

Vin interjected. "I tested random samples of the water. None of them showed up positive for the formula. But a handful of the grappa bottles did."

"So we quarantined both product lots just to be safe," Erika said.

Devlin nodded. Ascari continued, "Rasmus just told me both restricted lots are gone. Shipped during the night, not by Aurora's crew. Outsourced express courier, who recorded simply that 'an Aurora employee' arranged it."

In the momentary silence that followed, the beeping of Scotti's heart monitor increased its tempo. Scotti was the first to speak. "POTUS and the Brits' prime minister are among the guests of the Italian PM at the summit. Not to mention the thousands of other attendees." He cleared his throat. "We can't just pray they're not thirsty."

Devlin's stomach fell. "Contact convention security. Stop all incoming shipments from Aurora. And halt any and all distribution of the company's product."

Erika stepped forward. "Devlin, be reasonable. Aurora would never recover from an all-out embargo."

He opened his mouth to protest, but Erika pushed forward. "Organizers have been storing our promo distribution of water, grappa, and wine since last month, before any of this even started. Let us at least dispense these shipments among the participants. They're clean."

Erika had a point. The mayhem had begun only as far back as the Monaco race.

After a moment, he said, "Allow disbursement of the time-tested presummit deliveries. Halt any and all distribution of shipments…received in the past two weeks."

Erika pressed her lips together and clenched her fists. But she did not verbally disagree.

Ascari nodded. "Will do. But, Lucky, it gets worse…"

Before he could finish, Marisse rushed into Scotti's hospital room. Disheveled and panting, she struggled to catch her breath. The bruise on her head from the spa incident still appeared red and swollen.

Marisse, holding her side as if to quash a runner's cramp, panned the room until she spotted Erika. "*Mon Dieu*, Erika," she said. "*C'est terrible*! *Vous devez venir rapidement!*"

Erika jumped to her feet, clearly panic-stricken.

Marisse took a deep breath and attempted to collect herself. In a heavy French accent, she said, "I tried to find you. Nurse told me to come here. You must come with me."

Now Ascari got to his feet, since wherever Erika went, he went, according to the plan.

Erika's phone buzzed, and she took the call. A look of abject terror stole across her face. She hung up and quickly informed them. "Leif has been MedFlighted to the hospital. A ski ranger found him on a mountain. They just brought him into the ER. Along with Philippe."

Marisse nodded vehemently. "*Oui*, and Philippe. Let us go there now." Marisse didn't wait. She simply tore off down the hall.

Devlin snagged Erika's hand and tore quickly after Marisse. Running down the flight of stairs, a thought sped through his head.

Back to the emergency room. Was this Aurora as strong a fighter as his sister?

Chapter 34

Devlin barely remembered his mother. He certainly couldn't remember if he'd ever seen her cry. She'd died when he was an adolescent, a tragedy he'd borne courageously like Marcello, with the help of Scotti and the crew. His wife Ella had briefly cried tears of joy at Marcello's birth. And though he'd observed tragic suffering in war-torn countries, he was unaccustomed to the sorrow of a mother with whom he was familiar.

That's why the anguished keening of Marisse LeFleau for her son chilled him like nothing he'd ever heard.

While the medical staff worked feverishly to repair Philippe's maimed body that lay dying inside the ER, Devlin tried in vain to comfort Marisse. He placed his arm around her shoulders, calmed her with consoling words, and offered water, a chair, and a blanket. The distraught woman finally turned to him, politely declined his help, and asked him to leave her alone.

He acquiesced and headed toward Leif Aurora's room. Erika stood outside the windows of the ER unit, watching the doctors treat him.

Erika didn't wail, as Marisse did. She didn't dwell on her little brother's idiosyncrasies or past failings. Instead, she focused on the positive attributes that she so loved about her baby brother, especially growing up. At least, that's what she told Devlin as she fingered the tiny gold crucifix that hung around her neck.

Vin stepped between Devlin and Erika. He held something like an eyeglass case in his hand. Devlin knew that another vial of the lethal formula's antidote lay inside.

A short doctor with large hands who used too much hair dye around the ears exited the room. He handed Erika a stainless steel flask.

"We dislodged this liquor flask from the patient's fist once the seizures dissipated." The doctor sighed, radiating an arrogant disapproval for the patient's reckless behavior. Apparently he was unaware of any poisoning due to the undetectable nature of the lethal serum. He was also unaware of his horrible bedside manner.

The physician continued "The patient imbibed excessive alcohol, resulting in overdose. Seizures, respiratory depression, and vomiting ensued. We administered oxygen and thiamine, a dextrose solution and saline flush, and applied hemodialysis." The doctor's pager beeped, and he silenced it. "The short-term issues are under control…"

Erika inhaled sharply. "My brother's going to be okay?"

He put up his hand and nodded. "I must emphasize this warning: If the patient continues to drink this heavily, the long-term damage from alcohol toxicity could be severe."

Erika exhaled slowly and rubbed her temples. Devlin and Vin exchanged a knowing glance.

"At this point, we've been able to ward off the onset of blindness or liver damage, but we've sent him to the ICU," the doctor said. "He's very weak, and the risk of dehydration is our primary concern right now. We'll need him to stay a few days for observation."

"Can I see him?" Erika said. "Please…"

Her pleading expression pulled on his sympathy muscle. "I'll call the nurse. You have ten minutes before she kicks you out." He spun around and retreated through the double doors.

Vin spoke up. "Erika, let's go see your brother immediately. The antidote should mitigate any residual effects of the poisoning, but we need to administer the serum ASAP."

Poison. The culprit had struck the Aurora clan again.

Erika straightened her shoulders and wiped her eyes. "Let's go, then."

The three sped past another ER unit, empty but for the body on the table and the grieving mother by his side. There, the beeping machines connected to Philippe's body indicated that life still flowed through him. Erika sunk her nails into Devlin's shoulder and muttered, "That's the bastard that tried to kill my family."

Chapter 35

After Vin had administered the antidote to Leif's IV bag, Devlin was nothing less than astonished. Erika and Leif had not only inherited their Nordic mother's external beauty, but more importantly, her Viking mettle.

Both siblings had rocketed to death's door on a lethal methanol-induced roller coaster. Though Leif had nearly plunged across the threshold, the two of them had rebounded well. Erika's ride had thankfully derailed early, and she appeared stronger by the minute. Leif's experience had left him unconscious, vomiting, and dehydrated. But thanks to Nordic genes and Vin's antidote, they both would recover.

Philippe LeFleau was another matter entirely. His bashed face and crippled torso made Devlin wonder how the hell he had survived his ski crash.

Philippe's doctor had told Marisse that the young man's prognosis did not look good. He'd handed the overwrought mother a sedative and escorted her to a bed in a quiet wing down the hall.

Nonetheless, if indeed it was Philippe LeFleau who'd just spent the last couple of weeks wreaking murderous havoc, Devlin hoped the kid's path to Hell was a short one.

While Vin had added the lifesaving serum to Leif's liquid lunch, Devlin and Erika had run through the laundry list of evidence against their prime suspect, Philippe.

"Look at those tiny, lifeless feet poking out of the blanket, that bastard," Erika said. "Philippe enticed Leif to ski on a whim, knowing Leif would jump at the chance to play hooky from work." She proffered the canteen that the doctor had extricated from Leif's seizure-tight grasp. "Philippe knew Leif always carried this flask skiing. So the bastard poisoned it."

Devlin slapped on a latex glove he'd borrowed from the emergency ward. He bagged the piece of evidence and added it to his backpack.

Erika continued her rant. "That mountain ranger, Frederick, told me he saw the whole thing. He said my brother and Philippe were having it out on the slopes. And when Leif collapsed, Philippe just left him there! Tore off down the hill while my brother was having a seizure!" Her breathing had grown rapid, and her face burned red with fury. "Smashing into that tree was the best thing that ever happened."

Devlin rested his hands on her shoulders. "Getting crazy won't help your brother. The nurses won't let you in to see him like this. Plus, you're still recovering from your attack." He led her to a chair.

"How can you stay so calm, Devlin?" she asked. "Philippe tried to kill you too. Back on the tram ride, on your first day at the vineyard, he was there."

Devlin recalled that Philippe had introduced himself right after the gondola hijacking and the sniper shooting. He could easily have shot at them, and then skirted over to the vacated control tower to ram them. Devlin said to Erika, "The gondola ride was the perfect opportunity to wipe out one or more company heads in one fell swoop. Capped off by the perp's later conquest, when he pushed your sister into the grappa vat."

Erika lowered her head and clenched her fists tighter.

"That's when I found the first syringe…the one that led Vin and me to the poison…" he said. "Then there's the other syringes, the ones I found inside Leif's office safe."

"Philippe probably planted them there," Erika said. "Though how he figured out the combo, I still don't know. Because not even Leif had it. Philippe planted the syringes to frame me…or frame Leif…or both. But why?

"In fact, why would Philippe disparage my brother, or try to kill him? It's not like Philippe would stand to inherit the company with Leif out of the way. Same-sex marriage isn't recognized in Italy." Erika shook her head and sighed. She stood and gazed vacantly into Leif's room.

Why kill Leif indeed, Devlin wondered, without any basis for legal ownership anyway? Why not run the company together with Leif, employing their similar activist schemes? Together they might've proved an unstoppable force against Erika's agenda.

Perhaps Leif's plans had begun to differ dramatically with Philippe's. Perhaps conscience interfered with the radical tactics of Watery Grave, headquartered in their Swiss chalet. Was it Philippe who'd given the attack order to the hostage-taking psycho BASE jumper, or the Vitreuve plant bomber, in the name of activism? Or someone else?

As if those questions weren't enough to blow his mind, the one stickler that had started this whole mess still demanded an answer.

What was the motive for poisoning to death auto racer Giancarlo Venchi? Had someone meant to kill Runa, but accidentally killed Giancarlo? Or was this just another way to ruin Aurora's reputation, by linking Aurora's products with gross negligence, akin to the "anonymously authorized" Aurora-labeled shipments of tainted product at the summit?

From the hall, Devlin sized up the mangled mess that was Philippe LeFleau. Then he flicked his eyes to the unconscious Leif Aurora. He willed them both to wake up and give him answers. But his questions would keep. Because the murderer wasn't going to get up and walk away anytime soon.

Chapter 36

One last look, Leif thought as he roused from his stupor. *Philippe took one last look back at me on the mountain.*

Leif peered through his long eyelashes at his surroundings. But the light stabbed his eyes, and he squeezed his lids shut before he could gain any insight. He licked his lips. His tongue felt coarse and swollen. His head pounded mercilessly, so he kept it resting firmly in place.

He felt…hungover. Only this was the worst hangover he'd ever experienced. He was lying in an elevated bed, probably in a hospital room judging by the antiseptic smell. He recalled that he'd had a seizure. Evidently he'd survived it. Though he almost wished his aching body would just let him slip away. Then again, Philippe had taken that one last look back at him before skiing away…

And crashing into a tree.

Leif tried to raise up on one elbow. The sudden movement jarred his brain, like getting smashed with a frying pan. He slouched back against the pillow.

"Easy now," a female voice purred gently in a distinctly Veronese dialect. "No need to raise your heart rate on my account, sweetie."

Leif opened one eye, then the other, painfully adjusting them to the overhead fluorescent lights. A young, attractive African-Italian nurse in powder-blue scrubs stood beside his bed, marking a clipboard.

"Philippe?" he heard his own hoarse, gravelly voice mutter aloud.

She ignored his question. "You're in the intensive care unit," she said. "Had a scare. But it looks like you're on the mend, pretty boy. Close your eyes now. Sleep will speed recovery."

"Philippe?" he muttered again.

The nurse moved to another bed behind a curtain about twenty feet away. She pulled back the drape to reveal a patient in far worse physical condition.

The blond male's face, swollen red and purple, had been badly damaged. His long, lean body lay prone in traction. His only discernible feature was the pair of tiny feet poking out of his blanket. Philippe.

Leif's heart pumped so fast that he wondered if his chest might explode. He drew in a sharp breath that ended in a choked sob, and the nurse rushed over.

"Sweet Jesus, I thought you were seizing again. Easy, honey." Noticing his distress, the nurse glanced over at Philippe.

"This must be the patient they brought in with you. I'll be honest…it's bad. Honey, I'm sorry."

There were no words. The despair that he felt crushed him like a solid weight. He lay back, and he let the tears come.

She patted Leif's hand. Then she jotted something on her clipboard, shook her head solemnly, and returned to Philippe's bedside. After a minute, she sat down at a metal desk in the corner of the room and entered information into a computer.

Leif remembered the handsome face of the young man who'd swept him off his feet less than two years ago. On his first day of Advanced Chem at EPFL, he and his lab partner, the young, brilliant, beautiful boyish Philippe, had nearly burned down the lab by exposing potassium to water vapor. Philippe had suggested that they cut the day's classes and go skiing. He had met his perfect match. Philippe had been adventurous in life, passionate in his beliefs, and desirous to be with someone who finally understood and accepted him.

He wept. Philippe LeFleau, a man of many talents and strong convictions, might not ride out this life alongside him.

"Fam…family," Philippe mumbled, likely through a morphine-induced haze.

Leif twisted his head toward Philippe in the next bed. Pain seared through his already throbbing skull. He gritted his teeth and wiped away tears so that he could see Philippe clearly.

The nurse stood and checked Philippe's monitors. Then she shot a glance over to Leif and nodded reassuringly, as if to say,

"Talk to him while you still can." She returned to her desk to give them some privacy.

Philippe mumbled again, slightly louder and more coherently, "Leif. My…my family. Always…love you." He groaned with the effort.

Leif felt some small relief in their communication. There was so much that he wanted to say. In soft whispers, Leif poured out his heart to him. He rehashed old memories, apologized for past transgressions, and promised that he'd still be there for Philippe through whatever lay ahead.

He heard the nurse sniffle. She stood and left the room.

Philippe silently listened through the remainder of his soliloquy. Leif wondered at times if he'd slipped back into repose, but he prattled on, saying things he needed Philippe to hear. When he finished, he heard faint crying from the other bed.

"Never meant…to hurt you," Philippe murmured through his tears. "You were always there…when I…an addict, world was too much." A pause for breath. "My family…no father…controlling mother." Another pause, then he said, "*You* were my world. Leif, you're…my family."

Leif garnered every bit of his strength and reached his arm toward Philippe's bed. He had to let him know he felt the same.

It was then that Erika and Devlin Lucchesi entered the room. He expected his sister to overreact with concern when she spotted him exerting himself. But the last thing he expected was her banshee-like screech of rage.

Red-faced, she glared at Philippe. “Leif, don’t even speak to that freak.” Her tone would’ve made a pit bull cower. “Don’t you know? Philippe tried to kill you on that mountain!”

***

Erika tucked his arm securely beneath the blanket and bent to kiss his cheeks. His sister sat beside him and cradled his head in her arms. She’d done the same thing when their mother had died when he was two, so young he could barely recall her face. Leif grew weary with grief and fatigue, and he slept.

When he awoke, she and Devlin explained that he’d been poisoned. Devlin’s colleague had provided an antidote. The onset of his seizure had been harsh, and recovery would be slow. The toxin had ravaged his body far worse than when she’d been poisoned earlier that day.

“You were poisoned?” Leif said. “Are you going to be alright?”

Erika smiled and stroked back his hair. “My symptoms were caught early. I received treatment quickly. I just…” She looked at Devlin. “I got lucky.”

Leif remembered the scene that had transpired when Erika and Devlin first entered the ICU. “You think Philippe did this? But there’s no way. He’s…my family. He would never…” His head throbbed with pain. His sister was out of her mind. He glanced at Philippe, who lay silent and immobile in his hospital bed. He lowered his voice. “You think he tried to kill you, Erika, and then me? Not possible. He and I went skiing…”

"I was attacked around sunrise this morning. Do you know exactly where he was then?" she asked.

"He was…sleeping…and then…I woke up. He was gone. He'd taken a drive," Leif said slowly.

"And your poisoned flask, he had access to it?" she said.

Leif's eyes widened. "Look at him! You think he tried to kill us? And then what? He smashed himself into a tree?"

She nodded. "I think the bastard got what was coming to him after he tried to murder us!"

Philippe moaned through his morphine. He must've heard their rant. "*Merde*," he mumbled in French. Then he said, in accented English, "You are…full of shit."

Erika's jaw dropped. Devlin grasped her elbow as if to ground her.

"Not…what happened," Philippe murmured.

She glared at the damaged man in the next bed. "Okay, Frenchie, you're telling me that you're not the one who poisoned Leif's ski flask?"

"Did not…do it," he answered.

"You didn't attack me, and poison me, early this morning? When Leif was sleeping and lost track of your whereabouts?" Erika huffed.

"Not me," Philippe replied.

"You want us to believe that you haven't been trying to target every one of my family, including Runa? And disparaging my company from the get-go?" she said. "You hit your head harder than I thought."

"Okay," Philippe said.

"Okay, what?" she said.

"I admit it…"

A look of puzzlement, and then sheer triumph danced across her face.

Philippe continued, slowly gurgling the words from his broken face. "I disagree…with the way you run Aurora. I run a group…of activists…out of our home…mine and Leif's," he said. "But Leif's not part of it. My group…we believe…everyone has right to free water. And I admit—"

Devlin pulled a tape recorder from his backpack and turned it on. "Philippe LeFleau, you have the right to remain silent…"

Philippe silenced him with a raspberry, a full-on burst of spit from his lips.

Devlin's eyebrow shot up.

"That was me…waiving my rights. Hear me out. Please?" Philippe mumbled. Devlin and Erika sat back and listened.

"I'm responsible…for the flybys…the vandalism…the BASE jumpers. Those people…work for me. Tactics… to bring attention to Aurora's aquifer." Philippe winced, groaned, and continued. "I was the one…leaked news of aquifer. Felt the world should know…"

Leif swallowed. Philippe had deliberately endangered his company's reputation. Philippe's news leak, and its subsequent court-imposed injunction, had had a harsh impact on his company's production and imperiled its very existence.

"Leaked news…long time ago," Philippe said. "Before I knew about…Leif's water value initiatives. BASE jumpers…wanted to scare Erika…halt bottled water line."

"You held my winery guests hostage." Erika gritted her teeth and narrowed her eyes. "You killed my dog."

"Told crazy redhead…to scare you. Never wanted…to hurt anyone…too extreme. I'm sorry," Philippe said.

"You didn't mean to get extreme?" Devlin said. "You shot at our gondola lift. You shot at us in San Remo, and blew up Vitreuve's bottling plant."

"Not me…I swear," he groaned. He grimaced and took a minute to resume normal breathing. "Not me. Redhead and others…got erratic…not the group's core ideals," Philippe said.

Erika huffed and shook her head in obvious disbelief.

Leif spoke up. "What he said about Vitreuve's plant…it's true. In San Remo, Philippe and I left. Philippe had become offended after you'd brought out that syringe, Devlin. He took off down the road. I caught up with him. We called a cab to take us to the train station and left San Remo together. We only heard about the explosion and the shooting after the fact. I can vouch for him, Erika."

She settled her gaze on Leif. Solemnly she asked, "Why are you covering for him, Leif? He's killed people. Philippe tried to kill you."

Leif shook his head. He refused to believe that his partner had tried to kill him, or his sisters. What Philippe had just explained about his activism added up, made sense. But murder?

His heart and his mind told him that Philippe just wasn't capable of it. But if not Philippe, then who?

An alarm on one of the monitors sounded, signaling a problem. The nurse in the powder-blue scrubs shooed Erika and Devlin from the room and called for a doctor.

Philippe moaned, louder now. Each moan trailed off into a whimper of anguish. Leif tried to rush to his aid, but he collapsed with the effort. "Please hold on, Philippe. Nurse, please get a doctor! Where's Marisse? Someone please find his mother."

Devlin retreated through the door just as the doctor rushed in. Erika exited too, but she stopped to take one last look at Philippe. Pity? Forgiveness? Or hatred? Leif couldn't be sure through his tears.

Another gut-wrenching cry of pain tore from Philippe's lips. The alarm continued to wail.

Leif wept. He was losing the love of his life. It was almost too much to bear.

Another nurse dashed inside with a cart bearing medical equipment. A doctor closed the curtain, separating him from Philippe.

"Fight, Philippe. Fight, my love," he shouted through the chaos.

The medical team bustled around Philippe's bed. One of them knocked the curtain aside with an elbow. Leif saw Philippe's face on the other side.

"Philippe," Leif shouted. "Nothing else matters. You're my family. I love you, now fight!"

With a wrenching groan of tremendous pain, Philippe turned his head. He peered toward Leif ever so slightly. Just an inch, just enough for a smile…

…And one last look.

***

Leif awoke to the sound of murmured voices. His head felt thick with fog again. Had they sedated him?

He heard the nurse speaking to someone in a hushed manner. Philippe's doctor answered her. And the realization that Philippe no longer lived came crashing down on him.

He wished he could escape back into the dark gloom from which he'd awakened and stay there forever. Philippe was gone.

He heard crying, and he recognized the quiet weeping of Philippe's mother. Leif didn't open his eyes. He wasn't ready to face her yet. His own grief consumed him.

***

Leif rustled again. This time he determined to open his eyes and face the world. Slowly, gingerly, through the haze of his slumber and medication, he peered out into the light.

Grimacing down at him was the face of pure evil.

He lay there in his hospital bed, paralyzed, transfixed by fear.

Her eyes were the same eyes that had glared at him with disdain as a young child.

The nose that protruded from those eyes was not the witchlike beak of old, but rather a clearly sculpted nose of plastic. An improvement on the crooked hook that had decorated the beast from his childhood.

The roots of jet black, so well hidden just above her collar beneath the perfectly coiffed platinum-blond bob, jogged his memory too. Back to the raven-black, long-haired rat's nest that had haunted his dreams for years growing up.

Perfectly white veneers capped her front teeth, disguising the crooked yellow molars at the back of her gaping maw.

It was she. The migrant worker. The one whom his father had regularly bedded. The same one who'd hauled off and smacked him in disgust. The one who Erika and his father had banished from their family's vineyard during the great earthquake twenty years ago. She had returned.

Back then, she'd been the epitome of hideous, filthy refuse. How was this demure, soft-spoken fiftyish beauty the same wretch who'd haunted his nightmares as a child?

She now stood over Leif's weakened, prone body. She glared at him with a grimace that radiated both anguish and hatred. He wondered if he might die from fright.

Marisse LeFleau raised both fists above her head. Her grimace contorted to form spoken words, and her voice issued forth like thunder. She bellowed, "Everything good is gone from this godforsaken world. My son has passed. And yet, you still live!"

Chapter 37

From the bowels of the hospital's ICU, Marisse LeFleau shrieked like a Valkyrie.

Out in the waiting room, Erika shot up from her chair. *The attacker's come back! My brother! Marisse! They'll be killed!*

Erika and Devlin rushed to the ICU entrance. Erika stood frozen at the threshold, unable to process what she was seeing.

Marisse was bashing her closed fists against Leif's head, over and over again. Lacking the strength to defend himself, her brother moaned and writhed in pain as Marisse pummeled his chest and face.

Erika rushed to Leif's bedside and threw her arms over his face to protect him from further blows. "Marisse, stop it! Get a hold of yourself. Marisse!"

The woman intensified her punches.

Erika looked up into the woman's bloodshot, manic eyes. She hauled back and slapped Marisse so hard across the face that her open palm stung. The force of it halted the onslaught.

Devlin stood by Erika's side, ready to pounce, but he gave her space to handle it.

A nurse dashed into the room. "Get me security!" she yelled into the hall.

Though her arms had slumped to her sides after Erika's blow, Marisse's lunatic expression remained. It was marred by an inflamed cheek, seared red with the mark of Erika's wallop. Marisse took a deep breath and released another flurry of punches against her brother.

Devlin's six-foot-four frame loomed behind Marisse. He wrapped his arms around her waist and hoisted her, still flailing, to the other side of the room, far enough away from Leif to do any more damage. Marisse pulled and tugged until she broke free of his grasp, and she fled the ICU.

A doctor rushed in and checked Leif's monitors. "Everyone out of this goddamn room!" he bellowed.

"Please," Leif begged the doctor. "Please, let me speak to my sister. I need her."

The doctor turned to him. "You've been through enough. Don't you—"

"Please, my partner has died." Leif nodded toward Philippe's empty bed. It stood clear of any sign of his lover's vain struggle for life. "Just let my sister stay until I fall asleep."

Erika shot the doctor an imploring stare.

The doctor nodded reluctantly. With the nurse, he made a few adjustments to ensure Leif's comfort and treat his bruises, and then left.

Devlin looked at Erika, then Leif. "I'll be standing guard right outside this room. Take as long as you need."

Erika edged beside Leif on the bed and gripped his hand. A tear trickled down his cheek, and she wiped it away.

She chuckled softly. "I never slapped another woman before," she told Leif.

Leif mumbled something she couldn't make out, and she squeezed his hand. "I'm sorry she hurt you," Erika said. "Marisse is clearly distraught over Philippe, as are you. I'm so sorry he's gone. My heart breaks for your loss. Tell me what I can do to make things better."

"Do you remember the day of the big earthquake?" Leif said. His voice was low and somber. His breathing appeared shallow. "I was filled with so much fear. Of our father dying from a broken heart. Of not having a mother. Of the land opening up and swallowing us when it shook. Of that migrant worker who used to hit me."

She nodded. She cradled his head in the crook of her arm and stroked his hair.

He continued, "And today, I'm still afraid. Runa's gone. Someone poisoned you. Then me. But it's taken until now for it to finally hit me."

He took a deep breath. She peered down at him.

"All of the fear that I felt twenty years ago." His voice cracked. "It just came crashing down on me."

He grew quiet and she pondered his statement. She recalled their tumultuous Aurora history, in its inception and in its recent past.

Something tugged at her consciousness. Some hidden fact that she'd taken for granted, a truth that had dangled out in the open, too obvious to be seen clearly, ever since their father's death.

When Leif spoke next, it felt to Erika as if the earth shook and a great spring burst forth from the ground. And she knew.

She locked eyes with Leif. Trembling, Leif then confirmed, "She's back."

Chapter 38

"Get me eyes on Marisse," Devlin told his HELL Rangers.

At the same time that Erika had sat down to console Leif, Devlin had taken up guard protection outside the ICU, dialed Scotti's room, and rustled up all his men through Vin. With Scotti out of action, Vin was his interim crew chief. "I don't want the hospital in panic mode, so we need to proceed carefully. Have Helio tap into the facility's surveillance and track down Marisse LeFleau's whereabouts. She freaked out in the ICU and ran off, but she couldn't have gone far. I'm still acting on a hunch. After her outburst, I want eyes on her ASAP."

"Got it," Vin said.

"From now on, Ascari's covering Erika on guard duty. Montoya never leaves Leif," Devlin said.

In Scotti's room, Vin voiced both sets of direction to the crew, then told Devlin, "On their way."

"Lauda and Hunt at the summit?" Devlin said.

"Scotti ordered them there an hour ago to oversee Aurora shipments. Solid progress, but a bit of a shitshow… our safety restrictions cut the water supply in half, so, lots of thirsty, and ornery, attendees," Vin said. "Two hours until the opening party…a lot of important people are likely planning on drinking. Things are bound to get even more dicey."

"Send over Graham, Senna, Montoya, and Alonso. To help out the Aurora unit," Devlin said.

"Where do you want me?" Vin said.

"Better get to the Aurora lab. Cook up more of that vaccine. If the shit does fly, we'll need all the antidote we can get."

"Uh…I got digits from one of Scotti's doctors," Vin said. "I might be able to get keys to the hospital lab…save some time."

Devlin smirked. "Get on it," he said. "Give my best to Scotti. Stay in touch."

Ascari's two hundred fifty pounds of lean muscle arrived then, chewing on an unlit Montecristo Espada. Another man of few words, Montoya, was popping sunflower seeds.

Devlin updated them. Montoya pocketed his seeds. He stood outside the room with arms crossed and feet spread, eyes glued on his ward through the window of the ICU.

"I know your hands were full with Erika the past hour," Ascari said. "You should know the shipment situation at the summit is under control for the moment."

"Vin told me Scotti sent over four of our crew to help the Aurora team," Devlin said.

Ascari held Devlin's gaze. "There's been a development. On the way down here, Prost called from Siena."

Devlin's stomach dropped. Siena. Palio. Marcello.

Ascari continued. "Prost confirmed that product expedited from Aurora Vineyard this morning arrived in Siena in the past hour. But we'd already issued our warnings on tainted product before distribution. Good news is…the Siena crew is sitting on those morning deliveries."

Devlin held his breath, knowing Ascari wasn't quite finished.

"Bad news is…last-minute grappa shipments and water pallets had already arrived in Siena late last night," Ascari said. "The tracking numbers that Rasmus texted them around noon today match those shipments…they're half the quarantined lot of grappa and water that Vin had tested positive for the poison formula."

Devlin's heart pounded in his chest. "Hell, no."

Ascari nodded grimly. "There's no significant infrastructure there. No real security or manpower to distinguish between the shipments…so the tainted product was already dispersed among the *contrade*." Ascari's face had turned ashen, and he rubbed his stubble. "That's ten Palio-participating neighborhoods…leaders, members, guests, tourists, children…all planning on eating and drinking at one of the biggest block parties of the year."

Devlin dialed Lupo. After three agonizing rings, Lupo picked finally up. Harried, excited, and raising his voice among revelers in the background, Lupo said, "*Ciao, Devlin, aspett'un momento!*" Hold on a minute? He didn't have that kind of time.

Devlin shouted into the phone, "Lupo, the wine, the grappa, the water…they're poisoned!"

"Sorry, I had to move into an alcove." The background noise had diminished, but Lupo still shouted. "It's crazy here! Thousands of people. Dude, what'd you—"

Devlin gripped the phone tighter, and shouted into the receiver. "Get rid of the wine. Find Marcello. You need to…" He punched his hand through the corridor's drywall. "Don't drink the water!"

***

Three hours by plane. Five hours by car or train. Devlin knew that by the time he or any of his crew dispatched from Verona to Siena, it would be too late to prevent circulation of Aurora's tainted product. By then the good people of Siena might've been poisoned, Marcello among them.

Lights suddenly flickered in the hospital corridor. Devlin flicked his gaze to the window at the end of the hall. Haze of midafternoon had turned to black of night. Lightening flashed. Huge raindrops splattered against the pane.

He, Ascari, and Montoya spent the next ten minutes teleconferencing with Lupo, Prost, and Chiara in Siena. The two men paced the hospital corridor and formulated a solid strategy for handling the tainted product there.

Vin texted him: "Helio tapped surveillance. Eyes on Marisse. Morgue. Sitting vigil over Philippe."

Devlin exhaled. Fires had been doused, for the moment. The summit was secure. Marisse had been located, and was stationary. HELL Rangers had been assigned to prevent her escape. And Lupo had designated Prost as head of his Palio security team. Though the group was small, they were working with local police in each contrada to gather and confiscate all Aurora product.

Ascari had also texted a half dozen other HELL Rangers still in Rome to drive to Siena. They'd arrive in time to lend a hand with the Palio post-race festivities later that night.

Chiara had located Marcello. He and his grandparents had been headed to the Palio rehearsal dinner for their Aquila contrada. The mayor had refused to cancel it, and the show would go on. Marcello and family planned to bring their own drink boxes.

Lupo hadn't yet worked out a backup plan for partygoers who planned to drink anything at the dinner that evening. Last-minute BYOB might lead to rioting. Devlin's poisoned racing colleague flashed through his mind. Convulsions. Death. A riot problem was far better than the alternative. Bring Your Own Booze might just save the day.

The group finally hung up. Ascari stood guard alongside Montoya outside the ICU. Devlin knew he should update Erika and Leif. But he took a moment to breathe and gather his thoughts first, just outside the hospital.

Though deep purple clouds still hovered over most of Verona, the one that had pelted rain over the hospital had cleared. It left steamy, sticky summer haze behind.

Regardless of the heat and humidity, Devlin ran. He lapped the hospital once, pumping his arms and legs full of vigor, working his heart muscle until it felt like it would burst. He slowed and reentered the hospital. As he walked back through the sliding doors, Devlin scrolled through Hamilton's incoming text message He smirked. His hunch had proved correct. The jaunt on which he'd sent Hamilton had turned up the proof that he needed.

Marisse LeFleau was going down.

Chapter 39

"She's a murderous slut!" Erika told Devlin as he strode back into the ICU.

"Marisse?" Devlin said to her.

Erika glared at him. "You knew?"

"Had my suspicions, but no real proof until minutes ago." Devlin pulled up a chair, spun it around, and sat with his arms crossed over the back of it. The Jack Daniel's box cutter that Veronica had gifted him jutted from his back pocket. He pushed it further down so he wouldn't lose it. "I was just coming in to fill you in on evidence we gathered. When did you two find out?" he asked.

Leif explained his revelation brought about when Marisse had loomed over his bed and attacked him.

Devlin nodded. "She went ballistic. Erika and I thought she was acting out in grief. But the subsequent proof the HELL Rangers gained shows that she must've poisoned your flask. When you survived, and Philippe accidentally crashed and died, it's clear now that she attacked out of rage and vengeance."

Erika said, “We have to find her. She’s out of control and capable of anything.”

Devlin held up his hand. “We’re monitoring her. She’s in the morgue, lamenting Philippe. We’ll give her a few more minutes to grieve her dead son. Then we’ll call the police and haul her in. With all the evidence that Hamilton found on her in France, she’ll be locked up until she rots.”

Leif and Erika stared at him, waiting for answers.

“I sent Hamilton to Marisse’s leather company outside Paris. With Marisse away at the summit, her staff there was minimal—”

“But with her gone, wasn’t the security tight?” Erika asked.

Devlin tipped his head and smiled. “The HELL Rangers are pretty good at circumventing such measures…and getting into computer files…and safes…” He winked at Erika. She rolled her eyes.

“Ham hacked a file named ‘MeOH’ that outlined her entire plan,” Devlin said.

“The chemical symbol for methanol,” Leif said.

“Must be her code name for her highly potent poisonous formula,” Devlin said. “The one she used to harm you two and murder your sister.”

“As in, foreshot and tail?” Erika said. “Marisse is killing people with the by-product of fermentation, that stuff we ditch when we’re making grappa?”

“Exactly,” Devlin said. “If someone ingested the methanol by-product from your fermentation process, they’d get sick from alcohol overdose. Just like people did sometimes when they made moonshine during Prohibition. Now, people know better. Or if they don't, they're treated. They typically recover before either blindness or seizures overtake them."

Erika and Leif both nodded.

"Marisse formulated a new concoction that ramps up the potency of methanol. Her formula increases its negative effects on the body, in less time."

"How?" Erika said.

"Cowhide," Devlin said.

Leif shook his head in understanding. Erika gritted her teeth and cursed under her breath. "She's a leather chemist," she muttered.

"Philippe told me that his mother married his father, LeFleau, the owner of a small leather factory, when she was in her midtwenties," Leif said. "The guy put her through school. She graduated top of her class and later improved the leather that he was making. He died of natural causes, though now I wonder if he died by her hand. Marisse turned it into one of the biggest leather companies in the world," Leif said.

"Before that, Marisse must've tried to worm her way into Aurora," Erika told Devlin. "Her earlier outcry jolted my memories of her. Now I remember this young woman who came to the vineyard over twenty years ago as a migrant. Always worked with my father in his little wine room—cutting vines, mixing varietals, and whatever." She rolled her eyes. "Maybe Marisse's MO has always been to shack up with a padrone, learn the trade, and then bump him off..."

Devlin interjected, "I stumbled upon Augustus Aurora's journal. Read about a methanol formula he was working on. Likely she stole it and left. After getting a degree and working the leather trade, she probably figured out the cowhide additive would max the potency of his polymer," he said.

Leif nodded.

"She didn't just leave," Erika said. "We kicked the bitch out on her ugly fat ass."

"Thank God we did," Leif said. "She might've been planning to marry our father, murder him, and take over the vineyard. She probably offed Philippe's father for sole ownership of the leather company."

Erika gazed out the window. "When the water sprang up, the bitch slapped my baby brother, and Dad kicked her out. Twenty years ago…to the day. But then…"

"What?" Devlin asked.

"Oh God, looking back…I recall…Marisse was pregnant. Not huge, but showing. Back then, I just assumed she arrived at the vineyard that way." Erika turned her gaze to Leif. "I was just a kid. I didn't put it together. I didn't think…"

"What?" Leif said.

"I didn't consider the possibility that she might've been carrying our father's child." She gulped and looked up at Leif.

"Pregnant with our father's child? Twenty years ago?" Leif groaned. "That means…she must've been pregnant…with Philippe." Leif sank further back into his pillow.

Erika and Devlin exchanged a glance. He swore he saw her grimace in disgust, but she recovered quickly. Instead, Erika smiled gently at Leif. "Philippe was a lovely man in his own way. No wonder you cared for him so deeply." She turned toward Devlin and shrugged, clearly ill at ease. Leif's partner in life was his brother from another mother.

As if struck by a thought, she abruptly turned to face Leif. "How did Marisse learn the combination to Augustus's safe? She probably secreted the syringes inside, to frame one or both of us. Daddy never told anyone the combo. And I just guessed that it was the date that he took our family in."

Leif rolled his eyes. "I was four. I used to sneak around the farm, playing spy. I'd gone into Daddy's bedroom looking for chocolates. I didn't want to get caught, so I hid, and…they were having a private moment. After that, he told her the date we first arrived at the vineyard."

Devlin fought back a smirk.

"Ugh, disgusting," Erika said. She shook her head. "I still can't believe that loud, black-haired, bucktoothed witch is the same demure, high-class CEO whose leather goods I adore. She used to saunter in and out of the vineyard, checking on Philippe now and again, right under our noses. Come to think of it, she came on the scene shortly after Daddy died. She probably figured that it was high time that Philippe inherited the company…"

Leif nodded. "That slut introduced us. Up at school. She was giving a guest lecture in my Advanced Chem class. She made sure Philippe and I were lab partners." Leif struggled to sit up, and Erika helped him. His rosy cheeks had regained a significant amount of color since learning his boyfriend was his step-brother.

"Marisse must've planned this from the start," Erika said. "And when our father died, she probably wanted to ensure that their son, Philippe, would inherit the entire Aurora estate. So Marisse tried to pick off the rest of his children, one by one."

Devlin nodded. "Her MeOH file outlined this exact plan. Like a journal, the file documented her every move, including when she blew up Vitreuve's water-bottling plant."

"*She* blew up the plant?" Erika sighed. "Makes sense now. She did it to increase Aurora's industry market share, and then she could hand over a more profitable inheritance to her son," she said. "Poor Vitreuve."

"Vitreuve is a huge competitor," Leif said. "Pinning the rap on him, and knocking him out of the game, would have made our company surge."

Erika's eyes scanned the ceiling as she rubbed her temples, likely sifting through the events of that night. "The slut shot at us, too!"

"She had help," Devlin said. "The radical activists that Philippe told us about…her mercenaries. Ham texted me photos he copied from the file." He opened his messages and held up two pictures. One was a petite blond man, and the other was the psycho BASE jumper who'd run off the cliff with Erika's dog.

Erika pointed at Devlin's photos. "That's…the other murderous slut!"

Devlin forward the file to his entire crew with the clear message that the enemy was armed and dangerous. The small blond man must have been the sniper who'd shot at them from the vineyard's pine tree on the gondola ride up the mountain, the perp with the tiny feet. And the other was the redheaded psycho bitch, whose body remained unaccounted.

"There were one or two other accomplices, but we don't have a visual ID on them," Devlin said. He looked up from his phone. "Ham also found the missing Aurora surveillance footage that Rasmus reported as stolen."

Erika shook her head. "Not missing. Remember, I saw Runa turn off the monitors in the grappa plant. Looking back, she was probably just guarding her intellectual property. Research was everything to her."

"Not that footage," Devlin said. "Footage from the day I first arrived on the gondola, the perimeter coverage—it went missing. Marisse stole it to cover up her little blond sniper. And, Ham told me, to hide the fact that Marisse was the one who sneaked into the control booth and tried to ram us."

Erika threw up her hands in frustration. "I was on a conference call with her when she tried to ram the gondola…I was her damn alibi!"

Devlin nodded. "You'd later returned to the controls, and she'd already gotten away."

"Slut," Erika said.

Devlin stood. "We have enough evidence to put Marisse away for a long time."

Leif shook his head. "I can't believe it. Marisse used Philippe, her only son, as her pawn. As a means to take over our company. And with Augustus's three sibling owners out of the way, Philippe stood to inherit the whole company when he turned twenty-one next year." Leif's eyes welled with tears. "Who knows if she would have killed him too, to get a piece of it for herself?"

"I don't know…that's one mother who's really devastated over the loss of her son," Devlin said. "She still hasn't left the morgue."

Erika stood up from the edge of Leif's bed. "Now that Philippe is dead, she'll do anything to destroy Aurora's reputation. The only thing worse than a murderous slut is one planning revenge."

Devlin dialed Helio, who was monitoring Marisse's location from the computer in Scotti's hospital room. "Perp still in the morgue?"

Helio confirmed that Marisse had not wavered from her vigil over her son's dead body and that Sneakers still covered the morgue's external door. "Good, I'm going in through the hospital entrance," Devlin told him.

Devlin stepped to the threshold of the ICU. Montoya was still standing guard there. "Guard both Erika and Leif," Devlin told him. Then he nodded to Ascari. "Let's go get her."

Chapter 40

The trip to the morgue began with a fight. But Devlin ultimately relented—Erika could come to the morgue too, on one condition. If trouble arose while Devlin was apprehending Marisse, Ascari would escort Erika away before she got hurt.

Erika, Ascari, and Devlin descended the four floors to the morgue in the elevator. Still on his call with Helio, Devlin asked him for another update on Marisse LeFleau.

"She hasn't budged from her chair," Helio said. "Security let her in a while back. She was all crying and whatnot. She's been sitting on a stool, crouched over that body, her head bent like she's praying or something. Kinda boring TV, actually."

"Anyone else in there?" Devlin asked.

"Quiet day. No other dead bodies came or went. A nurse went into the office area. Think she's still in there—"

"You *think* the nurse is still there?" Devlin said.

"I never saw her leave, must be doing paperwork. Office is tucked out of sight of the camera," Helio said. "Also a couple technicians came in. One adjusted the thermostat. Another laid out a table of funky-looking tools, probably expecting an autopsy. They left. A janitor came in with a bucket and mopped the floor. He left. Told you, boring TV."

When they reached the main lobby, Devlin, Ascari, and Erika descended another elevator to the basement.

"We're almost there, Helio. Keep an eye on Scotti, in case this gets crazy," Devlin said. "And Sneakers is still posted at the morgue's back entrance?"

"Affirmative," Helio said. "Hey, one more thing. There's a sign on the wall right above Marisse's head, been staring at it on the monitor forever. But I don't know Latin. What does this mean: '*Taceant colloquia. Effugiat risus. Hic locus est ubi mors gaudet succurrere vitae*'?"

"Tells those who enter the morgue that it's a place of respect, where Death rejoices in teaching the living," Devlin said. *But I am in no mood for taking lessons from the dead today.*

Devlin dialed Vin next. "Status on the vaccine?"

"My doctor friend came through. Gave her the gist of what I was working on, and she gave me a couple pathologists to help out. We've got some antidote stored, and we're cooking some more," Vin said.

"Can your friend also get me through morgue security?" he asked.

"On it." Vin hung up.

The elevator doors opened into the basement. The San Daniele Hospital in Verona had been around since the Second World War. But Devlin knew that renovations had transformed it into a top-notch facility, one of the most renowned in northern Italy. Except for the basement.

Pea-green cement blocks greeted them in the hall off the elevators. The smell of formalin and pine-scented cleaner led the way to the morgue. It stood about fifty yards down, at the end of a fluorescent-lit corridor. As they approached, Devlin spied a lone security guard, of reasonable stature and in his midforties, standing outside the room talking into his cell phone.

Whimpering, sniveling, choking sobs sounded next to him. He turned to see Erika openly weeping. "My brother, Philippe!" she bawled loudly.

Ascari and Devlin exchanged a glance. Devlin instinctively reached out his hand to console her, and she clutched him close.

At the door, the armed guard surprised them. He offered a tissue, smirked, and winked at Erika. Apparently, Vin's doctor friend had come through, and Erika's theatrics had proved unnecessary. The guard turned a key and opened the thick soundproof metallic door to the morgue.

Devlin shook hands with their accomplice. "Erika stays with you," he said. The bald guard nodded his assent.

Devlin and Ascari quietly entered the twenty-five-by-twenty-five-foot cement-block room. Brick-colored walls and tiled floor, for obvious reasons. A shiver ran through him. Devlin first attributed it to the room temperature, which felt like it hovered just above freezing. But then he spotted Marisse in the middle of the open viewing room, dressed in a navy blue pantsuit and practical leather mules. This room was where the living came to identify their dead. Perched on a wheeled stool in its center, her back to Devlin, she hovered over her only son like a vulture over its prey. She remained immobile, seemingly unaware of their presence. Devlin sensed that she was the true source of the frigid atmosphere.

Devlin quickly scanned the rest of the interior layout. A bank of refrigerated cabinets lined the left wall—cadaver storage. On the opposite wall, ventilation fans whirred just beneath the painted Latin inscription. In front of it stood a table of shiny metal tools connected to wall outlets, as well as a washbasin and a hazardous waste bin. Another door marked "Work Room" stood behind it, likely where autopsies were performed. An enclosed corner office was positioned opposite the morgue's entrance.

On the other side of the room was the exterior exit. Sneakers was stationed there, outside, to prevent Marisse's escape.

Devlin flicked his eyes to Ascari, then to the corner office and back again. Ascari nodded, stepped to the threshold, and peered inside. He shook his head, signaling that no one else was home. Ascari checked the workroom—locked. He leaned his back against the wall and crossed his arms, ready for anything.

"I'm sorry for the loss of your son, Marisse," Devlin said aloud. "But you have to pay for what you did to Giancarlo Venchi, Runa Aurora, and the others. It's time to go."

She'd flinched when he'd spoken her name. An ounce of pity seeped into his resolve at the loss of the woman's son. Until

Giancarlo Venchi's painful death resurfaced in his mind. Devlin planned to drag this perp away kicking and screaming if necessary.

"I think you should see this, Dev," Ascari said. He was examining the handle on the waste storage bin and a red blinking light next to it. Devlin cringed. Marisse must've planted an IED on the waste bin. He'd handle it. But first things first.

"Marisse, let's not make this difficult. The Aurora family knows what you did, and we have evidence to prove it," Devlin said. "Say your good-byes to Philippe, and let's go."

Two wheeled tables, both empty, stood on either side of the one bearing Philippe. His body was covered by a sheet, including his badly damaged face, all except his telltale tiny feet, one of which bore a toe tag with his name printed on it.

Devlin shivered again and took a step forward. He placed his hand on her shoulder. "Marisse. Now," he insisted.

She didn't appear to be crying. He wondered if she'd fallen asleep. He gave her shoulder a squeeze. Only then did he notice the red hair at the nape of her neck, beneath the blond wig. An impostor.

Ascari said, "Devlin, about this IED…"

The woman pretending to be Marisse leapt to her feet, knocking Devlin's arm from her shoulder as she did. She bounded backward a few steps to catch her balance, swiping at him with gleaming metal weapons in both hands. She held a hooked hammer in one hand and a chisel in the other.

Devlin jumped back a step and reached for his Glock, coming away short. He'd been forced to leave it with hospital security.

The woman's wide eyes gleamed. Her teeth flashed in enthusiastic rage. Spittle flew from her lips.

Ascari, also unarmed, grabbed a scalpel from the table of autopsy tools and faced Marisse, ready to fight.

But Devlin put up a hand to stop him. Keeping his gaze on the rabid lunatic, Devlin said, "Ascari, you take care of the IED. I've got her." He heard Ascari grab more tools from the worktable and set to work on the explosive attached to the biowaste bin handle.

"Where's Marisse?" Devlin said to the woman. She was shifting and striking, recoiling and jabbing at him like a prize pugilist, while he ducked and shimmied out of her reach.

"Marisse is gone. She has work to do." The woman slashed blindly at him. "Ensuring that the water rights of all people are equal and just." Her taunting, manic smile never faltered from her lips. But her blond wig now hung askew, revealing the bold red rat's nest beneath it. It was the psycho BASE jumper.

Bobbing and weaving to avoid her assault, Devlin eyed the two exits. Too far to reach. Too soundproof to call out to Sneakers or the armed guard for assistance. Soundproof, to protect the vitality of the living outside from the noisy business of death inside. He spotted the buzz saw. He wondered what using it on the psycho would feel like.

"Bitch must've just armed it," Ascari said. "Got one more minute. It's rigged from the inside of the locked workroom. Waste bin must connect on the other side of the wall. Won't be able to bust through the deadbolt in time. Let's get the fuck out."

"You somehow survived death once on the vineyard cliff. Doubt you'll make it out alive a second time," Devlin said to her. He lunged with a left hook and knocked the chisel from her hand.

She waggled her middle finger at him. "Ever hear of a backup parachute, asshole? Besides, I'm prepared to die to ensure every human's right to clean water. How about you?" She jumped up, grabbed a water hose that dangled over the washbasin, and yanked it toward her. She snatched the high-powered water cannon nozzle midair and torpedoed him in the face with a torrent of ice-cold water.

Devlin lunged through the cannon-spray and tackled her. He knocked the nozzle from her grasp. He clutched the arm that gripped the hammer hook and shook it. But the bitch had muscle, and she refused to let go.

Water continued to stream from the nozzle, and the two sloshed and rolled on the slick tile floor. She bit and thrashed and clawed. He grappled and punched, until he finally got his hands around her neck.

But Devlin and the redhead smashed into the legs of a table, and Philippe's cold, dead corpse thunked down on Devlin like a sack of potatoes. The odd thought struck, *He's still warm.*

He was pinned to the floor beneath Philippe's corpse. The woman, now bloody and bruised, jumped to her feet.

Ascari ran toward the redhead and punched her to the ground. He stood over her and gripped the hammer hook. When he tried to yank it from her hand, she picked up the chisel with the other and slashed deep into his upper thigh. He howled in anguish.

Devlin glimpsed Ascari's skewered leg. A two-foot poker jutted from his flesh like a hunter's spear. Blood seeped but didn't spew from the wound. Not an artery; he would live.

Ascari walloped her square in the face with a closed fist. She went down. He slumped to the floor, weakened by blood loss. Though it had been a great punch by any standard, the bitch fought on, kicking and screaming in Ascari's face.

Devlin heaved the dead weight of Philippe's couple-hundred-pound cadaver off of him. He scrambled to his knees and groped for the psycho's leg. Found it. He tugged hard. But she clung to the handle of one of the cabinet drawers. And as he yanked her toward him, the metal bin rolled all the way out with them, confining them both between the wall and the drawer, which was filled with a refrigerated three-hundred-pound male torso.

The redhead flipped onto her back and slashed Devlin with the hammer hook. But it met with his belt loop and stuck, just missing his abdomen and intestines. She released the hammer, tucked her flexible frame, and rolled through the few inches between the open drawer and the floor until surfacing on the other side. No way could his six-foot-four body fit underneath there.

Devlin watched the wily woman crawl her way to the exit. He struggled to shove the drawer closed, but he was unable to heft back the man's weight while wedged between the drawer and the wall.

Devlin spewed curses as he shimmied the heavily laden drawer mere inches at a time to break free. He couldn't let this crazed psycho out into the hospital wielding a chisel. And on the other side of the door was Erika, who didn't stand a chance against her.

His eyes darted around the room. Spotted the power tools, and the blinking red light of the time bomb. Spied Ascari downed by his wound near the door. Then he shifted his gaze to the psycho slithering her way toward to the same exit.

Devlin shouted to Ascari, "I got a plan. Get the hell out, and get away from the door. Now!"

Ascari had already pulled himself to standing on one leg, the chisel from his wound discarded on the floor. The redhead sprang up from her hands and knees, and Ascari punched Red in the abdomen. But it didn't slow her down, just made her mad.

Red grasped the chisel from the wet floor, raised the hammer hook like a talon in the other, and ran straight at Ascari.

Ascari blocked the hammer hook with his left arm. But he lost his balance on his one good leg and grabbed for the wall with his right. She drove the chisel back into his open wound.

He growled at her through gritted teeth. Ascari wrapped both hands around her waist, upended her, and slammed her head down onto the ceramic tile floor.

Leaning heavily on one leg, Ascari groped along the wall and tore open the door. Devlin saw the stunned faces of Erika and the guard. Ascari slammed the door behind him.

The tenacious, feral she-beast slithered through the bloodstained water toward Devlin, again wielding death instruments in both hands.

But just as Ascari had exited the morgue, Devlin had pushed the immense corpse from the open drawer to the floor. He'd slammed his own body atop the rubber body bag inside the sliding cabinet. And he'd pushed off, toward the chamber, using the tile crevices for leverage.

"Nooooo!" he'd heard the redhead shout.

The bomb exploded just as the drawer he was in banged shut.

A tremor coursed through the pitch-black wall of drawers with the force of the blast. His ears rang with the deafening assault. Devlin smelled C-4 and charred barbecue.

Devlin, safely shielded inside the refrigerated chamber, knew the psycho bitch had to be seeped in carnage and shrapnel. Because the explosive rigged to the hazardous waste bin would've spewed vile human waste from floor to ceiling inside the morgue's main room.

But it got better. The redhead had teetered on the edge of death before and survived. But not this time. Devlin made sure of it. Before he'd escaped, he'd untethered the cord of one of the plugged-in power drills, bitten off the end to reveal bare wire, and tossed it into the pool of dirty water outside his sanctuary. Death by electrocution would've zapped the psycho right back to Hell where she came from.

Within the chamber, Devlin shimmied his phone from the inside pocket of his jeans and dialed Ascari. "Cut the power before anyone comes in. Perp's cooked. I'm good. The dead guys I'm hangin' with are pretty chill. Call HAZMAT, get me outta here quick. All eyes on the water summit. I'm sure Marisse will stop at nothing short of genocide."

Devlin impatiently waited to get sprung from the morgue by taking lessons from the dead.

Chapter 41

Showered and shot up with antibiotics, Devlin and Sneakers convened in Scotti's hospital room with Ascari and Helio for a full report.

"You two still reek," Scotti said. He sat upright in his hospital bed, holding a closed fist to his nose.

Devlin sized up Sneakers. He'd borne the worst of the morgue's human waste explosion. "You really got it bad," Devlin agreed.

"And I was the one posted outside," Sneakers said, shaking his head. He rubbed a dry bar of deodorant soap over his neck, face, arms, and hands. "I'm so pissed she got away from me."

"You were run over by an ambulance. You're lucky to be alive," Helio said.

Devlin still couldn't believe the story Sneakers had told him after his release from the cadaver cabinets. Sneakers had shown him the rubber hose dangling from the ceiling. Marisse's impostor had used it to Tarzan across the room, bust through the emergency door, and smack headlong into Sneakers. She'd escaped electrocution and had marinated Sneakers in hazardous biological goo.

Though Ascari had dialed Sneakers to alert him to the perp's escape, the IED, and the electrified room, Sneakers had missed the call. The seven-foot Kenyan-American was busy colliding with a speeding EMS vehicle. Sneakers had brushed himself off and was listening to Ascari's voice mail when the redhead smacked into him harder than the ambulance.

The fact that the crazed woman had gotten away confounded Devlin. Still, he glanced over at the bandaged Ascari, now sidelined by the double chisel stabbing, and was relieved that both men had survived her wrath.

"Erika headed over to the summit," Scotti said. "Montoya's got her back. The morgue security guard is now posted outside ICU for Leif."

Devlin nodded his assent, but he didn't like the scenario. Though Erika had a job to do as head of Aurora, her life was at stake. Marisse and her radical activist underlings were right now targeting Erika and the thousands of attendees at the global water summit. He'd deduced that much from the chatty redhead in the morgue.

"Lauda and Hunt are already scouring the convention center with a handful of Aurora's security team. Looking for Marisse, the little blond sniper, and the red-haired kook. No sign of them yet," Scotti said.

Helio spoke up. "Hospital surveillance outside the morgue showed the redhead escaping on foot, heading off down the street toward the summit. I'm still checking early footage for any sign of Marisse, but she hasn't surfaced."

Scotti said, "The morgue's corner office was the only area outside of our surveillance, and Red must've been there waiting. Don't know how we missed the switch."

Helio grunted his commiseration.

Devlin nodded. Costly mistake, but they could only move forward. "Any Palio update from Lupo or Prost?"

"No word from them," Scotti said. "Also, Ana Malia told me she helped Lauda gain access to summit surveillance a couple hours ago. No update there either." Devlin's crew chief pointed to him and Sneakers. "You two get over to the gala," he said. "Remember, Marisse has a small but powerful contingent, and she's avenging her coveted offspring. Be careful."

***

Devlin debated hot-wiring a motor scooter, but decided he and Sneakers would likely reach the Veronafiere convention center faster hoofing it rather than dodging city traffic.

On the way, Devlin made calls. The humidity made clutching his mobile difficult. He nearly dropped it four times into the puddles from the earlier storm.

First, he tried Lauda, and then Hunt, but both of their phones went right to voice mail. He also tried Ana Malia, to no avail. Finally, he texted Erika to let her know that he and Sneakers would arrive shortly. He asked if she and Montoya would meet them at the south entrance.

As he drew nearer, Devlin read the enormous banners flying high in the waning daylight. They mostly touted various desalination techniques: "Forward Osmosis, Forward Thinking"; or "Solar, Nuclear, & Freeze-Thaw: Low-Cost Relief for All"; or "Nano- & Bio-Membranes Are Our Future."

Sneakers snorted. Devlin looked over to see if he was suffering from his impact with the ambulance. But he was chuckling. He gestured to the enormous sewage recycling and treatment exhibit as they ran past it. The convention organizers must have insisted it remain outside the enclosed venue. A vague manure odor cloyed at the dank, humid afternoon air.

Devlin recalled that Singapore's government had espoused wastewater recycling for its five million poverty-stricken sandbar inhabitants as an effective and economical means of solving their water scarcity and pollution issues. Singapore employed this process of ultrafiltration and reverse osmosis of any and all wastewater (so-called NEWater), and then conserved the resulting crystal-clear, drinkable, super clean water in an enormous cistern. Though Singapore's plan proved highly successful, global industry leaders still had trouble convincing the rest of the world to forget exactly what it was that they were drinking—recycled sewage.

"Someday, push may come to shove, Sneaks, and if I'm thirsty enough, count me in," Devlin said. Sneakers smirked and shook his head, wiping sweat from his brow as he ran.

The south entrance loomed closer with every footfall. Devlin dialed Lupo. That call too went to voice mail. But Lupo called back a second later, panting and out of breath. "Sorry I missed you…almost got the shit kicked out of me…then I flashed him my pythons and let fly on his ass," Lupo said.

"Who the hell are you fighting?" Devlin said.

"Everyone. It's a madhouse. This is what the zombie apocalypse is gonna be like," he said. "The next time I tell you I'm Contrada Captain, just shoot me. I got twenty-five thousand Sienese spectators crowding the streets, sitting down to dinner in row-upon-row of fifty-foot tables. They're all hungry, and they all wanna get drunk. I've got loads of fettuccine and bread. But then we told them it's Bring Your Own Beverage. There's no grappa, and there's no wine, and not even water…fists started flying. Men, women, even children…the children are crazy!"

"You mean all you planned to serve was Aurora beverages? No backup?" Devlin said.

Silence on the other end.

After a few moments, Lupo began shouting into the phone again. "There's break-ins all over our contrada. All the shops are closed for the big dinner, so people are doing smash-and-grabs. They're stealing wine, beer, water, espresso, grappa… everything…from the stores and restaurants. Some of them have knives, man!"

Devlin stopped running. Sneakers jogged in place beside him. Devlin demanded, "Where's Marcello?"

"Chiara insisted on keeping him home tonight, *grazie Dio*."

Devlin exhaled. *Thank God for small favors.*

"Prost has been working with the local police," Lupo said. "He even shipped in *carabinieri* from surrounding towns."

"What about beverage help from a competing contrada?" Devlin said.

"Bite your tongue, man. I'm not groveling to any competitor," Lupo said. "Plus they've all heard about our dilemma and they're hoarding it, especially Pantera contrada. They're having a big laugh at our expense."

Devlin shook his head at the massive screw-up.

"People are crazy. A couple guys found the Aurora grappa stash that was locked up at town hall. Started passing it out in the back parking lot. One of them started convulsing and vomiting from just a few sips. Guy's in the hospital, don't know if he's gonna make it. Prost was able to shut it down. Police locked up the perps. But we think a case of the quarantined water got past them."

"What?" Devlin paced. He could always count on Lupo as a solid wingman, but his best friend had no military training. Crisis mode had never been his strong suit, so he usually cut him some slack. But right now Lupo needed to get his head out of his ass, because lives were on the line. "Lupo, where are you now?"

"Prost cleared the riffraff out of the town hall, and I stayed back to lock up. Ran into one of the selectmen, who tried to kick me out, and that's who tried to beat me up," Lupo said.

"Listen to me," Devlin said. "Get to the fire department. Now! While we're talking…go! Get out of the town hall, go down two streets, and grab all the fire trucks you can. Bring them back to the contrada dinner tables. The firemen can either hand out free water, or they can hose down the detractors."

"Good fuckin' plan!" Lupo said.

Devlin continued, "Graham, Senna, and Alonso should almost be there by now from Rome. I'll tell them to haul ass to one of the million wineries in Tuscany, buy up the inventory, and truck it in. You'll look like a hero for handing out free wine. Until then, keep it together, man."

Devlin dialed Graham. He ordered him directly to the Siena hospital to drop off the stash of antidote that Vin had cooked up and left with them in Rome. This would aid those unlucky Palio revelers that happened to imbibe the poisoned Aurora contraband trickling through the city.

Senna and Alonso had driven up separately and were already passing through nearby Montalcino. He ordered them to Castello Banfi winery, where each HELL Ranger would buy up a truckload of wine, water, and grappa, and give it away to anyone who'd drink it inside Lupo's neighborhood.

Devlin redialed Lupo. "The crew should arrive at the Palio party in about an hour," he said. "If not, hose 'em all down." Devlin hung up, and he and Sneakers bolted for the summit.

Chapter 42

With just over an hour until the summit's opening gala, Devlin knew that it was time-critical to stop Marisse and her cohorts from wreaking havoc. The activists would step up their game, because a worldwide public spectacle would enhance visibility for their cause. And Marisse would stop at nothing short of murder to avenge the death of her son.

Devlin was confident in Leif Aurora's security at the hospital. But the threat to Erika Aurora's life increased every moment she was exposed to Marisse's murderous whim. He hated that Erika had refused guarded seclusion. But he understood Aurora Vineyard's livelihood depended on successful public relations at the gala.

Presidents, prime ministers, and other VIPs would be congregating inside the enormous Grand Ballroom for the evening cocktail party. Aurora's famed grappa and wine, and their new FONS water, exclusively graced the menu. Devlin knew Rasmus's team and summit security had successfully barred all tainted fare. But inevitably, Aurora would exhaust their limited and rapidly diminishing pure supply. How would Aurora appease the masses then?

The panic-stricken look on Erika Aurora's perspiring face at the entrance gave Devlin the answer. She had no idea either.

But having run the long mile in the sweltering heat from the hospital to the convention center, all that mattered to Devlin was the venue's air-conditioning. He pushed past Erika and through the double doors to discuss matters in the cool interior. But the hot, humid air lingered inside too. He turned to Erika for confirmation.

She nodded in visible dismay. "No power. Storm that ran through an hour ago knocked it out. The building's running on emergency generators. That means no AC."

Sneakers groaned.

Ana Malia and her cameraperson joined the group. "It also means Wi-Fi is down, and intermittent cell disruption. Power crews are here, but there's no word on when we'll get full juice." Perspiring through her silk blouse, she fanned herself with notepaper. "I'm betting Marisse killed the switch, but who can be sure?" Ana shrugged. "All I know, there's a lot of thirsty people headed into the ballroom, and the servers are already rationing. This could turn into a riot."

Ana turned to Erika. "Letizia and I are headed to the VIP suite. Leaders are holding a press conference before the gala. I'll meet up with you before it starts."

Erika nodded.

The journalist dashed away with her press pass clutched firmly in her hand. Devlin saw her flash it to security, allowing her passage to an area cordoned off by velvet ropes and enclosed by bulletproof glass. Amid the microphones and cameras stationed inside sat a throng of media reps. Influential suits strolled in a few at a time, accompanied by their not-so-secret-service personnel.

Erika's phone rang, and she issued instructions in Veronese dialect. As she paced, Devlin's crewman, Montoya, acted as her interim bodyguard. He maintained visual on her surroundings at all times.

Devlin contacted Rasmus, Lauda, and Hunt with his location and instructions to meet him as soon as possible. In the meantime, he assessed the Veronafiere convention center. It was nothing more than a huge warehouse. He spotted armed security posted around the interior perimeter, similar to what he'd seen outside. His trained eye also picked up on the occasional plainclothes security that infiltrated the population.

The venue housed an extravagant ballroom and three ample auditoriums, now closed for the evening, as well as one enormous central atrium subdivided into plush cubicles. These nooks, some larger and more elaborate than others, were built to accommodate exhibits, presentations, and small panel discussions.

The diverse exhibits included castle settings with bridges and moats, beach scenes, and replicas of international wonders. The one across from the press room impressed him. It boasted a thatched-roof hut, a pirate ship, nautical rope barricades, and potted palm trees. He wasn't sure what the theme had to do with water conservation, but it fit the tropical climate inside the venue. Devlin sized up the participants scurrying about in professional attire, wrapping up the day's business in preparation for the evening gala. Every last one of them appeared drained and ready for a drink.

Erika ended her call, clearly flummoxed. "I've tried every other venue that I can think of…the amphitheater, the local school auditorium, the soccer stadium. But they're either booked or can't accommodate the large group." She bit her thumbnail until it bled.

"I have my shipment manager coordinating with the local fire station," Erika said, wearing a path in the ceramic tile floor. "We'll be able to ply them with tap water…but, oh God, this was the perfect opportunity to showcase our brand-new product line and hawk our anniversary grappa…what an epic fuck-up this is!" She immediately placed another call and continued pacing.

Aurora's security chief, two of his men, and two summit guards appeared. They flanked Erika. "I have more intel," Rasmus said. "The driver who delivered the anonymous shipments last night is not on the Aurora staff." The Swede held up his phone and showed Devlin and Erika a picture of a seedy-looking man with a ferret's face. Devlin recognized Marisse's henchman from the pictures that Ham had texted him from France. "A couple of my men spotted him here earlier, but they lost track of him," Rasmus said.

Devlin shared with Rasmus's team the visuals of the psycho redhead and the blond sniper. Rasmus issued orders to his group. A guard armed Devlin and Sneakers with Berettas and ammo, then they dispersed. Rasmus took his post beside Erika, freeing Montoya from the job.

Lauda checked in via text, letting Devlin know where to find him and Hunt outside the venue. Devlin sent Montoya to the north entrance to meet them, while he and Sneakers exited south. Passing the press pavilion, Devlin spotted Ana inside, seated amid the rows of gathered press corps. They shot questions to the long table of dignitaries with a rapid flurry of raised hands.

Sneakers gestured to the pavilion. "Looks like every major head of state's in there. Except China and Russia."

Devlin eyed the long row of distinguished speakers, including the newly elected American president. All of them were vying desperately for face time. All except the Italian prime minister.

Pale and drawn, the Italian leader sipped from a bottle of San Pellegrino like a man stranded on a desert island. Devlin spotted him slip away from his seat at the end of the row and furtively depart the media room, flanked by two bodyguards. The leader leaned against one of the security men, who clutched his shoulder and angled him toward a rear exterior exit.

The heat must've gotten to him, Devlin thought. That would be news if the Italian prime minister blacked out in the middle of the summit.

Nearing the exit, the Italian leader and his entourage briefly disappeared behind a privacy curtain near a hydroelectric waterfall display. That's when Devlin spotted the blond sniper. The same guy who'd shot up the gondola. The shooter who'd chased him and Erika from Vitreuve's vineyard. Now from atop the thatched roof of the pirate display, the blond sniper was taking aim at the Italian prime minister.

The sniper must've lain in wait all day for a ripe opportunity. He was barely visible amid the prodigious pirate flags. He'd only captured his attention after the shiny spur on his cowboy boot reflected a strobe light at the right moment.

Devlin was close enough to see the shooter shift his prone body, adjust his finger on the trigger, and exhale. But Devlin was too far to accurately shoot his 9mm Beretta across the crowded floor of the arena. A sharp surge of adrenaline coursed through his body. He nudged Sneakers and pointed to the sniper at the top of the structure.

The sniper again repositioned and exhaled to ensure precision.

Whether the bullet was truly intended for the prime minister, or for another prominent summit leader, or possibly for Erika Aurora, Devlin didn't know, because he didn't stop to ask.

Instead, Devlin and Sneakers tore off running. Devlin grabbed the exterior metal moldings supporting the thatch-covered hut. He swung up and over, crashing atop the sniper's body.

Too late to stop the shot.

Luckily, the bullet lodged in a wood carving of Niagara Falls. Dead center of the Canadian horseshoe. Missing the Italian prime minister, who'd been escorted past the exhibit seconds earlier.

The shocked shooter flailed and shimmied to break free of Devlin's hold. Devlin ripped the rifle from the man's hands and bashed him in the face with the butt of the rifle. Knocked him out cold. Then Devlin broke the man's trigger finger, on both hands.

Devlin kicked him from the roof, and the sniper landed at the feet of arriving security. Devlin sat back and smiled. He now had a lucky rifle to go along with his Beretta. All the better to shoot Marisse with.

***

Devlin was thrilled when Ana Malia and the summit security team had vouched for him and Sneakers, sparing them from detainment. But when local Veronese carabinieri dragged away the shooter, he was miffed that they'd kept his lucky rifle for evidence.

Chaos had cleared the media room. The press sought interviews from the prime minister, now fully composed and rattling on about the foiled attack. The two dozen other world leaders canceled all further appearances, until the next day.

The bureaucratic lull also gave busybody Jacques Vitreuve, Aurora's longtime competitor, time to accost Devlin outside the

Veronafiere convention center. "Devlin, *mon frère*, to what do we owe this distinct pleasure?" he asked.

"Gotta keep moving, Jacques. Catch up later," Devlin said as he and Sneakers cut through the crowd at the exit. "I thought it was one down, two more thugs to go," he told Sneakers. "But I could definitely be convinced to shoot Vitreuve."

"Please, just do it, man," he agreed.

As the sun set further into the mountains, the two men met Lauda, Hunt, Montoya, and Erika outside in the vicinity of the wastewater conversion display. Ana stood with the group, in full view of the service entrance. There, a half dozen fire trucks pumped fresh water into dispensers for the gala attendees. The fire trucks were accompanied by six other unlabeled white tank trucks. *Milk haulers?* Devlin wondered.

Pockets of activist rallies seemed more prevalent, and louder and angrier, now that the gala was underway. Vitreuve had caught up with their group outside. His incessant chatter annoyed Devlin even more than the vociferous mobs.

But Ana and Erika helped him out. They engaged the French vintner by stroking him for information on the reconstruction of his demolished water-bottling facility, while Devlin further updated his men on the sniper melee.

In turn, Lauda explained to Devlin how he and Hunt had followed Marisse's ferret-faced activist through the kitchen service area and out back to the fresh water delivery. The two wrangled him down before he could tamper with its distribution.

Hunt found capped syringes in the perp's pockets before handing him over to local carabinieri.

Devlin imagined the dire consequences if the Ferret had successfully tainted the venue's water supply. Mass casualties. Unacceptable.

Devlin was nearly unhinged by the thought that the Palio event, involving his own town…his own family…and dear God, his young son, had nearly suffered a similar fate. Unacceptable.

He and his crew needed to find the psycho redhead before she carried out another lunatic attack. More importantly, they needed to track down Marisse LeFleau. What else did the twisted, vengeful bitch have in store?

Chapter 43

"More tankers? What the hell is this?" Ana Malia said. She pointed to four more unmarked milk haulers trundling down the back road to the ballroom's service entrance. They joined the six others already being emptied into massive cisterns. "You planning to serve milkshakes, Erika?"

Erika Aurora shot Jacques Vitreuve a grateful smile. She knew full well what the hell those tankers were. He winked back at her. Why not? He'd just saved her CEO ass.

"Six tankers of red. Four tankers of white." Erika glanced around to ensure that no one among the meandering convention attendees could overhear her secret. Then she lowered her voice to a whisper. "Compliments of HydroVino," she said.

Devlin held back a smirk and continued to scan the area for Marisse or the redhead while gaining status updates with the various HELL Rangers and Aurora security personnel scouring the grounds.

Erika applauded Vitreuve in homage. "My compadre saved the day. When organizers heard about our latest product contamination threat, they understandably nixed our entire contract. To satisfy our customers and save face in the industry, we needed fresh allocation of our entire product supply. But we only had an hour until the gala…"

"That's insane," Ana said.

Erika nodded. "No way Aurora could gather and ship that much fresh product in time. But Jacques overheard my dilemma. He rerouted shipments HydroVino had scheduled across town over to our venue instead. He's a lifesaver!"

Vitreuve beamed.

"Why?" Ana glared at Erika. "Why would your competitor do such a thing?"

Devlin posed another pertinent question to Erika and Vitreuve. "Has security authenticated the safety of Vitreuve's supply? After all, Marisse did sabotage your company once before, Jacques."

Vitreuve frowned. He hiked up his jeans, which were spilling into his penny loafers, and mumbled a few French vulgarities in Devlin's direction.

Erika smiled. She rested a hand on Vitreuve's shoulder. "Devlin has a point. Due to Marisse's threats to both our companies of late, I'd already had one of Rasmus's security men run chemical tests on every tanker. The wine is potable, Devlin, and delicious, Jacques."

Jacques harrumphed his satisfaction.

Devlin shrugged and rolled his eyes. He sauntered closer to the sewage treatment display and inspected an ornate metal manhole cover. A second later, he placed another call.

Erika turned to her journalist friend. "Ana, you can report that Jacques's help was also a good faith gesture. No further recompense or recognition, other than payment at cost."

Clearly impressed, Ana said, "Is sainthood what he's after?" She chuckled. "Nice gesture, Jacques, well done. Let's be sure to squeeze in an interview later on the rebuild of your water-bottling plant. And that new filtration technology you mentioned."

Jacques nodded, bashful with praise. One of his staff approached him with delivery questions, and he stepped away to sign papers.

Ana pounced on her chance to discreetly divulge information into Erika's ear. "My source, also your beau-hunk blond lawyer with the fine ass, had information on the injunction—"

Erika smiled. "You already told me the news yesterday. Injunction lifted. That's why Aurora's here today. Is there more?"

Ana nodded, "Sadly. Word is…the injunction may be reinstated."

Erika's stomach sank. "What do you mean? Can the courts do that? They just—"

Ana nodded. "Opposing counsel provided the court new environmental evidence. Initially it was assumed that your aquifer lay within the borders of a single sovereign nation, Italy. New evidence suggests it may be part of a freshwater system flowing down from the north, fed by Swiss or Austrian resources. Which means—"

"International law governs," Erika muttered.

"Exactly," Ana said. "An international tribunal will get involved. Another injunction imposed. The whole thing starts over."

Erika said, "The right to use my own property's freshwater is completely up in the air again, indefinitely. What happens to our FONS water line? Not to mention the exorbitant cost of shipping in water for wine production. It's…" Gears turned in her head. A perfectly delicious idea formed. Maybe not delicious, but strategic and extremely lucrative. Erika smiled and gave Ana a hug. "Not a problem. I just figured out how to fix it. But I may need your help along the way…"

Ana Malia flashed her brilliant on-camera smile. "Always, Sister." She stepped away to confer privately with Letizia.

Jacques's colleague left, and he turned back. Erika flicked her eyes at him, leaned in close, and squeezed his arm tenderly. "Jacques, Aurora thanks you so very much for everything. I can't—"

"It's my pleasure," he said. "Marisse LeFleau has shamefully victimized both of our companies."

Erika nodded in agreement.

"But, I admit, I was shameful too," he said.

Erika was thrown off guard. "In what way?"

"Many months ago, when you released your anniversary grappa, commemorating your twentieth year of making the most superb product on the market—"

"And, coincidentally, marking twenty years since the discovery of our own little Fountain of Youth," Erika told Vitreuve. She chuckled. "Did you know? The earthquake was twenty years ago to the day."

Devlin jerked his head her way. He looked at her quizzically. Then he whispered something to Montoya, and the two men headed back toward the venue.

"*Oui*, congratulations. But I must tell you…I purchased a batch of your sweet grappa through a distributor, and I…" Jacques lowered his gaze. "I attempted to copy your recipe. I failed badly. But I feel bad about trying to replicate your formula. I'm truly sorry," Jacques said quietly.

Sneakers nudged Hunt and Lauda. The three men left Erika with Jacques, in the capable hands of her security detail, and headed back inside.

Erika smiled. There was something quite charming about the silly, overbearing little Frenchman. Something almost…sickeningly…disturbingly…sexy… in a Mr. Bean or Nutty Professor sort of way. His harmless confession about his industry-standard copycatting of the grappa only endeared him to her more. This, combined with her gratitude for the epic save at the gala, and her need to develop alternative freshwater resources for production…*Why not consider a merger?* she thought.

"Could you ever forgive me?" Vitreuve asked.

Erika waved away his confession. "Water under the bridge, Jacques." She slipped her arm through his and asked, "Won't you show me your filtration exhibit?"

Jacques's eyes sparkled with enthusiasm. "It's just over by the wastewater treatment display." He and Erika drifted slowly through clusters of visitors toward the exhibit. Rasmus and his two men formed a wide circle around them both as they did.

Vitreuve preened, "My technology is patented, you know? Also, I started out filtering the salted Mediterranean to irrigate my San Remo soil. But it's even more revolutionary than that. It doesn't just filter salt water, no, and not just sewage. My technology filters chemically altered water, anything polluted by lead or toxins or—"

As they passed the rank sewage display, Erika interrupted with a brilliant thought. "So let's just say my company is bogged down with a warehouse full of tainted, poisoned, useless product...are you telling me that your industrial filtration technology will convert bad grappa, water, or wine back into—"

"Ultraclean, fresh water," Vitreuve said. "*Exactement!*"

Sparks suddenly flew into the sky on the north side of the forum, drawing everyone's attention. They seemed to emanate from an elaborate irrigation demonstration. The sparks were followed by a series of popping sounds, and then the bitter smell of burnt rubber and smoke.

In those few seconds, Ana and her camera assistant had bolted toward the commotion to cover the story. Vitreuve had raised both his arms over his head and crouched low for protection. And Rasmus and his two dependable guards had instinctively aligned to form a circular barrier between Erika and any potential threat.

But the psycho redhead tackled her from the air, leaping from the top of a nearby display structure. In full-force-rage mode, she slammed Erika to the ground.

On her back, Erika looked up into the face of the thrashing, biting, kicking banshee. The bitch had threatened the welfare of Aurora's valued customers. The woman had killed her childhood dog. She'd stabbed Ascari and tried to blow up Devlin. The bitch was fighting with her hands, Erika realized. No gun. No blade. Only bare hands.

Erika fought back.

Rasmus bellowed orders to his men. They clicked off the safeties on their guns, but Erika cried out, "Holster your weapons! This bitch is mine!"

Fired up by all the anger, betrayal, grief, and stress of the past few weeks, Erika landed all the well-placed jabs and hooks that her father had taught her growing up.

The psycho redhead punched, kicked, and clawed her in return. But Erika inhaled deeply, and then she bucked the woman so high that she rolled them both over, leaving Red on her back and Erika on top. Just the way she liked it.

Erika closed both fists and pummeled the woman in the face until blood spattered them both.

Red howled through clenched teeth. She gripped Erika by both arms and tossed all of her buck-and-a-quarter pounds through the air. Erika landed on her side beside the sewage treatment exhibit. Her head nearly landed in a metal tub of slop. The stench overwhelmed her.

Slightly dazed, Erika watched the beefy redhead come for her. Red trudged the few-foot span like a steroid-enhanced wrestler.

Erika didn't budge. She put her hands over her face in self-defense and waited for the hit.

Red lunged.

Though Erika lay immobile on the ground, she was ready. She grabbed the woman's shoulders with both hands, pulled her close until their noses touched, and kicked her high heel straight up into Red's radical activist crotch. Hard.

The woman crumpled inward. Her face turned the same shade of red as her ridiculous head of flaming hair, and then to pea green. The redhead was about to spew all over Erika whatever bile was traveling up her pipes. But she thrust Red's shoulders sideways and pushed clear in the opposite direction.

The psycho bitch face-planted into the tub of raw sewage.

A smiling Rasmus grasped Erika's hand and pulled her to standing. She flicked back her still-gorgeous hair and straightened her skirt. The Aurora company believed that recycling refuse was indeed the new big thing in water conservation. CEO Erika Aurora smiled into Ana Malia's live TV camera to prove that she'd done her part.

***

Lucky for Rasmus, the summit's security team had converged on the scene in moments. They'd handcuffed the stinking, dripping, filthy redhead, then hosed her down with recycled irrigation drainage, and dragged her away. Ana and Letizia reported the whole thing.

Rasmus ordered his charge back inside the facility. "Erika, you've had your fun. But your life remains in danger as long as Marisse is roaming the summit. I insist, whatever work requires your attention, conduct it inside the guarded, bulletproof media room."

She knew he was right. Summit organizers were shutting down exhibits and panel discussions until the next day. The conference president urged cancellation of the gala, but participants and press who demanded their share of free booze threatened riots. He acquiesced. The show would go on, even in light of Marisse's threat, or perhaps because of the spectacle it drew.

She told Rasmus, "Let's get to the fishbowl, then. I have work to do."

Her security chief nodded, conferred with his agents, and placed a call. As the group shuffled toward the venue, she told Vitreuve, "Jacques, it's been fun. Thank you again for your generous supply of vino. Let's talk more tomorrow about future plans."

Erika paused to kiss Vitreuve on both cheeks, and then she turned to face her journalist friend. "Ana, I understand if you need to go and cover the gala. But do you have any word on Devlin's whereabouts?"

Ana shook her head. "I saw him heading toward the north entrance with Montoya about a half hour ago. Hunt, Sneakers, and Lauda are inside looking for Marisse. Maybe he's with them."

Erika's path to the fishbowl was blocked by a mass of summit participants. They milled about the central atrium with wine glasses, talking and laughing as if nothing was amiss. She glanced at the ballroom's double doors. Both sets overflowed with drinkers spilling out of the immense hall looking for a party. Erika shivered. Was Marisse among those revelers? What would the spiteful evil queen do next?

Erika spied her Aurora detail, a dozen summit guards, and a few HELL Rangers intermingled with the guests. But she couldn't spot Devlin Lucchesi among them. Where the hell was he when she needed him the most?

Rasmus must have noticed the same thing. "Erika, this place is like a beehive, and it's only a matter of time until you get stung. I strongly advise that you leave the summit until Marisse is found." He took a call, giving her a moment to consider his warning.

Aurora was the summit's sole sponsor. If she didn't remain a visible presence, Aurora's reputation would suffer. However, it wouldn't do the company any good if another of its chief officers was assaulted or murdered.

Rasmus hung up. He was visibly stunned by the call.

"What is it?" Erika said. "Is my brother alright?"

Rasmus nodded. "Scotti believes that Marisse never went to the summit. Only her cohorts."

"What? Where the hell is she?" Erika said.

"Helio just picked it up on hospital surveillance," Rasmus said. "When Marisse planted her impostor in the morgue, she fled the facility in an SUV. The monitor showed the vehicle entering the highway behind the hospital, headed north."

Erika gasped. "Oh God, that was well over an hour ago, almost two." Her hands and feet grew cold. Her breathing started coming up short. Shit, she was going to hyperventilate.

"Marisse could've crossed over to Switzerland by now, or Austria…she could be anywhere." Erika began to tremble. She felt entirely out of control. Control was her thing; she always maintained it, and now she had none. "All this time, we thought she'd be coming after me at the summit. Now, how will we find her? How can we ever stop her from ruining our lives? I can't even—"

Rasmus put both hands on her shoulders. "Erika, it's going to be okay. Helio just told me…" He sat her down on a folding chair, knelt on one knee, and looked into her eyes.

"Devlin has a plan."

Chapter 44

It was his racing crew's lengthiest pit stop ever. But any highlight reel surely would've ranked it as one of the best.

Devlin's crew's performance ran like any other day at the track, with one minor variation. His pit boss typically barked orders to his men from inside the pit. This time, Scotti conference-called his commands through a cell phone, from his window overlooking the hospital parking lot.

As usual, the crew jockeyed to complete their tasks with precision. Their goal? Getting their driver back on the track in record time to win the race. Now, winning meant beating Marisse LeFleau at her game before it was too late.

Devlin wished all of his men were there to help him transform his Formula One chassis into a souped-up racing machine, capable of handling rain-slicked mountain roads at night. But some of his crew played other vital roles, like guarding the Aurora clan and preventing poison massacres. Just another day among HELL Rangers.

In the fading light of day, Helio, Vin, and Montoya rolled out from the Lucchesi team trailer both Devlin's race car and his engineered prototype. Scotti had showcased the mock-up to the Monza racing board before his heart surgery pit stop at Verona Hospital. Little did they realize they'd be taking it out for a trial run.

With his turbocharged 1.6-liter V-6 engine already firmly planted between the seat and rear axle of his racing car, much time was saved from the install. Scotti insisted on adding ballast for better weight distribution and stability on the slick, curved Dolomite roads. Devlin shoveled in parking lot gravel until Scotti nodded his approval.

Helio and Montoya bolted on treaded Pirelli Cinturato wet-weather tires to handle the rain-soaked roads from the earlier storm. Scotti argued for full wets to handle the larger puddles. But Devlin made the executive decision to go with intermediaries—they sacrificed some grip but were more durable. Marisse already had a solid lead, and shaving seconds off his drive time would be critical.

Ascari leaned on his crutch and juiced up the car with petrol from the ambulance fuel pumps. Devlin had ditched the idea of the straight and speedy A22 highway route, in favor of the narrow, winding SS12 heading north from Verona *centro* toward Trento. Not because the route was breathtakingly scenic. But because the SS12 was far shorter, and his fuel capacity topped out at forty gallons. Besides, he could handle the curves.

Helio and Montoya finalized installation of the headlamps. These weren't part of the original plan, but they were conveniently borrowed from an Alfa Romeo 4C Spider parked nearby for safer, sexier nighttime driving.

He slid into his single-seat open cockpit. Helio installed the steering wheel that would allow Devlin to change his eight-speed gearbox with paddles on the handle. His car was capable of rocketing to a max speed of 225 miles per hour, and he buckled his six-point seat belt. Marcello would've demanded it of Lucky.

He donned his gloves and helmet. He checked his mirrors, and his water intake tube. Devlin had entrusted his faithful backpack full of evidence to Scotti, because in the cramped quarters of his monocoque, something had to give. And for the tenth time, he made sure that the extra syringes of antidote that Vin had cooked up, and his 9mm Beretta, were securely holstered to his cargo pants.

Devlin signaled to Scotti through the hospital window. He waited for his chief's indication that no other vehicles impeded his quick exit from the pit lane.

When his men finally jumped out of the way, Scotti gave him two thumbs up.

Riding high on a protein bar and gumption, he tore out of the parking lot and raced toward a life-or-death finish.

***

Devlin headed for the SS12 roadway that Marisse had navigated less than two hours earlier, according to hospital surveillance. She had a hell of a head start. But she was driving an aquamarine Lancia SUV, renowned for its luxury rather than its performance. That improved his chances of catching her before her next exploit.

He zipped onto the single-lane Strade Statale regional highway 12, and he breathed easier when he found no other cars on the road. If one surfaced that he'd have to pass in a fraction of a second, he prayed for a shouldered straightaway instead of a winding cliff. He lit his headlamps even though visibility of the surrounding landscape was still clear.

When he'd first proposed his race car idea to Scotti in the hospital, his pit boss had looked at him like he was crazy. Devlin reasoned that his race car would shorten a forty-five-minute ride in a typical SUV to roughly fifteen minutes. Scotti told him it was suicide. But Devlin explained his rationale for Marisse's probable location and what he thought would be her magnum opus. Scotti acquiesced, and the HELL Rangers were all in.

Devlin had formulated his theory back at the summit. During Erika and Vitreuve's verbal love fest, Devlin had noticed an ornate metal manhole cover that was part of the outdoor sewage treatment display at Veronafiere. The cover reminded him of the decorative medallion in the center of Aurora Vineyard's courtyard where the aquifer had first come to light.

The couple's banter had also reminded Devlin of the date of the aquifer's discovery, a landmark moment in the establishment of the family business. The date was twenty years ago on this very day. According to Erika, it also represented the torrid banishment of Marisse LeFleau from Augustus Aurora's love nest for tormenting his child, Leif. No one at that time, save

Marisse LeFleau, had been aware that Augustus was actually banishing his unborn child, Philippe, on that same occasion.

Devlin fishtailed his race car at one hundred miles per hour, but he gripped the wheel and lowered his speed. He adjusted his aerofoil wings to maximize downforce and minimize drag, allowing for higher speed while cornering the tight curves. Would this race end as dramatically as his Monaco showing?

All this time Marisse's goal had been to preserve Aurora and murder its heirs, to secure Philippe his rightful inheritance of the lucrative winery. Now, with Philippe dead, what better way to exact revenge on the Auroras than to destroy their company altogether?

He spied a car ahead. He lowered his speed, downshifted, passed, and resumed his breakneck speed. He sipped water through the tube in his helmet and maintained focus on the road. He gauged his fuel. It would hold until the vineyard, roughly eight more minutes away.

He wondered if Marisse was aware of her cohorts' failures. The psycho redhead, the blond sniper, and the ferret-faced thug had botched assassinations and mass murders in Siena and Verona. Marisse's radical activists were nothing more than watered-down minions. Now, she was on her own.

He recalled the redhead's rant inside the morgue: "Marisse is gone…with work to do… ensuring that the water rights of all people are equal and just." In the morgue, he had assumed this meant Marisse would seek vengeance by targeting Erika Aurora and the company's reputation at the summit. But her failure to surface alarmed him. Her minions' escapades were mere diversions. Marisse pursued a loftier vendetta.

Devlin spied the perimeter lights of the vineyard atop the winding mountain. He chanced a glance at the antidote syringes Velcroed to his pant leg.

One more curve and he hit the turbocharge. The race car sailed across the finish line, into the parking lot of the estate.

In the lot sat an aquamarine Lancia SUV. Was it definitely Marisse's vehicle or a similar one that belonged to an Aurora employee? Then he knew it must be hers. The license plate read: MeOH, the chemical symbol for methanol.

Devlin prayed he wasn't too late.

Chapter 45

Lanterns illuminated Aurora's landmark medallion that denoted the fateful aquifer's plentiful spring. Devlin half-expected Marisse LeFleau to be standing there. Dead center of the courtyard. A syringe in her hand. Waiting to stick it to him.

But the rolling estate and accompanying buildings appeared deserted. Only Marisse's SUV and two muddy field trucks stood in the lot. He'd panned the acres of grapevines but saw no sign of field-workers. There'd been minimal traffic on the mountain, and no other vehicle had yet passed the vineyard. The five million inhabitants of the Veneto region were probably cramming Veronafiere to guzzle Aurora's free booze.

Devlin heard his footsteps echo through the courtyard. Erika Aurora had called for her employees' evacuation of the vineyard upon Marisse's escape from the hospital. Also, Rasmus had gathered most of his troops to secure the summit. But the chief had stationed a half dozen personnel to guard the production plants from possible destruction. He spied none of Rasmus's guards now.

Was she lining up Devlin in her sights at that moment? She'd already used Aurora's surveillance to scout the property for anyone who might stop her in the recent past. Marisse was an intelligent, cunning woman. And, reminiscent of the movie *Aliens*, she was a bloodthirsty mother she-devil looking for vindication. He was damn sure he would not underestimate her.

He pulled the Beretta from his waist and held it in front of him, using the gathering shadows thrown by the property lights for cover. He scanned the overlook to the mountains and valley, where the redhead had taken her flying leap with Erika's dog. The sun had just set behind the queen mountain, Marmolado, to the west. No sign of Marisse alongside the cliff or near the dark gondola lift station.

He scanned the woods ahead of him, right up to the top of the pines where Marisse's other henchman, the blond sniper, had hidden himself. Nothing amiss.

The mountain air was damp. The temperatures were cool. Any fog was kept at bay by a light breeze that eerily rustled the leaves. The cantina, the villas, the office building, and the production plants were all visible in the gloom due to the security lighting. He wondered why Marisse had chosen to keep the estate illuminated. He figured it was somehow part of her plan.

Aside from the fluttering leaves, silence choked the property like a noose. Devlin instinctively tugged at the neck of his shirt. His footsteps crunched on the gravel. He halted and cursed himself. *More stealth, Lucky.*

He peered at the ground around the cantina for a quieter route. A spattering of animal tracks traversed the courtyard toward the woods. A single pair of work boot prints, perhaps belonging to a guard, led toward the villas.

After closer inspection, he noticed a fresh set of high heel footprints. They could only have been pressed into the rain-soaked soil after Erika had gone. He'd bet his lambskin racing gloves they belonged to Marisse. They led toward the grappa plant, which housed the company's laboratory. Seemed like a logical place for a mad chemist to produce more lethal formula. Maybe too logical, but he had to start somewhere.

***

With stealth, Devlin crept down the main hall of the grappa plant. He shone the flashlight he'd stored in his cargo pants. He trained his gun forward. Was Marisse in the lab, mixing more poison? Was she drawing him into the lab only to ambush him? He'd deduced that the vineyard was where Marisse would exact her payback on the Aurora family, but to what end?

He hadn't spotted any explosive charges along his route so far. But that didn't mean she didn't intend to blow up the entire estate. Case in point—Vitreuve's bottling plant. But no, the Aurora family could always rebuild.

Perhaps Marisse had chosen a technological approach—blow up the company from the inside, with a computer virus that would destroy company records and intellectual property. Companies rarely survived such an attack. But Erika, Leif, and

Runa had likely installed backups and firewalls to prevent such a business catastrophe. Plus, the value of the company didn't reside in any office. Aurora's worth grew in its fields, where the grapes were sown.

Devlin reached the outer doors of the grappa plant. He employed the high-tech dumbwaiter that Rasmus had shown him, a more clandestine way of sneaking up on Marisse inside the plant.

He continued to ponder her next big move. Marisse's attempts at intimidation and assault had proved only partially effective. True, she'd been successful in murdering Runa Aurora. But subsequent attacks on Erika and Leif had failed, due to Vin's antidote. Plans to mar the company's reputation through tainted product at the summit and at Palio had fizzled, thanks in part to the HELL Rangers' efforts. But Marisse was inventive. She would devise a new plan to destroy Aurora and vindicate her son.

He exited the industrial dumbwaiter onto the plant floor, directly behind a grappa vat. He peered up the length of it. It was the same grappa vat in which Runa Aurora had been poisoned and left for dead.

This secluded entry allowed him a visual of the glass-enclosed, fluorescent-lit lab on the opposite wall of the plant. He scrutinized every inch of the lab's interior from his shelter, but he didn't spot Marisse. Unless she was inside the inner equipment lab?

He crept quietly around the grappa plant's perimeter to the base of the lab steps. There he smelled the perfume that Marisse LeFleau had worn to Runa's memorial. The scent was tinged with a whiff of something else, even more fetid.

With his gun thrust in front of him, he climbed the stairs. He peered inside the outer lab. Empty.

The door to the inner lab was open. He put his sleeved hand to his nose to cover the rank odor in the room. He lurked near the threshold of the inner lab, ready to fire. Empty.

She had been there a short time ago. He could smell her. Had she become alerted to his presence? Where was she now?

Devlin glanced about the room for evidence that Marisse had been mixing up formula. On the counter, alongside assorted syringes, beakers, and tools, sat a rack of vials topped with platinum-speckled dirty-brown liquid.

Then it hit him. Lingering above the floral scent of Marisse's perfume was something "barnyard" in nature. The smell of cow manure. Vin had mentioned that an element of cowhide had something to do with the methanol's increased potency. And right now, the lab reeked like an animal farm in the middle of July.

He exited the room, careful to cover every corner of the plant with his weapon, and edged back down the stairs. At the bottom, he cut in the opposite direction from which he'd come. And stumbled over the uniformed dead body of a guard named Lorenzo.

Devlin recognized Lorenzo only from his uniform's name tag. The man was otherwise unrecognizable. Devlin noted the thick, bloated body. Whatever remained of the dissolved skin and muscle on his skull congealed with foaming vomit and blood. A needle protruded from the corpse's right arm. The guard must've confronted Marisse, but she'd injected him with a syringe of her lethal formula.

Wherever she was on the property now, she was packin' heat.

Devlin racked his brain for Marisse's next move. He stole toward Leif Aurora's office safe. Augustus Aurora, the man who'd rejected Marisse LeFleau two decades earlier, housed his most personal documents there. Devlin again cracked open the safe and routed it. There had to be something of his belongings that would indicate her next move.

Letters, bonds, deeds…they formed a mountain of proof that Augustus Aurora had become a giant in his industry. During his investigation, Devlin had discreetly conferred with the man's friends, suppliers, distributors, and lawyers. The one thing on which they'd all agreed—Augustus Aurora had been salt of the earth.

Devlin shook his head. He was missing something. Something that teetered on the edge of his brain. He left Leif's room, checked Runa's former office, and ended in Erika's. No sign of Marisse, but plenty of Augustus. In every office, he had passed by framed photos and sentimental tokens of their father. The man truly had been the salt of the earth.

In the shadows of Erika's office, he abruptly halted his gait. Salt of the earth?

What better way for a jilted paramour to get back at her man? The man who'd taken her into his field as his migrant worker, and later into his bed as his lover. A padrone that had banished her and their unborn child, his only true seed, from his estate. Banished, in favor of his adopted children. How does one exact vengeance on such a man?

Salt his earth. Destroy the fields around which the entire estate was built. Kill the fields, kill the company.

Armed with the poison that would destroy the Aurora fortune, and ruin any chance of rebuilding it for future generations, Marisse LeFleau had in her hands the means to avenge her son. She would infuse the vineyard's irrigation system with the formula, and all crops would be lost.

In the darkness of Erika's office window, he peered out at the fields that sprawled for acre upon acre from the estate.

He spotted Marisse then. She stood atop the medallion landmark in the center of the courtyard. With a beaker of speckled auburn liquid in her hands.

***

Devlin dashed from the window. His heart pounding in his chest, he ran down the stairs to the exit. He pushed through the door and out into the courtyard.

Marisse spun around to look at him. Her wild sapphire eyes gleamed against the backdrop of her formfitting blue-green dress. Marisse's lips parted into a horrifying grin.

"You've graduated from syringe to beaker, I see," Devlin said.

Marisse replied in a thick yet refined French accent. "As in 'graduated cylinder.' Good humor, smart man. Fuck off. I'm busy."

"Let's talk about this." He inched closer, attempting to close the gap between them.

With about fifty feet between them, she said, "Stop walking, *s'il vous plait*."

He edged closer a few more steps, until she raised the beaker as if to smash it. He halted, unsure what would happen if she did.

"Want to tell me what you're planning to do with that cylinder?" He said, stalling her until the moment when he could strike.

"Throw down your weapon, and I'll think about it."

He weighed his options. Then he tossed the gun aside. It clattered out of reach beside the cantina door.

He finally asked the question that had been burning in his mind since the start. "I get why you wanted to murder Aurora's chief officers—so that Philippe would inherit the company all to himself. But why kill Giancarlo Venchi?"

She rolled her eyes. "Collateral damage. My mistake. I tried to get rid of Runa Aurora by flavoring her grappa with my chemical compound. How did I know that she would give the bottle away?" She shrugged her shoulders. "Too bad, really. Your race car friend, he was always a good lay."

Devlin fumed but kept it together. "Marisse, you're a bright woman. You know this can't end well. Think of Toujours, the company that you built into an empire. Turn yourself in, and your reputable company will continue to flourish…for your workforce, and for the benefactors of your charities. End this, and honor the memory of your child."

"Lovely speech, *mais casse-toi*!" Marisse said. "How dare you speak about Philippe? As for my leather company, *je m'en fous*. My activist son deplored my use of cowhide. His shame in my company is the reason why I worked so hard to grant him his birthright in Aurora Vineyard. Goddamn those children of Augustus. They were not the fruit of his loins. Our son was his legacy," she shrieked.

Marisse's eyes blazed and her face burned red, her blood now fermenting with rage. "This land is my son's rightful dominion. But now Philippe is dead. Since my son does not live to reign over his kingdom, then I shall kill the kingdom."

Kill the kingdom.

At that moment, Devlin knew that this was about more than just salting the fields and destroying Aurora's future. For Marisse, without Philippe, there was nothing left to live for. A widespread massacre was her only revenge. "You plan to poison the aquifer," he said. "Right where you stand."

Her eyes glimmered with power and satisfaction.

He knew that pouring the poisonous formula into the aquifer would ruin Aurora's artesian well and, by extension, their irrigated land.

Far worse than that, he knew from investigating the property that the Aurora water source naturally flowed down the Dolomite mountain. Through rainwater, runoff, and subterranean discharge, the aquifer fed the Adige river and the many alpine lakes and streams spanning the Veneto region of Italy.

The names of Marisse's poisoned victims trickled through his conscience—Erika and Leif, Runa Aurora, Giancarlo Venchi, and Lorenzo, the faceless Aurora guard.

Then like a waterfall, the faces of millions of men, women, and children poured through his mind. Innocent people and livestock would suffer painful, violent deaths simply from imbibing fresh drinking water or eating tainted fruits and vegetables. And for how long? Months, years, decades…there was no telling how long it would take to flush the poison from the ecosystem, or how far away it would travel from its source.

Marcello's face appeared in Devlin's mind. What if Marisse's poison somehow found its way to his son's fresh drinking water?

Adrenaline shot through him. He lunged forward, knowing that his speed would overcome Marisse's reaction time. He'd cover the distance, grasp the poison in one hand, and beat the murderous bitch down with the other hand.

But he must've flinched before he'd charged.

In a heartbeat, Marisse lowered one of her hands, clasped the beaker with the other, and pulled a small trinket gun from her waist. She shot him in the arm.

It stopped him cold. And made him angrier. He sprang forward again, this time covering half the distance.

She shot him higher, near the same shoulder.

He growled in pain. Kept moving. Dodging left and right like a footballer to avoid a shot to the head.

She shot again. Missed. She snorted loudly like a pig.

Two more feet and he was finally on her. Grateful the beaker was capped, he grabbed the glass vial with his hand as he clutched her gun hand with his bad arm. He grimaced with pain as he shook the petite Frenchwoman like a rag doll until she dropped her weapon. He tried to boot it away but only kicked up gravel.

Glaring at him with a sardonic smile, she opened her hand and released her hold on the vial, jerking it from his grip as she did.

He lost it but dove to prevent it from shattering, and he grasped it once more. When he did, she made for the gun at her feet, grunting heavily with the effort. He tried to kick the tiny pistol away, but again the thick gravel prevented it.

Now he had the beaker. But Marisse had the gun. Pointed straight at his head only a foot away.

He heard her grunt again, like the swine that she was. He realized that his last moments on Earth would feature a dame who snorted like a pig, smelled like cow shit, spoke like a frog, and reckoned on contaminating the farm's water trough. In the name of George Orwell, he would fight to his last breath to take this bitch down.

Clutching the cask like a pigskin in the crook of his arm, he ducked low and rammed her.

That's when the wild boar that had been nosing about with his incessant grunting charged them both, taking them down like a sack of potatoes.

Sandwiched in the tangled heap between him on the ground and the ferocious boar on top, Marisse flailed her arms and legs, struggling to break free.

While the animal focused its gnashing teeth on her cheek and throat, one of the boar's tusks impaled Marisse through the eye. She screamed in terror. The gun was thrown from her hand. He saw it land on the cantina's patio, too far for either of them to reach.

Pinned beneath the wretched, filthy she-beast, and the massive three-hundred-pound boar, Devlin wrestled to maintain the integrity of the glass beaker. At the same time, he dodged powerful projectile hooves like a fighter in a ring.

Blood suddenly spewed above him like a geyser.

Marisse gurgled a scream. She floundered like a hooked fish, grasped at her throat, and choked on her own blood, as if poisoned.

Marisse's dead weight crumpled atop him, the bristled gouge in her throat now visible. The boar must have gored her jugular.

He was next. He had to get the hell away from the beast or suffer the same fate. But he was now pinned by both the boar's weight and that of a dead woman.

The boar bicycled its clawed hind hooves against Devlin's chest in an effort to gain traction and sprint away. Though Marisse's corpse acted as a shield against the heaviest blows, he still reeled from the hard jousts of the squealing, drooling swine.

He shot an uppercut to the boar's underside. Then he punched again. The boar found his calf and bit down hard.

Devlin bellowed. He sought to crush its testicles in an effort to weaken the beast. But a lack of them proved she was more of a bitch than he'd first thought. Just like Marisse, one angry mother.

He didn't know how much longer he could hold out. Either the boar would impale him with a tusk or a hoof, or he'd lose his grip and shatter the poison flask that was still in his fist. He rolled back and forth, hoping to gain enough leverage to roll both Marisse and the boar off of him. But the solid weight of both bitches was reducing his air intake. Would he live to watch his own evisceration, or first asphyxiate from crushed lungs?

He continued to rock side to side, teetering the dead woman and the walloping, gnawing pig above him. Until, finally, he got what he needed from his back pocket.

The shit-brown, platinum-speckled lethal contents lolled and splashed sickeningly inside the beaker gripped in his left hand. With his right hand, Devlin stabbed the blade of his Jack Daniel's box cutter into the meat of the beast.

The gorgeous, smiling face of his benefactor, Veronica Griffith, flashed in his mind. He withdrew the blade she'd gifted him, reared his arm, and lanced the swine's thick underside again. Blood spattered his face and neck this time, might've hit a major vessel. The boar squealed louder than ever. Kicked him in the forehead so hard he saw spots.

He shook it off and tried to breathe beneath the weight. If he passed out now, the boar would gain her footing, likely turn on him, and feast on his blood-soaked flesh.

Pull back, jab.

Pull, jab.

Pull, jab. Devlin sought the femoral artery in the boar's thigh, but with only one active hand, coupled with the occasional hoof to the face, it was difficult to tap a vein.

Marisse's body suddenly slid to one side. The thumping, butting boar finally toppled her carcass off his chest. Half the weight gone, Devlin sucked in more air.

He eyed a clear shot to the boar's underbelly, and he thrust the blade forward. This time it did not meet flesh.

With Marisse's body out of the way, the boar finally had gained solid footing on Devlin's torso. She propelled her bleating swinehood off him and ran, squealing her high-pitched siren as she tore through the woods seeking refuge.

Alone at last.

He set the beaker of poison safely atop the ground, within reach of the maniacal scientist who'd created it. He collapsed on his back and breathed long, full breaths of air into his compressed lungs.

He held up the box cutter still in his grasp to the starlight above and smiled.

Who knew Jack Daniel's would save the world's water supply?

Epilogue

Veronica Griffith took the lead at the IndyCar race on the seventieth lap, bending her car around the hairpin turn and rocketing down the Second Street straightaway. The way she was hauling now, there was no way she'd relinquish her first-place title this weekend. Devlin was thrilled that he and his crew were there to see it happen.

Lupo nudged him. "Veronica's got a shot at making IndyCar history. First female winner in—"

Devlin shot him a glare. "What's the matter with you? Do not jinx the lead driver so close to the end." He elbowed his best friend and grinned. "Would be great, though, wouldn't it?"

Veronica inched further ahead of the nearest competitor as she aced the Elm Street straightaway.

Lupo laughed and poked him in the ribs. Marcello joined them with a heaping tub of popcorn. Devlin settled his son between him and Lupo in the enormous box he'd bought to seat his crew, as well as his honorable guests, fifty or so wounded military veterans and their families.

Marcello tried to edge back against the cushioned seat but had a bit of trouble, because the rucksack he was wearing prevented it. He adored his son's newfound habit of hauling around a backpack, like Devlin had been doing for his more frequent HELL Ranger missions.

Aside from the backpack's essentials, like Legos, trading cards, and a baseball, Marcello also toted Ella's book of tales. Devlin had given it to his son just before the Palio horse race, subsequently won by their contrada's horse. Treasured as a token of luck, the bedtime stories were a perfect way to spend time with Ella's memories.

Veronica's race car sped past the waterfront, just as Lupo took a call from Ana Malia. After a few minutes of romantic chatter, he handed the phone to Devlin. On behalf of the BBC, Ana inquired whether Devlin, as IndyCar's guest of honor, could meet her down at the track for an interview. Marcello chose to hang with his godfather, Lupo, and Devlin promised to meet them later at the winner's feast.

He stole another glance at the track. Veronica Griffith was still in first place.

***

On Second Street near the course's finish line, Devlin joined the rest of his pit crew. They were clustered near one of the barriers, scrutinizing the drivers' and mechanics' strategies.

Ana was interviewing Scotti, healthy as ever on his fish-and-vegetable diet. She asked him about resuming his crew chief duties in Devlin's upcoming Formula One British Grand Prix. But Devlin overheard Scotti touting Veronica, the woman who'd saved his life, and who appeared on the verge of a history-making run here in America.

Four laps remained. Veronica Griffith had just pulled ahead of the legendary Juan Pablo Montoya by nearly a quarter of a lap. Though Devlin's crewman, Montoya, always rooted for his namesake, he was hoping Veronica would pull this one off.

With three laps to go, Juan Pablo Montoya was closing the gap between him and Veronica Griffith. When Ana Malia finished speaking with Scotti, Devlin deferred their meeting until the dinner celebration. Ana's imminent interview with the IndyCar winner would be tantamount.

Devlin grasped the metal barrier with both hands and focused on the last couple laps around the track. He was profoundly impressed with Veronica's technique in edging out Montoya on the Lake Street curve. His stomach tightened. His heart pounded. He sent a prayer to Ella for help with a win.

Erika Aurora interrupted his reverie with a hug and a kiss on the cheek. "It's been months, Devlin. How's my hero?"

Devlin felt his face flush, and he embraced her. "It's great to see you, Erika. You look gorgeous as ever. Almost…glowing."

Now it was her turn to blush.

"Congratulations on the merger with Vitreuve," Devlin said. "I see Aurora-HydroVino has soared to the top spot in the beverage industry—water, wine, and grappa. You two must be very happy." The union of Aurora Vineyard with HydroVino had astounded the world, let alone the industry. Not only had they assumed the top level in market share, but their water conservation and filtration techniques had instigated a global water values revolution.

Erika nodded. "Very happy." She thrust her left hand between them. A ring on her finger flickered flecks of light on her face in the summer sun. "Platinum," she said and winked at him. "We have a solid appreciation of each other's assets."

Devlin laughed. He grasped her hand to admire it. "Merger and marriage. *Auguri!*" He kissed her, impressing his well wishes on both cheeks.

Devlin gestured to Scotti's brother, Vin. Hunkered over a race monitor beside him was Erika's brother, Leif Aurora, in sunglasses and a Red Sox cap. The two had remained close friends, and after Leif's full recovery, they'd worked together to secure the remainder of the formula and antidote.

All potentially tainted Aurora product had been safely "ultrafiltrated" using Vitreuve's patented technique. Vin's antidote was locked up at the Grotto. Additional serum was produced and distributed to the hospitals in Siena and Verona as a precaution.

"Just between us, there's more to it." Erika slyly raised an eyebrow. "The ink on our latest merger is almost dry…"

Devlin's eyes widened. "Another venture?"

Erika nodded. "We're merging with Leif's company…into a veritable conglomerate."

Devlin looked at her quizzically.

Erika continued, "Apparently, the original founder of Toujours leather company had equally bequeathed his shares to Marisse and Philippe upon his death. Though Philippe spurned the cowhide factory while living, in death his viable shares nonetheless passed to his next of kin."

"His mother, Marisse," Devlin said.

"Nope." Erika smiled and shook her head. "My brother and his partner had secretly married in France months ago. So Leif, his spouse, inherited Philippe's shares of Toujours. Then, when the former migrant Marisse croaked without any next of kin…"

Devlin took a breath and exhaled deeply. "Leif became sole shareholder of Toujours."

"Exactly," Erika said. "Marisse LeFleau's worst nightmare has come true…the Aurora children have saved their own company and are now taking over hers in its entirety."

"And somewhere out there, your sister Runa is laughing her ass off." Devlin squeezed her arm with affection.

She smiled. "Thanks, Lucky…"

Suddenly, the cheers of the spectators grew louder. Erika leveled her gaze at the track and then pointed. "Holy shit, I think your friend Veronica's going to win this thing."

He jerked his glance to the track and gasped.

Seven seconds later, history was made. Devlin beamed.

***

After driving her victory lap, the first female IndyCar champion Veronica Griffith hugged every member of her crew, twice. She jubilantly hoisted her trophy, then graciously accepted interviews, selfies, and tokens of appreciation from the press and adoring fans.

During Ana Malia's live BBC interview, Veronica inquired whether she might also include the race's special guest—Formula One racer, and potential future IndyCar driver, Devlin "Lucky" Lucchesi. Broadcast on the track's Jumbotron, fans of both drivers cheered with excitement. Devlin agreed. Then he and Veronica gave spectators what they really wanted to hear…a promise to compete against one another in a future IndyCar race. The crowd went wild.

When business icon Erika Aurora presented her company's sponsored driver with a gift—a bottle of their new product, called Marcus A. Grappa—a collective gasp escaped the crowd, followed by a resounding, "No!"

Veronica smiled. The driver took a long, deep swig of the 120-proof grappa and handed it to Devlin, who did the same. "Thank you, Sister," Veronica said, throwing Erika a wink. The crowd roared.

When the cameras finally dimmed, Veronica grasped Devlin's hand and meandered beneath the canopy of her team's pit garage. "Catch up with you later?" she said.

"Maybe tomorrow. Tonight, you and your crew, and the rest of the city, enjoy your well-deserved victory feast," he said. "Go make it a night to remember."

Veronica stepped close to him. She exuded an intoxicating blend of jasmine and gasoline. He grabbed her, pulled her jumpsuit-clad body against him, and kissed her. She kissed him back, like a champion.

"How about tomorrow we make our own night to remember…and you cook me dinner?" Veronica asked.

"Love to." He reached into his pocket. He held up his prized Jack Daniel's box cutter. "How about wild boar…with some fava beans and a nice bottle of Jack?"

THE END

If you enjoyed this book, please leave a brief review at your online bookseller. Thanks.

Check out the first book in the HELL Ranger series, the action-packed thriller that started it all...Gina Fava's The Race: A HELL Ranger Thriller.

Be the first to get updates on new books and giveaways...sign up for Gina Fava's Newsletter at www.GinaFava/newsletter.

ACKNOWLEDGEMENTS

Special thanks, as always, to my readers. I appreciate your book reviews, letters, emails, posts, and tweets. Please continue to spread the word about my books to your friends, family, and co-workers. You can learn more about my next novel at www.GinaFava.com.

I am indebted to Stephen King, Daniel Silva, Dan Brown, and Marcus Sakey, who have shown me the way. To JJ Abrams, Damon Lindeloff, and Carlton Cuse, because when all is Lost, I am found. To the vintners at Vinitaly, it's all about the *terroir*. To the residents of Italy who fed me endless pasta and information, "Salute e mille grazie!" To the water specialists: David Zetland, Alex Prud'homme, Maude Barlow, and Seth Maxwell. Any mistakes are mine. Please drink responsibly.

To Bruce Skinner, my cover designer, for changing water to wine to blood; it's a mystery. To my editor, Eliza Dee for your amazing eye for detail. To Cheryl Perez, who always has my back, and my interior design.

Deepest gratitude to my parents, family, and friends. To Jamie, Sabrina, and Mario, I love you. Blood, wine, and water are precious. It's all we've got.

28636761R00236

Made in the USA
Columbia, SC
14 October 2018